THE REBELLION

OF STARS

R.V. WILBUR

THE REBELLION OF STARS

*To anyone who embraced the darkness
for love of the stars.*

*And for those who became it
in order to survive—
it is okay to mourn what was
stolen from you.*

AUTHOR'S NOTE

This book contains scenes depicting childhood trauma, loss of agency, war and violence, genocide, dark magic, death/loss and grief, discussion of SA, murder, mild language, on page spice. No children or animals are physically harmed in this book.

PLAYLIST

Pompeii (Acoustic Version by *waybackwhen*
Empire Now by *Hozier*
Her & the Sea by *CLANN*
Solas by *Jamie Duffy, Sarah Cothran*
Behind the Mask by *Ivy & Gold*
Empire Now by *Hozier*
West Coast of Clare by *Niamh Parsons*
Circus by *Britney Spears*
I don't have feelings anymore by *Roses & Revolutions*
Burn Your Life Down by *Bleachers*
Notre Dame by *Paris Paloma*
Empire Now by *Hozier*
Never Forgot by *Kendra Dantes*
Empire Now by *Hozier*
Lullaby by *Chxrlotte*
Porcelain by *Rachel Taylor*
I Hate Everything About You by *Angry Bard*
Still Here (Acoustic Version) by *Digital Daggers*
A Midsummer Night's Dream by *Hexperos*
Echo by *Jason Walker*
Stories by *Paden*
The Albatross by *Taylor Swift*
Storm by *Wendy Child*
Kingdom Fall by *Claire Wyndham, AG*
Come What May by *The Last Bison*
Chopin: Nocturne No. 20 in C-Sharp Minor by *Mikhail Pletnev*
Teeth by *5 Seconds of Summer*
Narcissistic Cannibal by *EarlyRise*

Castles Crumbling by Taylor Swift, Hayley Williams
Hunter by Paris Paloma
Dawn of the Mage by Peter Gundry
Hate Me by Eurielle
Numb by Tommee Profitt, Skylar Grey
Nobody Wants to Be Alone by Christian Reindl,
    Atrel
Heavy in Your Arms by Florence + The Machine
Whiskey Lullabies by Janet Devlin
Freak of Nature by BROODS, Tove Lo
Dangerous by Sleep Token
Island by SVRCINA
Moods Calm - Piano and Cello by Mario Vinuela,
    Ardie Son
Pentecost (Reworked) by Christopher Galovan,
    Ardie Son
Rabbit Hole by Mindy Gledhill
Animal (Epic Trailer Version) by J2, Keeley
    Bumford
Sound of My Youth (Acoustic Version) by Jamie
    Hannah
Life's Divide by Peter Gundry
Lovers in the Dark by Sophie Morelli
To Be Loved by Askjell, AURORA
Facade by SKY
Forest Fires by Lauren Aquilina
Church by Lawless, Valen
Disarm by Carrie Manolakos
Ace of Hearts by Zella Day
moved by LACES
My Heart's Grave by Faouzia
Can't Love Me by It's Alive
Jaws by Sleep Token
I love you by Billie Eilish

PAINT ME BLACK *by Ben Hazlewood, Mali-Koa Hood*
BLEEDING LOVE *by Ni/Co*
GIVE *by Sleep Token*
ATLANTIS (ACOUSTIC) *by Seafret*
ALL I ASK *by John Saga*
GODDESS *by Laufey*
HOW DID IT END? *by Taylor Swift*
THE RULES FOR LOVERS *by Richard Walters*
RUIN IN THE STARS *by Kendra Dantes, Sleeplore*
DON'T LET ME GO *by RAIGN*
GOODBYE *by Apparat, Soap & Skin*
DAUGHTER *by Beyonce*
WE MUST BE KILLERS *by Mikky Ekko*
ALL THAT YOU ARE (FROM "LOST EMBER") *by Solid
Audioworks*
YOU'VE CREATED A MONSTER *by Bohnes*
GUNS FOR HIRE *by Rachel Hardy, Garrett Weyenberg*
INNOCENCE *by Nathan Wagner*
TO LIVE AND BREATHE *by Eurielle*
IRIS *by Stillman*
WISH THAT YOU WERE HERE *by Florence + The
Machine*

THE WORLD OF BRETERIA

THE RAELTACH (RAIL-TACK), OR GREAT THREE:
The Paladin of Stars
The Warden of Time
The Muse of Darkness

THE STARS:
Isteriaeth (is-ter-ee-aith)

THE AWDURON (AW-DUR-RON):
Mage
Form Forger
Faery
Elfin Folk
Einherjar

THE KOLLAPSAR (KOHL-LAP-SAR):
Axion
Vacare
Eoten
Hrotesk

THE ELÉRYND (EL-LAE-RIND):
Humans with magic living in their hearts/souls (who believed in magic) who were sent with the Awduron to Breteria.

THE FIVE STRANDS OF MAGIC

ATMOSPHERIC MAGIC
Bestows the ability to conjure items from the air itself.
MAGIC OF FORM
Bestows the ability to forge the bearer's physical form into
whatever animal or creature they wish.
ELEMENTAL MAGIC
Bestows the ability to control and manipulate the four elements.
TEMPORAL MAGIC
Bestows the power to defy time and the ability to halt and bend
it at will.
TENEBRESCENT MAGIC
The strand of magic, carried by beings of darkness, that ushered
in the end of the Age of Stars and brought about the fall of the
Trifolium Thrones.

GLOSSARY

TRIFOLIUM: (Try-foal-ee-um)

The clover that represents the four Thrones and rulers united to serve the realm of Breteria.

INFLAMEL: (In-fla-mell)

The kingdom at the heart of Breteria.

OBARIAN: (Oh-bar-ee-an)

The northern kingdom of Breteria.

GRIMOIRA: (Grim-oy-ra)

The western kingdom of Breteria.

TAURIELLIS: (Tar-ee-ell-is)

The southern kingdom of Breteria.

PROVINCE OF WESTORAM: (Wes-tore-am)

Province in western Breteria.

PROVINCE OF CULWYRT: (Cull-wirt)

Province in northern Breteria.

PROVINCE OF STRAGIUM: (Stra-gee-um)
Province in central Breteria.

PROVINCE OF STONESTIDE: (Stones-tide)
Province in eastern Breteria.

DHUST: (du-st)
The visible representation of magic.

STRAND: (Str-and)
The form of magic.

BESTOWED: (Bee-stow-ed)
The point of time within an Isteriaeth's first decade of life in which their strand of magic is revealed to them.

MOONRISE:
The rise of a full moon, occurring once every seven calendar months.

DEWYNIOL (DEW-WIN-EE-OLE):
The tree of the faeries. The last source of the dhust mines, ancient as Breteria itself.

AWDURON BONDS:
Manifested physically, in things like telepathic speech. Manifested intrinsically—a sharing of energy, power, and mortality. Some archaic variants connect human to creature, even beyond the strand that allowed form forgers to shift their appearances.

ISTERIAETH TETHERS:

Not mere links between souls or magic, but everlasting ties broken only by death.

A Shared Tether: The most common according to Isteriaeth history, entered into willingly by both parties and broken only by death.

A Star-Blessed Tether: The most rare. A gift given by the stars to those found to honor them. It tethers two lifelines as one, and will fade should one life be laid down for the other.

A Seized Tether: A connection in strand alone, possessing the same strength as the other two, but with only one side as the benefactor. It can never be shared, is limited to the boundaries dictated by the bene-factor, and can be broken in death alone, be it natural or through an attempt to seize freedom.

PRONUNCIATION GUIDE

Elric: (Ell-Rick)

Graecerys: (Gray-sair-ess)

Falchion: (Fal-key-on)

Blenheim: (Blen-hime)

Auger: (Aw-gr)

Kathrina: (Kath-ree-na)

Gevallester: (Gev-val-less-ter)

Stargell: (Star-gel)

Auriana: (Aw-ree-anna)

Jacian: (Jas-ee-an)

CATHAN: (Cath-han)

DENFRIN: (Den-frinn)

FENDO: (Fen-do)

GANCH: (Gan-ch)

TOWLES: (Tow-less)

SNELL: (Sn-elle)

HUBART: (Hugh-bar)

ARLYS: (Arr-lis)

LYRA: (Leer-uh)

LLEWYRENNA: (Thoo-wren-na)

TIMOTHIUS: (Tim-oath-ee-us)

NELLUENYA: (Nel-lou-en-ya)

MILO: (Migh-low)

REGINALD: (Reg-inn-ald)

ISPERI MAGE: (Is-pair-ee Mage)

Breteria
The Grimm Sea
Grimoira
Australis Ocean

Inflarian Strait
Borealis Ocean
Inflamel
Taurian Strait

THE LEGEND

Once upon a forgotten time, there was magic upon the earth. Magic so brilliant it rivaled the sun. So powerful it could shift mountains and carve valleys. So gentle it danced upon the air itself, drawn into every lung and whispered across every surface.

Until it was no more.

Until it was rejected by humanity. There was no room for magic amid progress. No place for fantastic beings within reality. Its hosts, discarded by fate and time, were purged from a society that had outgrown its enchantment and become numb to its wonder.

But....

What is life to tell a dream to cease breathing?

What is reality to inform wishes of their doom?

What is the world to suffocate the very thing that might restore its life?

Five eternal strands of magic fought their way from the earth, beyond the clouds, through galaxies, piercing the constellations until they were reduced to no more than dust strewn across the heavens. They collided with dying stars and bound together as one, creating a realm that had not existed before—opening a world of perfect impossibility. Four kingdoms formed of stars and magic where they alone could thrive.

Beings that were once cast aside, unwanted, opened their eyes to a second life after dancing a short time with death. Elfin folk, winged faeries, beings able to shift their appearance, mighty conquerors and their legendary descendants—each one unable and unwilling to relinquish the magic coursing through their very souls—awoke to a new existence, the authors of their own freedom.

But with them came beings of a different sort of magic—a power drawn from the darkness left in its wake, pulled from a cold ruin and brought to life with the promise of violence. They were monsters carved from stone and shadow, demons existing only to feed the insatiable lust for power that magic alone could satisfy. They rose unbidden, ready to usher in an endless collapse.

But all was not lost.

A ruler was chosen from each of the four kingdoms, and together they stole away into the mountains high in the northernmost reaches of their realm. Together they raised a stronghold—a castle laden with bricks of each magic, forming a foundation strong enough to withstand the test of time. And there, with the greatest sacrifice, they poured out the very magic that had given them life to forge four thrones. Each ruler bound their fate to their crown, forsaking their own flesh and blood in order to cleave to one another.

Joy and prosperity, peace and providence reigned over the realm in the middle of the stars. The lands thrived, magic was cultivated, and its people flourished under the rule of the four thrones. Within each kingdom, a field of clover bloomed. Each bore four delicate leaves—the very world itself paying homage to the united rulers who poured themselves into the realm to preserve it, just as the strands and stars had once done for them.

The Trifolium Thrones, as they were then known, reigned through time from their Keep high in the mountains, their mantle passed down from generation to generation, no two strands of magic alike sitting on the Throne at one time. But while their power flowed deeper into the land, delving through rock and sediment to the remnant bones of the fallen stars themselves, the darkness at its core began to shudder and grow.

Beings in every form of malice rose under the banner of Kollapsar and burst forth. Having grown cunning over time—not resting while peace reigned but strengthening and waiting—they waged war on the four kingdoms, cutting down life, land, and creature with no discrimination. The greater the battle won, the more magic they consumed, and the more infallible their power became. One by one the kingdoms began to crumble, and still they marched, undaunted, daring the High Kings and Queens to come down off the Thrones and save their people.

The first Throne to be lured away was the conqueror, the mighty Einherjar, from the kingdom of Obarian. But rather than be consumed for the very magic he had protected and saved, the King of Obarian sought to save his own life. He turned his back on the world and led the demons to the foot of the mountain itself. And so the first leaf of the Trifolium blackened and died.

Weakened by their loss, the remaining Thrones held fast to one another until the great Trifolium Keep was breached, only fleeing at the final moment to their own kingdoms, each to take one last stand for their people.

The second to fall was the Elfin Queen, from the continent of Grimoira. She stole away with her kind, weaving their magic like a shroud to conceal their presence—vanishing from time itself. And so the second Trifolium leaf broke from the stem.

The third to fall was the King of Faeries, delicate wings and wishes doing nothing to stop the full-scale slaughter of his people. Fleeing into the depths of the forest, into the trees of Tauriellis so thick that no man could carve a path, the faeries retreated to the source of their strength—forever to be hunted. And so the third Trifolium leaf curled into itself before crumbling to dust.

The final Throne rallied what forces they had left to the city within the kingdom of Inflamel. Isteriaeth, mages, beings who could forge their form at will, all came together to defend the final tie to their world, and beneath a rain of stardhust and magic, they fought until they could give no more. Until they had no choice but to take one final action. And there, under the banner of the clover sigil with death breaking through their door, the last force of magic threw their saving grace from the world. The final Trifolium leaf froze, neither living nor dying, forever preserved in time.

The Kollapsar overtook the world, swallowing everything in their path. Faeries, mages, and form forgers alike either fled or were consumed, and each kingdom was set to rule by a new crown under a new banner. Inflated with power and believing themselves to be untouchable, the Kollapsar marched upon the four vacant Thrones at long last. And when the most powerful, malevolent, and darkest of terrors rose to devour them, the great Thrones sent a surge of magic through the realm—shaking the stars and time itself—and shattered the Kollapsar leader into shards.

With their figurehead felled and their stolen magic broken, the Kollapsar retreated, weakened and desperate to regain power.

Silence descended upon the four kingdoms, desolate and cold as an unrelenting winter. The Thrones stood empty, high in the mountains over the world, their magic alive but dormant.

Waiting.

The fields of clovers in each kingdom withered and died,

their ashes strewn through the skies and into the heavens themselves, floating on the air, desperately seeking their lost rulers.

But none could be found.

For nearly four centuries, the realm of Breteria plunged into a bleak existence devoid of magic, lost and forgotten, where it remains to this day.

Some now recall the Thrones as legend. Others as tragedy. But they are all correct, for what is there to live on after tragedy but a story to be told?

PART I
THE SEA

CHAPTER ONE

One drink, uninterrupted, in anonymous bliss. Was it truly too much to ask?

Apparently, yes.

Elric had no way of knowing how long he had been unconscious. The sack over his head made it impossible to view his surroundings. He would remove it to confirm were it not for the coarse rope binding his hands at the wrist, lashed to the same about his ankles, but he surmised from the rocking and rolling of the floor beneath him, and the pungent scent of mildew and saltwater, that he was on a boat.

The groaning shift of wood; the cold too frigid to be that of Inflamel—the kingdom he called home; and the preternatural moisture that clung to his skin, transferred from the floor itself, banished any doubt from his mind.

His thoughts raced alongside his heartbeat, the panic rising like bile in the back of his throat, threatening to choke him. He forced his breathing to remain even, controlling it despite the nearly paralyzing terror that seized him. He was not the same confused boy trapped in a dark and watery coffin. He was a man. A star fallen to the realm his people had helped forge, the embodiment of the powerful dhust used to save all magic. And he needed to keep his wits about him.

Pulse slowing, he searched his memory, grasping for pieces that formed the portrait of how he came to be in this place. An alehouse in the city of Inflamel. The urge to drown his thoughts and numb his feelings. A chatty sailor who had seated himself across the bar. He had kept a respectable distance from Elric.... But the drunkard who elbowed him in the side of the head had not. In hindsight he wagered they had known one another. So was it the knock to his skull that had pricked his skin with a sedative, or was the distraction just enough to allow his ale to be tainted?

Either way, they hadn't let him finish one Thrones-damned drink.

Could he have had one in the castle? Yes. Should he have remained there, especially with the restlessness encroaching upon their borders? Indeed.

But why make anything easy on himself?

It was only one drink.

And one second, one mistake is all it takes.

He groaned and rolled, the inertia of the tilting boat moving him from his back to his stomach. The bag over his head was a thick weave making it hard to breathe in much more than the dubious, fishlike stench clinging to its fibers. It needed to go, but his hands did not quite reach, so....

Propping himself up the best he could, he pulled from within, calling on the atmospheric strand of magic woven to his very bones. It awoke the dhust in his chest and released it, the warmth running through his veins and into his palms where he knew a radiant blue cloud would now be visible. Stars tickled his fingers, slipping to the ground, and the moment he felt a small, cold blade in his palm, he relaxed the strand.

Not that long ago he would have been mercilessly stuck, unwilling to use his magic so openly. But now there was no use in hiding it. Everyone knew who he was—knew *what* he was—the last Isteriaeth in the Realm of Breteria, advising the King and Queen of Inflamel from within the safety of their borders. No one would dare risk open war by touching him. At least they wouldn't have...*before*.

He made quick work of the rope binding his wrists, slicing through the abrasive twine that would undoubtedly leave burns on his skin, before tugging the hood off his head to find the deep brown eyes of a very tall man smirking at him just beyond the bars of the cell he sat within.

His chestnut-colored hair was long and unkempt, reaching down to his chin, its waves blown back as if he'd just come out of a breeze. His forearms—crossed at his chest—were corded, his biceps thick as saplings, and judging by the fur-lined boots and fleece tunic he wore, he was from the north.

Obarian.

Damn.

"Well, that was entertaining to watch," the man remarked in a deep, youthful voice, shifting his weight from one foot to the other and cocking his head.

Elric glared at him, and when he gripped the knife beneath the sack, the man made a tsking noise that stopped him in his tracks.

"Ah, ah, ah, Master Isteriaeth. You may have power we cannot keep in check, but I have a duty. And I take my job very seriously."

The accent thick on his tongue confirmed his origin, and Elric cringed. "Your job is to kidnap innocent men trying to have an ale?"

"My job is to ensure the safe transportation of valuable goods to the Kingdom of Obarian."

Elric stiffened. "Are there goods I am unaware of, or are you referring to me?"

The corner of the man's mouth tipped up in a half smile that was both belligerent and keen and revealed the hint of a dimple. "We can make this working relationship as easy or as difficult as you wish. Me? I'd prefer easy, so I will start us out on the right foot. My name is Falchion Drisbane. And you are?"

"Valuable goods," Elric replied dryly. "That you have stolen from the King of Inflamel."

Falchion threw his head back, laughing loudly. "The King of Inflamel. I will make a deal with you, Isteriaeth. I will return you to your master the second he notices you are gone. Do we have a bargain?"

The words cut deeper than if Elric had stabbed the knife in his fist through his own heart. Shaking his head, he hurled the blade and drove it point-first into the floor between them, wedging it easily an inch into the wood.

Falchion watched the handle quiver, a lone eyebrow raised in approval, but Elric only regarded him coldly. "What does Obarian want with me?"

The man assumed a stance far too at ease for the strength his dhust-wielding prisoner had just displayed, but Elric refused to be offended. "I would think it obvious, Master Isteriaeth. Do you have a name, perchance? Isteriaeth is a bit much to wrap my teeth around."

Elric blinked slowly, a bored expression relaxing his face.

Falchion pressed on. "Are Isteriaeth given names? Or are they a mystery none may know?"

"My friends may know, but you may refer to me as you are, thank you."

"Oh, come now. I have been nothing but pleasant to you," the man replied, extending his arms in goodwill, his voice containing a hint of humor. "I was raised and trained to respect those in station above me...as well as my elders."

Elric snorted at the man who looked little more than three decades. "Commentary on my age. How original."

"You cannot hold the novelty against me, though I expected

someone more advanced in age. Not a man of three decades with oaken hair that shines more red than silver. Were it not for the Isteriaeth blue of your eyes, I would not have identified you," Falchion said, taking a small step forward. "I heard many a bedside tale of the fallen stars who walked the realm. Passed down by my parents who learned from their parents in the same way for generations. And you were alive for them all."

Wonder marked his tone with curiosity, but Elric remained undeterred. "And were your ancestors and their many generations involved in the hunting and extermination of my own?"

"We are getting off subject," replied Falchion with a small nod before turning on his heel and striding for the set of stairs at his back.

"If you wish to be friends, you might start by treating me like a guest and not a commodity," Elric called after him. "Allow me above deck instead of here, in the company of boxes and barrels."

"Ah, but we do not yet know the extent of the magic you possess, Master Isteriaeth," he called over his shoulder. "Additionally, we are not that good of friends. I still haven't got a clue of your name."

His boots were heavy against the wood leading him up and out of the belly of the ship, abandoning Elric to its relentless swaying and shuddering. He wasn't fond of ships, but he *despised* the sea, and prisoner or not, he refused to be trapped below it any longer.

He rose, taking a moment to get his legs properly beneath him, then began to inspect the bars of his cell. If he could find the lock, he might be able to summon a key, or at the very least a hair pin, to open it.

The memory of pulling pins from golden hair, releasing waves that smelled sweet like lilacs, slammed into him, knocking the air from his chest.

Kathrina.

One second late is all it takes.

He steadied himself, knuckles white around the bars, and once he regained his composure, he straightened and resumed his search for the lock.

Only there wasn't one.

The bars were solid, their joints smooth to the touch with not so much as a hinge in sight. It was almost as if the iron bars had been built *around* him.

Or built with him in mind.

Both thoughts caused him to shudder. The former for his paralyzing fear of the ocean that he was now also a prisoner to, caged beneath its surface, and the latter because anyone who had gone to such lengths to imprison a being of magic and ensure that—no matter the strand—they would be unable to escape was formidable.

Formidable and clever.

He summoned all manner of tools and weaponry to himself, succeeding in adding a few small chips in the metal bars, and then slumped back to the ground in an exhausted heap.

Allowing his strand to slacken and his dhust to burn too quickly was not a viable option—not while he was still so vulnerable. But he would find a way out of that Thrones-damned cage, even if it killed him.

Because, at the end of the day, it was certainly better than whatever unknown fate lay ahead. And it might even be better than the ruins he left behind.

CHAPTER TWO

Falchion continued to be the only other individual Elric saw, bringing him heaping portions of food that he firmly rejected in favor of the moderate dishes he could summon for himself.

The hull of the ship was a long, cavernous space—far larger than any fishing boat Inflamel possessed, and considerably bigger than even the vessel that had brought Elric to her shores as a young boy, which led him to wonder how it had remained off the shore long enough for his captors to carry out their mission. How they had gone undetected by not just the Inflamelian guard, but the elfin as well?

Judging by the cargo within his shared space, he was not being held by a mercenary, or even the lawless marauders who kidnapped faeries and trafficked illegal wares in the southern waters off the coast of Tauriellis. But the wood was also not well maintained enough to be of royal origin, though his prison certainly was, so the question remained: Who had orchestrated his capture, and what lay ahead?

Another full day's worth of rejected meals later, he received his answer in the form of a storm building above deck. Shouts carried on the roaring wind that echoed down the stairs, followed by a deluge of seawater released in torrents with each dip and roll of the ship.

Food forgotten, Elric lay on his side against the bars of his prison, his legs curled up to his chest and his arms holding his knees close. He did not care how undignified he might appear on the outside, because within his mind, he was trapped inside a barrel, bobbing and drifting in the hull of a sinking ship. The boards cracked around him, splitting and allowing the ocean to seep in…. And he was too small and powerless to do more than hold on to himself and beg for either rescue or a swift end.

He had not been ready to die then. And while it might be a welcome relief now, he didn't want to drown. He didn't want to sink. He didn't want to be where the stars could not find him.

The boat lilted much too far to the left before violently changing direction and surging back to the right, pitching over and over.

The motion was enough to drive a weathered sailor to madness, yes, but the *sounds.* The inescapable howls of the wind and crashes that threatened to break the world around him. He had known people, born sailors, who were soothed to sleep by the sound of the ocean, but not him. He would never forgive the waves for how desperately they had tried to choke him when all he'd ever done was beg for borrowed air.

He squeezed his eyes shut, furious to be so shaken by a memory he had long since buried, and forced his thoughts to burrow past. They drove down to the roots of his being and returned him to a time and a place long before the traumas and terrors that haunted his waking moments.

He may have sunk low, with further still to go, but even after everything else failed him, he could still cling to the stars.

The door above crashed open and Falchion tumbled down, skipping every third step as he fought against the inertia driving him up and down all at once. Concern etched the tight lines drawn across his forehead, his obnoxious dimple and easygoing mirth nonexistent when he met Elric's eyes with a mixture of distress and disgust.

"If my presence is this disagreeable, may I suggest leaving me alone?" Elric quipped, sitting up enough to grasp the bars for dear life with both hands.

Falchion snorted and shook his head. "'Tis not your company, Master Isteriaeth. We had hoped to reach the western coast and weigh anchor in the cape town of the Province of Westoram. They were prepared to secure your passage for the remainder of the journey, but a storm approaches from that direction, cutting off our course."

Elric frowned, silently considering the words before voicing his musings aloud. "Assuming we sail on the Inflarian Strait, storms would approach from the east. Unless I am wrong and we are not in the Strait and you have lied about our destination."

Falchion's disconcerted stare met his. "Your assertion is correct and my words were true, yet the clouds build deep in the west—dark and foreboding. I do not presume to know your power, nor make the assumption that you would help us, but I must ask. Is there anything you might do to draw aground on the southern coast? If we continue directly into the gale, we run the risk of being pulled out and dashed upon the rocks of the Grimm Sea. Or worse, cast ashore within the boundary of Grimoira."

Elric shuddered but weighed his options. The Grimm Sea earned its name in blood, both from the rocks and the monsters that lurked below its surface. Being caught up behind the cursed boundary of Grimoira, however, might be a reprieve...except their borders let none who enter leave, so that would be a prison all its own. Which left him with the final option—willingly aiding his captors in completing their journey to Obarian.

Maybe the Grimm's monsters aren't as bad as they sound.

He stood slowly, hauling himself up the bars hand over hand. "I carry the strands of atmospheric magic. I summon things to myself, I do not command the elements."

The hopeful light bled out of Falchion's eyes, but a heartbeat later it was replaced with steel. "If I bring you above, will you try?"

Above. The hull groaned and popped under the strain of the waves, the strongest sending everything in the hull pitching to the side. Elric grimaced, then gave the soldier a terse nod. "I will see what I can do."

He did not notice what triggered the release of the bars, but they retracted from the deck above, receding into the floorboards below his feet, the mechanical *tick-tick-tick* of a pulley deep within the bowels of the ship drawing the confirmation from his mind.

Not only had the cage been made for him, but the entire ship as well.

Falchion clasped him by the elbow and hauled him toward the stairs, pushing him forward with a small shove. "Up you go, Master Isteriaeth."

Elric tumbled up the steps, falling into the wall and rail more than once, before breaking into the deluge above. The ocean churned a midnight green—the whitecaps' cavernous jaws threatening to snap closed around the ship. Clouds, high and towering over them, raced across the sky in an unnatural flow, billowing a gray so pallid, it tinged purple.

It cannot be the Isperi Mage.

Violet eyes rose to the forefront of Elric's mind. Their hue was evidence of her temporal strand of magic, and the malevolence behind them a testament to her violence, but neither produced dhust that commanded the elements. Besides, she would not be outside of Inflamel. The last she had been sighted was in the Deorc Weald...*after.*

Elric flinched. It had been well over a year since she had

been seen. Three since they had first pursued her into the Weald. Since she had destroyed the lives of the people he loved most. Since he had failed to protect them.

One mistake.

He felt it then. Hanging on the gusts and assaulting him from within every droplet.

Dhust.

This storm was a result of magic after all.

His own stirred within him, and he searched his mind quickly. He could not summon the land to them, that would surely sink them. And he dared not try to call the sun or moon forth to clear the sky.

He had summoned elements once before, but it had been different. A fire had raged all around, uncontrollable, and they were losing the fight against it. He had concentrated then, desperately wishing for water to pour from the sky, amplifying the efforts that were already being exhausted. And that's when his strand had quivered and hummed to life. Dhust had rushed to his fingers, and what felt like his entire being had pulled clouds into the sky.

This time, he did not want the clouds. He was desperate for a clear sky. For the sun. The warmth on his face and a sea that looked like glass. A canvas swathed in blue, erasing the terror splattered in dark greens, grays, and violets.

"A break!" a voice called on the wind from the crow's nest above. "A break in the storm!"

Elric and Falchion's heads snapped to the right, out across the water where—sure enough—the clouds were ever so slightly brighter. Where a crease revealed not only a break in the storm, but a way out.

Falchion's eyes widened, then he met Elric's. "Whatever you are doing, I beg you to continue."

"I don't know that it is—"

His strands silenced him, a tremor so vibrant it stole the

breath rattling within his lungs. He fixed his eyes on the sky. On the crack splitting it open.

He envisioned the sunlight as golden waves, soft and warm, rippling like curtains while the scent of lilac kissed his face.

He was desperate for it. Longed for just one more touch.

Then he pictured an endless expanse, brilliant blue with tufts of ivory clouds like lace across its delicate—

"The storm is yielding! Make for the break!" Falchion shouted, ordering his crew as he strode toward the helm himself.

Elric turned away from the man and withdrew his hands from where he had concealed them in his cloak. Star dhust raced across his skin in the sapphire of his strand, not with glittering blue alone, but green swirling on its edges in a harmonious dance.

Two colors of dhust.

It meant two strands of magic.

But how?

A rogue wave stole Elric's thoughts, crashing over the deck and sweeping him off his feet. The world gurgled and plunged into silence for a heartbeat, his body pinwheeling weightlessly through darkness. Terror seized his chest, then gravity rushed back in with the *slam* of his back against the side of the ship.

Men cried out, yelling over the din, but Elric remained still, staring at Falchion half a boat length away from him. In his mind he saw men, sailors not unlike the ones he watched now, holding on to whatever they could to secure themselves.

They had not realized it would be a fatal mistake to do so.

But which was a worse fate? Drowning or being dashed to pieces on the rocks?

He heard their screams either way....

Before him, Falchion clutched the wheel for dear life, lashing a rope to hold it fixed toward the horizon, toward the break in the storm. Now the gap was much larger and wider. They were almost—

The crack and snap of wood and rope was the only warning Elric had before a beam swung through the deluge to deliver a blow against his head.

Then he heard and saw no more.

CHAPTER THREE

The light behind his eyelids was too bright, the throbbing in his head too great, but Elric forced his eyes open anyway. Instead of the blue sky above, the bottom of a cot greeted him, and beneath him was not sand or soil but soft blankets. The call of gulls carried in on the breeze flitting through the window at his bedside, and the crescendo of waves brought about an instinctive wince, thought short lived as reality snatched his attention.

Gulls. Breaking waves. The sun.

He sat up slowly and swung his legs over the side of the bed. He wore the same clothes, but his jacket was gone, leaving him in his tunic, trousers, and boots alone.

He tried to take a step, but his leg resisted and a rope knotted around his ankle pulled taut.

Grunting in frustration, he summoned a knife to his hand and sliced through the twine in a blink, then turned back to the door now filled by Falchion's frame.

"Just in time, I see," he remarked with a smirk. "I trust my quarters treated you well?"

Elric looked around. Not quite captain's quarters. But not barracks either. "What sort of ship is this?"

"The kind you saved," Falchion replied, sincerity warming his tone. "Only two men were lost when we all should have perished. I owe you a great deal of thanks."

Elric stood, kicking the rope toward Falchion with narrowed eyes. "But not enough to convince you to return me to my home, I presume."

"Not quite. But I can offer you a hot meal," Falchion said with a chuckle.

No sooner had the words left his mouth that Elric had an apple in his hand. "I am set, but thank you."

The man before him raised a lone eyebrow, then a shallow dimple returned. "Spiced ale, then?"

Mid-bite, Elric froze before slowly nodding. "That I might agree to."

"Then follow me," Falchion said with a dip of his chin.

Elric proceeded cautiously, taking careful steps out of the room and down the hall to a small galley. He accepted a flagon filled to the rim with warmed ale, its spices tickling his nostrils. The delightfully sweet foam soothed his scratchy throat, warming him from the inside out, and he drank half in one long drag.

Falchion tipped his own mug to Elric in salute, then drained it, but not quickly enough to hide the fact that he was consuming water.

Elric frowned. "You are not a captain, yet you captain this vessel. You fail to answer to another, yet you live in the ranks as if you were a common boatswain. This ship was constructed specifically for my retrieval, undoubtedly requiring an enormous sum of money, so you cannot be a mercenary, yet you do not drink as a royal sailor either."

Falchion was silent a moment, watching him take another

sip from the flagon, then he inclined his head. "Follow me above, Master Isteriaeth."

Elric did as he was told, carrying the rest of his ale with him. He was unsure where they were or how long he would have before being dragged to their final destination, but he was certain he would need every ounce of liquid courage he could muster.

Or at the very least enough to numb his impending misery.

When he reached the deck and followed Falchion to the rail, however, he realized he was far closer to it than he thought.

The ship had beached upon the shore, run aground carefully instead of dashed as he knew they should have been. Nothing and no one was in sight, just the wide, open countryside of Obarian with its long wheat-colored grass, rolling bluffs, and small deposits of snow though autumn had yet to depart.

"It hasn't changed a bit," he murmured under his breath. "But where are the people? The farms? The villages?"

Falchion eyed him closely. "You have been upon these shores before?"

Elric did not answer, but drained his flagon instead, resting it on the side of the vessel and leaning forward, the warmth of the drink filling his insides and relaxing his mind.

Looking at the man beside him, he smiled. "You don't happen to have another flagon of ale available for your *cargo*, do you?"

Falchion's stoic stare melted into a slow smile and he shook his head. "I believe we can scrounge one up. But I will need to shackle you again."

Elric shrugged, extending his wrists before him. "I will simply remove them again."

The man laughed, clasping the manacles against his skin before turning to stride away.

"Elric."

The word stopped Falchion in his tracks, and he turned back.

"You may call me Elric."

Falchion's eyes widened in a surprise that he quickly recovered from by snapping his heels together. With one arm at his side and the other in a fist across his chest he gave Elric a small nod that resembled a bow. "Thank you for trusting me with your name, Master Is— Elric. Master Elric."

Elric snorted. "It is a name, nothing more. Do not let it go to your head."

Falchion's rumbling laughter carried back on the breeze as he walked below deck, but Elric smiled, pleased with himself for tricking the man into revealing his hand. The salute proved he was none other than a soldier of the crown. A trained dog who would snap to attention at the least of recognition. Which meant not only had he been retrieved for the Throne of Obarian, it had been a mission set forth by the *shtrone* of *Odaian*.

Elric startled and shook his head, as if to clear his thoughts.

Orvalian.

He shook his head again, his face tingling and the world fuzzing along the edges of his vision.

Orderrien.

Orber…berry…

He reached helplessly for the side of the boat, but the wood slipped right out from under his fingers, and he slumped to the deck.

Looking up, he noticed men staring, all curious but none making a move to his aid. Almost as if….

Boots appeared in his vision, and he lay down to focus on them. It felt decent lying down though the world still moved beneath him.

Damned-Thrones sea boats.

He tried to focus on the man standing above him, and

attempted a scowl, but whatever look Elric's cheeks gathered into only made Falchion laugh.

"I think one was enough, though you were not meant to ingest it so quickly," he remarked. "However, the envoy has just arrived. So the sooner you close your eyes, the faster this will all be over."

Over....

Oh, this ridiculous, soldier-shaped child of a man had no idea what he was talking about.

The ocean may have been the source of Elric's nightmares, but his horrors were far from over.

And as the rest of the drug-laced ale took hold of his body and mind, rendering him unconscious, Elric slurred, "Over? It has barely begun."

CHAPTER FOUR

Clouds, long and hazy, broke up the monotony of the night sky and concealed the stars. It had been hours since Elric started staring at them, the sea becoming a distant thought. Normally that would have brought him joy, but it did nothing to fortify his heart now.

A stone archway with great iron gates passed overhead, and he blinked slowly. He must have been unconscious for some time. He hadn't expected to see it so soon.

Or ever again, for that matter.

The wagon's wheels smoothed out on the cobble path, a far cry from the grass and dirt it had traversed to get here, and though Elric did not have the strength to sit up, he knew what lay around him.

A courtyard with painstakingly placed stonework covering the expansive ground to the left of the carriage path they drove upon now, made for parties and soirees beneath the sky, safe behind the iron gates that surrounded the oblong building at the center of it all.

To the right of the road was a labyrinth garden, if one could call it a garden. It was mainly a maze of hedges that towered above even an average man's height. Sparse flowers—primarily roses—grew both in and around the shrubbery, one of the few plants that could weather the brutal winters of the north. Their large petals, velvet and inviting, lured you close, their sweet fragrance drawing you farther into the maze of dirt-covered walkways. In and out, around and through, it led in every direction and nowhere at once, until all you knew were pointed leaves of green so dark they erred black, pristinely sharp thorns, and the traitorous, smiling blooms. Representing the beautiful yet ruthless kingdom itself, the palace grounds made you feel as if you could explore and discover all its opulence while remaining firmly within its prison.

His prison once again.

At long last, he was home.

He wished he could draw apart his thoughts as keenly as his body felt separated from his brain, his desires unable to spark movement from any of his extremities. But the farther they traveled inside the gate, the more acute his anxiety became. The sharper his fear pricked. The closer every nightmare he had buried deep in his mind clawed to the surface.

The wagon stopped in the shadow of the palace, and after a moment, Falchion's head came into view.

"Ah, you're awake," he said pleasantly. "Up you come."

Two more soldiers appeared, opening the side door and hoisting Elric out, standing him upright with his feet flat on the frost-covered ground, though they still supported his weight. Falchion crossed the stone before him in slow, even steps, dressed head to toe in fur and armor—the full regalia of a soldier of the north. After a moment, he stopped pacing and cocked his head to the side.

"Loosen your grip on him," he ordered the soldiers supporting his weight. "But slowly. He said it would take a few moments to disburse once the Isteriaeth was roused."

Sure enough, about the time the furthest edges of the sky

bled from indigo to periwinkle, Elric found himself standing on his own. And though he still felt weary, though his clawing fear threatened to empty his stomach on the soldiers' boots, he kept his expression slack and unbothered.

Falchion met his eyes one more time before turning on his heel to face the grand doors. "Right, then. We enter."

The entrance was the original ornate, gilded arch, framing thick wooden doors as pristine as the day they had been erected. Inside, the carpet was the same rich red leading to the grand staircase with its square landings, sharp turns, and wooden banister, painted white and carved in endless winged filigree.

The halls and floors above, with their tall ceilings, were all unchanged. It was as if time had not progressed since Elric last passed between the palace walls, but instead of warmth filling the space like sunlight on a bleak winter morning, it was empty as a tomb. Its life had frozen into a ghostly apparition, waiting to haunt him with its bitter familiarity.

Because that's all it was to him. Cold and dead.

They reached what he knew to be the throne room, where the wide, twin oak doors were already flung open. He was accompanied to the center of the caramel and black parquet floor, their steps echoing against the ivory trim carved into the vaulted ceiling until he was halted before the vacant throne, then hemmed in by his accompanying guards, all waiting expectantly. The golden chandeliers, delicately woven to appear like vines supporting blooms of light, illuminated the high back of the hallowed chair, carved with the twists and curls of the Trifolium sigil—the four-leaf symbol of the four rulers who had once united their realm from high in the mountains on the Obarian continent itself. But differing from the depiction he had grown accustomed to in Inflamel, where the sigil stood alone, these were surrounded by thousands of hand-etched stars.

From the shadows beside the dais, a man stepped forward. His uniform was pristine, his jacket a deep blue, and his pants a few shades lighter than leather. He was ceremoniously dressed to reflect the kingdom itself, all depthless sky and endless fields of wilted vegetation. Yet around his core, from left shoulder to right hip, was a brilliant gold sash, and pinning it in place, a medallion of the same precious metal.

He strolled forward, hands behind his back, and circled Elric. His dark-silver hair, mustache, and goatee clipped to a point off his long chin caused his brown eyes to sharpen in contrast, and when he stopped in front of Elric once more, his head bobbed in approval, like he was accepting a well-harvested crop.

"Well done, Falchion. I must say, I questioned your ability to succeed in this task, but it appears your youth was an advantage. Your men speak not of the lives lost, but of how you commanded the vessel in the storm to prevent any more. A true mark of greatness that will certainly be commended. Your future is bright."

Falchion snapped to attention and bowed, fist over heart, preening in the glow of such high praise. "It was my honor, Lord Blenheim."

The lord returned his gaze to Elric, his eyes probing and prying, though Elric refused to show weakness or look away.

"Long has it been since an Isteriaeth graced these halls," he remarked, taking a step toward Elric. "Well over the days since the Fall of the Thrones."

False, Elric thought, but he did not allow his denial to slip. No one need know how long he had called this palace home. How long the Isteriaeth had survived, hidden in plain sight.

"The Obarian kings of old were warriors," Lord Blenheim continued, resuming his stroll around Elric. "The people here demand such, and while the nobility since have attempted to cultivate that might and iron will, they have rejected it, rising up against their benefactors. We have long sought what we must do to regain their goodwill, to restore our kingdom to greatness, and have settled on one thing our ancestors had that we do not. One piece that might call our people to heel—magic."

Elric snorted. "It would appear you have some form of sorcery afoot. Unless you are not the *he* your lackey referred to as I learned how to stand upon my own limbs again."

The lord came to a halt in Elric's view, close enough that he could smell garlic lingering on his breath. "'*When dhust doth bind Isteriaeth to king, the strands shall sing with stars' blessing.*'"

Elric stared blandly at the man before him, the adage sending a chill instead of the comfort it would have in days of old, and he shook his head. "Obarian has no king."

"No," someone said from behind him. "They have a queen."

The voice rang clear and cold, bells on the winter wind heralding a warning. When the woman strode by him, the soldiers within the room dropped to a knee one by one. Her robe was cerulean, with gold embroidered filigree kissing every edge of the train as it slid behind her purposeful gait. Red tresses were caught up in a net on the back of her head, braided beneath the golden twine, allowing no wisps to fly free against her alabaster skin. And when she reached the throne and turned, her deep-sapphire eyes pinned him to the tile.

"Where did you find him?" she said to no one in particular.

"Inflamel, my queen, as the reports said," Lord Blenheim replied.

"And you are certain he is unclaimed? You are sure he is the last?"

The familiar sting of the inquiry was a vicious stab to the heart while standing in the halls of the place that made it so. All eyes turned to Elric.

"I am the last," he confirmed, allowing no one else to answer for him.

Something shifted in the queen's eyes, a wave of bitter disappointment lost in a midnight sea. As quickly as the emotion crested, it was gone, and a sardonic smile played on her lips instead. "Then I herald your return to Obarian, Fallen Star."

Elric returned her smile with derision. "You are gracious, my lady, but I regret to inform you that Obarian's reputation is not that of a place one would wish to live within or visit. So forgive my reluctance in accepting your welcome."

A lone eyebrow raised, and he saw a glint in her eye that tempted a real smile to her face, though she kept her features carefully schooled. Was his abrasiveness *amusing* her?

"Gracious lady I am not," she replied, sitting on the throne and folding her hands in her lap. "But you may call me Queen Graecerys—or my queen, if you so wish."

"I do not wish," Elric replied sharply. "Stealing from a fellow kingdom, be it goods or living beings, is a crime. You are not, nor will you ever be, my queen."

The glint vanished, replaced by flat, cold eyes, and her lips drew together in a tight line. "That privilege is something you lost the moment you touched my shores. Now on your knees, sir."

Silence fell upon the room as Elric stared at her. "Pardon me?"

"I said on your knees, sir. Now."

He did not have the chance to retort. With an even push against the back of his legs from the soldiers flanking him, Elric's knees hit the stone, a *crack* echoing across the silent hall—though he wasn't sure if it was his heart or dignity breaking. He had entered this room with a solid will and fortified confidence, but it all *whooshed* from his chest, evacuating his lungs with the air they rejected when he was shoved to the ground. Gravity had always been a prison, but he had never felt so trapped beneath it.

"Now," said Lord Blenheim, stepping forward once more and crooking a finger at another man that Elric had not noticed lurking in the shadows. "Restrain him."

The hooded figure stepped forward, green eyes sunk into his face, surrounded by dark circles that made his skin appear a pasty hue. He held a coil of rope in one hand and a jagged blade in the other.

Elric recognized it immediately, the long wooden weapon carved from a single Tauriellan tree limb and honed to a deadly point. But not just any tree. Dewyniol—the tree of the faeries. The last source of the dhust mines, ancient as Breteria itself, and the only thing capable of draining an Isteriaeth of their dhust and their life.

Or worse, binding them.

Realization dawned, chilling him to his very core. He had never feared life, but there was always something far worse than death.

"Isteriaeth, you have been returned to our shores to be bound by ancient rule in the eyes of the stars," Blenheim prattled on, as if delivering a proclamation of life and death at once. "As you have shown no acquiescence, this tether will not be shared for mutual benefit, but instead seized and claimed. Your life shall be henceforth under the command of our queen, until the day her soul passes beyond the realm of the living. You will go as far as she allows, you will obey her command alone, and your power will be hers to call upon and use as she sees fit. And now that you understand why you are here, let us begin."

All warmth leached from Elric's body and his pulse raced in his ears. He blinked, certain this had to be a nightmare carried on far too long, but no amount of clarity in his vision erased the reality before his eyes. He was to be imprisoned and indentured, used as a siphon for dhust whenever power was demanded. Where a shared tether would have been reciprocal, one that was seized could not be denied.

He had known darkness. He had walked so long in it that he no longer worried what might find him there. But of all he had lost, his freedom—his very life—was the last thing he could protect.

He pulled against the soldiers that held him, struggling to knock any of them off balance, eyes never leaving the knife or the man shuffling forward with an awkward gait.

"Restrain him," warned Lord Blenheim again, and the hands on him tightened like fetters.

But Elric, Elric *fought*.

He grappled for the upper hand, clawing and thrashing wildly like a man possessed. Protecting the last spark of light he had left. The one thing that had not been taken from him. The sole virtue that, once lost, he would never recover. Freedom.

But the man drew closer and the soldiers doubled in number. Elric never stopped fighting, but his strength was no match for a dozen men. Before he knew it, his cheek was pressed to the stone, his prone body held unmoving on the floor.

It broke something within him, and though his battle against the hands restraining him was useless, his voice *roared*. His animalistic growls and cries echoed louder and louder, but they did nothing to change what he was about to face. If these would be his final moments whole and unbound, he would not go quietly.

The four men holding his right arm turned it over, palm up, the shift in their bodies allowing him to see the throne once more. He sought out the eyes of the woman watching with rapt attention, searching for any hint of mercy.

There was none to be found.

Whatever she felt was carefully concealed behind the mask of a queen who would have her prize no matter the cost.

A sharp bite in the center of his palm caused him to flinch, but it was nothing compared to the slow and torturous burn as his skin split in a straight line down over his wrist. He screamed while his forearm was flayed open, the blade only stopping once it reached the crook of his elbow. When the wooden edge retreated, he succumbed to the pain, embracing the ground as a steady anchor to the agony that was his own blood pumping freely across the floor.

The motion was repeated on his other arm, but Elric did not fight now. He did not scream. He did not struggle any longer. But he did not accept his fate either, though he knew it would be sealed the instant his blood turned from red to glittering starlight. He lay in pain, in trepidation, in choking fear, his racing heart aiding the speed in which his life fled from his body. And then, as his mind and vision clouded with the sluggish thump of his heart, he heard a sharp gasp, and a luminous shimmer filled the room.

He felt it then, the crude and perverse words spoken above him awakening the stars in his veins. The strands stretched and rose from the trenches carved into his flesh, dancing along his bones and caressing his skin, beckoned forward like an invitation from a lover. The binding was something meant to be beautiful, something natural that the stars longed for and his magic craved. Everything within him wanted to be tethered—to live, to die, to serve, to fulfill the ancient calling that was so heavy a burden, but so great an honor for an Isteriaeth to bear. But the instant the strands recognized that this was not an oath but a forcible taking, the dhust within him froze.

The words punctured his flesh, driving deeper still with razor-sharp talons, ensnaring the strands of magic that were now desperately trying to retreat within him. It pulled and tugged, both forces at war beneath his skin, causing excruciating pain that he was powerless to stop. The strands tore away, and an undignified scream ruptured from his lips. His body twisted in the hands of the soldiers, contorting unnaturally in a physical display of the takeover happening at his very core.

The tether anchored deep inside his heart, capturing his strands and imprisoning the stars' dhust within him. He was strung like a dog on a lead to the woman before him who only watched, head cocked in cold curiosity. He knew she must feel something from the ritual taking place, but her placid interest remained focused on him alone—on his suffering. On the wicked violation of his freedom and the exploitation of his being.

Every inch that the noose tightened, trapping and severing his own power from his control and lashing it to her wrist, he felt his autonomy slip away like innocence lost, once held but never to return again.

The tether snapped into place, like strands of iron caging the thread of his magic to the royal who showed zero remorse for taking what was not hers. She drew in a breath, inhaling his life and exhaling the remnants of his freedom. And when her eyes found his, the small smile stretching across her face ignited a hatred deeper than the fires of Hades within him.

The hands restraining him retreated, the odd man's chanting ceased, but Elric did not rise. He curled onto his side, pulling his mutilated arms against his chest to try and ease the raw, open, and bleeding wound that he imagined gaped from his heart too. He knew that no physical indication would remain once his body healed, no scars would tell his tale, but he would carry the burden of this loss right beside the others for the rest of his life.

The life that was now claimed by the Queen of Obarian.

He was chained to the woman who wore the very crown that had ensured he was the last of his kind. He was bound to the throne by a dagger that was still stained with his family's blood. Obarian had left him destitute and alone once before, and he would never be the same again.

The world grayed at the edges. Blurred images danced in brilliant color before his eyes.

And then nothing.

Elric's head shot up. His vision clear and fixed on the man before him. Not a face, but a mask.

Gloved hands rose to its edge, pulling away the ivory, its gold filigree glittering in the torchlight, and as a curl tumbled across the man's forehead, his kohl-lined green eyes welled with tears.

"It is me, brother."

The words stopped Elric's heart, and he stumbled forward, throwing his arms around the soldier's neck—the friend he was certain he had lost—and grasping a fistful of his cloak for dear life. "T. At long last I have found you. You live and I have found you."

"That is why you are here?" T asked in fearful admonishment. "You have endangered your life, risked your freedom, to find me?"

"We believed you to be dead. Kathrina and I, we all—"

"Were better off believing my demise," T interrupted, pulling away and meeting his gaze.

Elric felt the curtain fall between them, his friend and brother growing cold as stone beneath his fingers.

"You must let them believe I am dead," he continued. "I am no good as anything more."

Elric swallowed. "If that is what you wish, I will honor it, but, Timothius, why? What is this you have become? Why are you here?"

Timothius hesitated, then pressed on in hushed words. "We do not have much time, and though I dare to try and separate us for good, to send you away where you might never touch this wretched city's soil ever again, I fear I cannot. I need your help, your strength, to rally the people beyond the walls. To find the elfin folk. To raise a rebellion. To free Inflamel once and for all."

"Against the king? How can you...." The words died on Elric's tongue, confirmed, though his friend's face held no tells. "You are the king's most trusted weapon."

Timothius nodded. "And when the time comes, I will become his reaper. But that is a long way off. I need you, Elric. I can be none other than the faceless soldier. Timothius is dead, but the executioner will lie in wait."

Elric shook his head. "How can you become this? Accept this sentence? The boy who saved field mice becoming the man a kingdom fears."

Timothius was silent for a moment, the echo of footsteps overhead catching his attention. They passed and he leaned in, his form emotionless but his eyes unable to hide the monstrous depths of his pain. Elric feared the truth of what his brother may have already endured more than the hushed words he shared.

"Do you remember those mice? The game we would play? The lies we crafted to the rat catcher to steal them away, promising we would bait them for prey? And the more callous and cruel our tale, the more he would give us? The more he would trust us? You play the part, Elric, no matter how hard it becomes to breathe. You do not remove your mask until it is time for them to see your victory—until it is time for the game to be won. You do not stop playing until the mice are well and away. And then you pray to feel the sun again before they strike you for the final time."

"You cannot mean that," he hissed, voice cracking. "Your life, your freedom, is worth more than this fate."

Voices sounded from the wall above, and in an instant, the alabaster mask had returned to his brother's face. But his eyes...his eyes held more pain and love than Elric could handle. An errant tear ran down his cheek, and Timothius spoke again.

"My life and freedom for your life and freedom. Either we both die prisoners or you live for the both of us. Fate has made this decision, and as a result, I have saved you. I dare say I will not be able to again. You must go, but know the part I play will never reach my heart. My love will always be for you."

Elric embraced him one last time, squeezing his brother of the heart, before Timothius retreated slowly back into the shadows of the castle. "Go, E. I will find a way to reach you. I will always find a way to you."

CHAPTER FIVE

THERE ONCE WAS A GIRL ON THE EDGE OF THE WORLD. She dreamed with the wind in her hair, and the song the waves beat against the cliffs was a lullaby to her soul. She loved the land with its hills and bluffs and the horses that ran free across its expanse. She adored the people with their kind, simple admiration and the way they cared for her without question simply because of who she was.

Because of who her parents were.

And she cherished them the most.

Yet despite everything, when the world grew quiet—when it was nothing but her and the sound of the ocean—she looked beyond it all. Tugged away from her limited world, she was pulled toward more.

She was drawn to the stars.

They comforted her on the nights her father was called away and her mother was not well enough to leave the bed. They kept her company in the dark when the candles burned low, and sometimes when she woke before

THE SUN, THEY STILL TWINKLED OVERHEAD, WAITING WITH HER TO GREET THE SUN AS IT ROSE BEYOND THE CLIFFS AND WAVES.

BUT SHE WAS ALONE THE MORNING THE STRANGE, STERN MAN ARRIVED. HE DID NOT REFER TO HER MOTHER AS LADY LIKE EVERYONE SHE KNEW, BUT INSTEAD QUEEN. AND WHEN HE GREETED HER, HE BOWED LOW AND CALLED HER HIGHNESS.

THAT'S WHEN HE REVEALED THE LETTER IN HER FATHER'S HANDWRITING—THE ONE THAT ASKED HER TO JOIN HIM. THE SAME ONE THAT BROKE HER MOTHER'S HEART.

THE GIRL SPENT THAT NIGHT BENEATH THE STARS AND BETWEEN HER MOTHER'S ARMS. HER MOTHER SPOKE EXCITEDLY OF HOW SHE'D GAIN HER STRENGTH AND JOIN THEM AT THE PALACE, AND WHEN THE GIRL'S LESSONS WANED, THEY'D RETURN TO THE CLIFFS TO CELEBRATE MOONRISE.

BUT THE GIRL DID NOT WANT TO RETURN BECAUSE SHE NEVER WANTED TO LEAVE. SHE WANTED HER MOTHER, THE WAVES, AND THE STARS IN THE ONLY HOME SHE KNEW, WHERE HER FRIENDS WERE THE FOAM TRACKS LEFT ON THE SAND AND THE SHELLS SHE COLLECTED IN HER POCKET—HER TREASURES.

SHE CARRIED SOME WITH HER ALL THROUGH THE CARRIAGE RIDE ACROSS THE KINGDOM. SHE MET SCORES OF PEOPLE WHO LOVED HER FATHER, WHO ASKED FOR HER MOTHER, AND TOLD HER HOW BELOVED SHE WAS FOR BELONGING TO THEM. THEY SMILED AND WAVED, THOUGH THE COACHMAN CRIED, "MAKE WAY!"

AND WHEN THEY FINALLY ARRIVED, AND SHE LEAPED INTO HER FATHER'S ARMS, THEY BOTH CRIED.

HE WAS BUSY AND THE PALACE WAS LONELY, AND THOUGH THE PEOPLE WERE KIND, THEY WERE NOT THE SAME ONES WHO HAD RAISED AND TAUGHT HER, WHO'D TENDED TO HER MOTHER AND SNUCK HER CANDIES.

HER LESSONS WERE DIFFICULT, BUT SHE DEDICATED HERSELF TO THEM, WRITING TO HER MOTHER DAILY AND READING HER REPLIES OVER AND OVER AGAIN. AND AT NIGHT, WHEN THE PALACE GREW

SILENT, SHE KEPT THE CANDLES BURNING TO KEEP THE DARKNESS AT BAY.

MONTHS TICKED BY, GROWING INTO A HANDFUL OF YEARS THAT MARKED HER FIRST DECADE OF LIFE. HER FATHER BECAME MORE DISTANT—DETACHED FROM HER. SHE VISITED HER MOTHER EVERY SUMMER, THOUGH SHE WAS RARELY WELL ENOUGH TO VENTURE FROM THE HOUSE. AND THE GIRL NO LONGER LOOKED FOR THE STARS, SHE ONLY WATCHED HER MOTHER SLEEP.

THE PEOPLE CEASED CALLING TO HER AS SHE RETURNED TO THE PALACE. THE GUARDS URGED HER TO REMAIN AWAY FROM THE WINDOWS, TALKING OF RISK AND DANGER BECAUSE OF WHO SHE WAS. BECAUSE OF WHO HER FATHER WAS. AND WHEN SHE ARRIVED BACK AT THE PALACE, SHE WAS MOVED TO A NEW ROOM DEEP AT ITS HEART WITHOUT WINDOWS TO THE SKY.

HER STUDIES CONTINUED THE SAME, YET DIFFERENT. SHE WAS NOT PERMITTED TO DO THE THINGS A PROPER LADY WOULD, BUT WAS INSTEAD INSTRUCTED ON THINGS A PRINCESS SHOULD KNOW— WHAT A QUEEN WOULD NEED. SHE BEGAN TO RESENT THE LESSONS AND THE WAY HER TUTORS REMINDED HER THAT SHE WAS MADE TO BE A QUEEN. THAT HER VERY NAME WAS ONE MADE FOR STRENGTH. THEY ASSURED HER SHE HAD NOT BEEN NAMED FOR MUSIC OR STUDIES OR NEEDLEPOINT OR GALAS.

NO, SHE HAD BEEN NAMED FOR A THRONE.

AND SHE DESPISED IT.

AND THOUGH SHE MET EVERY EXPECTATION OUTWARDLY, SHE RETREATED INTO HERSELF MORE AND MORE EACH DAY.

LATE ONE NIGHT, LONG AFTER THE PALACE HAD GONE TO SLEEP AND WELL PAST THE TIME A GIRL OF NEARLY TEN SHOULD BE SLUM- BERING, SHE TIPTOED ACROSS THE PALACE AND CLIMBED THE FLOORS UNTIL SHE FOUND WHAT SHE SOUGHT—A ROOM WITH A BALCONY.

BUT WHEN SHE WALKED OUT INTO THE NIGHT, SNOW FALLING SOFTLY ON HER HAIR, ONLY CLOUDS FILLED THE BLUE.

AND THERE WERE NO STARS.

$\mathcal{E}$lric opened his eyes once more to a different bed in a strange room. But to his utter misery, it was yet again beside a familiar face.

"You again," he grunted. "Wonderful."

Falchion snorted. "We do need to cease meeting like this; however, I was charged with ensuring you woke once your body finished mending."

Elric glanced at his arms, clean and devoid of blood, the wounds now gone and his skin brand new, as if nothing had ever happened.

Though he could never forget that it had.

He felt his dhust, the stars, warm inside his veins, but they were not alone anymore. Invisible chains ran beside his strands, their shadow an uncomfortable weight. The tether now lay between him and every bit of peace he once knew. He was no longer his own.

He scowled at his intruder. "I'm awake. You may leave."

Falchion shook his head. "I am also here to escort you to dinner. The queen is holding a banquet to honor your arrival and to commemorate the turning of the tide."

"The tide of what?" Elric grunted, forcing his aching limbs to a sitting position. While the stars within had sealed his wounds, his magic was not all-healing, and he felt every bit of the hundreds of years he had roamed Breteria.

"The revolution," Falchion replied matter-of-factly.

Elric knew all about the revolution that had sparked into a flame over the last months, the people of Obarian rising up against the woman taking the crown after her father had driven them to near destitution, but he would rather hear it from the horse's mouth.

Or rather the ass's jowls.

"The last I checked, Isteriaeth do not possess enough magic to bring about peace, especially between innocents and tyrants."

"They do not. But magic is in short supply here and you are now bound to the queen, which changes things in the eyes of a people who value their history."

"Short supply is a quaint way of describing the genocide of the Isteriaeth and subsequent devaluation of the kingdom that once blossomed under the eye of the Thrones. Which I'm certain Obarian's people remember, if they truly do hold their history so fondly."

Falchion sighed deeply and pushed to his feet. He crossed the room to the cracked light trickling in and flung open the curtain, revealing wide windows.

Elric blinked in the light, brow furrowing as he registered the dimming sky above a setting sun. "It is eventide?"

"I said I was escorting you to supper, did I not?" Falchion muttered, striding to a wardrobe and withdrawing a traditional Isteriaeth robe.

"How long was I indisposed?" Elric asked, eyeing the arcane garment with disdain.

"For a night and a day," the soldier replied. "Now please, dress quickly. I have been sitting here for hours and am famished."

Elric eyed the clothes thrown on the end of the bed, namely the bulbous ceremonial robes of the Isteriaeth cut from crushed velvet, and the brilliant stars embroidered on every hem staring back like a ghost from his past. "I am not wearing that."

"You will have to address that with the queen, as the only garments known were the ones recorded in the books of old." Falchion sighed impatiently. "Now please, rise and dress. The washroom is through that door."

He nodded to the single door opposite the room.

When Elric rose, instead of making for the washroom, he attempted to stretch his aching muscles and hobbled over to the curtains. Upon closer inspection, he realized that they were not large windows, but in fact glass-paned doors with bronze handles that led to a spacious balcony three floors above the ground. But when he tried the handles, they failed to turn.

"They do not open," he remarked flatly.

"Nor do the windows," Falchion added without missing a beat. "They shall remain so until it is assured that you will not pitch yourself off a turret once left unattended."

"I still have dhust in my veins, I would not die."

"No, but you strike me as the kind who would continue trying regardless."

Elric ignored him and glanced around the room, eyeing the seam of a door concealed by the decorative molding of the wall almost directly beside the bed. "And that door?"

Falchion glanced at it with a raised eyebrow. "Impressive of you to notice. That leads to the queen's suites. It is to remain unlocked in case she is in need."

"A door concealed in a wall is not as peculiar as its remaining unlocked with no handle on my side."

"As I said, in the event that *the queen* has needs. She is not to be disturbed by you, and you are allowed privacy until needed. Your privileges will be gained as trust is garnered."

Elric tried to keep his hands from smacking dejectedly

against his sides as the curtain slipped from his fingers, and he refused any slouch in his posture when he turned and strode through the washroom door, but once it was shut firmly behind him, his resolve bent and cowered, and his shoulders slumped.

He had barely been given a moment to heal, to recover from the whirlwind of losses that had been his life for greater than the last three years, and now he needed to brace himself for the reality he swore he'd never have to face again.

The memories of his life before Inflamel.

The days he spent in darkness, cold and starving.

The nightmares of the ocean that had carried him to a new home and family—to safety—but not before it rendered him a lone survivor once more.

Was that all his existence was good for? To be the last? He had believed otherwise, for a short while...until—

He shoved the thought down and pulled on his strands, their familiar caress flooding him with a peaceful warmth, tickling beneath his skin as it traveled to his palms. Blue dhust filled them and spilled over, and then he was holding a pressed ivory collared shirt, clean pants in onyx, and a vest of rich charcoal with silver stitching.

After washing up, he took his time dressing, summoning a comb to brush his auburn locks back into a neat wave, then removing any sign of facial hair from his cheeks. Once finished, he took a deep breath, watched all light drain from his light-blue eyes, and returned to the bedroom.

The guard raised a curious eyebrow, mischief toying with a smile at the corner of his lips. "Those clothes are not the style of Obarian. Unless there is a tailor living in your washroom that I am unaware of."

"He resides alive and well below the basin. Do remind me to feed him later," Elric deadpanned.

"You carry atmospheric magic alone, then," Falchion remarked, ignoring his response.

Elric bristled, lacing his boots. "You knew this. You watched me attempt to escape my prison on your ship with nothing more than thin air."

"This is true, but I had wagered you carried elemental," the soldier replied, strolling toward the door. "What you did in the midst of the squall was unnatural. It could have fooled me."

His words resonated in Elric's mind, revealing his own curiosity over his inconsistent abilities as of late, but he thrust his arms through the sleeves of the atrocious robe and glowered at Falchion instead.

The soldier hid his smile with the back of his hand at the sight of Elric in the giant, billowing travesty of a garment, then cleared his throat before turning the handle. "Well then. Shall we?"

The banquet hall was opulent, though darker than Elric remembered. Candles were lit in the eight-armed fixtures suspended above the floor, showering soft light onto the diamond tile, but what should have radiated upward to illuminate the gilded walls died below the dazzling hems of gowns and shiny boots of the various nobles milling about.

Elric focused on the spectacle and the laughing upper crust in their finery, sipping wine from goblets, though most cheeks were already flushed. He refused to look upon the faces of the portraits surrounding him. The history painted in vignettes on the walls.

History he had learned at his mother's knee.

It was miraculous any history was preserved at all, as rule in Obarian had been passed to many family lines since the Fall of the Thrones. Whether by external force or internal coup, the blood-soaked crown was handed from ruler to ruler all through violent and tumultuous means, with each new king seeking to exterminate the memory of the prior from realm. The people of Obarian, ever the traditional and superstitious beings, believed it to be a curse—the unrest an eternal punishment for their kingdom being the first to bow to the Kollapsars, paving their way to victory over the Trifolium Thrones. Yet through it all, they appeared to have saved as much of their proud origin as the oldest kingdom in Breteria as they could, celebrating its prestige instead of their reputation. It was easier to remember their greatness than their culpability in the Fall of the Thrones and the bickering, betrayal, blood, and bravado that continued every few decades, stopping for a while only to start again.

At least they were still consistent.

Elric focused forward, and above the revelry, he spotted the throne occupied by the woman with deep-red hair braided about her head like a crown, though she did not wear one. Beside her, Lord Blenheim stood, surveying the room as if studying it for imperfections, but while his eyes roamed, hers were fixed on Elric.

He stared back, unflinching, though Falchion's low growl sounded in his ear. "You will show respect to the queen."

Elric's eyes flashed to him for a heartbeat, then returned to the sapphire orbs flaying him alive. He twisted his wrist with a flourish, ending palm up with his first three fingers outstretched and the last two folded in, then tipped his forehead to the ground.

Graecerys smirked, though her eyes held no humor, and without breaking their connection, she lifted her glass to him in response.

Lord Blenheim caught sight of her gesture and followed her gaze to land on Elric. Raising his arm in the air, he signaled to the musicians cloistered in the corner, and the room fell silent.

"Noble people of Obarian, favored of the crown, thank you for assembling on this most festive of occasions. You were promised a celebration, and a celebration we shall have, for our queen has been blessed by the stars themselves. And tonight, I introduce you to the new Advisor to the Crown—the favor of the Stars bestowed upon us, and the final Isteriaeth in the Realm of Breteria."

Whispers filled the room, a chorus of wonder and skepticism mingling as one. The louder it grew, the higher Elric's eyebrow drifted, the stiffer Falchion straightened beside him, and the harder the queen's stare became.

"What is this discourse?" she snapped. "Speak plainly."

A man stepped forward, dressed not unlike Lord Blenheim, though he was considerably younger, with fair green eyes and sand-colored curls that hung against his neck. He bore none of the medals or air of pageantry that the other man did but stood with the same measure of confidence in his posture, and when he spoke his voice was strong and assured. "My lady, it is simply that the people believed the Isteriaeth departed this realm. How do we know this is truth and not a parlor trick conjured by the sorcerer Blenheim hides?"

The silence that descended upon the room was deafening, and before Elric registered that he had moved, Falchion had pulled the man from the crowd and forced him to his knees. "You will address the *queen* with respect and the lord by his station."

The man's laugh barked across the room, causing a tittering of glass as partygoers jumped at the caustic interruption. "I will show honor when her rule is ordained and she has a crown upon her head. And Blenheim is no different a man than I, though he has long forgotten. But do you know who has remembered? The people. Even now they will storm this palace if any harm comes to me at the hands of this circus."

The metallic slide of a sword being unsheathed rang through the air, but as Lord Blenheim stepped forward with blade in hand, the queen stood and spoke so clear that Elric felt as though she were only paces away, not across the room. "Mind your tongue, Lord Jacian, or you might find that you no longer have it. And if it is tricks you want, allow my Isteriaeth to show you his power." Her attention cut to Elric. "Or should I say *our* power."

All eyes turned to Elric, whose gaze remained fixed on the queen.

She only smoothed her dress and sat down again, though straighter this time, and if Elric didn't know any better, he would think she had postured herself within arm's reach of her own weapon, ready to strike.

He made no move to obey, but when a prickling beneath his skin began to tear like claws along his arms, fire burning at the center of his chest, he realized with sickening clarity the true weight of his curse: To reject her wishes was to refuse their tether. And to refuse their tether meant his very being would riot. The stars within his dhust—the very thing that so often comforted him—would be his executioner.

"Come now, Isteriaeth," she prodded, her words a poisonous balm to his needling skin. "Show us what makes you so all-powerful that the lords insisted I needed you to officially claim my throne."

The boldness of her statement tickled his mind, and he quickly filed it away, but before he could respond, the point of a sword tipped into his ribs.

He glared at Falchion, who had returned to his side, but then Lord Blenheim's voice rang out. "Master Isteriaeth, there is a ripened plum on the tray here beside me. Call it to yourself."

The queen's stare became searing hot blood in his veins, and Elric winced under the scrutiny, bracing himself only a heart-beat before the fruit appeared in his hand.

A small gasp went up from the crowd and they drew nearer, wide-eyed as flecks of blue dhust fell from his palm. And then the demands began.

"Isteriaeth, take the feather from my hair."

"Isteriaeth, fetch me more wine."

"Isteriaeth, can you summon my wife? She's wandered off this evening."

The crowd pressed closer, and fire of another kind burned beneath Elric's skin. He had been stolen, stripped of everything, and dragged to the last Thrones-damned place he wanted to be, and for what purpose? To be mocked, ridiculed, and turned into a spectacle. What he wouldn't give to snatch every flickering flame in the room to himself, to steal their light and return it in an all-consuming fire that reduced their world to rubble. Vengeance called like a siren to his dhust, his heart racing with the desire to rage, but beside it the shackles of the tether tightened, an invisible tourniquet that strangled him under the guise of saving his life.

With each loathsome request, he felt the queen's intentions remain firm, and though he was given no choice but to silently obey, his anger festered.

He could no longer keep track of the voices, their demands all blending together, their faces losing shape. His coiled tension snapped and broke, and the last bit of fight within him rained to the floor, mingling with his dhust and washing away his bitterness, leaving him stained. He detached from where he stood and let his mind drift, wondering what it might be like to refuse. What it would take to let himself burn to ashes on her opulent floor instead of facing a lifetime as her puppet.

Finally, Graecerys clapped her hands and stood, silencing the room.

"I believe that is enough for one night. I need my advisor rested for tomorrow, and I have barely begun to stroke the surface of his abilities myself. Tell all of what you've seen. As for you, Lord Jacian, spread word to your connections within the revolution's camp that the stars have smiled upon Obarian's rightful queen. And do not test my goodwill again. I assure you, while my power is now limitless, my patience is not. Do not provoke me."

The man sketched a short bow, glared in the direction of Lord Blenheim, then stormed from the ballroom.

"See he finds his way beyond the palace gates," the queen ordered, her eyes following him, and Falchion clasped his fist over his heart and strode out.

"What are we standing around for? Eat, drink, dance," she ordered, sinking back down on the throne and reclining into its velvet cushion.

The music began with the scratch of strings, and with it, women in gowns and men in their finery swooped onto the dance floor, fanning out like flower petals in a rainstorm.

A few nobles passed Elric by, some stopping to run a hand along his robes and others to gaze into his eye or to examine his face like he was an old statue, but even they started to ignore him. He had served his purpose, been used for entertainment, and now he would be forgotten until needed again.

But while his obedience to the tether was dictated, his free will was not. He would not be able to wander far, but there was no one there to prevent him from seeing just how much distance he might put between himself and this spectacle.

He took one last hard look at the throne, at the woman perched above it all, and with a curt bow that no one saw, he strode from the room.

CHAPTER SEVEN

The halls of the palace were long, cavernous in the darkness despite the flickering lanterns on the wall, and yet Elric still knew them. Their familiarity came back to him the farther he walked, though the finer details remained absent.

Isteriaeth lived brilliant lives, burning in the night sky as stars until their death. Fallen stars were then born to a new existence in Breteria—their conception a rare and beautiful phenomenon—with both strands and dhust giving them life as much as air and sustenance. Elric had been the last of the fallen stars to open their eyes on Breteria, or so he had been told, though no one knew why they ceased being born into the realm. Could it have been because the stars stopped aging and dying? Or had they still perished in the sky, yet refused to enter a world that itself had fallen?

Either way, he had no memory of his life as a star, nor the start of his childhood when he reached his first decade of life and stopped aging—the dhust living within his being failing to fall from his hands and usher in his next stage of growth until he was well away in Inflamel centuries later. The years in between, however, all blurred into fragmented moments within these halls, endless days hidden away with his loved ones, and then cold, empty, silent darkness.

Elric shook off the memory, and instead of returning to his room he walked until he reached the grand staircase. He followed its great spiral down to the receiving hall, but before he could exit to the courtyard, the flickering of the lamp on the wall drew his eye to a room tucked beneath the stairs. The door had been left ajar, and his heart skipped a beat as he took in the frames, aged in various patinas, crammed along its walls. The closer he drew, the faster it raced, until he pushed the door open fully and the face of a woman came into view. One he had not seen since he was far too young, but one imprinted on his heart as much as his mind.

Her long, dark-chestnut hair was caught up in pearled pins and her pale-blue eyes shone in sharp contrast, though there was nothing pointed about her countenance. She was beautiful, bold but delicate, gentle yet powerful, and her smile was warm with a steady strength that bled off the canvas. He reached out as if he could touch her face, like she possessed a tangible hand he could hold, but when he brushed the frame, all he felt were the cold bevels beneath his fingertips.

Of everything he had ever lost, he missed his mother the most.

He moved to the next frame—his uncle—and then the next. Down the line he drifted, from one side of the room to the other, greeting each portrait like his own family were arriving at the palace for an evening together. Their ghosts smiled and laughed, their eyes in every shade of blue—a hall-mark of the Isteriaeth race—recalling another story to his mind. He flipped through the frames leaning against the wall, careful not to topple their stacks, and heard their voices. He smelled the peppermint that had clung to his great-grandfa-ther's coat, and if he concentrated hard enough, he remembered exactly what it felt like to be embraced by each of them.

They shone in his mind like the stars they were, forever lighting up the night sky of his thoughts and illuminating his path forward, dark and desolate as it was.

And when he stepped back to take it in, something within his chest twinged and gave way. He could not bear the weight of it all. Not alone. With one last lingering stare on his mother's face, he left the room and closed the door softly behind him.

The air was bitter as he descended the steps into the courtyard, and he pulled the ghastly robe tighter, though it felt like a vice digging deeper into his skin. The irony that he had only worn it a few hours and was already accepting it struck him and halted his steps.

What would become of him if every bit of his resolve faltered this quickly?

He ripped the garment off, left it in a heap at the bottom of the stairs, then crossed his arms against his chest and stalked into the courtyard. Hedges rose around him on either side, the stone pathways weaving in and out in a patchwork maze, but they sheltered him from the wind, so he continued. The closer he drew to the outer gate, however, the sharper a pain dug into his flesh, like a hook around his neck assuring he did not wander too far from his captor. He subconsciously knew he would not set foot outside the gate again—at least not without the queen—yet part of him wondered how far he would make it if he continued walking. How close could he get to the shore before the tether tore him apart entirely?

He wandered aimlessly through the hedges, and about the time he accepted that he was well and truly lost, the pathway widened and each trail converged in an open, circular patio. At the center stood a stone fountain, the water falling in a slow trickle—the cold taking its toll—and in the middle of it was a statue that stole his breath.

A man, crown in the hand by his side and water flowing from the outstretched palm of the other, stood with his head tilted to the stars. The water glittered, reflecting the luminaries that surrounded the pool, making it appear as though stars shimmered like diamonds and cascaded through his fingers to the inlaid rock below.

Elric walked along the edge, gazing at his own blurred reflection in the water, until he reached the front where he looked up at the face of the man, worn down and faded through time.

Gevallester. The first King of Obarian. The one the stars had ordained to rule over the land they called their own. His charge was to balance doctrine and dhust, and he had done just that as both a gracious ruler and a stalwart warrior until just before the Kollapsars rose. For reasons unknown, he then passed the Obarian crown and Trifolium Throne to his most trusted friend—the fabled Einherjar Warrior who had fought as a commander by his side to claim Breteria for the Trifolium Thrones. The same Einherjar who would later betray the entire realm.

But it was not the statue that drew Elric's focus.

"If you are determined to lurk, have the decency to do so in shadow," he grumbled aloud.

There was a moment of silence, and then Falchion eased around the corner of the hedges Elric had just emerged from. "I was unsure if you would know your way—"

"Of course I know my way," Elric snapped. "This palace was my home before you were an inkling in your mother's mind."

The soldier froze, surveying him quietly, assessing him, though the Isteriaeth refused to look away. Finally, Falchion broke their stare and nodded to the statue. "Did you know him?"

Elric shook his head tersely. "I knew of him. Stories told to me by my mother who remembered him fondly. He was first and only of his name, then he passed his crown to the Einherjar who became king not long after my ascension."

"Ascension?" the soldier asked, leaning against the fountain's wall and removing a cork from a bottle. "I am unfamiliar with the term."

"Because it is not Breterian. It is one the Isteriaeth use. One would think that a star dying and coming to earth might be a loss, but to us it is ascension. There is no greater honor than to walk the world that gave us life after death."

"You lived an entire life as a star, then died and started over here?" Falchion asked incredulously.

Elric only nodded.

Recognition dawned on the soldier's face. "Every Isteriaeth began again here…and then they were…."

"You know the history," Elric responded quietly after a heartbeat of silence.

Falchion stared at him, face unreadable, but in his eyes, Elric saw something soften. "The time for compassion is over and gone," he added flatly, resting both hands on the stone wall and leaning forward, peering into the water. "Do not pity me now."

Falchion said nothing, looking away and gazing up at the sky for a long while. When the soldier moved, it was toward Elric to hold out a second corked bottle.

He stared at it. "The last drink you offered me was laced. How confident of you to assume I would accept another."

Falchion shook his head, a measure of sadness and regret wrinkling his brow and the skin about his eyes. "As you astutely indicated, I have no need to drug you now, Master Elric. I simply thought you may need it, if for nothing more than a dreamless sleep."

He did not wait for Elric to accept the peace offering, setting it on the wall beside his hand before striding back to the pathway they had come from.

"By the way," he added, the words floating over his shoulder, "exit the path at your back. It will circle around to the side of the palace. You will enter a different hall. One without portraits."

Elric's eyes widened and snapped to him, but there was no mirth or mocking on the soldier's face when he turned. Only understanding. "Have a good evening, Master Elric."

Elric remained frozen in place long after Falchion left, then finally gave in, uncorking the bottle and taking a long drag of the dry, dark wine. It warmed him from the inside, and he drank deeply again, realizing he should exit the maze before draining any more. There were few imports he missed from Obarian during his time in Inflamel, and of them, the wine was his favorite.

His mind drifted back to Inflamel as he walked, and despite his hopeless circumstances in Obarian, he found them easier to dwell on than the painful thought of the kingdom his heart had always called home.

Another gulp of wine and he recalled the tree home he had lived in—the sweet memories made there.

Another tip of the bottle and he swore he heard his friend, the one closer than a brother, laugh. Though it did not sound right. It was not full of joy, but something else entirely. Something much darker.

He drank again, and all of it melted away to a voice he would recognize above any rabble—that of his sweet Kathrina. But it, too, was wrong. Her words were too breathy and barely there.

"Oh, the way I love you."

He tripped up the final step into the palace, then drained the bottle to silence the noise.

Noise.

The last time he had existed within this palace the silence was the thing that tortured him. Sound had, in fact, saved him from it all. He wondered if that room of beautiful noise still existed, if he might find it and hide there once more, though he wasn't sure if he would know how. He had never entered it from this side of the world. He only knew it from within the walls.

But maybe he might focus on locating it instead.

Not on the ghosts of his family, cut down by the kingdom imprisoning him now.

Not on the brother and later sister he had discovered family in—though they shared no blood—then betrayed, failing to safeguard them when they needed him most.

Not on the seconds he had been too Thrones-damned late to save the love of his life.

No, maybe he might become a boy once more. Hidden away, imagining a different life, playing pretend. He had survived that way once, maybe he might do so again.

By some sort of miracle, Elric found his way back to his quarters, stumbling past the guards stationed at either end of the hall, then shut himself firmly inside.

He threw his vest aside, slipping from his boots and unbuttoning his sleeves and the top few buttons of his shirt before collapsing on the bed. The world spun gently around him, warming his cheeks and dizzying him in delightfully soft waves as the intoxication latched deeper. He smiled.

He could almost convince himself everything was fine. Almost....

He saw nothing when he opened his eyes again, but the pounding of his heart told him where he was. And he was alone.

The rocking of the darkness lifted a tide of devastation in his chest, and a panicked fear sank its claws into his mind as the water rose higher.

But then he smelled it.

Lilacs.

And he was not lost at sea any longer. He was home. With Kathrina. He had not lost her. He had not buried her on their wedding day.

Gentle hands held his own. Tender kisses pressed to his face. A laugh. A caress. The slide of silken skin against his body; golden hair falling in his face, wrapped around his fingers. Soft gasps and warm sighs and hot breaths mingling so close they became one.

Here, stories were whispered and vows were stolen beneath the stars. Here, Elric could breathe again. Here, in his dreams, in this place where her heart still beat—where he had not been seconds too late—she was hidden away safe in his memory. And no one would touch them there.

CHAPTER EIGHT

The sunlight was a jarring white against the rich blues and greens of Elric's quarters. It brought no warmth to his skin but did serve to increase the pounding behind his eyelids.

It was far too late in the morning, and for the first time since his kidnapping Falchion was not there staring down at him. There was no one to witness him lying in last night's wrinkled clothes, still in a post-drunken haze, and for the first time since his kidnapping, he felt a small sense of relief despite the trepidation.

Elric shut himself in the bath chamber, summoned water to his basin, and eased into the steaming tub. His muscles relaxed in the heat, and as he stared at the ceiling, watching the candle flicker in the sconce, he found himself recalling Falchion's words.

"I had wagered you carried elemental. What you did in the midst of the squall was unnatural. It could have fooled me."

Elric was no stranger to testing the bounds of his magic. From the time it was finally bestowed on him—a few short years after his arrival in Inflamel—until he had physically aged well past twenty, he had done nothing but hone his skill.

In truth, he could not have done much else. His adoptive family, fearing for his life, hid him away in the forest so no one learned of his true identity. So none would steal his life away as they had now.

In another age, his dhust would have been celebrated, blossoming naturally after his first physical decade of life instead of remaining dormant and leaving him a child for hundreds of years. His extended childhood days with his family had been a blessing, one he wished he had not taken for granted, but as an adult, he wondered why they had not found his lack of dhust concerning. It should have emerged so they could guide him, test him, and help develop his strand, ferrying him into adulthood, but that was not his lot. Alone, he had taught himself as much as possible with the very basic lessons he remembered from *before*, learning the ins and outs of his ability through trial and error alone.

But what if some of his capabilities were not loopholes? What if more than one strand of dhust had been bestowed upon him, thinly veiled as the same atmospheric blue?

Elric stared at the candle. How many times had he summoned flame to wick? Was it called, or had he instead generated it from thin air? And upon the ship, he had not decided how to approach the storm and yet they found a break. Was it luck, or had it in fact been him forming a clearing?

There was one way to learn more, and he was in the correct place to do so, but that would mean returning to the place his family had lived and worked—if it still existed. If any of their journals had survived. And if their portraits had been hidden away in no more than a closet of a room, who knew where the Isteriaeth's tomes resided now.

He rose from the bath, summoned himself a fresh shirt,

pants, and vest in a deep shade of caramel, then laced his boots while munching on a biscuit he had called to his fingers—unable to stomach the thought of eating a full meal, but knowing he needed something to absorb the remnants of wine inhabiting his system.

When he faced the door, however, he paused. It had been oddly quiet so far that morning. Would he truly be allowed to walk freely within the palace walls?

He approached hesitantly, grasped the knob that was shockingly cold to the touch, then turned it fully.

Unlocked.

Adrenaline surged through his veins, the stars moving beside it, but the moment he swung the door open, a large body stepped before its frame.

Elric sighed, glowering at the soldier. "I knew you wouldn't be far."

"I thought you might like your privacy after last eve," said Falchion brightly, a conspiratorial smile revealing the dimple in his cheeks. "But I am here now to escort you to the Diviner's Wing."

Elric froze. "The Diviner's Wing?"

Falchion stopped a few paces down the hall, turning back to face him. "Yes, do you know it?"

Elric closed his door behind him with a *click*. "I do. I…spent many days within that wing. I just did not believe it would still be intact."

"Understandably so," Falchion continued, speaking as they made their way down the hall. "It has been preserved by each bearer of the crown. Some say it was from shame. Some say it was in hopes that the stars might see it as a sign of goodwill and return once more. Either way, it has not been disturbed."

A chill ran across Elric's skin, and though he kept a steady pace with the soldier—despite his stride outpacing Elric two to one—he felt everything slowing around him, and his heartbeat echoed inside his head.

His mother's firm kiss pressed to his forehead. Lingering.

Soft hair grasped in his small fists.

A shawl wrapped around his shoulders with her favorite brooch to hold it tight.

It smelled like her.

Even after the world grew silent, and his tears soaked it through in the darkness, it smelled like her.

"Are you well, Master Elric?"

Falchion's words jolted Elric back to the present. He realized he had stopped climbing the staircase at some point and stood with a palm flat against the wall to ground himself.

Blinking quickly, he gathered himself and cleared his throat. "I am well," he replied, a rasp betraying him.

Falchion nodded slowly, but didn't look like he believed him for a moment.

"I am just a bit winded from last night's libations," Elric added, continuing up the stairs, though he found himself trembling. "Thank you for that, by the way. It has been far too long since I last experienced Obarian wine. I forgot how easy it is to enjoy quickly."

Falchion snorted. "I shall not judge if you find you need more. Just do not let it become a nightly habit. You may be called upon at any time, and all will undoubtedly require you to have your wit about you, though I will try to warn you of their arrival ahead of time."

Elric hummed. "You are my warden, then."

"Not at all," laughed the soldier. "Consider me your bodyguard."

"Handler."

"Assistant."

Elric snorted. "Assistant in what?"

"Ascending staircases. Wine supply. Library…needs?"

Elric shook his head as they reached the top landing and proceeded down the hall.

"Or I dare say you may call me a friend."

Elric glanced at the man who stared straight forward, as if avoiding his own words. "A friend who kidnapped me at an alleged usurper's behest and brought me to a kingdom in which I was to be imprisoned?"

"I never said you had good taste in friends, I merely said you might call me one."

Elric could not help it, he laughed. And with it he felt the tension bleed from his body, chasing away the last of the heart-broken pieces pitted in his stomach. "I feel as though we are too far ahead of ourselves. But I might consider it. Eventually."

Falchion nodded. "You have all the time in the world, I hear."

Elric rolled his eyes. "We have already established that jokes about my age are beneath you."

Falchion hesitated, then after a heartbeat, slowly asked, "How old are you exactly?"

"How old do I look?"

"Well, you appear to be my age. You have seen three decades at least."

"And I have. Plus over three centuries."

Falchion peered at him closely. "But that would mean you were born to this realm during the age of the Trifolium Thrones."

"Yes."

"And yet…this palace is familiar to you."

"Yes."

"Then if the Isteriaeth within this kingdom were hunted to the last, how is it that you as a child survived?"

Silence fell between them, but Elric offered no more information.

Finally, before the last door, he spoke. "We are not that well of friends yet."

Falchion met his eyes, but instead of pressing or prying, he nodded. And if Elric didn't know any better, he thought he recognized a grim respect in his gaze. "I will remain here. If you have needs, you may relay them to me, and I shall only interrupt if you are summoned."

Elric looked at the door, then back to the soldier. "You would leave me unattended in a wing that contains a realm's worth of knowledge from a powerful family line?"

Falchion turned, posting himself facing down the hall they had just walked. "I would leave you to confront whatever it is that stops your thoughts while walking and drives you to drink at night."

Elric hesitated, studying the candelabra winding up the wall, affixed to it like a vine, then cautiously spoke. "You talk as if you understand what it is to lose. To be without a home and a family."

Falchion did not move, he did not waver from his post, but when Elric gave up waiting for an answer and reached for the door, a reply came. "I was young but already helping on my uncle's farm in the Province of Westoram. My father was a fisherman, and my mother had just given birth to my little sister." His voice warmed at the mention of her but began to tremble as he continued in hushed tones. "She was a surprise, but a welcome one, and my world spun around the smallest of her fingers. They were accompanying my father on a short trip around our coast. I was left behind on the farm, as they were only meant to be gone a day, but…something went wrong."

Elric stared at the soldier who continued to gaze unflinchingly down the hall. "The raided boat and lifeless bodies of my mother and father washed up on the southern shore. My sister was but a babe, and it is not possible for her to have survived, yet her body was never found. Still to this day I cannot accept a reality in which she, too, is gone. Many have tried with good intent to help me face the inevitable, but that is not for them to decide. I have mourned in my own way and my own time, and if grief is all I have left of my family, none will take it from me. Much has been stolen from you. This need not be another."

Falchion blinked, one lone tear falling from his eye and rolling down his cheek. He quickly brushed it away, and Elric cleared his throat, turning away out of respect for the man's grief. "I thank you, then, for your kindness. And for sharing something so vulnerable. You did not have to."

The soldier finally cleared his throat and turned his head, the mischievous gleam in his eye once more. "It is what a *friend* would do."

Elric sighed and shook his head, turning the knob and throwing his shoulder into the door, which opened with a loud *POP*. "Handler."

"Assista—"

The word was cut off as Elric closed the door behind him. After taking a deep breath, he straightened his vest and stepped up the four stone steps into the circular room.

Memories bowled him over instantly, fleeting snippets that felt more like distant dreams than his own lifetime.

The walls stretched high into the tower's turret, their shelves reaching all the way to the peaked ceiling. Light filtered down from the windows in the roof, illuminating the aged spines and the single ladder tall enough to retrieve them all.

Just ahead was an arched doorway leading to what he knew would be an office, and off to the left was a spiral staircase that would lead to a second landing with a small balcony that over-looked the room.

He had silently climbed that staircase so many times, crouching behind the wall, hastily folding paper, then waiting for the perfect moment to launch his small bird toward the long table that now sat to his right.

It was covered in dust, but the papers strewn about appeared to have been thrown there recently.

At least more recent than his time.

It was true that he had ascended to Breteria before the Fall of the Thrones, and while most Isteriaeth had perished during—including Elric's grandfather, who served the Throne of Inflamel—the history that had been passed down in Obarian regarding the age after the fall was inaccurate. There *had* been Isteriaeth who survived, remaining alive and well in places where they were protected. But as that safety slowly eroded, they, too, fell and suffered far worse fates. Ones that the proud Obarians did not wish to remember.

What came next, he refused to recall—a time in his childhood so dark that it vanished into the furthest reaches of his memory, far enough away for him to escape altogether. That is, until he had stood before his mother's portrait.

Until he remembered the last time he saw her face.

Until he looked about this very wing.

Here, his past would not be ignored.

Why his magic had been delayed, he did not know. But why they abandoned him, why his mother would leave him behind, alone, he would never understand.

Elric physically shuddered, shaking himself out of the cold clutches that were churning what little food he had in his stomach. Walking gingerly to the doorway, careful not to disturb the books strewn about the floor, he rested his hand on the arch.

The audible *POP* of the door sounded, and he sighed. So much for being left alone with his ghosts and his grief. He turned, fully expecting to see the annoying guard insistent on befriending him, but caught his composure quickly when he met the eyes of none other than Queen Graecerys.

Her gaze moved over him, to his feet then back up again, and she tilted her head to the side, a disapproving look slackening her face. "You do not care for the wardrobe curated for you?"

Elric's eyes narrowed. "I do not care to wear clothes I'm

certain my great-grandfather and his grandfather before him would have possessed."

"And you do not approve of the Obarian style either? Surely *that* was not provided to you here."

Elric looked down at his ensemble before turning his gaze to the queen once more. "I know what I like and what I do not. And if you can believe it, I enjoy using my dhust for convenience."

Graecerys stepped forward, folding her arms. "Interesting. That is not something I would have surmised last night. You seemed quite irritated showing off your striking power."

"My own convenience," Elric replied, words clipped. "Striking power begets striking wardrobe."

A small smile toyed with the edges of the queen's mouth, her eyebrow twitching upward before she schooled her features and strode slowly about the tower. The action was so reminiscent of the night he'd arrived—the night he was bound to her—that it gave him pause. He had suspected then, but he was certain now. She *was* amused by him. But not for show or in entertainment. No, she enjoyed his cynicism, and of all things his dry, bitter wit.

Interesting, indeed.

"I see they wasted no time bringing you up here," the queen continued, her voice echoing about the room as she stopped to peruse the shelves.

Elric folded his arms and leaned against the frame of the door. "They? Do you make a habit of blaming others for carrying out your wishes?"

"Queens do not wish, they command," she replied, rising onto her toes to read the spines on the shelf just above her head.

"And though you are queen, it is Blenheim who seems to control the palace. Is that true?"

Her shoulders stiffened, but she did not turn or pause her careful examination of the tomes. "Blenheim was my father's second-in-command. When my father passed from this life, it was his wish that Blenheim steward my path as queen."

"Yet so few accept you as their queen. Is that why I am here as your advisor? To improve upon his progress?"

"An important part of his plan to assure my reign is you," Graecerys replied, disdain dripping from her tone. "Obarians hold fast to rite and ritual. My ascension to the throne followed neither, and my claim as the sole child and heir of the appointed king proved insufficient in their eyes. You are a means to an end to earn their favor."

"And have I been successful?"

Graecerys rose onto her toes, flashing a wry smile over her shoulder. "No, just an irritation."

Annoyance flared within Elric. "Maybe instead of hunting me, your efforts might have been focused inward. Perhaps what Obarian needs is not an Isteriaeth, but a ruler they can respect."

The soles of Graecerys's shoes smacked the floor, and Elric allowed a slow, derisive smile to fill his face as she turned. Her fair complexion was mottled red with anger, and though she laughed, he could see the raging tempest in her eyes.

"I did not want you here. I still do not. Your kind does nothing but herald reminders of suffering, of the darkest days this realm has ever seen."

Elric tsked. "Bold of you to blame darkness on a star."

"And brazen of you to speak down to me when you walk the same fallen earth that I do," she fired back.

A throat clearing loudly from the doorway reminded Elric they were not alone. He straightened and glanced to where Falchion stood, but the guard only shifted from one foot to the other and continued staring down the hall.

He turned back to Graecerys, whose midnight eyes threatened to burn him alive, though he refused to back down when she took a step toward him. "Respect is a luxury in Obarian. One even a queen cannot afford. But you can be certain of this, I am controlled by no one. And if I am to be any sort of ruler, I will be my own first."

She spun back to the shelves, her light-green dress fanning out around her, then snatched a book off the shelf, tucked it to her front, and marched toward the stairs without a word.

"Good day to you as well, Your Grace," Elric muttered, and he did not move until the door slammed at her back.

Strolling to the place where she had stood just moments before, his eyes ran over the titles on the shelf and he frowned. Of all the records and knowledge hidden in the tomes of the wing, she had been looking at Breterian history. And out of every book, she had taken the second to last timeline of Obarian history.

Elric snorted. What sort of ruler was still learning about their own kingdom? Surely someone whose father was already king—who was inevitably raised to be queen—could remember the details of the history, the very foundation of their land, that lived in every soul born to Obarian soil?

He shook off the peculiar interaction and finally turned back to the office he had only partially entered before. It was small but bright, the walls hardly anything but windows, with a low ceiling and an oddly clean desk. It had never been clean before.

Walking around it, he slipped the center drawer open. Parchment and a fresh quill lay inside, and when he flicked a lever within, the false backing of the drawer fell away. He gently gripped the wafer-thin metal within and pulled out the hidden treasure. Staring at the glasses in his palm, a single strand of silver hair still caught in the arm drew his eye.

His great-grandfather had also possessed atmospheric magic —all the men in his mother's line had—and Elric could not count how many times the man had sat at that very desk, spotted Elric peeking in the door and called him to his knee. Objects would then flit in and out of his hands. Small toys, sweets, occasionally something useful he would inevitably *lose* and need Elric to help locate later. Elric never knew the burden he carried, never understood why he disappeared so suddenly. And he didn't want to know now. He only wanted to hold on to the joy he always saw reflected in the glasses he so delicately held.

Elric had never known his father. His mother shared as many tear-stained memories with him as she could for him to understand that he had been lost in the Fall of the Thrones, and though Elric was surrounded with enough love to not dwell on that fact, he always wondered what strand his father possessed. His mother, on the other hand, possessed elemental magic—a glittering emerald cloud that danced and spun on the breeze, gently beckoning the elements forth. It all obeyed her, adoring her as much as everyone who knew her. But none loved her more than Elric.

His sank into the chair, the weight of each recollection finally too much to hold, and rested his elbows on the desk. He had lost so much, more than he ever truly allowed himself to absorb, and to hold something that once belonged to someone he loved was an indescribable gift.

Yet it wasn't enough.

He would always have the memories, but even they were discarded in the recesses of his mind. He did not want any of it. Not while he was still trapped within these walls alone. He had falsely allowed himself to feel free for a short while, but the chains of the past locked around his heart had never fully released, and now it was their turn to lead.

He rose from the desk and left the office, surveying the tower and wondering where to start. Leafing through the stack of papers on the table, he stiffened. It was article after article detailing Isteriaeth law.

Particularly vows and tethering.

The queen had used his own family's work—his own history —to capture and claim him.

Acerbic bitterness churned in his stomach, flooding his veins with anger and a ravenous longing for vengeance, though it went against everything in his very being. Isteriaeth did not ascribe to the same laws as the other beings that walked upon Breteria—neither the other Awduron races who founded the world nor the Elérynd humans who did not carry dhust, though they believed in it. No, Isteriaeth respected the word of those who ruled, but their own code and laws were strict. Handed down from the Great Three—called the Raeltach—who came together to preserve the exiled magic and knit together the realm of Breteria, there was no doctrine more ancient or sacred to them.

Their currency, their worth, was weighed in mercy.

It was the price their power demanded, an equal payment for the life they had been given, and any above or below the stars were held to it. But mercy would not work here. It did not exist any longer. Not in Obarian and hardly anywhere else in Breteria. Not when you were desperate to survive.

There was nothing more valuable, more sought after, than dhust. The Isteriaeth had been killed for it, the elfin folk hid because of it, and the faeries were still hunted for the same. And while Awduron and Elérynd alike clamored greedily for the power it provided, the Isteriaeth had refused to barter in power. And it had led to their demise.

If Elric was expected to exemplify their law, he would end up joining his ancestors faster than he thought. But if he intended to survive, to rid himself of this place and return to whatever future had been ripped from his hands in Inflamel, then he had no choice but to withhold mercy. And if he were already doomed to reject their favor, what prevented him from disgracing them more? What stopped him from severing his tie to Graecerys and freeing himself?

The thought chilled him but the vision, the memory of Timothius's words rang in his mind.

"Play the part. No matter how hard it becomes to breathe. Until it is time for the game to be won."

The words had been an explanation so long ago, but they had returned to him now as a weapon. And the more he considered it, the more he realized there may be no other choice.

If he were to escape, to be free again, he would need to end the life of the Queen of Obarian.

CHAPTER NINE

Falchion turned out to be as reliable a vintner as he was handler, and Elric didn't complain each time the guard left a bottle of wine in his room. He just allowed him to think they were consumed responsibly over the following weeks as he summoned more to himself and sent the empty bottles away when he woke.

He longed to be back in Inflamel, his heart begged for all he had lost, but in the end, he was not only trapped in servitude but imprisoned in life with no way to seek out joy. It had all been stolen from him, one way or another, and he had finally stopped fighting long enough to be crushed by its reality.

Each day that passed, every morning that he woke to the reality of his entrapment, was an unimaginable weight pressing down on him like gravity itself, making it near impossible to rise. There were a thousand things he wished he could do, an entire life of freedom he did not have as he passed day after day in the ashes of his lineage and the carefully curated prison of his quarters.

But there is one thing I might do. One way to break free.

The dark call for vengeance whispered in his mind, begging its deadly musings to be entertained. They kept him awake at night, staring at the midnight sky from the inside of his locked balcony door, breeding bitterness in his soul. The barrier blocking him from the stars threatened to drive him mad until his heavy hand poured just the right amount of wine, allowing him to silence the thoughts and slip into his dreams—his lone source of comfort. It was after one such night that he stepped out of his quarters and stopped with a jerk backward.

Falchion was nowhere in sight.

"You there," Elric said, approaching a soldier at the end of the hall. "Where is my guard?"

"Mandatory training for his regiment today, Master Isteriaeth. You are permitted to your wing alone, unless you are uncertain of the way, in which case I shall call you an escort."

"None needed, thank you," Elric replied, curious that this had not been thought of. "Unless you fancy a walk."

"I move when the queen moves."

He looked at the only other door along the hall. "She is still in her chambers? At this late hour?"

"I commit to memory the comings and goings of my men, not my queen, Master Isteriaeth, though I expect her soon," the soldier said, facing forward at his post once more.

"Well then. I will leave you to it." Elric nodded, making his way down the hall blissfully alone.

It was halfway up the stairs to the Diviner's Wing that he paused.

He wondered....

Turning on his heel, he retraced his steps and continued down the stairwell to the second floor. He wandered its path until he found the short corridor branching off to the right.

A corridor that contained a series of small rooms.

He felt ill, cold sweat beading on the skin at his hairline, panic billowing in his mind and swirling around the shrouded memory he refused to let clear. And when he reached the door that sat exactly below the wing he inhabited day after day only floors above, he took a deep breath and turned the handle.

The once open space was now crowded with tables lining the walls in long, low rows, obstructing his view of the stone surface. Apart from the stain on the carpet that correctly identified the room—the very one he had caused—there was nothing familiar about it. No books. No benches.

"Might I help you, Isteriaeth?" a voice all but hissed.

Elric jumped, turning to find himself face-to-face with a man he had not seen since the night he arrived—the man who had wielded a blade and bled him to dhust.

In the daylight, he appeared less menacing, though he was shorter than even Elric. He couldn't tell if it was a result of the way his frame hunched—adapted to working over a desk—or his given stature, but his eyes were an unnatural shade of green so fair it tinged gray.

"I…my apologies, I was unaware this room was occupied," Elric replied, realizing he had no good reason for his presence there.

The man lifted a dark brow. "That you knew this room existed at all is a fascination. That you sought it out from every other door in this wing is a peculiarity."

"I am familiarizing myself with my new residence," Elric said simply, shaking off the gnawing discomfort of the man's scrutiny. "I don't believe we've been properly introduced. In fact, I don't believe I've seen you since…."

The man smiled coldly, his skin wrinkling in tight lines that looked more like gouges across his face. "You would not. It is not my job to be seen, but to do the watching."

He stepped forward, forcing Elric back into the room, then slipped by him like no more than a breeze, slinking around the table and returning an empty dram to a shelf.

"I am the magnificent Augur," he declared, fingering a line of vials, all filled with colorless liquid, before choosing one. "And you are Elric. Son of Llewyrenna."

Elric stiffened at his mother's name. "You are a spy, then?"

"I need not spy when the walls and waters tell me all I need know," he said, the vial in his palm flaring a deep green.

Elric's eyes snagged on it, his mind piecing together his experiences with the man before him. The knowledge of the ancient tongue, the ability to execute a tethering, even though he possessed no dhust, and now the elixir in his hand all pointed to one dark, perverted form of magician.

"You are a thaumaturge," he bit out in disbelief. "You seek out power unnatural to this realm, pervert the strands given by the Raeltach. Pray tell, what speaks to you from the walls and waters? Are there strands, dhust alive and well within the stone itself, or do its shadows whisper to you?"

The man smiled cruelly. "My talents are magnificent to behold, as you have seen. Yet that is a bold accusation to make. You must know the kindness being shown to you, allowing you to inhabit the palace freely. Your strands could be plucked from the prisons. An Isteriaeth only need retain an ounce of life for their tethered to reap the benefits."

A chill prickled Elric's skin, invisible fingers tightening around his throat and knotting his gut. Was the demon of a man simply threatening? Or did he know the exact manner that death had come for Elric's ancestors?

"Ah," Augur drew out. "Are those memories hiding behind your eyes? Or do you wonder even now what became of your people? Would you like me to tell you?"

"Do not pretend to know me," Elric snapped, unnerved by how easily his thoughts were perceived. "I would remember an urchin such as you leached to the walls of this palace. I knew Obarian had fallen, but I did not know they would stoop so far as to invite perverse magic into their midst. I suppose it now makes sense how I was subdued. Tell me, where do you source the dhust for your tinctures? How many faeries have you slain?"

"None," Auger replied. "The Obarian lords of old were careful with their Isteriaeth, wasting not. They were only ever missing one of the five strands. But as it would seem, the temporal strand is not needed to subdue a star—you already bear the weight of time's curse."

Elric stared in cold loathing at the creature before him. The one who had used the remnant dhust of his own family to bind him. And at the look in his eyes, Augur smiled at him through crooked teeth.

"You and I are not unlike the other, Master Elric. Power much darker and more vast than what we carry shackles us to this place while our own bitterness serves as a paralytic. Freedom, liberation, comes when such entrapment is learned and wielded as a weapon. When the binds that tie are turned on those who hold us and we may witness the life choked from their eyes."

"I am nothing like you," Elric responded through clenched teeth.

"No? Then you've not been here long enough. But do not worry. It is a matter of time."

The man chuckled low in his chest, and Elric turned to leave, flinging the door back before Augur's words stopped him once more.

"Take note, Isteriaeth, that this wing is one of the eldest in the palace. It dates back to the Age of the Thrones, though its use was not known. In more recent years, before the last royal line was overthrown, these rooms were used for private studies of sorts. In fact, when I came into possession of this one, there was just one item within."

Elric's heart fell, his hopes dashing to pieces on the cold stone floor of reality, though he was not certain why they had bothered to rise in the first place. He gathered himself quickly and turned to face Auger. He wondered if the man suspected why he had come there, afraid he might be sifting through his mind even as he stood there. "And what was it?" he asked coldly, but he already knew the answer.

"Why, this was the music room. It contained only an old piano."

CHAPTER TEN

THERE ONCE LIVED A GIRL BY THE CLIFFS AND THE SEA. SHE LOVED THE WAY THE SNOW FOGGED ON THE MOUNTAINS, THE WAY THE ICE SPRAYED FROM WAVES AGAINST THE ROCK, AND THE WAY THE SHELLS LOOKED LIKE CRYSTALS TUCKED INTO THE SAND AS THE WATER WAS CALLED BACK TO THE DEPTHS. BUT NOW THEIR DIAMOND-STUDDED PATTERN FADED INTO VELVET CUSHIONS, SKIRTS AND CORSETS, AND HAIR PIECES SHE WAS NOT ALLOWED TO TOUCH. HER WORLD OF FRESH AIR AND WILD HORSES HAD VANISHED, AND A NEW WORLD LAY BEFORE HER.

BUT THE GIRL FOUND SOMETHING ELSE SHE LOVED—SOMETHING THAT SUSTAINED HER WHEN THE NIGHTS GREW TOO QUIET AND THE DAYS TOO LONG.

MUSIC.

SHE EXCELLED IN HER STUDIES FAR BEYOND ANY OTHER INSTRUCTION GIVEN, POURING HER HEART INTO EACH PIECE, MEMORIZING EVERY PLACE HER FINGERS DANCED ACROSS THE IVORY KEYS IN A SMALL MUSIC ROOM IN THE ELDEST WING. SOON THEY PLAYED IN THE AIR, NO MATTER WHERE SHE WAS, PLUCKING OUT THE MELODY, THOUGH NO SOUND COULD BE HEARD. AND WHEN SHE WAS TOLD TO REMAIN STILL, REMINDED TO ACT

BECOMING OF A LADY, SHE WOULD IMAGINE THE MOVEMENT IN HER MIND AND WAIT.

THEN AT NIGHT, WHEN THE CANDLES BURNED BRIGHT AND THERE WERE NO STARS TO KEEP HER COMPANY, SHE STOLE DOWN TO THE ROOM, SAT UPON THE BENCH, AND PLAYED UNTIL HER HEART FOUND REST.

SHE PICTURED THE NOTES FLOWING FROM THE PAGE, BALANCING ON HER FINGERS, THEN FALLING THROUGH THE KEYS BEFORE BEING CARRIED OFF, OUT OF THE PALACE AND ACROSS THE FIELDS, RACING LIKE A HORSE AGAINST THE WIND, OR DANCING LIKE SHE MIGHT HAVE WHEN SHE WAS WILD. THEY WERE ADVENTURES SPUN FROM HER HANDS, STORIES BUILT FROM HER SOUL. THEY SANG WHAT HER HEART FELT, WHAT HER MIND COULD NOT EXPLAIN, AND WHAT HER MOUTH WOULD NEVER UTTER, AND THROUGH THEM, SHE WHISPERED, SCREAMED, LAUGHED, AND CRIED.

THROUGH THE MUSIC, SHE LIVED.

IT WAS ONE SUCH NIGHT, PLAYING A PIECE BY HEART—HER EYES WATCHING THE CANDLELIGHT FLICKER ACROSS THE ROOM LIKE GRACEFUL DANCERS—THAT SHE NOTICED THE WALLS FOR THE FIRST TIME.

THEY WERE CIRCULAR, ROUNDING THE ROOM ITSELF TO CENTER THE PIANO, WITH SQUARE PANELS HAND CARVED INTO CURLS AND TWISTS THAT FRAMED IT INTO SECTIONS THREE-TIERS TALL TO THE CEILING.

ONLY, THE PANEL THAT HER LIGHT REFLECTED ON WAS DIFFERENT FROM ALL THE OTHERS.

SHE WASN'T SURE WHAT LED HER TO HALT THE SONG AND APPROACH IT, BUT WHEN SHE DREW CLOSER, SHE NOTICED THAT THE CARVINGS SEEMED TO BE ETCHED TOO DEEPLY INTO THE WOOD ON ONE SIDE...ALMOST LIKE A SEAM.

THE GIRL PRESSED ON IT WITH BOTH HANDS, AND INSTEAD OF REMAINING FIRM BENEATH HER PALM, IT SAGGED IN AND THEN RELEASED WITH A PUFF OF DUST.

EYES WIDE, SHE SHIFTED THE SMALL STACK OF BOOKS ON THE FLOOR OUT OF THE WAY AND PULLED HER CANDLE CLOSER, PEERING INTO THE DARKNESS OF THE DOOR IN THE WALL.

IT WOULD HAVE BEEN EASY TO MISS THE SMALL FIGURE IN THE SHADOWS, BUT SHE WAS DRAWN LIKE MOTH TO FLAME, AND WHEN SHE SQUINTED, HER EYES MET THOSE OF ANOTHER CHILD—A BOY JUST SHORTER THAN SHE—WHO PEERED BACK.

"HELLO," THE GIRL SAID, DIPPING INTO A CURTSY. "I AM SORRY TO DISTURB YOU. DO YOU LIVE HERE?"

THE BOY STARED AT HER WARILY, AND THEN QUICKLY GLANCED TO THE LEFT, AS IF PREPARED TO RUN DOWN THE PASSAGE HIS DOOR HAD CONCEALED.

"YOU ARE NOT IN ANY TROUBLE," SHE HURRIED. "UNLESS YOUR PARENTS DON'T KNOW YOU'RE HERE. BUT MINE DON'T EITHER, SO YOUR SECRET IS SAFE WITH ME."

THE BOY FROWNED, LOOKING AT HER WITH ODDLY ASSESSING EYES. SHE TOOK HIM IN—HIS GHOSTLY PALE SKIN, THE DIRT ON HIS HANDS AND FACE, AND THE PACK THAT HE CLUTCHED TO HIS CHEST.

"DO YOUR PARENTS WORK WITHIN THE PALACE?" SHE ASKED CURIOUSLY.

HE DID NOT REPLY, AND THAT'S WHEN SHE NOTICED THE BLANKET IN A HEAP AT HIS FEET, BUNCHED UP ON ONE SIDE OVER A BOOK FORMING A MAKESHIFT PILLOW.

HER EYES WIDENED. "YOU'RE ALONE, AREN'T YOU."

NOT A QUESTION THIS TIME, AND THOUGH HE REMAINED SILENT, HIS SHOULDERS SAGGED AND HIS KNUCKLES LOOSENED ON HIS BAG, AS IF THE STRAIN HER WORDS PLACED ON HIM ADDED MORE WEIGHT THAN HE COULD CARRY.

SHE CHANGED COURSE. "DO YOU LIKE MY MUSIC?"

THE BOY SWALLOWED, AND SHE HOPED HE MIGHT SPEAK, BUT HE ONLY LOOKED PAST HER AT THE PIANO AND NODDED.

"WILL YOU COME SIT WITH ME?" SHE ASKED.

HE STEPPED BACK INSTINCTIVELY, FARTHER INTO THE SHAD-

OWS, AND SHE FROWNED. A BOY, ALONE IN THE WALL. WHY WOULD HE BE THERE? HOW LONG HAD HE BEEN THERE? AND IF HE WAS SO AFRAID, WHY WAS HE STILL STARING AT HER? SHE STOPPED HERSELF FROM VOICING ALL OF THE THINGS SHE WONDERED. HER TEACHERS OFTEN TOLD HER THAT SHE TALKED FAR TOO MUCH. NOW WAS THE TIME TO PUT HER INSTRUCTION TO THE TEST.

SHE TURNED AND STRODE TO THE ROOM'S ENTRANCE, FIRMLY LOCKING THE DOOR AND PLACING A CHAIR BEFORE IT FOR GOOD MEASURE.

TURNING BACK TO THE DARK VOID IN THE WALL, SHE PLACED HER HANDS ON HER HIPS. "THERE. NO ONE CAN GET IN, AND IF ANYONE APPROACHES, I HAVE GIVEN YOU ENOUGH TIME TO HIDE BEFORE THEY ENTER. BUT YOU SHOULD KNOW IT HAS BEEN WEEKS AND NONE HAVE SEEN ME HERE. OR THEY HAVE AND THEY DON'T CARE, WHICH IS ALSO POSSIBLE. EITHER WAY, YOU ARE NOW MY FRIEND AND YOU ARE SAFE HERE. I WILL MAKE SURE OF IT."

AFTER WHAT FELT LIKE AGES, THE BOY STEPPED OUT FROM THE SHADOWS, LOOKING AROUND AS IF IT HAD BEEN YEARS SINCE HE'D SEEN A SPACE SO VAST. THE GIRL SAID NOTHING, SHE SIMPLY RETURNED TO HER BENCH AND RIFLED THROUGH A MUSIC BOOK ABSENTLY. BUT ALL THE WHILE SHE KEPT A KEEN EYE ON THE BOY, WHO WAS INDEED FAR TOO THIN, AS HE WANDERED ABOUT IN A CIRCLE, THEN FINALLY ARRIVED AT HER SIDE.

HE CAREFULLY RAN A FINGER ALONG THE IVORY KEYS, TAKING THEM IN WITH AWE, AND WHEN HE PRESSED DOWN ON ONE, HIS LIPS PARTED AT ITS SONG.

SHE SURVEYED HIS CLOTHES, STAINED WITH DIRT AND MUCH TOO LARGE FOR HIM. "HOW LONG HAVE YOU BEEN HIDING?" SHE ASKED, THE WORDS SNEAKING OUT BEFORE SHE COULD STOP THEM.

THE BOY AVOIDED HER EYES, INSTEAD STROKING A FINGER ALONG A SINGLE ONYX KEY.

"IF I RETURN TOMORROW, MAY I BRING YOU FOOD?" SHE TRIED AGAIN. "MAYBE SOMETHING CLEAN TO WEAR? AND PROPER BEDDING? IT MUST BE TERRIBLY COLD IN THERE."

The boy's hand fell back to his side, and he slowly met her eyes. They were filled with a grief that the girl recognized from the nights she'd cried herself to sleep from loneliness—from the endless dark.

She smiled warmly. "I mean it. We are friends now. And you are safe with me. I will take care of you, and when you are ready, we will speak. But until then," she patted the bench at her side, "I will play for you. I might even teach you a little, if you would like."

His eyes widened, the first spark of light coming to life within them, and he nodded eagerly.

"But there is one thing I must know first," she pressed on. "Your name."

The boy eyed her carefully, and then in a clear and surprisingly confident voice, he replied, "Stargell."

The girl beamed and extended her hand. "It is a pleasure to make your acquaintance, Stargell. You may call me Auriana."

CHAPTER ELEVEN

The headache lingering behind Elric's eyes when he left his quarters the next morning was not a result of alcohol, but rather the tome—thick as a sapling—he had fallen asleep with his head on while sitting at his desk. After his unfortunate encounter with Augur, he had returned to the Diviner's Wing and, out of spite more than anything, retrieved the final volume of Obarian history recorded by the Isteriaeth. The idea of Graecerys being unable to locate it should she seek it next amused him, but it hadn't taken long for the words of the past to draw him in.

Still feeling Augur's unsettling gaze on him no matter where he went, Elric had finally retreated to his quarters. However, as he'd opened a new bottle of wine, he stopped himself, and instead of disappearing into the bottom of the glass, he vanished once more inside the old text until the sun woke him.

And now, to his disdain, instead of being left to walk to the Diviner's Wing in peace and silence, he found a far too energetic guard waiting for him.

"You look as though you had a restful sleep," Falchion said with a sly grin.

"You're already talking too much," Elric grumbled, pushing past him and down the hall.

"Are you under the weather? There's a rather nasty illness working its way among the soldiers. It begins with a headache and ends in the privy. I might see if there's a tonic that could help you."

Elric stopped, turning to the guard. "My pain tends to appear at my door nearly every morning and lingers above my head no matter what I do to rid myself of it. Do you have a cure for that malady?"

Falchion shook his head with a small laugh. "You missed me, I know it."

"Of all the things to know," Elric muttered, moving along down the hall.

"Truly, though, I might check with Augur and see—"

"I do not want anything from him, thank you. If I am ill, I shall send for something myself. I hear it is what I am useful for. Maybe I'll call the nobles in and set a jar on the floor at my feet to collect coins if they enjoy the spectacle."

Something hit him squarely between the shoulders with a *thud*. He spun in time to see it bounce once, then skitter across the carpet, and when Elric retrieved it, he realized that it was a roll of sugared dough.

He narrowed his eyes at Falchion who stared him down, slowly and methodically chewing a second roll before shrugging casually. "I thought you might enjoy something sweet. To take the edge off your bitterness this fine morning."

Elric had half a mind to hurl the pastry back at him, but he refrained and continued walking. Boot steps fell in line behind him, confirming that the soldier followed dutifully.

Shouts from outside caught his attention, drawing him to a window that looked out over the courtyard and beyond the palace wall where a cluster of tents were erected, thin plumes of smoke rising from their communal fires.

A crowd had gathered, their cries directed at the guards posted behind the gates, an unmoving wall between the unruly townsfolk and the entrance to the palace.

Elric frowned. "That is new."

Falchion stood at the window beside his own, looking out with lines of seriousness etched across his face. "Their numbers grow each day. They've moved from whispering in houses and taverns to shouting in the street."

Word of the growing unrest in Obarian had not been a secret, reaching Elric as far as Inflamel before he had been kidnapped. But outside of the speech made by Lord Jacian the night he was paraded before the nobles, he had not seen evidence of it. "And what do they want?"

"Revolution," Falchion said grimly. "They refute the queen's claim to the throne and demand change. And if they do not see it, they threaten to force it themselves."

Elric cast an eye over the empty fields, the places where farmlands should be flourishing. All that lingered were dingy shacks and broken fences. "I understand why, though I fear they've learned nothing. Obarian has not known rest, has not known sound rule, since the Fall of the Thrones. Every ruler since has risen to be cut down—replaced by another tree lacking roots. Far more innocent lives than nobles have been squandered along the way, yet the masses are so quick to jump to the fate that has betrayed them time and time again. It is a matter of time before they destroy the very thing that might bring them back to prosperity."

Falchion was silent for a moment, then spoke. "I believe that is the first kind thing I've heard you say of the queen."

"I do not believe I mentioned her," Elric replied, throwing him a glare.

"It was implied. She is the first successor by birth line, not force or coup, since the Fall. It is the first step toward unity. To a secured future."

"And that will make her a good ruler? Simply being born to the correct person at the correct time shall fix everything?"

"Not all, and certainly not right away. It is natural to feel a sense of loss with accomplishment. But I fear the people are so averse to loss that they see every pain as reason to raise arms against the wheel trying to bring them forward."

Falchion paused, and when he spoke again his voice was low, prompting Elric to step closer. "Some say she is weak; others say she does not truly want the crown. I say the only way to know is to ask, but none will. The lords try to advise her, but she is not to be tamed."

"And is that where I come in? I am to persuade her to thwart an uprising and heal a kingdom with land steeped in the blood of all who fought for loyalty and unity?"

Falchion met his eyes. "I believe no one changes the queen's mind without her affording them the ability to do so first."

He began to walk again and Elric followed, coming alongside him on the stairs. "It is just an observation of mine, but I have not heard a single majesty, grace, or highness. All she is called is queen. Why is that?"

Falchion faltered, but recovered quickly, Elric did not miss his hesitancy. "Her soldiers recognize that she is our queen. Queen of Obarian, as is her right. And out of respect, that is how she is to be known. It is 'yes, my queen,' and 'no, my queen' so that none may forget."

"And those who have forgotten. What becomes of them?"

"They suffer the consequences."

"Is that why the entirety of her people starve in filthy hovels?" Elric needled.

"This kingdom has long lacked prosperity," Falchion replied sharply. "She is not to blame."

"Yet her father would sacrifice his daughter on the altar of his faults."

Falchion wheeled on him. "You will not speak ill of either of them in front of me, especially my queen. I have sworn my loyalty to the throne, and I will protect it at every cost."

Elric smirked at his ability to ruffle the guard's feathers. "Good to know a coup is not alive and well. You've passed my test. Now have another roll, you seem increasingly acerbic."

He shoved the sugary treat that had hit him in the back toward the guard who did not move to accept it, his anger palpable.

"You are loyal to her. To a fault," Elric remarked, taking a bite. "How long before she uses that against you to turn the full force of her army upon innocent people?"

Falchion straightened, but instead of continuing up the staircase, he turned and began to walk back down. "Come with me."

Elric followed him to the ground floor, through the labyrinth of passages, and out into a stone archway-covered portico at the rear of the palace. A large courtyard sat between it and the barns along the back gates, and beyond, endless plains of long, wheat-colored grass bent softly beneath the wind coming down from the north.

The training exercises Falchion had taken part in the day prior appeared to be continuing, though a slow and steady rain fell—far more ice than liquid. Yet it was not the men engaging in swordsmanship, wrestling, and target practice that drew his eye.

It was the woman in the center of them all, her hair unbound in a sheet of brilliant red spinning in tandem with her skirt as she disarmed the soldier before her with a twist of her sword.

Elric watched, transfixed, as Graecerys, the Queen of Obarian, smiled and then gave the man a hand up. Her breaths came in even exhales of mist before her face, though his were rapids puffs. He stood, quickly clasped a fist over his heart and bowed, then moved to the side so the next soldier could step forward.

"I did not say we all agree with her," Falchion said quietly. "I said we respect her. And for us, it is easy. She is one of us to the younger men and has easy camaraderie with the elders. She does not trust the nobility in her circle, yet she will mingle with us unguarded. She cares for us more than most."

Graecerys's sword collided with the helmet of the next soldier, and he dropped to his knees, gripping the sides of his head just before she landed a firm kick to the center of his chest that sent him to the ground in a heap.

"I am concerned about what you consider fondness if that is your definition of caring," Elric murmured.

"It is a mutual understanding, unspoken between her and us," Falchion replied. "It is not easy to be a woman in this kingdom. Destitution brings out the ugliness in men of every rank, and when she sought refuge, the collective guard offered loyalty. She trained with us until she was confident enough to defend herself, and though we still keep watch over her, should harm befall us, she will raise her sword high to defend us as fearlessly as we will her."

Shouts from the men drew Elric's attention again, and his eyes widened slightly to see Graecerys drop to a knee, putting all her might behind the flat of the sword that held the opposing soldier's blade at bay above her head.

"You do not go easy on her," he remarked.

"Neither do you," Falchion replied, drawing a scowl from Elric that he met with a devious grin. "But you should know there are few things you could do that are more dangerous. There is no softness within her. Even she has said it perished long ago."

At that instant, Graecerys changed her hold on her sword, sliding the edge down to meet the hilt of the soldier's and dipping below him in a crouch. The shift of weight and balance sent his blade tip-first into the ground behind her and his body tumbling over her kneeling figure.

The soldier landed the somersault on his back, sword stuck

in the soil above his head, but before he made a move, the point of the queen's blade pressed beneath his chin.

Cheers and groans alike went up from the soldiers crowded around them, and money changed hands as the soldier on the ground clapped his gloves together in a breathless yield.

He rose and bowed, and Graecerys dipped her head to him in a show of respect as she, too, fought to catch her breath.

She sheathed her sword and, to Elric's surprise, withdrew a pouch from within her skirts, giving it to the soldier before her.

The weight of it dipped in his hand and his eyes widened as he dropped to a knee. "My queen, I cannot accept this."

She smiled warmly. "I insist. Take it to the storehouses and retrieve all that your family needs." She paused, reaching into her pocket once more. This time she withdrew a leather circlet no larger than Elric's palm, stitched with beads and a small shell to form a crown.

"Please see that your new princess receives her first crown," she added, handing it to him. "And remember to take a wooden sword for her brother to train so that he may protect her well against the world."

The soldier beamed, bowing his head lower. "I shall as soon as my leave allows."

"It allows," she replied, grasping him by the shoulder with wide, hopeful eyes. "Go to them now and remain until autumn's first frost. With my blessing."

The soldier bowed once more, clutching his fist to his heart and pressing a reverent kiss to the queen's hand with the other, before rising and striding with fervor toward the stables.

Graecerys watched him go, a faint smile on her face, and when she turned to make her way back through the crowd, her countenance held a hint of sadness that Elric could not place. It was unnerving, human almost, and entirely at odds with all he thought he knew of her. Or at least what he presumed to know.

The soldiers parted and bowed as she went, slowly returning

to their posts. She reached the portico and lifted her face, freezing before Elric and Falchion, then her face hardened and all hint of kindness was lost to the depths of her churning eyes.

Falchion clasped his fist to his heart and bowed, but Elric merely nodded to her.

"Care to do something with this rain?" she sniped, ignoring the soldier and sharpening her tongue on Elric's glare. "It is like ice."

"I have no dominion over seasons, though I hear spring shall fully begin once winter ends," he replied flatly.

She snorted. "I should have known you would not carry elemental. That would have been too easy. Regardless, I have a meeting with the lords of Obarian. We shall make our way there after I have made myself presentable."

"I'm sorry?" Elric asked as she pushed past.

She paused and looked back at him, eyebrows raised in haughty surprise. "You will accompany me to my rooms, then we will adjourn to meet the lords. As my advisor, your word will be needed while arranging celebrations for the next Moonrise."

"And why must I accompany you? Why not a guard?"

"Because I clearly have no need for protection and you could use a change as well. There is sugar all over your waistcoat."

Elric glared at Falchion who turned away to hide his smirk, then strode down the walk toward the barracks beside the barns, abandoning Elric to the queen.

He sighed. "Very well. After you, Your Grace."

Graecerys did not move, staring at him instead with eyes like daggers until he made the first move. She kept in perfect step at his side all the way back to the main staircase, where Elric's irritation with the silence finally won out. "Is there something about sugar that offends you? Or is it my general presence?"

"The latter," she replied sharply.

Elric couldn't help but smirk. "Ironic. I know how we might fix that."

"For someone who detests being here, ironic would be the fact that you found it acceptable to watch me when you did not in fact need to be anywhere near my presence at all."

"I was not watching you."

She barked a laugh. "Really? Then what exactly do you call it when you stand and observe someone with your eyes?"

"I go where my handler ferries me, and today it was for a delightful walk outside. You would do well to measure the level of your pride. Last I checked, even being royalty did not make it possible to *observe* people through the back of your skull. There is no way for you to know I was staring anywhere near you."

"Just like there is no explanation for the rain to ever so slightly warm the moment you approached?"

Elric faltered, nearly missing a step. It wasn't possible for him to have subtly changed the temperature...was it? Was his new magic truly so little contained that it reacted to his simple presence? And better yet, why did it not turn colder?

On cue, the queen shuddered, pulling her thick hair into a bunch over one shoulder, the ends dripping against her already soaked bright-blue dress. "Can you provide me with a towel or cloak or something to stave off this chill?" she demanded.

Elric summoned a towel to his hand, offering it to her with a glare that he poured all measure of scalding bite into, as if he could ignite her on the spot and spare himself the torture of her presence any longer. Graecerys, however, ignored it, and without thanks, wrapped the cloth around her hair and began to express moisture.

He folded his hands behind his back, waiting for her to walk again and allowing his eyes to wander around the hall before returning to the queen once more. Though physically she was addressing her hair, her gaze was fixed on the window—on the palace's front gate and the people beyond. *Her* people.

So subtle he thought he imagined it, he saw her eyes widen, fear mixed with grief as she took in their cries, their rage, their tattered clothing and too-small frames, and he wondered if she realized that the person with the power to change it all was not the queen indifferent to her own strength, but the woman who only let her guard fall when she was certain none were looking.

Swallowing down his anger, Elric cleared his throat and extended an olive branch. "I heard your exchange with the final guard," he said quietly so that no one beyond her would hear. "It was thoughtful. I believe the gesture, your kindness, meant a good deal to him."

Graecerys grew unnaturally still, her knuckles white against the towel wrapped around her dripping tresses. Elric opened his mouth to continue, but she ripped the cloth from her hair, spraying him with frigid droplets.

"Nonsense," she snapped. "You were not watching me. Remember?" And before he could reply, she stormed past him and up the staircase.

They reached their corridor on the third floor without speaking further, but when Elric turned the handle to his quarters, her voice gave him pause.

"Master Elric." He faced her where she leaned against the doorframe, her wet hair hanging limply over her shoulder, and —though stoic—he found himself disarmed by her effortless beauty. "You referred to me as royalty. Do you truly believe that?"

Elric swallowed, bartering for more time to formulate a smart response, but his words failed. "I do, Your Grace."

Something churned in her eyes, there and gone once more, and when a smile darkened her face, he knew he had played right into her hands. "Then do not tell me what to do. And the next time you choose to spy on me, have a towel ready."

CHAPTER TWELVE

Graecerys stared at Elric, picking him apart inch by inch, though he refused to meet her gaze. Instead, he surveyed the chamber they sat in. It was plain in appearance compared to the other rooms in the palace, containing a large oval table with chairs surrounding it, but the window overlooking the hedge courtyard made for a decent enough view. They were waiting for the lords to arrive, each representing a different province in Obarian, but after ten minutes of near silence, Elric was beginning to lose patience.

"Is there a reason why I was pulled away from my very important work reading history I have lived through and being spied on by a rodent-nosed man from the rafters?"

"If you don't enjoy being watched, maybe you should think twice before observing others uninvited," Graecerys replied pointedly.

Elric sighed, clinging to his last thread of patience. "The courtyard was filled with soldiers, why does my presence concern you?"

"I trust my guards, I do not trust you. And that is a rude assessment of your peer. Augur has a brilliant mind."

Elric hummed. "It has been some time since I've lived in this kingdom, but I'm certain the word *brilliant* still infers intelligence. Have you spoken with him recently?"

"Besmirching a member of my household, even thinly veiled as humor, is grounds for punishment," Graecerys said, glaring. "Do not force me to make an example of you, Isteriaeth."

"I wouldn't dream of it, Your Grace," Elric replied, meeting her eyes with a sharp smile. "It would take far too much time away from my being a fool at your parties."

Silence filled the space between them, and Elric took a moment to relax his jaw before speaking again.

"Is that truly his name? Augur?"

Graecerys stared. "It is. Why?"

"Are you aware that he calls himself the magnificent?"

"I suppose I could always call you the spectacular, since you're so fond of the attention you get from the nobility. Or would you rather something more illustrious?"

Elric glared at the woman, who showed no interest in allowing anything he said to slip by unanswered. "I prefer Elric just fine."

"Fine then."

"Fine."

"Fine."

Elric refused to allow her the last word. "In truth, why are we here?"

Voices passed by the door, and Graecerys shifted to get comfortable in the seat, folding her hands in her lap. "Lord Blenheim had an idea for a kingdom-wide celebration observing the next Moonrise in hopes that it will assure Obarians that the old ways are to be preserved. Word of your arrival has spread, and though it proved expeditious in quelling some unrest, there is still more to go."

"And you hope to earn your own people's favor by hosting a celebration, with my blessing, to honor the Isteriaeth that founded our kingdom and birthed our realm, though these are the same people who preferred to see them dead? Or do you simply assume that I might advise on hundreds-year-old observances?"

"Yes," Graecerys deadpanned. "Now please, stop speaking. The lords shall arrive at any moment."

The order grated his nerves, but when a long silence filled the room, Elric found himself grateful. Then, to his surprise and utter agony, the queen spoke once more. "Do you have any memories of it?"

"Memories of what? Talking?" he asked sweetly.

"No," she replied with a glare. "The Observances of Moonrise."

Elric did not answer, becoming lost in the quicksand of his own mind as his fingers traced the deep grooves of the clovers etched in the table.

"Will you not answer me?" she pressed.

"I would love to, but as it so happens, you have already asked me to stop speaking. I'd hate to offend."

Graecerys scoffed. "Oh yes, because you seem to long for conversation with me."

"My mistake, Your Grace," Elric sighed. "As you can imagine, being ripped from my home, incapacitated by questionable means, and stolen away to a foreign land to have my freedom stripped and seized by a stranger is undoubtedly endearing."

The soldiers posted by the door stiffened at his caustic tone, but when Graecerys lifted her head to meet his eyes, all she said was, "*My queen*. That is how I am to be addressed. And certainly never by anything akin to my given name."

Elric's retort was interrupted by the door swinging wide. Six men funneled into the room, many of whom Elric recognized from his introduction to the court, but only two that he knew by name—Lord Blenheim and Lord Jacian.

Lord Blenheim stiffened at the sight of Elric seated to the

right of the queen, yet quickly smoothed his expression as he assumed the chair at the head of the table directly opposite her. Each of the men nodded to her before sitting, though Elric noted that none of them bowed or addressed her formally.

"Thank you for joining us, Isteriaeth," Lord Blenheim remarked, his eyes piercing Elric. "I do not recall your presence being requested, but it is welcome all the same. Now, my lords, if you may regale the queen with an update on each of your provinces, then we may begin."

Lord Jacian's chair creaked as he settled into it, slouching against the high, straight back. He was directly to Elric's right, and though the lord did not glance Elric's way, he could feel his eyes tracking him.

"The Province of Westoram ports are half empty. Our fishermen have been unable to use our docks for some time due to the fog slowly engulfing the Grimm Sea," a man with a closely cropped white beard remarked from across the table. "Townsfolk are beginning to gather outside the manor, follow us when we go out, and ask what provisions are to be made if the bounties do not expand."

Murmurs around the table echoed the same sentiment, save Jacian, who remained silent, and one other man who appeared to be the eldest of them all. "The people in the north do not gather or question," the man stated coldly, "because the Province of Culwyrt is empty."

Silence descended on the table, and Elric's eyes widened. Beside him, Graecerys shifted forward.

"What do you mean *empty*, Cathan?" questioned Lord Blenheim.

"As you know, when we entered the spring, over half our population had been lost. The ground did not soften enough for crops to grow until late summer. Those without harvest left at first snow, but those who stayed to endure this winter have determined their stores will not make it through the end of the season."

"And where are your people going?" Lord Blenheim blustered. "Is there not enough strain on your neighboring provinces that you do not see it fit to retrieve them and return them to their rightful homes? Pilgrimage is not permitted here."

"Lord Cathan states that over half his population has been lost, with the rest facing starvation, and your concern is unauthorized relocation of survivors?" Lord Jacian asked, his flinty stare cutting into Blenheim from down the row. "Now, I believe, I have seen it all."

"Do you know where your inhabitants have gone, Lord Cathan?" Blenheim repeated, ignoring Jacian's words.

"They now reside safely here, in the Province of Stragium," Jacian replied loudly, surprising Elric who now stared at him outrightly.

Lord Blenheim turned to face him with reluctance, and Jacian smiled, leaning forward on the table. "Good afternoon, Lord Blenheim. How kind of you to acknowledge my presence."

Blenheim's eyes narrowed. "Accepting refugees is against the wishes of the crown, Lord Jacian. Or do you make it a point to use the law as a checklist of matters to ignore?"

"That we are discussing our own people, our Obarian brothers and sisters, as refugees is a more poignant matter," Jacian replied sharply. "I would not refuse any being in need, but to reject our own, to leave them starving and send them to their death, should be charge for treason. But I do not believe anyone at this table wishes to entertain that notion, lest we all find ourselves strung from the wall."

"*Anyone* at this table? Shall I be executed for not serving my kingdom well?" Graecerys's voice was clear and calm, and when Jacian swiveled to her, the malice melted from his face.

"My lady, I do not believe you to be a tyrant," he said openly, an earnestness in his voice that softened the rigidity in Elric's bones. "But if we do not intervene to help our people—your people—there will be no Obarian left to rule. This kingdom is not its land, its tradition, nor its history. It is its people. The revolution being screamed even now from the gate is the most desperate cry for help. You need only offer it. If you do not, I fear that yes, the people would see your demise."

Elric's eyes moved to Graecerys, but it was Lord Blenheim who spoke again. "You speak treason every chance you get, from your lack of respect for your queen to your support of the rabble that would sooner destroy this kingdom than preserve it."

"Names are irrelevant, but what is not are people dying," Graecerys said firmly, waving him off. "Culwyrt is our most northern province. Common sense would say to abandon it until milder conditions are observed, but Lord Blenheim mentioned there is additional strain. Are there other provinces suffering in the same way?"

The rest of the lords around the table shook their heads, murmurs of, "No, my queen," echoing from each, though beside Elric, Lord Jacian's irritation seemed to be mounting, his knee bouncing beneath the table with barely restrained energy.

Graecerys turned her attention to Jacian. "If the people of Culwyrt are in your care, then the palace will not withhold aid. Provisions will be provided to any who wish to return to their homes and additional stores given to support the Province of Stragium as they find themselves with more mouths to feed. When conditions in Culwyrt are improved, we shall send Obarian's best farmers back to test the land. The remaining unaffected provinces will be more than capable of supporting themselves, and extra hands will only increase efficiency of the trade before winter sets in once more."

Jacian nodded to her in acknowledgment, and though Elric saw Blenheim's mouth open from the corner of his eye, he only cleared his throat and pressed on. "With that settled, we will discuss the coming Moonrise. The realm of Breteria has not held an Observation since before the Fall of the Thrones. I believe it is a natural way we might show the realm at large that we are committed to returning to the ways of old, especially in light of the turmoil unfolding in both Inflamel and Tauriellis. And it will give our people an evening to forget their daily plight and erase the lines between civilian and nobility, uniting us all for a short time. Maybe then they will see that we are not the enemy. We are simply those who rule."

"Yes, because seeing the opulence that the nobility experience every day of their lives is enough to mend prejudice and heal our land. Especially on an empty stomach," Jacian mumbled, nearly causing Elric's carefully blank expression to falter.

"I, for one, believe it to be a pleasant change," Lord Cathan replied, pivoting to address the table. "There has not been celebration of any sort in this kingdom since before the nobility raised our late, great king to the throne. What better way to signify that his daughter, our queen in right, is different and will not falter in the way her father did during his last days."

At the casual mention of her father, Elric glanced at Graecerys out of the corner of his eye, searching for any sign of emotion that the subject might provide, but her expression remained placid.

"Do you agree that this is the best way forward, my queen?" Blenheim asked politely, though his voice held an edge.

To Elric's surprise, there was no retort, no sharp return, simply a demure smile that did not reach her eyes. "I trust you have the plans in hand, Blenheim. You always do."

Jacian's head turned to her as Blenheim clapped. "Excellent! Then it is settled. Now, Isteriaeth, I understand that during the Age of the Thrones, the Moonrise was held as sacred. In what ways did the stars mark its rise?"

Elric froze, every eye in the room moving to him, including

the fathomless blue depths to his right, though they were the sole pair that held any amusement. "I…am not sure," he replied. "I should need some time to—"

"Then how long did the celebrations last? The Observance of the Rise was ceremonial, but the Afterglow was often a more… informal time of celebration. What preparations should be made, and what shall we gather from the provinces for such an occasion?"

"More women than currently reside at court, I should hope," a lord Elric did not know remarked under his breath. A few snickers echoed around the room, and though Elric was growing increasingly uncomfortable at what felt more and more like an interrogation, it was the notion that made him bristle.

"I would think, my lord, in light of the previous conversation, we should not rely on the provinces to supply anything. The palace should provide what the people need so that the people may gather and celebrate properly, without strain or concern."

The chatter stopped suddenly, and Blenheim's eyes narrowed. "And this is how it was done in the days of old?"

"I do not know," Elric replied. "In truth, all I know of Moonrise are the stories passed down to me."

"Is there anything this Isteriaeth does know?" Lord Cathan asked incredulously.

"He seems to understand enough for my liking," Lord Jacian remarked, and when Elric looked at him, the man nodded imperceptibly in a show of respect.

"Then I charge you, Isteriaeth, with finding the tomes in which Moonrise is recorded. Bring us your findings in a month's time. We have much to plan before summer," Blenheim ordered, before forcing a smile. "I have no doubt that Moonrise shall be a great coming together."

"Provided that we can even see it," remarked Cathan. "The

last were obscured by cloud cover. What good is an Observance if none may view the sky?"

"Are you better with clouds than you are rain, Master Elric?" a velvet voice asked in his ear, and Elric startled when he realized Graecerys had leaned closer to speak to him directly.

He stiffened, tugging on the strand of his magic and allowing the blue dhust in his palm to wrap into a mug filled with steaming tea that he then handed to the queen. "To banish the chill, *Your Grace.*"

She glared at him but accepted the cup, setting it on the table without taking a sip.

"It is settled, then. We shall reconvene in one month and prepare for the first Observance in nearly four hundred years. Spread the word to your provinces and let us rally their hearts. Give them something to look forward to on the other side of this bitter winter."

"Yes, I'm certain a party shall prove an excellent motivator and distraction from the starvation," Jacian said, rising from the table. Turning to face Graecerys, he bowed stiffly at the waist, and without a word or glance to anyone at the table, he strode from the room.

The other lords stood gradually, all ignoring both Elric and Graecerys and talking among themselves as they wandered back into the hall.

"My queen, if I might have a word," Lord Blenheim asked, before adding, "in private."

Elric stood without hesitation, and after extending a flourishing bow to Graecerys, he nodded to Blenheim and exited the room, stopping just around the corner.

"Have you accessed his power?" Blenheim asked.

"I have not," Graecerys replied coldly.

"And why is that?"

"None of your concern," she shot back.

Silence. And then, "You sit in a precarious position, poised to lose everything should you not act. Is that what you want? To forfeit all you have been raised for and all I have given you?"

"What I want is inconsequential, as you have proven, else he would not be here. His dhust is not going anywhere. I shall be the one to determine when I have need of it."

Elric did not have a chance to hear Blenheim's reply, his attention catching instead on movement at the opposite end of the hall. There, Lord Jacian stood, staring at him intently, but before he could move closer or speak, Elric turned on his heel and left.

CHAPTER THIRTEEN

The sun hung without warmth over the open fields beyond the palace gate, the people upon it growing in number and agitation despite the bitter cold. Elric walked slowly down the front staircase, on his way to what was certain to be another stunning display of egotism from the lords, when the scent hit him.

It bowled him over, and he grasped the rail with both hands to keep from tripping down the final step.

It was not possible. And yet….

Lilacs.

He searched wildly for the source yet there was nothing. Only a single door on the landing to his right clicking shut.

Striding to it, he tried to turn the handle but found it locked. He raised a cautious hand, rapped on it softly, and his heart skipped a beat when it slowly swung open.

The familiar cottage on the opposite side brought a tightness to his chest as he stepped in. The oversized table along the wall, the deep sinks filled with fresh produce, and the jars of berry preserves lining the counters. It was whole—perfect—unlike the last time he had seen it. And so was the woman standing before the mantle in the small living space.

She turned, her long golden hair fanning out behind her, and with a radiant smile framed by full rose-colored lips, she ran to him.

He met her halfway, and when she leaped, he caught her behind the knee with one arm and wrapped the other around her waist, spinning her around the floor.

Her laugh was a song that filled his heart with life and shattered it all in a single note, and though he ceased turning and replaced her feet on the floor, her hands still clasped him around the neck.

"I have missed you, E," she breathed, her eyes alive in the dim light. "Moonrise is so soon I feared we might not keep our promise."

He shook his head, allowing their noses to brush. "No two Moonrises shall meet before we have seen each other. Nothing will keep me from you."

He consumed her lips, warm and sweet like the berries growing in the garden, but when they parted, he saw the first prick of frost in her eyes—a cold sorrow he knew he could not chase away.

"Do not think of parting," he murmured. "Not yet. We have the night, and we are so close to the time that I'll return home like this to you every day. Nothing will part me from you. I swear it."

A solitary tear fell down her cheek. Her complexion—leached of all color—turned a ghostly pallor along its trail, and his eyes widened in fear. He brushed it away, but her skin was like ice. It was already too late.

He was always far too late to save her.

"Not even death?" she whispered.

Another tear fell and he clasped her face. Her palms came to rest on his wrists, though they, too, were frigid.

"K, stay with me, please," he urged. "Just for now. This is the last place I have you—the only time my heart is whole."

"We always knew time was our enemy," she replied. "But I never imagined it would betray us like this."

Elric loosened a shaky breath, his eyes stinging and his throat raw with the tears he barely restrained. "I will not lose you here. I will not let my mind forget a single second, no matter the number of my days."

Her hand found his cheek, though now it was not sadness alone that filled her eyes, but compassion. "You will not forget me, Elric, but you will let me go, and that is all right. You need not live in the past."

"But do you know how desperately I need you?" he rasped, wrapping his arms around her, holding her to him as if his embrace might do anything to keep her from vanishing.

"And do you remember how madly I loved you?" she whispered in his ear, her breath the last bit of warmth left in her body. "It is something ages will never tarnish. While I will fade with time, what we had will last forever. But my darling, do not give up on life when you are the only part of me still living."

"I could never allow you to see me like this," Elric grunted, pulling back. "Your loss was the first, but now I have failed everyone. I—"

His voice broke, but her caress against his skin brought a comfort that allowed his eyes to fall closed. "You have failed nothing. In all my years of knowing you, even as youths, you never backed down. You never gave up. It is why I fell in love with you. In my darkest days, you were the star that guided me, reminding me that there is always something worth fighting for. Now you must find it."

Elric met her eyes, still full of vitality, though her lips were tinged blue and her skin was pale as death. "I am tired, K," he admitted, though he did not say aloud how much he longed for eternal rest. He did not need to.

She shook her head. "It is not your time. Not yet."

"You cannot know that."

"I know it because I know *you*."

Elric pressed his lips together. Fighting her would be futile. Adamant, stubborn, and determined, that was his K.

Was.

She took his hand, turning and leading him out the back door and into the garden where they lay in the rows, concealed by vegetation, and looked up at the night sky.

The air was cold, such that he could almost convince himself it was the night breeze and not death that had her in its clutches. And he held her that much tighter.

"Do you remember the night you told me you loved me?" she asked softly.

Elric smiled. "I remember you saying it first."

She gave him a good-natured shove. "I did not. You said it. And when you refused to repeat yourself, I told you that I loved you more, then you teased me for being so forward."

"Well, I must say, I am thankful you finally said it…I surely would not have had the courage had you not declared it first."

She gasped indignantly and looked up at him to argue, but he caught her lips instead, willing his reverent kisses to banish their chill.

"Do you remember the first time I kissed you?" he murmured, leaning away far enough to speak, his words quivering from the riot of passion and grief waging war on his heart.

"How could I forget? It was terrible." She smiled. "All of our firsts were, but I like to think they were perfect because we had them together."

"I concur," Elric replied, leaning in to rest his forehead against hers.

"Tell me a story?" she breathed, softly kissing his jawline before pulling back.

"Something new? Or 'The King of Wishes' again?"

"New. I fear I understand 'The King of Wishes' too well as of late," she replied, settling onto her side in the crook of his arm, her head on his shoulder and her hand over his heart. "But speak slowly. I am not ready for this night to end."

Elric drew out each word, painting pictures with every syllable and rhyme. He basked in her, the sun to his stars, her light reflecting off the moon to keep him company in the dark. And before he knew it, the soft lilac tickling his nose grew faint. The arm she lay on became numb, and he no longer felt her anymore. And when he reached over to brush her hair away from her face, it was only a cold pillow that he touched.

He woke with a start, shoving himself up from bed and to his feet. His stomach burned, his lungs could not hold air, and his chest *ached*. He wasn't certain if he would bellow, cry, smash the desk chair against the wall, or find a way to break through the glass door to free himself of this wretched prison.

He paced, unable to stay still, his lungs heaving, and he shoved his hands into his hair, gripping it by the fistful. The pain heightened his awareness and helped ground him to the floor, though it only reminded him that he was awake. Awake and alone.

An up-turned palm and small fall of sapphire dhust brought him a bottle. He did not bother summoning a chalice but removed the cork—snapping his fingers and calling it from the bottleneck—and gulped the liquid as if it were the answer to his existence.

He wasn't certain when he began crying, only that it made it hard to breathe while swallowing, and when he finally dropped the empty vessel to his side, he stumbled over to the settee and fell into the seat. Depositing the bottle on the table, he buried his head in his hands and wept.

Above his heaving sobs, he heard faint screams, startling him and causing him to suck air into his lungs so quickly that he choked. Fleeing to the washroom, he relieved his stomach of its contents, making him feel even more disoriented and miserable, but after dousing his face with frigid water, he returned to his room.

Hushed voices spoke in the corridor, and in the darkness, he made out the nearly imperceptible flicker of candlelight trickling beneath the door in the wall.

The wall he shared with Graecerys, whom he had not seen since the meeting with the lords earlier that day.

He took two steps toward the wall, then changed course, opening the door to the hall instead. Falchion stood just a few paces away, in deep, hushed conversation with the soldier who usually guarded Graecerys's door and—to Elric's surprise—Lord Blenheim.

All three men looked his way, but it was the latter who spoke.

"Return to your chamber, Isteriaeth," Lord Blenheim ordered sharply. "There is nothing we need summoned save a peaceful night's sleep. I had hoped otherwise, but it would appear that it is something you cannot provide."

The world spun before Elric's bleary eyes, and he frowned, unsure what Blenheim meant, when Graecerys's door opened and Augur slipped out.

Elric stiffened, and though the thaumaturge's eyes lingered on him longer than they should have, he turned to Blenheim and handed him a vial. "A draught for sleep. She refuses it now, but it may help yet."

"I will see that she takes this with her tea every evening," Lord Blenheim replied with a nod.

Augur gave a small bow, then turned, and with eyes that never once left Elric, he passed him slowly and slunk back into the shadows of the stairwell.

Elric shut his door firmly behind him, and though he was unsure why, he slid a chair in front of it, barring entry. He stood, waiting for his eyes to adjust once more to the darkness, but did not find the light from Graecerys's room again.

Adrenaline having worn away and his own trauma weakening his limbs, he stumbled back to bed and collapsed on the surface. He stared at the ceiling, replaying the last time he saw Kathrina over again in his head.

He held her while she took her final breath in his arms, saw her carried back to the garden where they should have been married, then watched as she was laid to rest beneath the trees. His eyes fell shut and he could almost feel the grass at her graveside—cool and moist with dew—where he had lain for days learning how to say goodbye once more. Just like he had so many times before.

Then he saw his brother, standing clearly before him, his own devastating heartbreak a result of Elric's failure to keep his vow—to protect his friends. Timothius's rage built louder, more violent, a madness that not even Elric might be heard through, leading him to give in to what he swore he'd never do. He left.

Now here he was in Obarian once again. He had escaped this prison long enough to ruin the lives of people he'd claimed as his family, then ultimately returned.

And if this kingdom was dead set on destroying itself, tearing its own people apart from the inside out, then they had certainly found the right advisor.

There was nothing he knew better than how to ruin a life.

CHAPTER FOURTEEN

$\mathscr{E}$lric tried not to mark the days that passed as weeks and then months. Late-winter bled into a spring just as bleak, and then summer dawned and finally brought warmth to the kingdom. The ground softened enough for some to return to their fields, though a robust camp still grew before the palace gates, crying for help and demanding change.

Sleep rarely found Elric at night and when it did, his dreams were plagued by memories. Some were welcome, but others drew a madness from beneath his skin that left him silently screaming. For that was all he could do. He was unable to find the best in his circumstances, resigned to a fate he knew deep down he was all too deserving of, and the oscillation between grief and anger was draining him of any and all vitality. Bitterness required more will than he had left, and he felt himself becoming empty and desperate for relief. Even the stars in his veins did not comfort him, forcing life more than they nurtured it, and he wondered if this was how his ancestors had felt after walking the realm for hundreds, even thousands of years.

He was no more than an apparition, though ghosts had it

easier. They could not be seen. He simply could not figure out how to disappear.

Graecerys, however, had. Or at least she made it her main goal to not only avoid Elric but withdraw from the public eye almost entirely. Blenheim conducted most of the daily tasks on her behalf, and when the lords convened and she emerged, it was with sunken eyes and a pale complexion that no amount of finery could hide. Yet on the nights Elric lay awake, begging sleep for kindness, he heard her relentlessly pace the floor, not even attempting to find rest. And it was finally during the late morning hours that he heard her own night terrors find her once more.

She did not command Elric, did not call upon his dhust nor summon him once for any reason, and while he was grateful for it, he did not entirely trust it. For if the exhaustion that bracketed her shoulders was any indication, whatever plagued her—be it illness or invisible weight—was waging a war that she was losing. So what was it that stayed her hand?

What kept her from reaching for his power?

The power in question was becoming more volatile by the day. There were times he would summon a shirt and banish the sun instead. Some days it took far more concentration than ever to bring the stars to life in his veins, and when it did, the dhust was reluctant to form. It was almost as if it had been poisoned or tainted, knotted up in a mass of incoherent power that did not look or behave as any true strand should, but instead was a perversion of them all.

Two strands of dhust was uncommon. Three or more was unheard of. What would he do if more emerged? What would he do if they became truly uncontrolled?

The words Blenheim had spoken harkened back to his thoughts, sending a chill over his skin.

"When dhust doth bind Isteriaeth to king, the strands shall sing with stars' blessing."

They had been spoken over the Einherjar king on the day of his coronation ritual, thought to be a blessing, and later believed to have cursed his reign. Most Obarians believed it indicated that a partnership between throne and strands must exist for peace in their land—hence Elric's current predicament. But others believed it to speak of the future, a prophecy that an Isteriaeth was meant to wear the crown.

Was it even possible? What did it say of Graecerys's future if she refused to secede the throne? And moreover, what did it say of a path for Elric beyond their tether? Would he ever truly be free again?

Today, however, those concerns needed to wait. The moon was about to rise high in the sky, and until the sun breached the horizon to usher in a new seven months of starlit nights, there would be no talk of war, conflict, negotiation, or revolution.

The entire kingdom had been invited to the courtyard of the palace for the celebration, and Elric would stand before them all to bless the skies and banish foul weather for the night—or at least attempt to. The people of Obarian would camp on the hills and bluffs, then the next day, the palace would open its doors and allow her people inside for tours and a gala that the nobility hoped might promote unity over strife.

And Elric already loathed every second of it.

"Is it age or stubbornness that brings you to scowl on what is the greatest celebration since the Clover's Bloom?"

Elric rolled his eyes at Falchion, who strode beside him in a crisp new uniform. "If I cannot recall the last time clover bloomed in Obarian, then you certainly cannot."

"Ah, but I have heard tales. They say the meadow before the palace in Inflamel blooms now, is that true?"

"Did you not see them when you came to kidnap me?"

Falchion clicked his tongue. "Sadly, no. It was dark, and we barely saw each other in the torchlight. Though I must admit I did try. It is something that always fascinated me as a boy. I couldn't imagine it in my mind."

"Then I have good news, for I doubt you shall struggle to see the enormous glowing orb that will hang in the sky tonight. I'm sure it will illuminate any of the subsequent…activities as well."

"And will you be joining in on any of the Afterglow *activities*?" Falchion asked, his voice drawing out in mischief.

Kathrina's face flashed in Elric's mind, and he gave a curt shake of his head, keeping his lips shut tight.

"Oh, come now. You have been cooped up in your wing with your routines and your self-imposed exile for months," pressed Falchion. "I have successfully kidnapped you once, I can ensure none are able to do so again. Come out tonight."

Elric only shook his head once more.

"Master Elric," Falchion said, grasping his elbow and coming to a halt. The seriousness in his face gave Elric pause. "You have been cloistered for longer than is healthy for any being, let alone an eternal one. I have made sure after the Observance ceremony that the night is yours. Join me in the courtyard and camps for one night, and tomorrow, I shall let you return to your misery."

Elric snorted humorlessly, then quietly found words. "The Afterglow is for those in love or lust. Not for those who have lost."

Falchion's brows tightened together. "Have you lost someone?"

Elric nodded.

"How many years?"

"It has now surpassed five. We always knew I would live beyond her lifetime, but this—"

It was not supposed to be like this.

How many times had he said the words inside his mind? Yet he could not bring himself to utter them aloud. "She was the sweetheart of my formative years and the great love of my life. I have no interest in company for a night, though I'm sure you are simply a delight to seek trouble with."

"I believe that is the highest compliment I have ever been paid," Falchion said, holding a hand to his chest in mock flattery, but then seriousness marked his gaze again. "I do not know such a loss, as romance has never been mine, but what I do know is that you deserve a reprieve from grief. Some pleasure may ease it, if just for a night."

Elric smiled but shook his head sadly. "I have only ever wanted one. I had her for a short while, and I shall be grateful. Bask in the Afterglow for the both of us tonight."

Falchion sighed. "I suspected you would not be swayed. Then allow me this—this eve, as you follow your pattern about your quarters, maybe leave yourself another few moments to linger by your balcony door."

Elric's eyebrows lifted as Falchion turned to walk away, then leaned back in with a wink to whisper, "Consider it a gift. For Moonrise."

He was a few paces away when Elric spoke again. "Why?"

The word stopped Falchion in his tracks. "Why what?"

"Why go out of your way attempting to become my friend? You are smart, you possess cunning, and you are a loyal soldier. If you were in my shoes, why should I trust you?"

Falchion considered his words for a moment and then shrugged. "In truth I would not trust me after all I have done. But I think that, with time, I would come to realize that we are not unlike the other, you and I. We are bound to fealty in our own ways. And while our pasts may not be the same, while our circumstances may be even more distanced, our futures will walk the same path. Why not have company along the way?"

His words echoed in Elric's mind long after the sun began to set where he stood upon the small, wooden platform erected at the center of the courtyard. Silken garland was strung across both the stone terrace and the labyrinth, catching the light from the gilded torches staked in the ground to illuminate the space. There were great tables and booths scattered about, the smells a medley of savory meat and sugared delicacies that complemented the rich, fruity tang of the wine flowing freely from casks all around the square.

The labyrinth's hedges were adorned with flickering lights, ensuring the path within would be lit should any venture there after dark, while the road that lay between the courtyard and maze, reserved to watch the rising moon, would later be used for dancing.

The great iron gates surrounding the palace were shut, and while the nobility and Obarian citizens all milled about the grounds together, the stark differences between them were jarring. The people wore what he knew with some measure of certainty were their best clothes, and the threadbare dresses, vests, and trousers—most all worn with patches covering inevitable holes—sent pain ricocheting through Elric's chest. They were thin, unbearably so, yet few dared touch the feast laid out in booths about the courtyard, their eyes snapping from guard to guard as if awaiting reprimand. The nobles, however, flitted about in loud and gaudy flocks, overindulging in the things they had available at their fingertips on any given day. And when their paths had the misfortune of crossing with a lowly citizen, they stared down their noses and gave them wide berth while they passed, as if afraid breathing the same air might afflict them with poverty.

Most of the Obarians kept their eyes downcast, though some remained proud with their heads held high, refusing to cower or bend to the nobility on display. It was a quiet show of defiance that Elric recognized all too well.

But there was one thing that they all had in common—they all gaped openly at him.

Used to being a spectacle at this point, he focused primarily on the sky, ushering away every cloud that drifted into sight, keeping the expanse open and clear. With the inconsistencies in his magic as of late it took far more concentration than usual, and he did not notice the moon itself until it was nearly in the sky. It rose slowly, regal and dressed in pure silver as it slid across the dimming purple horizon, close enough for Elric to spot its craters and dimples. Each one added pearlescent dimension to its stunning brightness.

The nobility in attendance cooed for a moment, then returned to their chatter, as if the marvel was simply another feat crafted for their pleasure, but the Obarian people soaked it all in with innocent eyes and open mouths. They did not speak, they did not move—even the smallest child enraptured by its beauty—and it struck Elric that when all was said and done, the only thing the people seemed to care for was the event itself. They had not come for pomp or indulgence but to take in the wonder of something larger and far beyond themselves.

As the light grew higher in the sky, illuminating their faces, he watched their hope alight too, inspiring them silently toward another day. Reigniting their desire to fight for one that may even be better, bigger than themselves. And when the sky was finally dark and the world properly bathed in moonlight brighter than any sun, a cheer rose from the ground, and music and dancing began. The flames of the torches and lanterns were diminished, alight just enough to cast elongated shadows across the stone, yet they invited the revelers to draw closer to one another. And they obeyed, pairings splitting off in conversation and dance, their lithe, fluid movements cloaked in the moon's ethereal beams. They had made the transition from Observance to Afterglow, and that was Elric's cue to disappear.

He retreated to his quarters, shedding his vest and untucking his shirt, but before he removed his boots, he paused to stare at the door to his balcony. Hesitation marred his steps, but he walked to it, then slowly grasped and turned the handle.

The lock sprang free with a soft *click*, and the door cracked open to the night.

Elric smiled to himself, shaking his head at the gift Falchion had given him, then slipped outside, shutting it firmly at his back.

He walked to the short, stone wall that framed the balcony and rested his hands on it, drawing in a deep breath of air that felt somehow easier at this elevation. The courtyard bustled below, lovers already taking to the maze of hedges, tucking around bends and corners in search of somewhere private. Some found places and others did not care, engaging in all manner of embrace in the open, the soft gasps and moans echoing up from the ground enough to make an inexperienced soul blush. From such a height, he could see it all, and he pitied anyone who believed they truly had privacy anywhere on the palace grounds.

The kingdom beyond the gates was also illuminated in a wash of moonlight, outlining the faded earth where houses had stood within the boundary of city limits—a proud capital, once bustling with life with the palace at its head. There were more makeshift homes erected now than there had been before, and he wondered if Obarians from other provinces were seeking refuge now as well.

Beyond them was the tent village—nearly triple in size—occupied by the members of the revolution who stood at the gate every day, shouting for change and demanding justice. His eye caught the flicker of a campfire, indicating that not all who resided there had accepted the palace's invitation, but outside of that there was no movement.

Elric looked up and let himself soak in the vastness of the sky, the size of the moon, the way the stars surrounding it studded the night like diamonds.

He wouldn't see this sight again for seven months. Every Moonrise that had come before, he wondered what might become of his life before the next—where the moon would find him at that time. Now he knew the answer. It would find him here. And the thought only brought pain.

He took a deep breath in, allowing his eyes to fall shut, then heard his mother's voice in his head.

"Shall I tell you once more how the Isteriaeth came to walk the realm?" she asked, pushing his hair back from his forehead.

She smelled soft like vanilla and the salty scent on her auburn hair tickled his nose. "How, Mother?" he asked, though he knew the answer already. He curled into her and ran a finger over the deep-blue stone of the brooch pinned at her neck, tracing the points of the lone white star that spanned its surface.

"When magic was first cast out, the Stars found it and had mercy. They called the Raeltach together and begged the Darkness and the sands of Time to catch the magic disappearing into the galaxies. Time promised to guard space for the Stars to gather it, but there was no way to hold the dhust together. That was when the Isteriaeth beseeched the Darkness, begging for her aid.

"All she had to give was her lyre—her most beloved possession, the music that formed the silent song the planets danced to—and when she snapped it, she threw the strands out like a whip and captured the magic in five parts.

"The Isteriaeth wove the strands, knitting them together and graciously sacrificing a part of themselves to bind the dhust to the strands. In doing so, the strands became a part of them—of us. And when we return to this world, when we have given a decade to learning from this land, the strands dormant in our being come alive and bestow on us their dhust. Through our magic, we become one with the realm."

"If we are one, then why must we stay inside for Moonrise? Why can we not look at the stars too?" he asked with a yawn, tipping his head back to meet her eyes. Breathing her in was like absorbing a gale off the midnight sea and basking in the light of her azure eyes was as breathtaking as any night sky could be.

"Some wonders are too precious to meet," she replied, tracing the outline of his cheek with a fingertip and rocking him softly. His eyelids drifted shut, heavier than his ability to hold them apart. *"And you, my dear, are one of them. But someday, I hope you behold them with joy and find rest in their skies. May you never go where they cannot find you."*

Elric opened his eyes once more, meeting the gaze of the moon again. There would be no rest for him, not tonight, but before he could turn in, a voice like velvet spoke.

"I always imagined you to be a stargazer, but a voyeur? I suppose you *can* learn something new every day."

CHAPTER FIFTEEN

*E*lric exhaled roughly, turning on his heel to meet the gaze of Graecerys. She looked regal in an empire waist dress of pale blue with a darker shade of gossamer fabric laid over the top that fluttered around her shoulders and gathered at the waist before ruffling along the skirt.

She fit in beautifully with the night, or at least she would were it not for her fiery hair, braided into a plait down her back.

Or, of course, her incessant speaking.

"A voyeur I am not, though it is interesting that you bring it up as you stand upon the same balcony. What does a lady of your station know of such things anyway?"

"Whatever I wish," she replied, tipping her glass of wine to him. That was when he noticed the second door behind her, and his eyes narrowed.

"It is not enough to have a door between our walls, but we share a balcony as well?"

"So it would seem, though I don't recall giving permission for your door to be unlocked. But I suppose since you're here now there's little I can do about that."

"Hm. Not *whatever you wish* after all."

Her eyes flashed with anger, and Elric couldn't help but smile. A thought occurred to him as he did. "I did not see you during the Observance." In fact, he had not seen her all night, though she was dressed for the occasion.

"I prefer to watch from a distance. I don't know if you've noticed, but there is a bit of tension among my people, and I was not provided with a proper sheath for a sword with this dress."

"I have not seen you carry a blade before," he remarked.

"Weapons are not meant to be seen, they are meant to be used. I refuse to entertain an audience, be it civilian or nobleman, if I fail to have a means to protect myself."

"Yet you do not mind being left alone with me."

Graecerys smiled slowly. "Why should I? Your strands are wrapped around my finger."

Elric glared at her, but before he could retort, she continued, "And unlike the lords, I am not foolish enough to believe an archaic celebration and free-flowing libations and debauchery will preserve peace in this kingdom."

"What do you believe might?"

Something faltered in her carefully constructed mask. Something youthful, hopeful even. Something strong.

But as quickly as it appeared, it was gone.

"I do not know that my beliefs matter," she replied. "As you like to remind me, I am not a queen in the eyes of my people. It does not matter what I do, what I say or think or offer, they want none of it because it comes from me. Nothing makes a difference."

Elric was quiet for a moment, then said carefully, "I take it the provisions have not served to ease tension."

"Nor the Moonrise Observance," Graecerys added. "The latter does not surprise me, and while I did not expect one show of goodwill to change hearts and minds I did hope...."

Elric widened his eyes expectantly, waiting for her to finish, but she took a long drag of her wine instead.

"The soldiers value your word. And though I am privy to your opinion, whether I wish to hear it or not, you were undeniably bred for the throne. So tell me why, when the lords convene, it is Blenheim's voice they hear the loudest."

"Would you rather it be mine, even if you are so oppressed by it?"

"Yes," Elric answered, drawing a slight eyebrow raise from the woman across from him. "If you are a ruler all of your own, as you once said, then why would you allow anything, anyone to silence you?"

She stared at him, silent, her face hard as stone. And though he knew he could push—knew he could prompt her to return to her quarters and leave him to a peaceful evening—he found that he did not have the energy to fight her. Not that night.

"Did you know the Moonrise was said to be observed over all four kingdoms of Breteria?" he asked, deftly changing the subject. "It was a time for all to pause and unite in remembrance and celebration of what the Raeltach brought together to form our world."

"The Raeltach," she said incredulously. "The Paladin of Stars, Warden of Time, and Muse of Darkness were folklore. Bedtime stories nursemaids told children to inspire them to get along."

"Oh, they were very real. Trust me, I would know."

"Ah!" She tossed a hand in the air, causing Elric to startle and her wine to slosh. "You do know something. That's a start. Please, continue."

"I'm beginning to think the unlocked door was a mistake," Elric muttered, turning away and regretting not sending her storming back to her room.

"Your being here is a mistake."

Her old, recited words prompted him to face her once more. "On that we can agree. See, we are making progress."

"I do not wish to make progress."

"But you do wish to bring up your disdain for me every time there is something you do not want to discuss. At least I have found some sense of belonging with your subjects, because while you insist that my presence is regrettable, it would appear they do not want you either."

Graecerys opened her mouth to speak, but to Elric's shock and awe, she slowly shut it. She looked away instead, approaching the wall not far from where he stood, folding one arm across her front and sipping from her glass with the other.

"The people here are destined to hate whatever the face of their ire might be. And how fortunate am I that it has become me," she said quietly, watching a gray bird soar over the courtyard.

"Then you accept no responsibility for your actions? For your culpability in both their lives and mine? You would do nothing differently?"

"As I said before, it would change nothing. There must always be someone to blame. It is the way of the world."

"Then blame the Isteriaeth, I hear we are easy targets."

"Why do my desires matter to you anyway?" she asked, pinning him with her razor-sharp gaze.

It was Elric's turn to slowly shut his mouth. He summoned his own glass of wine and walked to the balcony a fair distance away, leaning on the side and allowing his hands and cup to dangle precariously over the edge.

"It matters because the people of Obarian are strong," he said, keeping all harshness from his tone. "They are farmers outwardly, but they have the soul of their warrior ancestors and they communicate with the same fire. If you want to rule them, to be accepted by them, then you must gain their respect. And there cannot be healing until there is repentance."

"And you suppose they would be open to apologies and

amends? Surely you cannot be the bearer of such a simple epiphany when it has eluded the countless past royal families."

Elric's throat tightened, and without his permission, his mind drifted backward, dredging through the deepest recesses of his memory, to the fate he would have inevitably faced had he never escaped Obarian when he did. And for the first time, it struck him that while he had suffered greatly, he had been spared far more at an unfathomable price, paid by those who loved him enough to leave him.

"It could always be worse," he said, more to himself than anyone.

"Truly," Graecerys mused, though her tone was sharp. "I may be despised, but at least I have not gone mad like my father or the King of Inflamel."

"The King of Inflamel is not mad," Elric snapped. "Do not speak of what you do not know."

Graecerys's eyes widened a fraction. "Then what is he?"

If he didn't know any better, he would have taken her tone for genuine concern.

"He is—" Elric paused, grasping for words that did not pain him. "He is alive."

She hesitated, and he could almost hear her turning his words over in her mind, examining them before she spoke again. "I know what the lords have brought word of—what the court whispers of. But you are my advisor. So go on," she said, tone as gentle as she could seem to muster.

Elric took a steadying breath before quietly answering. "He is not mad. He is cursed. And not even I can find a way to free him."

The silence stretched just a moment too long between them. Graecerys turned back to look out over the kingdom. "So I not only have a rude and inconsiderate Isteriaeth, but a defective one."

"No, you have one who cannot contend with tenebrescent

magic," Elric answered with irritation. "One who never dabbled in it but wishes he had if for no other reason than to save a friend. Two of them, actually."

"You refer to the rebellion's queen?" she asked. "Now she I have heard plenty of. Her actions greatly inspired my people to rise against me."

"If you are talking about the High Queen of the Trifolium Throne, then yes. The king began his decay the day she was lost. The longer she is gone, the more he descends into darkness. I was a help to him for a while, a buoy in the waves of grief, but…."

Graecerys looked to him expectantly, and he took a long drag of his wine before answering.

"Not even I could pull him out," he finally admitted.

"Grief is not an ocean, it is quicksand," she said firmly. "You fight, rise, and leave it behind, or it will continue to pull you down."

He shook his head. "It is water. Capable of drowning, yet necessary and found in every bit of life around us. You cannot live without taking it in."

She shook her head. "I take only what I need to survive."

The vulnerability in her words sobered Elric, reminding him of where he was and who he spoke to. "Forgive me, Your Grace," he said, looking at her from the corner of his eye. "When did we begin talking about you once more?"

She froze, realizing her involuntary confession. "We did not," she asserted with every confidence of a queen.

"Interesting," Elric mused.

"What is?"

"That your people call you cold, stoic, and heartless. I have yet to see you as such. You are hardened, yes, but I wonder how much of it is to protect yourself. And why you allow it to slip so easily in my presence. Is it that I convict you? Challenge you? Or am I just favored?"

He waited for her verbal barb. Part of him even expected her to pull a weapon and stab him with it, but to his utter surprise, she smiled slowly and shook her head. "You're going to be a problem, aren't you?"

He shrugged. "You could save yourself the trouble of discovery and set me free."

Her laugh broke the night, light and musical despite the vastness in her midnight eyes. She turned and walked away, but before she entered her chambers once more, she replied loud enough for him to hear. "And where would be the fun in that?"

CHAPTER SIXTEEN

WHERE THERE ONCE WAS A GIRL, THERE WAS NOW A BOY, AND THOUGH HE SAW TRUST AS A FLEETING THING, A DELICATE PETAL, EASILY CRUSHED, SHE SAW IT AS A VINE GROWING THICK, PROTECTING ITS BLOOMS WITH THORNS. AND TOGETHER, THEY WERE LOVELY.

ON THE FIRST NIGHT, SHE BROUGHT HIM FOOD AND WATER, THEN RUBBED HIS BACK AS HER MOTHER ALWAYS DID WHEN HE GOBBLED THEM TOO FAST TO HOLD DOWN AND WRETCHED UPON THE CARPET.

THE SECOND NIGHT SHE BROUGHT MORE, WITH SMALLER RATIONS TO BE KEPT WITH HIM, AND A CLOTH TO CLEAN AND DRY HIS FACE.

BY THE TIME A FORTNIGHT HAD PASSED, A BIT OF COLOR RETURNED TO HIS CHEEKS. THE SHADOWS BENEATH HIS WIDE EYES DIMMED SLIGHTLY. AND HE WALKED WITH STRENGTH INSTEAD OF SHAKING LIMBS.

IT WAS SOME DAYS MORE, AS HE SAT BESIDE HER AT THE PIANO, THEIR SMALL HANDS COVERING THE KEYS, THAT SHE FIRST SAW HIM SMILE.

“DO YOUR PARENTS WORK HERE?” HE ASKED QUIETLY.

"My father does. My mother tends to our land, and I remain here for tutoring." Not a lie. And then with hesitation, she asked, "What happened to yours?"

The boy froze, but before she could apologize, he spoke. "They went away. But they left me here. They said I would be safe, but I do not know how. Unless...they knew."

"Knew what?" she asked.

"Knew you would find me."

They were silent again, the girl absently picking out a melody with her right hand. "Why would you be in danger here? Who would hurt you?"

The boy swallowed hard, and she watched him search for the words to answer.

"You do not have to say," she murmured, smiling softly.

"But I want to," he replied earnestly. "My family...they had magic."

The girl stopped playing, her eyes wide. "Real magic?" she whispered. "Do you have it too?"

The boy shook his head. "I'm supposed to, but not yet."

Reality sank into the girl's mind, and she looked away. Her instructors taught her about the Fall of the Thrones. She had seen the history depicted in art all over the palace. They had done their best to hide from her childlike ears what had become of the beings with dhust, but even the staff whispered about the benefits of acquiring it. The ways it was obtained.

The words were on the tip of her tongue. My father would— But she closed her lips. The father she knew, the one she loved, the one who cared for her and loved her in return, would not have harmed a boy. But the angry specter of a man who hardly glanced in her direction now....

She shifted on the bench, turning to face the boy who stared at his hands. "My teachers here speak of duty. They

SPEAK OF HONOR AND THE WORTH AND IMPORTANCE OF A NAME. THEY MAKE THEM SOUND LIKE SUCH PRETTY THINGS, BUT I DON'T FEEL ANYTHING WHEN I THINK OF THEM. BUT IF IT WAS MY DUTY TO FIND YOU, THEN IT IS MY HONOR TO SAVE YOU. THERE IS ONLY ONE PERSON I KNOW WHO I TRUST TO KEEP YOUR SECRET, THOUGH IT WILL BE MONTHS BEFORE I SEE HER AGAIN. WHEN THE TIME COMES, WILL YOU GO WITH ME?"

THE BOY'S EYES WIDENED, AND THOUGH SHE SAW HIS CONCERN, HIS MIND TRYING TO WORK OUT HOW SUCH A THING COULD BE POSSIBLE, SHE ALSO SAW TRUST. A CERTAINTY THAT ONLY APPEARED WHEN THEY SPOKE OF THE FUTURE. AND HER HEART WELLED, THREATENING TO EXPLODE WITH DETERMINATION AND SURGING HOPE.

SHE MIGHT NOT EVER HAVE IT FOR HERSELF, BUT SHE WOULD MAKE SURE TO GIVE THIS BOY THE THINGS SHE CRAVED ABOVE ALL ELSE—FREEDOM AND A LIFE OF HIS OWN.

THE BOY SMILED NOW, SMALL AT FIRST AND THEN WIDER. "WILL YOU STAY WITH ME?"

HER HEART FALTERED. FOR THE FIRST TIME, WORDS FAILED HER, AND SHE ONLY SHOOK HER HEAD.

HIS FACE FELL. "WHY NOT?"

SHE GATHERED HER THOUGHTS, PICKING HER WORDS CAREFULLY. "BECAUSE MY PLACE IS HERE. EVEN IF I WISH IT WERE ELSEWHERE."

THE BOY SURVEYED HER CLOSELY. TO HER SURPRISE, HE SLID CLOSER. "WHERE WOULD YOU GO?"

"WHAT DO YOU MEAN?" SHE ASKED, BROW FURROWING.

"IF YOUR PLACE COULD BE ANYWHERE, WHERE WOULD YOU GO?"

"I...I DON'T KNOW. I HAVEN'T THOUGHT ABOUT IT."

"TRY."

THE GIRL THOUGHT A MINUTE. CONSIDERED ALL SHE LOVED AND ALL SHE HAD LOST. WHAT MORE SHE STOOD TO LOSE. THEN SHE SAID SOFTLY BUT SURELY, "I WOULD BE NEAR MY MOTHER UNTIL I COULD NOT ANY LONGER, AND THEN I WOULD SET SAIL. I

WOULD SEE ALL OF BRETERIA BUT LIVE ON THE SEA. DISAPPEAR INTO THE ENDLESS BLUE WHERE AT NIGHT IT COULD BE ME, THE OCEAN, AND THE STARS."

"I SHOULD LIKE TO SAIL, I THINK," THE BOY ADDED. "I HAVE NEVER SEEN THE OCEAN."

THE GIRL SMILED AND CLOSED HER EYES. "IT IS PERFECT. ENDLESS. FATHOMLESS. I DO NOT THINK WHEN I SEE IT, ONLY FEEL AND LET THE SOUND CARRY ME FAR AWAY."

"LIKE MUSIC," THE BOY SAID.

SHE SIGHED. "JUST LIKE MUSIC."

"WILL OUR SHIP BE LARGE ENOUGH FOR A PIANO?"

THE GIRL LAUGHED. "OUR SHIP? WHEN DID WE SET SAIL TOGETHER?"

"WHEN YOU SAID WE CAN WATCH THE STARS. I WANT TO BE ANYWHERE I CAN FIND THEM. THEY ARE MY MUSIC."

AN IDEA STRUCK THE GIRL. "MIGHT YOU WANT TO SEE THEM NOW?"

THE BOY'S EYES WIDENED, BUT HE SHOOK HIS HEAD. "I DO NOT DARE LEAVE THIS ROOM. BUT SOMEDAY, MAYBE."

"IN THE SUMMER," THE GIRL REPEATED, NUDGING HIM WITH HER SHOULDER. "I'LL SING YOU THE OCEAN WHILE YOU PLAY ME THE STARS AND THEY CAN BE OUR MUSIC. DO WE AGREE?"

THE BOY SMILED AND NUDGED HER BACK. "AGREED."

CHAPTER SEVENTEEN

Elric did not sleep the rest of the night, and he already dreaded the long day that awaited. The palace doors were open and small clusters of Obarians were being guided through the main floor, though unlike the Moonrise festivities, they seemed keenly interested in the royal residence.

"Do they really think it wise to freely offer access to the palace when half these people would see it ransacked and those within it tried for treason?" Elric asked, sinking his teeth into a sugared roll.

"I don't believe they've thought at all," Falchion replied under his breath, taking in the crowd mulling about. "The guard is on high alert and the queen refuses to leave her quarters."

"Surely she will attend the gala this evening."

Falchion said nothing, and Elric turned to him. "She *will* attend, will she not?"

Falchion sighed. "Do you really believe she will obey anyone's orders?"

Elric shrugged, and he wasn't sure if it was his lack of sleep or their exchange on the balcony that led him to say, "Maybe she should not be ordered. A simple request may work."

Falchion snorted. "Who better to extend it than you? Your immortality is secure so long as the stars live in your veins, is it not?"

Elric finished his roll and summoned a napkin to clean his hands. Instead of disposing of it, he tucked it behind the leather straps that crossed Falchion's chest, patted it, then turned and walked away.

"And what exactly will you do when she strings you up and beats you like an old rug, Master Isteriaeth?" Falchion called after him, humor barely restrained in his words.

"I suppose I'll kick her, sir *vintner.*"

Falchion's full laugh echoed up the stairwell after him.

Once upon the third floor, Elric entered his quarters, strode to the door within his wall, and knocked on it loudly.

Silence greeted him.

After a few more raps, he heard the faint scuff of a chair being slid across the floor, then soft footsteps. He knocked once more, and this time the grating of a lock greeted him and the door swung open.

Graecerys's eyes—heavy with what looked like sleep, but ringed with darkened circles that indicated otherwise—pinned him to the floor, but instead of asking what he wanted, she said, "How did you know this was a door?"

Elric smirked. "When you know what to look for, it is easy to find what is hidden. Will you be attending the gala tonight?"

Her brow furrowed. "Why is that your concern?"

"Because though most in this palace call you queen and corroborate your claim to the throne, it would seem you are commanded more than you lead. And I simply wondered if your presence had been requested tonight, or if you had been ordered to attend?"

Her eyes narrowed. "I do not take orders from anyone."

"This I know; however, you are also stubborn, and in your stubbornness you would remain here all night. But what if you met your people? What if they are as concerned meeting you as you are to be in their presence?"

"Where did this come from?" Graecerys asked, placing a hand on her hip, her eyes shrewd. "Did Blenheim put you up to this?"

Elric snorted. "I care for your lords even less than I do you. I was simply offering a suggestion. The observations are mine and mine alone."

"Then you have decided to be my advisor now?"

Elric extended his hands, palm up, at his sides. "Is that not my title?"

Graecerys was silent, examining him, her eyes probing with fire. She glanced over her shoulder, looking to her own door before meeting his stare once more. He was surprised to see a neutral expression. Not vulnerability, but not the hardened mask of a queen either. It felt as though he were simply looking at Graecerys.

"What would you see me do?" she asked, folding her arms.

Elric's eyebrow raised, but he did not let his fledgling confidence ruffle his own carefully neutral expression. "Attend. Let the people see you. Spend time observing them from less of a distance. Allow them to experience a queen—an active leader— who sees them, and ascertain their wants and needs for yourself, apart from what the lords tell you. Let them form an opinion of you that is not fueled by what the revolution shouts. Observe each other, face-to-face."

She did not say anything, but he recognized the thread of anger that ignited in her eyes. "I will consider it," she replied, stepping back and starting to close the door once more. "Thank you for speaking."

Elric extended a hand, holding the door ajar. "That is it? Thank you for speaking?"

"Well, they are the most words you have said without mocking me since your arrival, so yes, I am appreciative."

"For a woman who hides in her room out of spite and fear of consequence, I am curious where you store the nerve to speak to me the way you do," Elric said, sarcastic wonderment filling his tone.

"Think on it and let me know your findings," Graecerys replied with a small head tilt and venomous smile. "We can't let all that wisdom you supposedly possess go to waste now, can we?"

"I never claimed wisdom. Your Lord Blenheim placed that burden on me."

"But is this not what you did for Inflamel? Advise them?"

Elric stiffened. "I was asked to serve and I did so out of love. They did not steal me away in the night. They did not take what did not belong to them."

She shrugged. "Maybe they should have. Maybe what you saw as kindness was a lack of deference. Or else we wouldn't be speaking right now, would we?"

Elric clenched his fists. "I told you before not to speak of what you do not know."

To his surprise, Graecerys took a step closer, little more than a foot away from him now. "Unlike you, I do not need to know everything. Just the right things. And if you would truly defend the king who threw you out of the castle, directly into our hands, over the land of your own people, then maybe you are not the dutiful, virtuous being they say you are."

"I am not virtuous. And if you knew what this land did to my people, if you understood loss in any form, you would know that a home is not soil. It is not birthright. It is love. And where you find home and love, that is where your family resides."

"Do not talk to me as if I'm an ignorant child," she lashed, her temper flaring, and for some reason Elric found satisfaction at the sight of it.

"Then shed your petulance and straighten your crown, because your people must see you tonight," he bit out, his eyes flashing above her head before returning to her eyes. "My apologies. I forgot you do not wear one."

Graecerys glared at him. "Do not patronize me."

"Then stop recalling what even I dare not speak of," he replied, removing his hand from the door and stepping back. "And be grateful for what you've stolen."

She pasted on a sickeningly sweet smile. "I am grateful— To be away from you."

And with that, she slammed the door in his face.

A surprising number of Obarians filled the hall, their modest clothing in dark shades standing out against the glittering finery of the nobility. Elric cringed from where he stood along the wall. Every aspect of the celebration had done nothing but further line the contrast between the two groups, and though they had been amiable, he feared they would have little to show for it on the other side. And certainly nowhere near enough goodwill for the people to accept Graecerys as their queen.

As if summoned by his thoughts, the door to the hall swung open and Graecerys strode in, silencing the room. The crowd stared, parting around her but failing to bow or even nod in respect as she moved toward the center of the room where Elric saw Lord Blenheim step forward to meet her, stopping to introduce her to a tall man with dark, close-cropped hair and a scar down the side of his face.

He watched them curiously, and when they parted the man did so with a dip of his head and Graecerys with a small, respectful curtsy.

"His name is Denfrin," a voice said to Elric's immediate left, startling him, though he recovered quickly. He turned to meet the eyes of Lord Jacian, a glass of wine in his hand.

"The man with the scar," he added.

Elric nodded, unsure why he needed to know that information.

Lord Jacian nodded in return, watching him, waiting for him to say something, and when Elric turned back to face the room, he took up post beside him along the wall.

"What is it you hope to accomplish from over here, Isteriaeth?"

He is truly not going away, is he?

"I assess people," Elric replied stoically.

"Assess them how?"

"I assess how long it will be until they make an ass of themselves."

Jacian snorted into his wine. "Funny, I thought someone who has existed as long as you would find some form of entertainment beyond simply watching people."

"Watching is what I do best," Elric quipped. "I have proven to give poor counsel, so perhaps becoming a vulture skulking from the shadows will accomplish what my wisdom and wit cannot. I hear it works for Augur."

"Auger may have been a vulture in another life, but that is not what I have heard of you," Jacian said, lowering his voice. "In fact, I heard just the opposite this evening. That it was you who spurred the lady of the hour to join us."

Elric's head snapped to the side. "How would you have heard such a rumor?"

Lord Jacian clicked his tongue. "The nobility does not do much, but what they do well is talk. A dress was sent for and before it was even donned, there were whispers in the halls."

Elric said nothing, watching Lord Blenheim lead Graecerys around the room and introduce her to different groups of Obarians, all of whom he presumed were from varying provinces.

"I see you rather often," Elric remarked. "Is your province near?"

"Quite," replied Jacian. "You are standing in it."

Elric's brow furrowed. "You are lord over the province in which the palace resides?"

"I am, though I carry no authority within the palace gates. Just outside her walls."

Elric raised an eyebrow. "Is that why you draw ire? Because you permit the revolution to grow just beyond the bars?"

"I permit nothing," said Jacian, a smile toying on his lips. "I just do not prevent it."

Elric stared at the man, but he only took another sip of wine, watching the path Graecerys carved about the room as he continued, "A lawless kingdom is a blight, but one that would starve its people in the name of justice is worse. They are not asking for us to provide, they are begging for our support. And we hesitate to extend even the smallest audience."

Elric laughed humorlessly. "There are few things worse than being a part of her audience."

"Yes, but at least those in her audience are given a platform. And though so many do nothing with it, there is no purer hell than to be given a place to speak where you are still forced to remain mute."

Elric was quiet, assessing the man at his side. "You seem to lack fear of what words may do to you. I do not believe you understand the meaning of silence."

"And you remain wordless, as if a blade might come down upon your head if you dare open your mouth."

Elric turned to face him, but before he could speak Jacian smirked.

"Rest easy, Isteriaeth, I do not mean to trap you. I believe you to be one of the few decent beings left in this kingdom. I just wonder where you stand."

"I stand against treason," Elric replied pointedly.

"Yet for your captor?"

The words silenced Elric, a restlessness brewing in him that he was afraid to acknowledge—but one he could not ignore.

"It is truly becoming impossible to heal when everyone in this Thrones-forsaken palace insists on bringing up my most painful memories," he hissed, voice low. "As if walking these halls with the ghosts of my kin is not enough."

"I wonder if that is enough," Jacian murmured, rubbing an invisible smudge on his cup with his thumb.

"Enough for what?"

"Enough to bring us both what we want."

"And what is that?"

Jacian's eyes snapped to Elric's, the fire burning in them unmistakable. "Freedom."

He fell silent as a few nobles milled past, and when Elric sought out Graecerys, he was surprised to find her not in conversation but cordially dancing with the scar-faced man under the watchful eye of Blenheim, who looked less than pleased.

"Denfrin is the face of the people's cause," Jacian said, his words prickling the skin on Elric's arms. "He leads their revolution, and though he is young, he has been brought up to love this land more than most. He is cunning and intelligent. There is nothing he will not do for Obarian."

"And he is allowed to dance with the queen he would see dead?"

"She is not aware of his position among us. And we do not truly want her dead. Most would see her forsake the throne and hand it to someone who may care for the people and heal our land instead. But I fear that favor vanishes with every life we bury too soon."

"*We,*" Elric repeated, drawing out the word. The weight of the admission, the implication, was like a boulder in his stomach. "And does the queen know a traitor sits at her table every week? Does she know who you truly stand for?"

"I am sure it is suspected, but I am careful to leave no cause for charges," Jacian replied, tipping his glass. "A delicate balance that I understand you may be familiar with from your days in Inflamel."

Clarity dawned in Elric's mind, and while he relaxed his posture, his spine remained stiff. "I helped gather a rebellion from the shadows to depose an evil king. I did not rally a revolution in the square to steal a throne."

"We do not wish to steal anything. Only take back what is rightfully ours for the betterment of Obarian so that we all may flourish once more."

"Force of any kind is difficult to recognize as a promotion of unity," Elric replied, shaking his head.

Jacian released a frustrated sigh, turning away, his gaze skimming the crowd a moment before he spoke. "See the people? Look at their faces. At the lifelessness in their eyes, the way their clothes sag on their bones. They have been trussed up, made to seem alive, every last one a presentable trophy for the crown, and yet they are mere taxidermy. Inside, they are dead." He fell silent, then as if to himself, asked, "When did it become a crime to fight for life?"

Elric did not need to look around. He knew Jacian was right. And part of him wondered if Graecerys did too, though he wasn't sure why he cared. The thought of standing in the space between her and such present danger put him on edge. And yet....

"She does not hold the power she would have you believe," Jacian added, stepping closer. "The lords seated by her side would see her under their thumb before a crown is placed upon her head. And she does nothing to assert herself over them."

"You mean Blenheim."

"Blenheim controls them all, the queen included, though she is a wild card. I believe you still afford her more credit than is due, but she has proven to possess a will strong enough to stop it all. If she wanted to."

"And you do not believe she wants to? Even after she learned the true state of the Provinces and moved to aid her people?"

Jacian snorted, swirling his drink. "And which do you believe is stronger? Intent or perception?"

"Whichever leads to the freedom you say we both crave the swiftest."

The man's eyes snapped from his drink to Elric and he took a step forward, lowering his voice to fill the space that had now vanished between them. "Then I suppose one must work faster. Shall you decide? Or I?"

Elric swallowed and stepped back, the implication clear. Beyond Jacian's shoulder, Blenheim swooped in to steer Graecerys toward the throne and the sight loosened his lips. "I will speak with her. We will see how much my words truly spurn her."

Jacian nodded. "It is all I ask. Your words may be the final attempt we have at a peaceful resolution."

Elric snorted. "It isn't like I have much to left to lose."

The lord assessed him slowly, then with a measure of warmth in his expression, he turned to face the wall so that his words reached Elric's ear alone. "Though the crown sought to starve out those who would recall the days before the great Fall, there are some that draw breath who were told the tales of old. They ascribe to the first days, when Isteriaeth called Obarian their home, and believe that this kingdom will not be whole again until the stars have been restored to the land…as our ruler."

Elric's head snapped to the side. "I do not want the throne. I do not want anything from this land. I only want my life."

"If that is what you wish, then the people will honor it. And if your words fall on deaf ears, then know you are still not without hope. There is, after all, a solution in which we all might gain what we desire most. I meant it when I said that the people do not wish her harm, but if it is the final path forward, I will not stand in their way. It is up to you if you aid us then, or if you step aside, but in either course, you will be freed."

A chill settled over Elric's skin, and though the words were hard, he saw a resigned sadness in Jacian's eyes as he nodded in respect, then turned to leave.

"And if I were to betray you? If I went to her right now?" he asked. "What then?"

Jacian paused, turning back to face Elric and raising his glass. "Then there will be no one left to stop them."

The lord walked away, and the full weight of his words settled on Elric's shoulders, rooting him to the spot and leaving him grateful to be alone.

The message was clear: The revolution—with a lord behind them—was extending one last olive branch to the queen through Elric. And should he fail, they would free Obarian and Elric in one fell swoop by taking Graecerys's life.

Only, there was another solution. One that had played in the shadows of Elric's mind since his first day in the Diviner's Wing. For if the palace fell, if peace dissolved too quickly, he might find himself—his dhust—as the last line of defense between the queen and her demise. But if freedom for the kingdom was at stake, if the people believed that his path was ordained for a crown and left him unharmed, would he be strong enough to defy the tether and rebel against the very stars?

Even if it were not his choice, was he truly capable of denying mercy and sending Graecerys to her death?

CHAPTER EIGHTEEN

Elric lit another candle and closed the glass of his lamp, replacing it above the desk in his quarters. It had been two nights since the gala, and he had spent nearly every moment combing through each word and phrase from the Isteriaeth's record of history, searching for any form of insight it might bring to his plight. Desperate for absolution from what he may face.

He had yet to see Graecerys again, and not from entire avoidance. She did not leave her chambers at all the day following the gala, and though she had a meeting with the nobility in the evening, she had not sent Falchion to retrieve Elric from the Diviner's Wing.

All conflict aside, Elric allowed himself a smile. He knew he had made her mad before going to the gala, and like a spiteful child, she was making him pay for it now. And he couldn't help the satisfaction it gave him to know he had gotten under her skin so badly.

He turned the page and his brow furrowed. The page on the right was missing half its text, ending mid-sentence at the center of the entry before continuing in an entirely new phrase at the very bottom. Sliding his hand across the parchment, he felt the groove of what appeared to be a note of paper that had fused to the original page with time, and with a few delicate scrapes with his fingernail it pulled free.

The familiar curls and swoops of the letters stole his breath. He ran his finger over the handwriting that he had seen scrolled so many times at his mother's side, following their lines, and the tension that had been coiled in his body all day released in a slump of familiarity and grief. He rested his elbows on the table, his eyes burning behind their lids as he shut them against reality and imagined another time and place where he was still a boy beside his mother. After a moment, he collected himself enough to continue reading.

What he found made him frown.

The Kollapsar race takes many forms—the warriors known as Axion, the unknown terrors called Vacare, the Eoten giants, and the winged Hrotesk. Still more may exist, as these forms did not before the Fall of the Thrones, but they will stop at nothing to consume the power that prompts their evolution.

Elric stared at the passage where the note had been placed, recounting the forming of the Obarian provinces by the first king. There was nothing that remotely overlapped with the note, yet it had been so carefully tucked into the page.

He wrestled the book on its spine and began to leaf through it one page at a time, finding another notebook scrap, this one in the middle of a section discussing the Fall of the Thrones and the hopes that someday the Trifolium might be formed, allowing the Thrones to rise in power once more. Only now the ink was largely faded from the paper, leaving a faint diagram with five lines across it and the words:

A host.

His brow furrowed, the words in the tome growing fewer and fewer as Elric raced toward the end of his family's—his mother's—timeline. Another shred of paper, folded in a portion of the book detailing the history of Obarian's reign and the extensive list of self-proclaimed royals who ruled long enough to be overthrown or assassinated, simply said the last words of a phrase:

...taken from within.

He leaned back in his chair, unsure what to make of it when a loud *bang* from outside startled him. He closed the book and walked to the balcony door but saw nothing.

Stepping out into the night air, far too chilled for late summer, he walked halfway across the balcony and stopped.

In the low torchlight, what appeared to be a small army of people stood in rows outside the gate. One man paced before them, his rallying cries agitating the guards and stirring up dissent among the people.

A door clicked behind him, and when he glanced over his shoulder, he met the eyes of Graecerys, a cloak clasped around her neck over a gown that did not quite resemble a sleeping garment.

"Do you always sleep fully dressed?" he asked.

"Not always," she replied. "Though night does not always mean sleep."

He tipped his head to the side as she came to stand beside

him, close enough to see the gates but far enough back to remain out of sight. "Do the nightmares find you every night?"

A muscle twitched in Graecerys's jaw, and she folded her arms. "That is none of your concern."

"I do not mean to pry," Elric replied carefully. "It is only that I struggle with them as well."

A long pause fell between them, then to his surprise, Graecerys spoke in terse, clipped words. "They come for me in the darkness. I sleep when and as I am able while there is light."

She did not offer any more information, and Elric was unsure how to ask for more details, though—against his good judgement—he remained curious.

"Do stars sleep at night?" she asked, the normalcy of the question surprising him, and at the look on his face, she hurriedly added, "That was probably inappropriate of me to ask. I did not mean—"

"No, Your Grace, the question was fine," Elric assured. "I was simply surprised you asked one at all."

She pressed her lips together and shifted on her feet, appearing to try and gain her carefully constructed composure again, but her eyes remained too wide—too curious.

"I do typically sleep at night, but I have not always," he continued. "I spent so much time alone, I used to only rest when my body signaled exhaustion. But that was no way to live, so I now observe a normal human schedule. I still prefer to work at night as opposed to the morning, but I suppose that might be the star in me."

Graecerys nodded, quickly looking away, though a small, pleased smile relaxed her face.

The silence grew between them, and the crowd grew louder. Elric searched for a reason to broach the subject of the sight before them, but he did not know what to say. He was unsure if it was his own guilty conscience plaguing him, or the restlessness that hung in the air, but something was different about the way she stood beside him, and somehow he knew this was not the right moment to speak about such things. She did not want to, and for once he did not want to provoke her.

"Don't you have another history lesson for me, Isteriaeth? Or a bedtime story, perhaps?" she finally asked, breaking the silence.

"I thought you were not interested in sleep tonight?" he asked with feigned innocence.

She did not meet his eyes, but her tone held a measure of amusement. "I'm not, but perhaps there's a chance you might bore me to slumber."

"Well, you did not appreciate my mention of the Raeltach, so I'm not certain what my chances are with another. And I am not convinced you are the kind to enjoy such tales."

"'The Ballad of the Great Three' was a song my mother would rock me to sleep to, it is not history."

"It is folklore."

"They are lullabies. Meant to appease simple minds and lull the restless to slumber."

"Not to me."

Elric's words ushered in another silence, watched over dutifully by Graecerys's keen eye.

"An Isteriaeth who never grew up. What a novelty," she quipped quietly.

Elric snorted. "I'm not a tinker toy, Your Grace, though I cannot help if innocence and simplicity call the magic within me to youthfulness."

To his surprise, she laughed, a soft sound that prickled his air-chilled skin with warmth. "Your *youthfulness* could have fooled me."

He eyed her narrowly. "Are you mocking my age?"

"I would never dream of it," she replied, eyes glinting with the smile she kept hidden safely behind her mask.

"Let me guess, a queen such as yourself was raised to respect your elders?" Elric asked playfully.

"You would be correct. However, I was fortunate to spend enough time under the tutelage of women to learn that you do not need youthful innocence to act like a child. One might just simply need to be a man."

Her words sank in, and Elric turned her, appalled more at her jest than her statement. "What a callous and rude remark from someone who deigns to be a lady."

She shifted to face him in return. "And what faux offense from a man—also my elder—who behaves like no more than a babe."

Elric couldn't help himself as he shook his head—he smiled. And it was one that Graecerys slowly mirrored.

"I—" she started, then broke off. Another question lingered on the tip of her tongue, Elric knew it.

"Yes, Your Grace?"

"I...what I am wondering is...is...."

"Yes?" he drew out, encouraging her.

"I— I just wanted to say that I really despise being called *Your Grace.*"

Elric raised an eyebrow, confident she meant the sentiment, but not convinced they were the words she wanted to say. She quickly turned to face the courtyard once more.

"Is that all?" he asked quietly, leaving the door open to her.

"It is."

"Are you certain?"

She looked at him incredulously. "Yes, thank you."

He didn't know what possessed him, but he took a step forward, their shoulders nearly brushing when he turned his back on the courtyard to survey the palace's stonework. "I have seen enough masks to know a carefully constructed one when I see it."

She inhaled sharply, then sighed, her eyes tipping toward the sky. "Silly me to think that would stop you."

"Ah, you are a fast learner. Only eight, possibly nine months and you are already figuring me out."

Another small smile graced her lips before a rolling sadness broke in her eyes. "It is cruel irony that it would come easier for me learning an Isteriaeth than my own people."

"What they want is not so difficult to ascertain."

"Yes, but what they ask for is. It's like they live every day as if the world will collapse beneath their feet, though they fight violently against the thought of it becoming solid. They will never be fully sated. They do not know how. And it is no way to exist."

Elric found himself wondering how much of her words were meant for the people, and how much she understood for herself, when she turned her head to meet his gaze. He realized then how close he stood to her. How intently he had been staring.

"I apologize," she said quickly, the waves in her eyes calming to endless depths once more. "There are few things worse than a weak, indecisive leader."

"On the contrary," he replied with a hint of a smile. "I believe that is the most strength I've seen you carry yet."

Graecerys looked away, and after a pause, shook her head. "I want to care for them. I would see them flourish and the beauty in this kingdom come to life again. Many push to see me lead with strength and assertion, but the truth of the matter is I just wish to be a queen who is beloved by her people. Who they will call to in the streets, and who might be among them, beside them, just as I am with my soldiers. But I fear it is too late. That I could give them all they ask for, give in to every demand, and it would not matter. I fear that if I do not surrender the throne, it will not be enough. And it is the one thing I cannot give."

"Cannot or will not?"

"Not everything is so simple."

"But what if it was?"

"Then I would believe in your fairy tales too."

Her words stopped Elric short, the vulnerability in them striking him to his core, and when she averted her eyes to the sky, he could have sworn he saw a glistening sheen in them.

He stood beside her in silence for a while longer, then with the flick of his wrist, produced a bottle of wine in one hand and two glasses in the other. She eyed him as he filled the glass on top, prompting her to remove it, then filling his own beneath. He sent for a chair next and gestured to it, inviting her to sit.

"Now, *Your Grace*," he emphasized with a flourish of his hand and a wink, "allow me to entertain you with a favorite tale of mine…'The King of Wishes.'"

CHAPTER NINETEEN

"They have doubled in number overnight and still more come undeterred. The time for force is now," the lord from the Province of Westoram blustered.

"I dare say I agree," Lord Cathan replied, "but we must ask what that will lead to. We have given them no reason to truly hate us. What will they become if we do?"

"No reason? *No reason?*" Lord Jacian repeated loudly, shaking his head and laughing dangerously. "They are dying. They are watching their families and brothers and neighbors waste to nothing while we sit in our finery with full bellies, allowing them to beg until they breathe their last. When did we cease to be leaders? Are we all kings on thrones too high to look down?"

"Interesting you should talk of leading, Jacian," Lord Blenheim said evenly, tapping his fingers together before his face and staring sharply over them. "The rabble grows on your lands. You allow them to threaten your queen, threaten all who reside in this palace. Is that the example of your leadership?"

"Infighting will get us nowhere," another far older lord said, exasperation in his tone. He shifted to face Graecerys. "I served from this seat beside your very father. I witnessed him lead from quiet strength into a man we knew was the best of us. Though he was not perfect—none could help the way his mind betrayed him—and though he was contested, he was never questioned. You are questioned in all things and remain too silent. You must do something."

Graecerys opened her mouth, but Blenheim's voice rang out instead. "How bold of you to assume you might tell the queen what she will and will not do."

"And how reckless of you to call her *queen* when she has not taken the sacred oaths before the people that should have come when her father passed," the lord retorted.

"Then we crown her," replied Cathan. "Tonight. We present her as queen."

"If you present her as queen without due process, the people will break down that gate and see her dead before sunrise," Jacian spat. "Is that what you want? Is that the fate you would send her to?"

Elric's head spun where he sat to the right of a silent Graecerys. He managed to steal a few glances at her, watching the war between the spitfire of a woman who refused to lose the final word and the lady who was raised for crown and kingdom.

"Hold audience with them," Elric said quietly, and when Graecerys met his eyes, he pressed on. "The time for negotiation is here. Hear them, then make judgment from there."

"We have heard them, Isteriaeth, more than once," Blenheim said, somehow hearing him from the opposite end of the table. Elric turned to face him, realizing the lord had been staring directly at him while he'd surveyed Graecerys. "Clearly it is not just food or shelter they seek, they also want to choose who wears the crown, and that is not their place."

"But does it give you a good enough reason to neglect them?" Elric asked stiffly.

The room grew quiet.

"No. It does not," Blenheim replied, leaning back in his seat.

"But all action carries consequence. If they want our favor, they will extend it in return. To their rightful queen."

"A queen you continue to silence," replied Jacian, turning to Graecerys. "Your Isteriaeth speaks wisely, my lady. May I bring word of a meeting to their camp? Will you hold audience?"

The voices in the room erupted, all conflicting one another—from Lord Blenheim's vehement refusal to Cathan's ambivalence. And when Jacian's arguments joined the fray once more, the rest of the lords, largely silent until now, all clamored and shouted to be heard.

It was not until Graecerys stood, shoving away from the table and storming from the room, that anyone stopped speaking.

It was well after dark, yet Elric surveyed his mother's notes once more, sitting atop the history tome and beside the new papers strewn across the desk. He had brought the scripts detailing the bonds between the strands and Awduron—beings who carried dhust in their veins, unlike their Elérynd counterparts—from the Diviner's Wing to his quarters, as well as the texts on vows and tethering that had lashed him to the storm he could almost feel brewing on the other side of the wall.

Though he had hoped to find a further indication of what his mother was researching, there was not much new for him to discover. Traditional Awduron bonds manifested physically, in things like telepathic speech between the bonded. Others were intrinsic—a sharing of energy, power, and mortality. There was even discussion of older, far more archaic bonds that connected human to creature, and still others that bound one to an animal within, even beyond the strand that allowed form forgers to shift their appearances.

Isteriaeth tethers, such as the one he shared with Graecerys, were none of those things. As the name suggested, they were not mere links between souls or magic, but instead everlasting ties fettered with iron—either sacred or a curse.

There were three forms: shared, seized, and star-blessed. A shared tether, the most common according to Isteriaeth history, was entered into willingly by both parties and broken only by death. Star-blessed tethers—the most rare—were a gift given by the stars to those found to honor them, and since it tethered their lifelines as one, it could not be broken in death but would fade should one life be laid down for the other. But a seized tether was a connection in strand alone, possessing the same strength as the other two, but with only one side as the benefactor—the one who had seized the tether in the first place. It could never be shared, was limited to the boundaries dictated by the benefactor, and would be broken in death alone, be it natural or through an attempt to seize freedom. Once seized, a tether could never become shared, and while a star-blessed tether would rule over all, there had not been one recorded since the Isteriaeth last walked the realm.

A chill spread across Elric's skin reading the confirmation of what he had known in his heart all along. Relief from his seized tether would only be attained through death—Graecerys's or his own. He had felt the pain that would split him from the inside out when he strayed too close to the limits she had set for him, but to reclaim his life through a forcible severing, through murder, would be freedom and prison all the same. Who might he become if he ran, but with blood-soaked hands? Could he ever fight for life, for goodness, if he had disregarded both so willingly to afford the right?

The click of a door and a silhouette at the edge of the balcony drew his attention, and he collected the pages, slipping them back in the book, and rose from the desk.

He had not seen Graecerys since her abrupt departure from the meeting, and though it discomforted him to greet the woman he had just contemplated assassinating, something about the way she had left—the way she had given up—unsettled him.

He emerged into the night, the air still unnaturally bitter, and shut his door firmly behind him, strolling forward.

"Just because we share a balcony does not mean we must share its space at all hours," Graecerys remarked, still gazing out across the courtyard.

Elric snorted. "Good evening, Your Grace. I see the rest of the day treated you well."

"I do not wish to talk tonight."

"Maybe I am not here to talk either. It is possible we are both simply here for a nightcap and some fresh air."

"Then summon one and leave."

"I do not wish to leave quite yet. If you are so offended by my presence, then either return to your chambers or lock my door once more."

She turned finally, and Elric suppressed a smile, knowing he had offended her straight into his trap.

"I am the queen. *No one* commands me."

"Today would beg to differ," he replied with a shrug.

She froze, her eyes on him but her stare far away, though his undivided attention did not waver from her. "That's it, then," she snapped. "You came out here to mock me, and now you have done it, so go."

"Come now, Your Grace. Spar with me," Elric prodded, stepping closer. "It helps pass the time and makes my shackles lighter in this life sentence I serve at your side."

She glared at him, and he waited for her next verbal barb. Instead, she crossed her arms. "You said nightcap. Do you not have one?"

A glass of wine appeared in Elric's hand, and he extended it to her, but before he could summon his own, the dhust died, leaving nothing behind but remnant stars.

Graecerys took it, drinking half in one go, then loosed an even exhale and angled her body to look at the courtyard once more. "I do not want to like you," she said coldly. "But you tend to make that difficult."

Elric moved beside her slowly, like approaching a wild beast. "Perhaps my magic is useful after all."

"It is useful," she mused, tipping her glass in his direction.

"Then why do you not seize more of it as your own?" Elric asked, almost afraid of the answer.

Graecerys froze, not meeting his eyes. "Would you rather I did?"

Elric laughed unsteadily. "Absolutely not. I suppose I just wonder why you do not use me. Why my strands are not drained for your own power. Experimented on, like my…."

He could not finish the sentence, but he didn't need to. Graecerys turned to face him squarely, her eyes betraying nothing. "I told you, I did not want you here. I have no interest in what you carry. You were a means to an end, to make me appear stronger and more worthy. Now tell me, is it working?"

Elric hesitated, but he had not backed down from the truth yet, and he was not about to start. "No. Not in the least."

"Then why would I take more? Is that not the exact thing that has put us in this place?" she extended her arm toward the night, and though he knew she meant the revolution growing violent beyond the safety of her gates, he couldn't help but look to the stars as well.

"From the very beginning of our time, greed has stolen everything," he replied. "Sometimes I wonder if progress can even be made without it. Yet I have seen beauty that comes from a world that is shared, not stolen. It is rare, but I believe it is possible."

"And it is what they destroy first," she added harshly, though when he met her eyes, they shone with a hint of pain—of remorse.

"Not always," he said softly. "When Breteria was created, the stars took form as Isteriaeth, and they met the Elérynd in the realm. Together they searched for the Awduron that had been rejected. They found the form forgers, the faeries, the Einherjar warriors, but it was not until the world fell silent during eventide that they noticed the trees. They had not come to Breteria but were born from it, their bark holding lithe and beautiful beings who carried blade and quill alike, poets and warriors sent as caretakers to the earth and guardians of their home."

"You refer to the elfin folk." Graecerys hummed along the edge of her glass. "The cowards who ran and hid away as the entire world fell, saving themselves through the abandonment of others to be consumed by darkness."

"No. They retreated into shelter to save their people. To preserve the guardianship. To watch over Breteria until leaders were raised up—until the Trifolium Thrones are united once more. They loved their home enough to understand that if they did not survive to defend her, no one would. Of all who walk upon the realm, Breteria belongs to no one more than the elfin folk."

"Do you have a story for everything?" she asked, feigning impatience, though he had watched the tension bleed slowly from her shoulders with his words.

"Nearly. When you have lived as long as I, memory is not always a stalwart friend, but I hold to what I can. I do not remember my first century of life, nor the second, but I remember the stories my mother told me. I—"

His words caught in his throat. He remembered them because he had repeated them over and over in his mind.

In the dark.

As the water rose over his head.

The first nights he spent alone again, in a tree in the middle of a forest trapped in perpetual winter, far away from the people he loved most.

And then to the love of his life as she fell asleep in his arms on so many stolen nights.

"They are a comfort to me," he finished quietly, and Graecerys's curious eyes watched him intently. "I have seen far too many days, suffered too much loss to dream up new tales, so I rest in the stories of old."

"I understand," she said slowly, her words careful. "Though I fail to recall the past well, I do not look to the future either. They are painful in equal measure, and I have not decided which is worse."

"To live within a dream—to be given the entire world—and then to watch it vanish in your hands. There is no worse fate. It would drive a person mad." Timothius crossed Elric's mind, the physical embodiment of what he felt inwardly. His own losses were etched on his heart, a weight crushing his lungs, but his brother's were scrawled on the walls and scratched into his skin. They both, in turn, were lost.

"Sometimes it is easier to allow that," Graecerys said quietly. "To let them think you mad rather than face the truth. To accept the weight of guilt from being the one who remains and pay the price instead."

"Or maybe we remain for a reason. For a purpose," Elric wondered aloud.

"I do not doubt that. But sometimes I wonder if that purpose is ever intended to be more than duty and death. Why be given anything if it is never meant to be ours? If it is only meant to be lost in the end?"

"I ask myself that every day," Elric replied, her words resonating in his chest more than anyone's had in some time. "And I have no answer. But I have to believe there is a reason. It is the only way I survive beyond my heart's death. There must be a reason. I just have not found it yet."

Graecerys was quiet for a moment, then she laughed to herself. "Your certainty is like armor. I wish I had it."

"You are welcome to borrow it whenever you like."

"Then forget the towel and have it ready for training tomorrow," she replied, turning and handing him her empty glass. "You never know when I might need it."

She started to walk toward her door, and Elric nearly let her leave, but before she touched the handle, he turned. "Your Grace?"

She stiffened at the name, but turned back to face him anyway.

"I believe you are facing your reason, your purpose, now. Maybe not the first, but one you were intended for anyway. You are a fierce ruler. It is a strength that would serve Obarian well. Use it."

He watched his words sink in, and though she lifted her chin proudly—the picture of regal grace—her voice trembled ever so slightly. "What would you do? What would you say to the people? How would you escape death, theirs or ours?"

Elric thought a moment. "An audience. Their leader, their most trusted, beside you and your most trusted. The lords need not attend, unless you trust them to assume the silent position they demand of you. Treaties and trust may always be forged, but strength of character is not easily broken. Show them who you truly are."

She nodded, then after a moment of consideration, replied, "Thank you. For finally giving me sound advice."

Elric sketched a bow, the lowest he had yet. "Thank you for hearing me, Your Grace."

"Your *queen*," her voice echoed from within her chambers just before the door shut.

Elric chuckled, turning back to face night and looking up at the stars. *Queen Graecerys.*

"Grace," he whispered to himself, and a small smile spread across his lips.

CHAPTER TWENTY

THERE ONCE WAS A GIRL WITH MUSIC IN HER SOUL, WHO LOVED HARMONIES IN MINOR KEYS AND THE SILENCE THAT EMBRACED THE FINAL NOTE. BUT SHE NEVER PAUSED LONG ENOUGH TO LEARN HOW DIFFERENT AN ECHO COULD SOUND.

THERE WERE ECHOES OF DARKNESS, OF EMPTINESS AND COLD. THE KIND THAT BROKE OFF THE CHORD AND BOUNCED BACK INTO YOUR HEART LIKE A DAGGER, STEALING THE AIR FROM YOUR LUNGS. THERE WERE ECHOES OF JOY THAT FELT LIKE LIGHT ITSELF—HAPPINESS GLISTENING IN THE AIR, FILLED WITH ALL THE VITALITY OF LIFE. AND THEN THERE WERE ECHOES OF REVERENT AWE. THE KIND THAT RANG ENDLESS LIKE A BELL, ABSORBED BY THE GRANDEUR OF ITSELF, YET PINGED SOFTLY WITH EACH TAP OF A HEEL OR SOLE, LIKE A CHIME CLINKING AT TWILIGHT.

BUT IN THE MUSIC ROOM, IN THE COMFORTABLE SILENCE SHE SHARED WITH THE BOY WHO SELDOM SPOKE, HER ECHOES CAME ALIVE.

AND THEN THE LETTER ARRIVED.

DELIVERED TO HER FATHER FIRST, THEN HER. AND A GRIEF UNLIKE ANY SHE HAD EVER KNOWN CLAIMED A PIECE OF HER HEART.

She lost count of days. Lost track of time. And it was only when she heard small scratches on her wall that she realized she had disappeared from life as effortlessly as her mother had.

She searched until she found the door, using brute force and stubborn determination to shove her armoire from its place, and then she opened the wall.

Stargell stumbled into the light, concern etched onto his tear-stained face, but when he saw her own, he froze.

The girl shook her head. "I am sorry, Stargell. I...."

Words failed her, and for the first time, her tears flowed freely. The boy wrapped his arms around her, patted her back with awkward yet earnest compassion, then helped her back to her bed and motioned for her to sit by the pillows.

She stepped toward the door to lock it, but he waved her away, fumbling with the bolt and then returning to her side where she handed him the letter. The one that had been given to her—the final one in her mother's handwriting—and she watched tearfully as he read her goodbye.

"She was alone, Stargell," she cried. "I should have been with her, but I did not know. They did not tell me she had worsened. They let me believe we would see another summer. I wanted to take you with me. To save you from this place. And now we are both trapped here. It is too late for me to even attend her burial. She was my best friend, and this letter is the only goodbye I have."

Stargell stared at the page, then set it down gently on the quilt before slipping his pack free from his chest.

Auriana sat up straighter, curious, as she had never once seen him remove it, and watched intently as he untied a leather rope in the seam. Something fell into his palm, and when he looked at her next, he held up a brooch.

It was a simple pin with a single stone of radiant blue surrounded by small diamonds, and in the center shone a long-pointed white star.

"This is all I have left of my mother," he said carefully. "She was my best friend too. And she saved me. She hid me and promised I'd be safe. The next person I met was you. I know she sent you to find me."

A single tear slid down his cheek when he handed her the brooch, and she didn't know why but it comforted her to hold a star in her palm.

"Do you think our mothers are together?" she whispered, placing it back in his palm.

Stargell's lip trembled, but he smiled, putting the brooch away and making quick work of the stitching. "I hope they are."

Auriana laid back on the bed, but when Stargell moved toward the wall again, she sat up. "Will you stay with me a while longer?"

He nodded, and she patted the blanket next to her, prompting him to amble clumsily onto the mattress and curl in beside her.

They both stared quietly at the ceiling before Auriana finally whispered, "I am afraid I will forget her. I forget things sometimes. Sometimes they're things I don't want to remember, and I don't mind when they disappear. But other times I can feel a piece missing that I meant to keep close. And it scares me."

"Even if you forget, she never will. She will be with you. My mother always told me that."

"I don't want to stay here," the girl admitted tearfully. "I still want to take you far away from this place, but I want to go with you. I want to get on a boat and go until we're far from here. Find somewhere to hide."

"But what if they follow?"

"We'll go where they won't find us. Live in the forest or hide in Grimoira where they can't bring us back. I just want to be free. You are my only friend, Stargell. You're the only good I have left."

"And you're the only thing I have left," he replied earnestly. "I do not want to be alone. Not again."

Silence filled the room, and though exhaustion hung like a steady haze in her mind, the girl found herself asking, "What if we did not wait? What if we left now?"

"I would go with you anywhere," the boy swore with a small yawn, and it brought a brief smile to her face as sleep finally found them.

Falchion was absent from the hall the next day. Luckily, Elric knew exactly where to find him. However, as he approached his guard's side, in the shade beside the portico toward the rear of the ring of soldiers, he noticed a bruised cheek and a grimace.

"What in Thrones' name happened to you?" Elric asked, suppressing a laugh.

"She is in a foul mood this morning," Falchion groused. "She has already challenged the entire first quadrant...and defeated them."

Elric's brow furrowed. Graecerys had been relaxed when she turned in the night prior, at ease even. But the woman he saw before him looked at odds with the one he had stood beside on the balcony—and she was awake during the daylight hours.

Fear seized him. Had she already tried to meet with the revolution's leaders alone? Had she encountered one, or more, of the lords?

The soldier she was fighting threw his sword on the ground, raising his hands in surrender and spitting a wad of blood into the dirt. She nodded to him and turned, swiping stray strands of hair back from her face with a forearm, her own sweat smearing grime across her cheek. Barely winded, she scanned the soldiers, looking for her next opponent. Her eyes locked on Elric's, and their dark circles like shadows had his feet moving before he realized what he was doing.

He broke into the training ring, the men around them chattering, but Graecerys looked offended. "You?"

Elric shrugged, picking up the sword from the dirt and flipping it from hand to hand, testing its weight. "I didn't bring a towel for you this time, but I will send for one if you wish."

She shook her head. "Have you any real experience with a weapon?"

"I have trained men and women alike younger than you," Elric replied, tossing the sword aside. Familiar leather brushed against his palm and a blade rose from a cloud of blue dhust, the stars within vanishing before they hit the ground. He examined it, realizing he had not seen it since the last time he visited his tree home, yet it was still perfect.

The glint of steel in the sunlight was the sole warning he was given before Graecerys attacked, throwing her body behind a blow that he deflected off the top of his sword, allowing her to slide past him and flip their positions within the circle.

"Fight with honor, Your Grace. We have not even properly saluted yet," he said with a smirk.

She shook her head, stalking toward him and crossing her blade over her chest. "You failed to mention you were a swordsman. Only a storyteller."

"I wasn't aware you wished to learn anything about me," Elric remarked, returning her gesture, and then in one sharp motion, they both surged forward.

"I do not," Graecerys retorted, barely winded as she advanced, and Elric frowned when her attack forced him back a step. He was rusty.

He flipped his sword to his opposite hand and parried anew,

gaining more than a step while Graecerys fought to regain her center.

"Have you taken action on what we spoke of last night?" he asked, giving her a moment to step back, on his guard as she began to circle him.

"I do not jump when something is suggested to me," she spat, venom filling her tone.

"I was not insinuating you did," Elric said, seriousness bleeding into his voice.

She waited for his shoulders to slacken, his sword arm to drop with the sincerity of his words, then lashed out. His mind raced to anticipate her next blow, only able to take defensive measures without dealing a strike.

He pushed off her weapon with his own, leaping back as she swung out, then he feinted to the left beyond the reach of her fully extended blade.

She tipped her head, laughing humorlessly at the sky, and then turned back to him. "Be careful, Isteriaeth. I am starting to think you will be my easiest match yet."

"Do not flatter yourself," he muttered under his breath, winded, though it boiled his blood to think of giving in to her.

"I don't have to, you do it well enough for me. You may drop the blade when you're ready to give up."

"I am only getting started."

He ran forward, switching hands at the last moment and engaging with her before she had a chance to react. Breaking away, she grunted in frustration. "Stop *doing* that!"

"Learn how to fight with every asset, Your Grace," he fired back, a cocky smirk on his face as he twirled the blade in his left hand first, then his right.

When their steel collided again, neither deflected, neither backed down, and they locked blades, each desperate to gain the upper hand and prove themselves better than the other.

Their eyes met, and Elric allowed amusement to fill his,

knowing that she was skilled but he was stronger, even if he was slightly distracted. He had never been this close to her before. And it would be easy to let the blade slip, for a tragic accident to wound her, or worse. But her lashes were long and soft, curling away from the half-moon shadows that darkened the skin below her eyes. Beads of sweat glistened on her forehead along her hairline, and for the first time, he noticed the faintest dots of freckles that had faded by her temple, a single small one that remained on the skin just below her ear....

"Shall I flatter you more by saying it is easier to appreciate your beauty this close?" he murmured.

"I would prefer you to do so from below me," she crooned back, that velvet tone sliding over him, sending a chill everywhere it touched. Places he did not realize a woman might still reach.

"Was my being on my knees once not sufficient for you, Your Grace?" he whispered, unsure why, but refusing to cower before her in any way.

What is happening to me?

She lifted her eyes, so dark a blue today they were almost pitch, and the fire he felt in his veins reflected back alongside a smile that tipped the corners of her mouth upward. "Hardly," she whispered.

Graecerys's blade began to slip, Elric's pure strength overcoming it, and as he unleashed his full weight behind the blade, prepared to take the win, she leaned back in one smooth motion and headbutted him clean in the cheek.

His head snapped to the side, his body shoved away by her sword, and his vision spun as the metallic tang of blood filled his mouth.

"Every asset. Is that not what you suggested?" she called above the howls of the soldiers surrounding them.

He coughed, spitting blood mixed with saliva on the ground, and turned back with his sword raised, but the moment he caught sight of Graecerys, something behind her shone.

He saw the glint rise beyond the gate. Saw it sail through the air, and it was as if time itself slowed to a standstill, then spun in reverse.

An arrow. An arrow was flying toward them.

He had seen this before, lived this moment. The perfect arc. The deadly tip fixed on its target, seconds away from stealing life.

It was happening too quickly.

It was going to kill her.

He was going to fail again. She was going to die cradled in his arms.

A fire so intense that it burned cold seized his body, and without thinking, he dropped the blade and rushed forward. Graecerys's eyes widened, but before she uttered a word, he grasped her by the waist—

And then they were beneath the portico.

Falchion yelped in surprise, leaping back and withdrawing his weapon, but Elric raised a hand just as a shout went up from the training circle.

"ARROWS! PROTECT THE QUEEN!"

Chaos erupted and every soldier leaped into action, some racing to the stables, others forming a perimeter, and at the center of it all one solider lay unmoving.

The same soldier that had stood beyond Graecerys only seconds earlier.

The woman in question shoved away from Elric, pushing his hands from her waist. "What are you doing? How did you do that? What is happening?"

Elric opened his mouth, but no words came out. He had no explanation for it. Somehow, he had moved them through the air itself. "I...I saw an arrow. It was flying toward you. I did not have time to act."

"Clearly, that is untrue," Falchion said with deep concern. "But you might discuss that later. To the queen's quarters, now, until the archer has been apprehended."

He gave them both a firm push toward the palace door, and soldiers filled in the space behind them, blocking them from view as they rushed inside and shut the door.

Elric moved hurriedly down the hall, his limbs trembling, though he was unsure if it was from the strain of the sparring or the adrenaline left behind by whatever he had done. He lifted his hands before him, watched their uncontrollable shaking, and— There it was.

The faintest hint of crimson dhust.

"Explain yourself," Graecerys ordered, stalking before him and coming to a halt.

"Your Grace, we need to take you to your quarters," he chided, quickly dropping his hands and nodding down the hall in an effort to distract her. "At the least away from the windows?"

She grabbed his hand, lifted it, and peered closely at his palm before lowering it with wide eyes. "You shifted form. But not into an animal. You *moved* us."

"I did," he admitted, swallowing the lump that failed to go down in his throat.

She stepped back, dropping his hand and shaking her head. "How is that even possible?"

"I do not know. I have never done that before, at least unassisted. I am unsure of its meaning."

Graecerys turned slowly and began to walk again. This time Elric rushed to keep up with her. Shouts were raised beyond the windows, and he instinctively grasped her elbow, guiding her up the staircase and only releasing her once they were on their floor, which was oddly devoid of soldiers.

"Your Grace, will you wait in my quarters?"

She stared at him incredulously. "I hardly think that is appropriate."

"I do not care what you think. There is something not right about today and you should not be alone."

"An attempt on my life is an inevitability. An Isteriaeth with powers none know of, however, is something not right."

"I did not say none know of it, I said I am unsure of its meaning."

"Then who knows, because I certainly was not made aware," she snapped, voice growing higher and louder.

Elric opened his mouth, but she cut him off. "Is this why you asked me why I had not sought your power? Would I have discovered it if I had?"

"No, not in the least."

"Then what prompted your change of heart?" she demanded. "Why seek me out after months of silence?"

"I did not seek you out," he replied angrily. "I stood upon that balcony on Moonrise well before you arrived. You did not have to remain, you chose to."

She took a step toward him, and though he was not intimidated, Elric had enough sense to be wary of her. "Then the conversation you were observed having with Lord Jacian on Moonrise had nothing to do with it?"

The blood froze in his veins, guilt gripping him like a vice. "What does it matter who I spoke with on Moonrise?"

"So you do not deny it?"

"I have conversed with many members of your nobility. Why does he matter?"

"I think you know exactly why," she replied continuing to stalk toward him. "Which is why you would see me hold audience with them, and why you brought it up again today. You are here to advise, not meddle, and certainly not control."

"I have no desire to control you," Elric said with barely restrained anger. "I do not even wish to be here."

"All the more reason for you to try." She smiled cruelly. "What did they promise you? My death for your freedom?"

"If they had, then why would I rip you from its clutches? Why would I have shown a magic that not even I knew I possessed? Why would I desire to protect you after you and this Thrones-damned kingdom stole everything from me?"

His voice echoed in the hall, but all Graecerys did was slowly shake her head. "You are all the same. Believing you're owed. Clawing for control, for power. But that is your weakness. And you are so blinded by the thought of it that you fail to realize it is my strength. For while you, the people outside those gates, and those within these walls all rage for what you have lost and what you might take from me in retribution, you fail to realize there is nothing I stand to lose that this throne has not stolen from me first."

A throat cleared from behind Elric, and he turned, coming face-to-face with Lord Blenheim. The man's gaze shifted between them, his eyes questioning, but Graecerys did not wait for him to speak.

"I want the lords summoned to the throne room immediately, Lord Blenheim," she ordered.

Elric's eyes found hers, and his anger burned hotter at the sight of her ruthless smile when she said, "If you want me to hold an audience, then that is exactly what I shall do."

CHAPTER TWENTY-TWO

Graecerys strode down the hall, sword still in hand, its blade glinting in and out of her skirts. Blenheim had gone on ahead, and though Elric seethed with anger, a sickness had settled in the pit of his stomach.

"Your Grace," Elric said evenly, but she ignored him.

"Your Grace." The urgency in his tone raised his voice louder. "Your Grace, you must—"

"*No,*" she spat, whirling on him and causing him to stumble back a step to avoid colliding with her. "You have been warned, yet you still dare to tell me what I must and mustn't do? And from the very beginning you were told not to address me as anything but your queen. Fail again and I shall see you imprisoned and drained."

Elric froze, her words effective in bringing him back to reality, and focused on slowing her anger. "I.... Our conversations. I had hoped to remind you of what we spoke about. You are angry—and rightfully so—but I would advise you not to react irrationally. There are many who stand against you, but it is not everyone."

"Our conversations? Did you really think a few stories

would sway me? Do you really believe there is any hope for us with *them*?" She pointed the tip of her sword at the window, the world beyond abnormally quiet. "You will stand beside me, silently, in unequivocal support, or I will ensure that you do not interfere. Is that clear?"

"I will not remain silent," Elric fired back vehemently. "I will not stand beside you in sanction as you take innocent lives in the way that my family was stolen from me."

"Then it was your mistake not to let that arrow pierce my heart," she declared, tipping her chin up.

Strong arms clamped around Elric's elbows, and he startled, instinctively trying to pull away, though he was held fast.

He met Graecerys's stare, but without another word, she turned and strode away.

Grunting, he struggled against the soldiers restraining him. As blue dhust started to gather in his hands, they released him and a stronger arm clamped around his shoulders, a hand covering his mouth.

"Do not use your power against us, Isteriaeth," Falchion warned in his ear.

Elric wrenched from his grasp, spinning to face him. "She cannot do this."

Falchion shook his head slowly. "It is already done. Your power…it is nothing here."

"Yet she needs it far too much to kill me," Elric seethed, stalking down the hall in the direction of the throne room.

The lords already stood within, but he paid them no mind, striding to the floor beside the throne where Graecerys sat with the sword laying across her knees and fire in her eyes. Each of their faces were marked by panic and concern. Even Jacian's brow held a crease of worry, and for the first time, Elric wondered just how under control he believed he had his people.

"My lords," Graecerys greeted them coldly. "I have called you all here because an attempt was made on my life. This cannot go unpunished."

They all blustered in tandem, agreements and outrage coloring their tones, though Jacian's expression grew uneasy.

"Jacian," Graecerys snapped. "These are your people. Your province. What would you have me do?"

Lord Jacian shook his head, folding his hands behind his back and shifting away from the throne. He wanted to appear at ease, but Elric knew a danger when he saw one, and Jacian was poised to strike. "It cannot be allowed to stand. Those responsible must be held accountable for their actions."

"And who shall I hold responsible? My soldiers were unable to find the one who fired the bow. Shall I call those beyond the gate in one by one? Question them? Or is there someone who might be leading them? Surely you must know."

"I do not know their inner workings," he said, a bite to his tone. "But dragging innocent people before the throne is hardly becoming of a queen."

Graecerys smiled, and though her face warmed, Elric swore her eyes filled with darkness when she stood. "And if I find one who is not innocent?"

Jacian hesitated, glancing at the sword in her hand as she stepped toward him. "That should be decided in fair process once you are certain they might be responsible. You just said you have been unable to locate anyone. Surely it will take time and patience."

Blenheim moved forward, partially blocking Elric's view. "My queen, if I may…." When he retreated once more, he held Graecerys's sword in his hand.

"Time is not a luxury I have, and patience is something I do not possess," she continued, stalking toward Jacian. "In fact, we appear to be devoid of both."

Jacian took a step back, his fleeting look toward the door

almost going undetected, but it was already far too late. Guards moved to either side of him, prepared to seize him with a simple order.

Shouts went up from around the room, the lords demanding answers, but Graecerys simply spoke louder, drowning them out. "Lord Jacian, I hereby charge you with treason. Your negligence has paved the way for the revolution to take aim and, by your own admission, an example must be made."

Every man in the room froze, even Falchion and the guards at his back stiffened at her words, but Jacian only laughed. "If an example is what you want, then an example is what you will receive. The revolution will serve your justice, and I trust that it will be painful as every second of your reign, but if I am to die for treason then I shall not go alone."

He squared his stance and brought his arm back above his head, but it was not until he flung the blade in his hand that Elric registered exactly what was happening—and that the blade was coming for him, not Graecerys.

The room descended into chaos. The guards snapped into action at once, and Falchion rushed toward him, his features marred with horror. Some lords cowered while others fled, though none were under direct threat. And before Elric could react to the weapon hurtling toward him, he fell to his knees beneath a wave of pain searing his flesh from the inside out.

He tried to scream, but his shout was no more than a strangled croak, his voice as paralyzed as his contorted limbs that failed to support his weight. His body slammed to the tile, the cool surface doing nothing to ease the firestorm tearing through his veins, and as he rolled, his eyes found Graecerys.

She stood before the throne now, her eyes leached of nearly all color—the blue replaced with midnight darkness. Her hand was outstretched, palm up with her fingers bared like claws in the air.

Jacian's blade soared harmlessly through the space where Elric had stood only seconds before, and though he had drawn a second and raised his arm high, he faltered. Another wave of agony slammed into Elric, his limbs writhing, his cries more like whimpers in his own ears, and that was when he saw it.

The blue dhust clouding in Graecerys's palm.

Jacian gasped for air, his limbs locking, and as the dagger dropped powerlessly from his hand, his face contorted in pain and then fell slack. His body collapsed in a heap, unmoving, and the pain in Elric's veins vanished, leaving behind an emptiness he had only felt one other time before—when his dhust was drained for the tethering. And when he rolled his eyes back to Graecerys, when the sapphire stars ceased falling from her hand, he saw what was clutched in her grasp.

Jacian's unmoving heart.

Graecerys had not only seized his strand and drained him, she had done it to take a life.

Every eye in the room was affixed on her, a mix of shock, horror, disbelief, and disgust on each face. But Graecerys only cast the fleshy mass on the floor and extended her arms.

"Now the stories are true. The Queen of Obarian is all her people say she is, and you have a ruler unafraid to wield the power of the stars. Are you satisfied?"

Her demand went unanswered, echoing in the cavernous room, and she pinned Blenheim with her stare. "Is this not what you wanted?"

Cathan was the first to move, stumbling back on his feet before fleeing the room. Another lord followed on his heels, while two more walked brusquely behind. The soldiers all shifted on their feet, looking at one another, then back to their queen. The one they respected. The one who, for all accounts, had just killed an innocent man.

Perception.

The word from Jacian's lips echoed in Elric's mind, but the meaning of it floated just out of reach. The world spun and Elric shut his eyes against the churning of his stomach.

"My queen," Falchion's voice said. "What shall we do with… with the…."

"String the traitor's body on the wall. Let it serve as a warning to the people that none come for what is mine. Make certain they know he moved against the Isteriaeth."

"And if they do not accept the reason? If they believe his death was unwarranted?"

There was a long pause, and though Elric could not force his eyes open, he recognized the hint of bitter resignation in the queen's voice when she replied, "Then do what you must to secure the kingdom. The revolution ends here. Let them decide if it is by choice or by force."

Elric was not sure when he was lifted from the ground, only that the air chilled around him as he was moved from the throne room back to his quarters. He was deposited in his bed, but when he looked at Falchion's retreating back as it departed his room, the world blurred back into darkness.

He fought the gravity crushing his bones and reached for the strands that weighed heavy in his being. With what sluggish energy he could muster, he dragged himself to the edge of the bed and forced his legs over the side, letting them drag him like an anchor down to the cold, hard wood.

His body collapsed beside his bed, everything within him raging against the events he had failed to prevent. He had allowed himself to imagine something more in Graecerys where there was only a hollow, self-serving lust for control. He had been swayed by foolish hope, beguiled by the chance that mercy and all he was raised to know might still prevail when he could, and should, have stopped her once and for all. Before it came to this.

But now it did not matter. He was being pulled farther and farther from the stars, he need not worry over what might keep him from them.

Now it was not time to play the game, but to end it. And he knew what he must do.

CHAPTER TWENTY-THREE

Night had fallen when Falchion knocked upon Elric's door. Physically, he was already mended, and though he had washed up and changed into a fresh vest, shirt, and breeches, his chest remained empty—devoid of dhust, of any warmth from the stars. The only thing he felt was anger and a thick, cloying bitterness that made him thirst for collision.

He wondered if this is what his family had felt when the walls finally closed in on them. Had they fought, screamed for what was right to the end? Were they depleted, empty, and tired from suffering so much loss? Had they been consumed by so much rage they did not hesitate to fight till their own death? Was he walking in their footprints now? Or was their shame just another loss he would bear?

He stepped into the hall beside Falchion, and to his surprise, Graecerys emerged from her door seconds later. She looked every bit a queen prepared for war—her dress was of deep, Obarian blue devoid of gilded ornamentation, but embroidered with black trim on the skirt and the tight sleeves that extended past her wrists. The bodice was a modest plunge that revealed a hint of the cream chemise beneath, and though she wore no jewels, a chain glinted from just beneath her high collar. Her cold, expressionless eyes fell on him, and she somehow appeared even more drained and exhausted than before, though he remained indifferent to it. He turned his back on her and began walking, but before he reached the landing, he was stopped by a shout echoing up the stairs.

"THE GATE IS BREACHED. SECURE THE PALACE."

Elric's eyes shot to Falchion who hesitated, but when he looked back to Graecerys, she nodded. "Go."

He clasped his fist over his heart, bowing to her, and then he turned to Elric and did the same. "Protect her," he uttered under his breath, his eyes lingering on Elric's with determination before he ran for the stairs.

Graecerys passed Elric, brushing his shoulder, and he did a double take. "I am sorry, Your Grace, you are following him for what reason?"

She paused with a hand on the rail. "I am going to meet with the lords who have not fled like cowards, as are you."

"They just said the gate has been breached."

"It is to be expected and will be fine. I trust my men to call for the reinforcements needed. We are simply facing a long night."

"And you are not concerned that your kingdom has descended into all-out war? You feel no remorse, no sorrow, no desire to make things right?"

Graecerys whirled on him, the blue only barely visible in her eyes once more. "You saved my life, I returned the favor in kind, that puts us on equal footing. Do not step outside the bound of my good graces, or I may find I have need of your power again."

Elric stiffened, his fists clenching and unclenching at his sides, begging to unleash his anger—to shake her to the sense he had believed might exist within her—but no dhust stirred.

Graecerys continued walking and as she reached the landing below, he chose to follow, preferring to keep his enemy in sight. He had just caught up with her when Jacian's face entered his mind. Recalling the lord's final moments chilled him, but it was his words from the gala that caused the hair to rise on Elric's arms.

Jacian was gone, and now there was no one left to stop the revolution. They were coming.

Graecerys and Elric reached the second floor easily, but it was walking down the hall to the meeting chamber, past the large windows facing out over the courtyard, that he slammed to a halt.

The gate was open wide, the courtyard burning, and the soldiers…well, there were none. Not as far as his eye could see.

"We are already late," Graecerys snapped. "We do not have time to—"

"The soldiers, Your Grace. Where are your men?"

She froze, then walked slowly to the window, and in its reflection, he watched her eyes search the courtyard, her face slackening, though she kept her posture secure.

As if summoned, three guards ran past them.

"*You*," she snapped, stopping one in his tracks. "Tell me what is happening."

"I am not certain, my queen. The men advanced as you directed, but something went wrong. The revolution fights from the front and back, and they have already driven our men to the doors. They say the palace may be breached."

A shout rose from outside, and as Elric and Graecerys turned, the glass behind them shattered with a club of fire hurling inside.

Graecerys stumbled away from it, shards of glass falling from her skirt, and when the soldier rushed to douse the flames, the sound of popping wood split the air.

Graecerys's head swung to Elric, a dazed look on her face, but he only shook his head in frustration, grabbed her wrist, and pulled her down the hall. They turned the corner, but a secondary fire blocked the path to the chamber. Elric stopped short, taking stock of their position within the palace before doubling back and pushing her inside the interior door closest to where he knew the Diviner's Wing lay above. He locked it firmly behind them and began to feel along the walls.

"What...what are you doing?" she asked incredulously, though her tone held no venom.

Elric did not answer, sliding a chair out of his way and continuing on, until he reached a portion of the wall partially concealed behind a bookcase. He threw his shoulder against the wood—once, twice, three times—shoving the furniture down just far enough to find the edge of the seam.

He pushed again and the wall swung inward, and as the palace shuddered, he turned back to Graecerys who had frozen in place with wide eyes. "Now would be the time to move, Your Grace."

She walked through the opening wordlessly, her eyes fogged over as if lost in concentration, but he shoved her in the passageway, swiftly closing the door behind them.

He strained for his dhust, scraping whatever traces he could find stuck to the walls of his mind, and a small candle appeared in his hand, barely casting a faint halo of light between them.

"This way," he said in a low voice, leading her down the wall, back in the direction they had come. The scent of smoke slowly dissipated, and he followed the corridor until they reached a ladder extending up through a space in the floors barely wide enough for a person to clear.

He doused the light and heard Graecerys's sharp intake of breath.

"We go to the very top. Stay close."

It was not until he cleared the first floor that he felt the ladder sag below him, confirming that Graecerys followed closely behind. His mind spun, unsure if it was wise to travel up and farther into the palace with the lower floors burning, but he was not confident of a way out through the passages below.

And with no visibility on the ground beyond the palace, there was no telling if they would even be able to get out.

The ladder ended, and he crawled from the hole and stood up, waiting for Graecerys to emerge. The thought crossed his mind to loosen the ladder, to knock her off balance and send her plunging to her death floors below. He could finish this once and for all and be long gone before any discovered her body. But his stomach soured at the thought of being so cowardly. He could not end her in the dark. Not in the passages that were nearly his tomb.

Elric cursed the mercy still clinging to his resolve, and felt his way down the ice-cold, cobweb-coated stone until he found another seam. He slid his hand to the small handle hewn in the rock, then with a grunt, pulled it open.

The night sky streamed in on the Diviner's Wing, and as he strode to the office, Graecerys tipped her head up, walking in a small circle and surveying the towering shelves of books as if for the first time.

Elric braced himself before the window and froze. From this vantage point, he could see the perimeter of the palace. The forces outside the gate were currently embroiled in battle with far more revolutionaries than had originally been camped there, and still more surged toward the palace, unopposed.

"It was a trap," he said, his words sharp.

"What was?" asked Graecerys, entering the office.

"The arrow. They wanted this. They meant to provoke you. And you ran straight into their hands."

Even in the darkness, her face paled. "I did not have a choice. I had to defend...my kingdom. I will not—"

"Your kingdom is gone, Graecerys," Elric said harshly. "The only thing left is you. And they will not stop until you fall as well."

She swallowed, but anger lit the waves in her eyes on fire. "Us. The only thing left is *us*."

Elric smiled, shaking his head and laughing humorlessly. "I will outlive you, Your Grace. And when you finally face your judgment by their hands, I will be free once more."

She opened her mouth to speak but a *crash* sounded just below.

"Graecerys!" Lord Blenheim's voice called, but before Elric could speak, she threw a hand over his mouth.

"Graecerys are you here? There is no time!" the lord called once more, his footsteps climbing the small set of stairs into the tower.

Graecerys released Elric, but instead of walking ahead to meet Blenheim, she turned the handle to the office door and slowly closed it.

"Graecerys," Blenheim shouted, and when his steps approached the office door, Elric's brow furrowed. Graecerys held the knob tightly with both hands—a knob that did not lock—and squeezed her eyes shut, taking a small inhale and holding her breath seconds before the knob began to jiggle.

It wiggled slightly yet held fast under her white-knuckle grip, and after a moment Blenheim's steps crossed the floor again, climbing up to check the loft, and then returning back down.

He paused once more, then with urgency, his boots hit the stairs and thudded down the hall away from them.

When they could hear no more, Graecerys exhaled slowly and her shoulders relaxed. Her eyes fluttered open, and if Elric wasn't mistaken, he thought he saw a single tear sneak from the outside corner of her eye.

"What are you—"

He did not have the chance to finish. A great cheer went up from outside the palace, and when their eyes met, they both knew.

The palace had fallen.

The revolution now controlled the kingdom.

CHAPTER TWENTY-FOUR

Elric held the rung of the ladder in one hand and a lantern from the Diviner's Wing in the other. He led the way through the maze of passages to the only other location he knew for certain, and with all his strength, he threw his shoulder into the hidden door.

They emerged in the old music room, now Augur's space, and closed the wall behind them, but before they could move toward the door, it flew open and slammed against the wall.

A tall, thin man stepped inside, a sword in one hand and a torch in the other. He held it aloft, illuminating his crudely crafted armor and worn clothing, and moved from Graecerys's face to Elric's, then back again.

"Well, that was simple," he said with a smile.

He lifted his blade menacingly, and Graecerys took a small step back, but instead of lunging, the man only looked at Elric. "Master Isteriaeth, we mean you no harm."

Two more men rushed in, stopping short behind him. "That is the Isteriaeth," the first man said with a nod to Elric. "But her, we take her to Denfrin."

Graecerys took another step back, steeling her expression in a mask of reticent determination—ever the fighter, she was prepared to face her fate. But it wasn't the emotions that made Elric pause. It was what hid behind them, deep inside the oceans churning in her eyes.

Fear. Unadulterated, panic-stricken terror.

The first man stepped toward Graecerys, but before he could make another move, Elric stepped forward and sent a swift punch straight into the man's neck. The man buckled, dropping his sword, but before it could hit the floor it was in Graecerys's hand and slashed across his throat. He fell to his knees and then flat on his face, making a terrible gurgling sound as the carpet darkened around his head, soaking through with blood as his chest stopped heaving.

Two more men rushed forward, setting the room alight with fire, but before they reached Graecerys, she had the dead man's sword aloft and was swinging it toward them. Elric followed, unable to call forth a blade of his own, but he grabbed hold of a third man's cape and yanked him backward, away from Graecerys.

His head jerked back, and Elric grasped it, swiftly twisting it to the side and severing his spinal cord with a *snap*. The man fell to a heap on the floor, and when something brushed Elric's spine, he spun and gripped the neck of his assailant, pushing them back against the wall.

Wide, deep-blue eyes met his as Graecerys stared at him. She dropped her sword and grabbed his wrist to try to force it away, but instead of relenting, he paused.

This was his chance. He could be free.

It would end all his problems if he finished this now, and she knew it. Elric realized then just how much power he truly held. All it would take was one motion and he would not only free himself but an entire kingdom.

He tightened his grip, raising her slightly off the floor. She did not kick or claw. She did not fight back. She simply held onto his wrist, her toes barely brushing the floor, doing what she could to hold onto life while waiting for the end.

An end that the darkest parts of him begged to provide. The power of death in his hands coiled like an invisible cloud of shadow around his fingers, beckoning them together and urging them to devour the light from her eyes. But through it, a small voice still whispered.

Mercy.

It was the very heartbeat of his strands. The legacy of the stars who watched him, even now. His thirst for freedom and the bloodlust it demanded pushed back, reminding him that if he ended her, he might appease them still—for death, though cruel, was a form of mercy, especially for beings so despised as her. Endings and beginnings would both be forged in that moment, his own future balanced between them, if he would only usher in her demise.

But was he capable of becoming like her? Could he lay claim to his own life in rebellion against the stars?

Graecerys jammed her eyes shut, waiting for him to steal her air, but the instant Elric relaxed his fingers, warmth surged through his veins in a wave that knocked him off balance. He swayed on his feet, leaning forward, and they both fell back, through the wall and a cloud of crimson dhust onto the cold, slate walkway of the portico.

Elric stumbled, staying on his feet, but Graecerys slipped from his grasp and fell back on the ground in a heap. She gasped, both hands flying to her neck as she looked around wildly, then up at Elric.

A voice hissed from across the portico.

"My queen? Master Elric, here!"

Elric glanced over and saw Falchion wave, a few soldiers huddled with him in the shadows, and he could not help but feel relieved to see the guard alive.

He strode to them, leaving Graecerys to rise and follow on

her own, and when he reached Falchion, the soldier clasped him on the shoulder. "Your magic is worth every bit its weight in gold, my friend. You have saved the queen once more."

Graecerys snorted, yet said nothing, but Elric ignored her. "What is happening?"

"The palace has fallen. The revolutionaries at the gates are inside, searching, and the rest are still engaged in battle with our men outside the palace. We sought to join them, then you fell out of the air."

"We must get the queen away from this place," another guard, who Elric recognized from training, whispered. "There might still be a chance at negotiation should she live."

"I agree," said Falchion. "I will create a diversion, draw their attention toward the skirmish long enough for you to take horses and escape to the north."

Elric's eyes widened, but Falchion was already unfastening his cloak, slinging it around Graecerys's shoulders, and motioning for another soldier to do the same with Elric. The matching midnight-blue wool was heavy, thicker than normal, and he realized there was a thin layer of armor woven in. Their cloaks were resistant to arrows.

"Hoods remain up," Falchion ordered. "Ride hard and ride fast, and don't look back. They may try to fell the horses, but in the darkness, it will be hard to discern which is the queen."

Voices drew nearer, and the soldiers all gathered closer, circling Elric and their queen.

"There is no more time," Falchion murmured, and when he stepped back with the other cloakless soldier at his side, he bowed deeply with both fists crossed over his chest. "My friends, may the stars guide you and the Thrones protect you."

They turned and ran along the wall, making a ruckus as they went, and though Elric paused with grief over what he was certain would be the last time he saw his unlikely friend, he rushed after the remaining four soldiers running toward the stables with Graecerys at their center.

He halted outside the stalls, watching them all make quick work of saddling the horses, and when Graecerys led a mare from the stall and handed him the reins, he asked, "Do you know how to ride or shall you accompany one of us?"

She stared at him in disbelief, her eyes turning skyward at the audacity of his question, then she turned, entered the stall beside it, and quickly harnessed the stallion within. Shouts sounded from the palace, orders were screamed along the opposite side of the gates, and the horses snorted, pawing at the ground restlessly.

Elric mounted his mare, the comfortable feeling that he had missed for some time sending a surge of adrenaline through his veins. It had been years since he'd ridden a horse. And though this was life or death, he could not help but feel the thrill of escaping the palace, even if it was toward another form of prison.

"All right," said the gravelly voice of the soldier leading the charge. "On my signal, we ride. Leave the doors open and turn out the rest of the steeds so that none may mount and give chase. Stay in a straight line until we reach the bluffs, and do not give them any reason to pick one of us as the queen. We make for Culwyrt Manor."

The horses burst from the stables, their hoofbeats thundering on the ground, drowning out the pounding of Elric's heart. Only one soldier rode behind him, bringing up the rear, with Graecerys before him and the final three soldiers leading her.

They reached the first bluff, rose to the top of its hill, then fanned out in a line straight across the horizon to the north. Elric knew they were not to look back, and he found he did not care to, but he did look up.

And the farther away they drew from the palace, the clearer it became to see the stars.

PART II
THE SONG

The sun had barely crested over the horizon when they reached the farthest reaches of the Province of Culwyrt. Elric's limbs ached, his eyes weighed heavy with sleep, and his head pounded to the rhythm of the horses' hooves, though they had stopped well before.

The fields and bluffs were now covered in a layer of snow, the long grass poking through in clusters that were becoming few and far between. While no ice or snow fell from the sky, the clouds above looked heavy, and the air carried a breeze of winter, ready to unleash and strip all warmth from bones.

Their convoy stopped at a farm, the horses safely hidden within a barn, and after a cursory search of the small house beside it, the soldiers offered Graecerys the loft inside for rest.

Fendo, the guard with the rough voice, ordered the youngest man, Snell, to the barn to remain with the horses. The other two —Towles and Ganch—had taken up post to the front and rear of the house, while Fendo himself took first patrol around the perimeter in case they were being tracked.

Elric, though exhausted, now sat alone on the first floor of the single-room farmhouse. A modest kitchen and pantry occupied the farthest wall, with an open living area outlined by a threadbare rug taking up the large remainder of the space. A ladder extended to the loft, and beneath that was a cot that he had made up as his bed for the night. He sat on the floor, however, staring at the ceiling, watching flakes of straw and wafers of wood chips flutter down as the woman above him paced the floor.

Finally, he could take it no longer. Climbing the ladder to the top, he stepped into the loft and ducked, though the roof cleared decently above his head. Graecerys stood with arms folded, gazing out the small, square window across the expanse of what was the start of Obarian's unforgiving north.

"There are soldiers sleeping in the cold and standing watch, even after riding all night, so that you might take rest," Elric said flatly. "It would be considerate of you to do so."

"Why did you save me again?" she asked without looking at him, her voice as cold as the frigid air.

Elric paused, her words catching him off guard. "I beg your pardon?"

"You not only saved me, you spared me," she continued. "You held my life in your hands, your freedom at the ends of your fingers, and you allowed me to live. Why?"

Elric swallowed, unwilling to answer, but unsure what he would say even if he did. He looked around the loft, then cleared his throat.

"Mercy is the currency of the stars. If it will help ease your mind, I did it for them, not for you." His eyes burned into her once more. "So now that you have your answer, will you rest?"

She glanced over her shoulder but did not turn. "You say you did it for them, yet you see me as responsible for their loss. Would you not have avenged them?"

"Vengeance, destruction, they are as much a part of this land as the snow and the bluffs. But they are not a part of the sky."

"Neither are you."

"Yes, but I despise anyone who can steal life so thoughtlessly. Why would I wish to join their ranks?"

Graecerys nodded at the thinly veiled insult, then turned halfway from the window and stared at the threadbare cot on the floor. Elric was struck then by how drained she looked. How, for lack of a better word, delicate. She was still forged from iron, but there was a fragility in the way she held herself that pulled at a softer part of him he could not help but despise.

"Sleep, Your Grace," he ordered.

"I do not wish to."

"I do not believe you were given a choice."

"Queens always have a choice," she retorted, her eyes finally meeting his.

"You might be queen to your soldiers, but not of Obarian. Not any longer. The people have deposed you, there is no rule for you here."

She huffed a laugh. "That is right. They favor you now, do they not?"

Elric did not reply, but Graecerys stepped forward, ever the predator, though the wounds she licked were still fresh and raw. "They will turn on you too, eventually," she said smoothly. "Their starlit savior who failed to help them when given the chance. You'll see that no good comes from straddling a line, yet choosing where to stand will only earn you enmity. And you'll understand then what it is to bear this crown."

"I do not want your crown," he uttered instinctively.

Graecerys laughed in derision. "You tell tales of kings sacrificing all to preserve a single wish, but you forget they are just stories. It does not matter what you desire when the world decides otherwise. There is no one here to hold your wishes."

Elric drew in a steady breath, controlling his anger. "I dig deeper every day for hope, and against all odds, I find it. That hole may someday become my grave, but I cannot stop. No matter how desperately I want to."

Graecerys regarded him with remorseless pity. "Bound to me, you will never know a moment's peace, but if we are ever unbound, know that they will never let you go either. You gave me power, but you inspire their purpose. It is a matter of time."

Elric shook his head. "It does not have to be this way."

"And yet it is," she replied, her eyes burning into him.

He held her stare, unwilling to cower as he considered his words, then cocked his head to the side. "You might have gone with Blenheim, but you hid from him. Why?"

Graecerys stood unmoving, stiff as a stone and barely breathing. Finally, she blinked and cleared her throat. "Queen or not, that was my choice."

His brow furrowed, but before he could speak, she turned her back on him. "I have decided I am tired after all. Goodnight, Master Elric."

He rolled his palm up, dipping his chin to her in a cold bow, and retreated down the ladder without another word. Lying upon the floor, he put an arm behind his head and stared up at the roof. The sound of Graecerys stretching out on her cot was the last bit of movement he heard before the house fell silent.

His eyes grew heavy, his body finally succumbing to the exhaustion of the last twenty-four hours, but when they fell shut, he wondered what was more curious—the fact that Graecerys had replied to his question at all, or that she had chosen to remain with him over her most loyal lord.

Scraping. Scratching. Whimpering. Then a sharp and sudden cry.

Elric sat straight up, his arm numb from being used as a makeshift pillow. He looked around wildly, but found he was still alone.

But then he heard it again, soft cries and pleading carrying down from above.

He leaped to his feet, hooking his needling arm through the rung and hoisting himself up with the other, pushing to the second floor with brute force and realizing halfway up that if Graecerys was in distress, he had no real way of defending her —unless his nap had managed to rally his dhust once more.

But when he stood, it was to an empty room, save for the woman asleep on the cot. Her face was contorted in struggle, and tears streamed down her cheeks. She lay on her side, but the arm she rested on was pressed against her head, covering her ear against a nonexistent noise. The other was palm-down on the floor, her fingers bared like claws, her nails tearing at the wood as if she could rip a hole in it.

Elric stepped toward her slowly. "Your Grace?"

She did not hear him.

Another step. "Your Grace."

And then he knelt by her side. "Graecerys?"

A scream tore from her lungs, wild and terrified, and her body curled in on itself before she kicked back out, thrashing at the thick, woolen blanket stuck to her skirts.

Elric lurched forward, grabbing her wrist. "Graecerys, you must wake up. Wake up, please."

Her eyes fluttered but did not open, and she cried out again, a panicked, animalistic squeal of desperate agony that made Elric's heart race. It sounded as though she was being attacked— as if something was *hurting* her.

"Graecerys, open your eyes. You must—"

Her free hand flew, backhanding him in the jaw with a force that caused his teeth to slam shut. He grunted in pain, but before it could fly again, he grasped it and pinned it beside the other with one hand.

He was only inches from her face now as she gasped for air, hissing and spitting with her cries. "Graecerys, wake up!"

Her eyes snapped open instantly, startling him with their darkness, though they remained unfocused, seeing nothing. She still struggled to free herself, her body bucking against his hold, and without thinking, he reached up and cupped her face.

"Look at me," he commanded softly. "Look at me, Grace. Find me."

As slow as fog dissipating over the bluffs, her eyes began to focus on his. "That's it," he said, releasing her hands while caressing her cheek with soft strokes of his thumb. "You are safe. I have you now. You are safe."

She drew in one long, ragged breath, like it was her first taste of air after being trapped underground for years, and when she blinked, her eyes focused and met his own.

The door to the cabin flew open below, and Fendo shouted, "The queen! Is the queen safe?"

"She is," Elric called down. Graecerys's eyes widened in abject horror and he released her, sitting back and adding quietly, "It was only a nightmare, nothing to be ashamed of."

The ladder creaked, and Fendo's torso popped through the opening. As soon as he caught sight of her—still tangled in her blanket, hair unbound and knotted—with Elric beside her on his knees, he reached for his sword. "Forgive me for the intrusion, my queen. I do not mean to embarrass, I just needed to be sure of your safety."

Graecerys visibly shook, and Elric could not help but reach for her once more, his thumb tracing a line along the back of her hand in a slow, soothing motion. "I— am well, Fendo," she said, unsteadily. "He stopped me. Before I...gave away our...our position."

The guard surveyed the scene, his eyes lingering on Elric's hand holding the queen's, but as her trembling eased and she regained her composure, he nodded and released the hilt of his weapon. "We will cover the perimeter, but so far it appears none were close enough to hear. Be well, my queen, we shall handle the rest."

After a moment, the cabin door shut, and its *click* seemed to startle Graecerys out of another haze. She leaned away, and Elric let her go, shifting back to give her space. She scrubbed her hands furiously down her face, streaking the dirt that her tears had moistened into grime.

Hiding behind her hands, she rested her forehead on her palms and forced her breathing to slow. Elric was struck by how calm she was—how methodically she worked through the motions—as if she'd done this a thousand times before.

Do you always sleep during the daytime hours?

Not always.

It occurred to him that she had refused sleep earlier not because she was rested, but because she had known nightmares would follow her. The queen who feared no man had been afraid to sleep.

"You think so loudly it's impossible to count my breaths," she said thickly from behind her hands.

Elric hesitated, all his questions damming up behind his lips. He could ask them later. "Is there anything that you need, Your Grace? Anything I might try to summon for you?"

Her hands fell and her strained, red eyes met his, the fractures breaking through their endless waves somehow cracking his heart.

He exhaled shakily, and when he tugged on his strands, the dhust rose with surprising ease. A porcelain cup of tea materialized, and he held it out to Graecerys. She took it with both hands, but instead of taking a sip, she frowned. "This...this is one of the palace sets."

Elric nodded. "Atmospheric magic will bring me whatever I wish so long as it is not a living being and only if I can picture it. I thought you may like this better than the clay set I used to call my own."

She sipped it slowly, the heat fogging the air before her face, and she held it there, allowing the warmth to coat her skin. Her eyes fell shut, and almost as if she forgot she was not alone, a single tear escaped.

Elric reached out and brushed it away without thinking.

Her eyes opened wide on him, but before he could speak—to make an excuse or apologize—Graecerys did. "Thank you." Her voice was still raw and scratchy but no longer unsteady. Now all that remained was exhaustion. "Had anyone heard, we would have been—"

"They did not," Elric reminded her gently. But then his tone grew serious. "Does this occur often?"

"Far more than I would like," she admitted, taking another sip of tea. "It is no use hiding, running, or even finding shelter if I give us away the moment I shut my eyes."

"And as I said, it is nothing to be ashamed of."

"True as that might be, it is a nonissue. You cannot feel pride or shame if you are dead."

Elric nodded once in acquiescence, and Graecerys looked away. "I don't suppose we can carry on from here yet?"

"I do not think so. I believe we are waiting for the horses to rest. And you should continue to do the same."

Graecerys finished her tea in silence, handing the cup back to Elric, who whisked it away with the flick of his wrist. "I have rested enough," she replied, rising to her feet. "I will have the guards come inside. They may take their rest while we keep watch."

Elric sighed, but nodded, her use of the word *we* not lost on him. "As you wish, Your Grace."

CHAPTER TWENTY-SIX

They remained in place until night fell once more, somehow more cold and bitter than the previous had been. Making their way farther north, they hoped to reach the manor that Cathan had vacated, but remained uncertain how far they would have to travel before locating it.

Graecerys stayed uncharacteristically quiet. She swayed in her saddle, refusing to stop until their convoy crested a bluff to find a small town before them.

Fendo and Towles pulled back with Elric and Graecerys, leaving Ganch and Snell to investigate, and after nearly thirty minutes, the soldiers gave the signal that all was clear.

The remaining company rode quietly in single file, but when Elric reached the soldiers he could see the deathly pallor on their faces.

"All these houses and not a soul hiding?" Fendo asked with scrutiny.

Snell looked at Ganch who shook his head. "There were, unfortunately, many souls within these walls, but none of them are among the living."

Graecerys's head snapped to the side. "These homes.... They're filled with...with bodies? The bodies of whom?"

"The townspeople, my queen," Snell confirmed quietly. "The entire town. They're deceased."

The air grew unsettled, and all four soldiers' eyes drifted to Graecerys. Elric was certain they had heard talk of what was happening. Whispers were always circulating the palace, though most in the ranks wrote them off as rumors used to stoke the anger of the masses. But now they had seen it with their own eyes, and when presented to the queen they'd staunchly defended, they were met with silence.

"Is there nowhere we can stay that is not occupied by death?" she asked, ignoring the words spoken and not.

There was a pause, then Ganch cleared his throat. "There is, my queen. A barn on the outer fringe. The horses will reside below, but there is a loft you might take your leave in."

She nodded, urging her horse on. "Then lead the way."

The soldiers led their group around the outer perimeter of the town, a soft flurry of snow fluttering down on their heads, and Elric was struck by how easy it was to peer through the boards that held the houses together.

Obarians were no stranger to the cold, especially those who lived this far north, yet the town showed signs of degeneration. There were no animals, the fenced-in fields were barren and untouched, and a hopeless desperation hung in the air, far more chilling than the unrelenting frost. And there were some homes nearly dismantled entirely, as if they had been torn apart piece by piece.

"Why are there only halves of houses?" he asked quietly, glancing at Snell on his right.

"It appears that the last of the survivors moved into a single home. They were burning wood from the others to keep warm, but...." He flinched, grimacing. "There were signs they had run out of food. That they had grown desperate. I cannot unsee it."

Elric swallowed the bile building in his throat. "They were the strongest of Obarians. The warriors, the stewards of the north, and they fell like this?"

"The bodies were undefinable. The men were hardly larger than their wives, and the children were all unnaturally small. Even the staunchest survivors cannot defy nature's course. But I do not understand why they did not ask for help."

Elric could barely meet his eyes, but when the soldier continued to stare expectantly—as if waiting for an answer he knew Elric had hidden away—he finally replied. "They did."

The silence between them was deafening, and after a moment they reached the barn, a large open building with a loft spanning half the room above. Setting the horses loose within, the soldiers secured the doors. Then with quiet bows and averted eyes, they left to stay in a shed nearby, claiming propriety, though Elric saw the wariness hiding behind their eyes. They needed time to discuss what they saw, what they knew, what they had believed, and he feared that in the end, they might come to admit what he knew had already taken root in their hearts. That the woman they were risking their lives for was, in fact, culpable for it all.

He sat on the edge of the loft, watching the horses below with more questions in his mind than answers, as Graecerys moved behind him. She had retrieved snow and was using it to cleanse her face, as if the most pressing need was presenting herself well.

His blood began to boil.

"I thought you sent aid," he bit out, his eyes burning into Graecerys's back.

She continued to scrub at the grime on her cheeks with damp fingers. "I did. I was not in every meeting with the lords for show alone. I listened to everything said, knowing they would lessen the blow to suit my fragile feminine mind. It did not take effort to surmise it was far worse. But clearly it was still an underestimation."

"Yet you did nothing more to ensure your people were well?"

Her hands fell into her lap, and she exhaled in irritation. "I do not make a habit of regretting things I cannot change. It was a mistake. And now we move on."

Elric stared at her in disbelief. "And how much of your population have died due to your unfortunate *mistakes*?"

She flinched, barely concealing it, but her words were sharp. "Do you see their blood on my hands? A sword hiding anywhere? The immortal and mighty stars may govern in mercy, but life upon this realm is harder to survive. It is impossible to save everyone."

Elric nodded slowly. "I am beginning to understand why your people would see you dead for your crimes."

Her eyes widened. "I have nothing to do with—"

"You have allowed all of this," Elric spat, using every ounce of his control to keep his voice low. "You were queen by your own acknowledgment and paraded about the palace as if you were in charge, but your own selfish cowardice kept it from being so. Did you never stop to think of the people themselves? That you might have bettered their world?"

Silence filled the loft.

Elric's heart raced in his chest, his breathing erratic as he fought to hold his barely restrained anger in check. He did not understand the woman before him, but he was unsure that he wanted to. She was intelligent and sharp-witted, and he had started to believe there may even be emotion and empathy lurking deep within her. But now he questioned if he had seen anything there in the first place, or if it had only been his foolish hope forming a mirage of what he wanted to see.

Graecerys did not back down or look away, but he saw pain laced in her eyes when she replied. "I tried."

Elric stiffened. "Is that what haunts you when you shut your eyes? Your guilt?"

Anger flared across her face, consuming all hint of weakness, though pain still lurked behind it all. "You do not know what you are talking about."

"It is not hard to figure out, Your Grace. A woman raised to be queen cannot know much of hardship—there is no suffering in your life that might prey upon you so ruthlessly."

She rose to her feet, stepping toward him. "You do not know me, and you know nothing of what I have lost. Of what tortures me."

"I know enough to understand there is no excuse for suffering. There is no pain that could ever justify the loss of innocent lives. And what was witnessed tonight is far beyond that. These people were made to serve a sentence they earned simply by existing. But you, who sat in your palace twiddling with a crown, now seek to become the oppressed because your own kind failed you?"

"You cannot fathom what has been taken from me," she shouted. "And until you stand in my shoes, you do not understand the fight I wage for my own mind and body, barely staying whole long enough to survive another day. Forgive me for not having the strength to then save and protect the kingdom."

"I do not discount what you may have endured, for Obarian is ruthless," Elric said evenly, though seething. "But it leaves no excuse for what you've done. If you did not want to take on the world, then you needed to step aside. Now it is too late."

Graecerys barked a laugh. "If only it were that simple. I could not have relinquished the throne if I tried."

"Why?" Elric snapped. "Help me understand what I seem to be missing."

She groaned in frustration and threw her hands up. "I cannot. And I do not have to. You do not understand what it is to shoulder the weight of a world, of collapsed expectation, of... of corruption and greed and lies—all of the *lies*."

"Lies that *you* perpetuated," Elric fired back, stepping forward.

"For good reason."

"There is never a good reason for a lie."

Graecerys stalked toward him. "It must be such a shame to be so virtuous that you have never lied to save someone you love. That you have never been forced to lay everything on the line, down to your very life, just to still lose them in the end."

Elric reared back as if slapped. "I have known love deeper than you will ever see. I have held my entire world, watched its blood cover my hands, felt it all slip away from me, and survived its abandonment, knowing it all came because of both who I am and what I cannot be. There is nothing I understand better in all the world above and below, and yet I still do not level destruction at the innocent. I do not even seek retribution on those who are guilty. It is why *you* still have breath in your lungs."

Graecerys smiled cruelly. "Then do it. If you despise who and what I am, if you know my darkness so well, then kill me. I'm sure even my guards will thank you by morning."

Elric considered it for only a heartbeat, then shook his head. "I refuse to be like you."

"Do you?" she asked, cocking her head. "Or are you so much like me that it scares you to entertain the thought?"

The doors below burst open, the suddenness causing both of them to jump. Snell rushed in and slammed them behind him, rushing to pull anything he could find to block the entrance.

"What is happening?" Elric called down, Graecerys suddenly at his side.

"We saw a house in the distance. Towles went ahead, thinking it was the manor, and it was, but it was filled with revolutionaries. They spotted him and ran him down. They are on their way here."

The doors began to shudder, slammed from the outside, and Snell rushed for the ladder, scrambling up to Elric and Graecerys. "It will not hold," he heaved. "We must pull up the ladder."

"Where are Ganch and Fendo?" Graecerys blurted, looking on as Elric helped Snell wrestle the ladder into the loft, cutting off any way up, but also their way down.

Snell shook his head. "They cannot accept the truth of this land. They believe you unfit and seek to stand beside the revolution. They are traitors."

His words landed like a blow, and she took a step back, resting a steadying hand on her stomach, the other covering her mouth as her face blanched white.

"We're trapped, aren't we?" Elric bit out, frustration coloring his tone. He ignored Graecerys and fixed his attention on Snell. "Do you have a plan?"

"When the doors open, the horses will run. We must find a way out and attempt to reach them before they flee too far. From there…it is only hope."

The door splintered, the horses neighing shrilly below, and more shouts surrounded them. Elric pulled on his strands, but the traitorous dhust was silent, and he slammed his hands down at his sides. He started to search the loft, throwing the stale straw and looking for anything that might aid them.

Graecerys stepped into his line of sight, and though he scowled, she simply lifted her hand, revealing a coil of rope clutched in her fingers.

He sighed, exasperated, yet grateful. "That will work."

He pushed by her to the wall and pried at the slats, yanking them with all his strength, attempting to form an opening. The ruckus he made was drowned out by the doors breaking below, and when the cold air finally rushed in against his face, the thunderous beat of hooves signaled that the horses had fled into the night.

The mob below began to search the barn, shouts and jeers sounding, their torches already filling the space with clouds of choking smoke. Elric surveyed the small opening, barely enough to fit a tall child, let alone an adult, but it would have to do.

"Snell, the rope," he grunted over his shoulder.

Reaching blindly behind, he grasped the coil being shoved into his hand, whipping around when his fingers met soft skin.

"Not you," he hissed, meeting Graecerys's eyes.

"Snell is a bit occupied at the moment," she scowled, tossing her head back over her shoulder.

He looked across the loft and found the soldier stomping furiously on the ground where a torch was quickly spreading flames.

Elric grasped the end of the coil, knotting it around the rafter and pulling it tight with the weight of his body before flinging it through the hole. He took a deep breath, then dropped his shoulder and rammed it into the opening. The wood splintered and cracked, then gave way, falling into the snow below, but effectively widening the space. All was silent outside, though he could see more torches bearing down on the town, their orange flickering brilliantly off the snow. He turned his back to the night and began to descend, letting his feet guide his path down the side of the barn, but the wood began to bow with the lilting building, throwing him off balance and sending him hurtling to the ground.

He landed flat on his back, pain shooting up his neck and down his legs as he gulped for air that simply would not enter his lungs.

Graecerys's feet hit the ground beside him, and she grabbed his arm, pulling him to a sitting position with surprising force. He gasped in lungfuls of air, and when she released him, his sleeve came away bloodied. She pressed her raw hands to her skirts, her palms ripped open from sliding so quickly down the rope. Before he could address them, the barn roof above gave way, collapsing toward the center of the crumbling structure. Elric looked around wildly, seeing Graecerys do the same, but his heart sank to find that Snell was nowhere to be seen. He had failed to make it out of the barn in time.

"Are you all right?" Graecerys asked, staring at him with wide, urgent eyes as he drew in ragged breaths.

"Fine. Unhurt," Elric grunted, wheezing as he forced himself to his feet.

"You do not sound unhurt."

"All men are infants, remember?" he retorted. "Your hands—"

"My hands are fine," she rushed. "But I'm afraid the horses are long gone."

He searched the night, but the only things surrounding them were darkness, fire, and their enemies bearing down on them.

Shaking his head, Elric looked back at Graecerys. Her shoulders sagged, and he saw it again—the pain lurking in her face. The steeled acceptance, as if she had known this would be her end all along. And then the fear, like her worst nightmares were coming to light. And it tugged at something inside him.

Something desperate for life.

Something that felt…*warm.*

He seized it, and the strand vibrated along his bones. When he held out his palm, red dhust began to cloud above their heads.

Panic settled in his veins. "Quick," he uttered, grasping her by the waist and pulling her against him. "I do not know where we will go."

Graecerys tried to step back, but he held her fast, and when their gazes met, hers were wide with unconcealed terror. "I thought you said you picture what you know?"

"That is for objects, I do not know how to harness forms that shift through air."

"Then think of something," she said hurriedly, her head whipping around as voices drew closer. "Somewhere, anywhere but here."

His tree home flashed in his mind, but the vision slipped away—fuzzy and fading. He pictured the Elfin Domain in Inflamel, the clearing with the soft lilacs blooming, but heartache banished the thought. "I do not know where to go," he stammered, his vulnerable admission racking him with pain.

I have nowhere to go.

"Try. Please," Graecerys rasped. The charred rope fell beside their feet, and when the barn started to crumble, the red dhust surrounded them entirely and blocked out the night.

Elric closed his eyes, then forced them open once more. The stars were brilliant now. Sparkling in his veins and covering them fully. He pictured the sky, the endless expanse of night against the horizon. And the mountains.

He landed with a *crunch*.

His entire face disappeared into a drift of snow, and when he tried to push up, it was as if the ground did not exist below. Just endless depths of sinking snow.

He looked around wildly, spotting Graecerys floundering in the same way only paces away. The wind howled, and there was nothing as far as the eye could see.

"What happened?" she shouted. "What have you done?"

"Saved us," he called back.

Finally wrestling to his feet, Elric searched the blowing snow for any sign of life—any indication of where they might be. And when he looked up...and up...and up, he saw the sky lighten. The first glimpses of the sun rising behind mountains.

He had sent them to the farthest reaches of Breteria.

They were at the foot of the Trifolium Mountains.

CHAPTER TWENTY-SEVEN

"Where are we?" Graecerys demanded, screaming over the howl of the wind and clasping her cloak tighter about her neck.

Elric reared on her. "I told you I was unsure where we would go."

She tried to step toward him, lifting her knee high to her waist and taking a single, stumbling step, but her skirts failed to sink in the snow and she tripped forward instead, landing on her palms in the snow. "What were you trying to picture?"

"I…I did not know what to picture. I saw stars and the night was calm and then…."

"Then *what?*" she spat accusatorially.

He swallowed. "I pictured the horizon line."

She paused and looked up. He knew the moment she realized the wall of darkness she stared at was indeed the Trifolium Mountains, because her eyes grew wide and her mouth fell open. But when she gazed back at him, her face was alight. "I know exactly where we are."

His brow furrowed. "How?"

"It does not matter how," she hurried, trying her best to

move through the drift of snow and failing. "We must head south."

"And what way is that?"

"The mountains rise in the east. They run from north to south. We are not in the mountains, we are at their foot, so if the range rises on our right we face north, and the left we face south. We go south."

"Wonderful," Elric shouted, matching her high steps but moving in the snow far better with his trousers and boots. "And how far south do we walk before we freeze to death?"

"There are cabins all along the foot of the mountains," she yelled. "Old ones, used during the Fall of the Thrones. We must make it to one."

Elric glanced over his shoulder at her, and she had barely moved, waving her arms and struggling forward with all her strength, which was not much if the exhaustion and strain on her face were any indication.

"Take my hand," he called.

Her head shot up. "Come again?"

"I said take my hand."

"Why?"

Elric grunted, his frustration building into a growl that he loosed to the sky. Turning around, he retraced his steps, forming new holes until he reached Graecerys. He took her hand, and without a word, started to walk back through his own tracks.

It took a little maneuvering at first, the weight of his dampened cloak oppressive, but it was his only source of protection from the elements. Elric found that if he dragged his leg through the snow, allowing small divots to form between foot holes, it was easier for Graecerys to walk forward in her skirt. Even if it did soak his clothes.

They did not speak, all their focus dedicated to moving forward and spotting any form of shelter in the blizzard. Elric lost all track of time. His mind was beginning to fog from cold and exhaustion, his limbs no more than lifeless weight being forced beneath him as he pressed on, and then suddenly Graecerys tugged on his hand.

"There!" she pointed.

He squinted, and, in the distance, he made out the peak of a roof. Summoning all his strength, he trudged a path forward, and when they finally stood upon the stoop, he reached for the handle and collapsed instead.

Graecerys stepped up next to his hunched figure, and her hands barely gripped the handle, the tips of her fingers discolored and the dried blood on her palms frozen. With every bit of determination etched into her face, she finally turned it enough to push it open.

She stepped through the door, stumbling on the firm wood floor, and she fell first to her knees and then prone across the ground. Elric pulled himself inside far enough to kick the door shut before his limbs gave out and he fell in a heap by her side.

The cabin was freezing, but airtight and dry, and after a few minutes, he looked to his left to find Graecerys staring at him. "If we survive this, remind me to thank you," she said faintly.

Elric snorted, and then his snort became a chuckle, and his chuckle a delirious laugh.

Graecerys only closed her eyes and rolled to her back, facing the ceiling. It was then that he truly took in her appearance, her soaked dress, trembling limbs, and the horrifying state of her hands. They were not safe yet, and he needed to act quickly.

He unfastened his cloak, leaving it in a wet heap on the floor, then heaved over and forced himself to his hands and knees, surveying the space. There was a sink and a table, a cupboard, a fireplace with a cauldron beside it, and a cot with a blanket and pillow. Crawling to the fireplace first, he pulled himself to a sitting position and reached for his strands.

Nothing answered.

He relaxed, picturing matches and summoning them to his hand. No dhust gathered. Not even a single star fell from his palm. He slapped his hands down on the worn, evergreen rug, already spent. But then a thought occurred to him.

Green.

He looked at the fireplace, focusing on the old coals, and instead of pulling something to himself, instead of forcing an action, he simply willed fire to appear. Just as he had begged for a break in the storm and longed for rain as the forest burned in Inflamel, he asked for what he wanted.

A soft vibration tingled in his arms, his hands, and when he lifted his palms, the grooves and lines in them sparkled a brilliant green.

A light flickered and he jumped away, thin curls of smoke rising from the coals. Soon they glowed red and orange, radiating a heat that burned his face. He crawled back to Graecerys, the warmth slowly reaching across the room behind him, and he grasped her under her arms and dragged her as best he could closer to the fire.

He pulled his own boots off, his soaking-wet socks followed, and then he did the same for her, though he realized removing her wet stockings did not matter if her dress was also soaked through.

Her eyes fluttered open and she groaned, turning to look at the fire with a dazed expression. "You found kindling."

He shook his head and couldn't help the small smile gracing his lips. "I summoned fire."

Her brow knit in confusion. "But that is…."

"True elemental magic," he replied.

She watched him shove to his feet with bewilderment. He moved to the cot first, stumbling like a drunkard but pleased to find that while there was just one pillow, there were two blankets made of a thick wool. Next, he shuffled to the cupboard, surprised to see bottles inside, though he was unsure of what.

And when he turned back, he spotted a trunk in the corner. He lifted the lid with a weighted creak and spotted still more blankets, a tunic, a pair of trousers, and one pair of long socks.

He carried them over to Graecerys who now sat up on the floor, shaking from head to toe.

"Here," he said, handing her the shirt. "I will face away. You must get out of that dress."

She held it up, assessing it, and—to his surprise—she nodded shakily and extended her hand. "Will you help me?"

He helped her stand, but when he moved to walk away, she added, "I cannot unfasten it myself."

He hesitated, but steeled himself and turned back. Graecerys tossed her matted hair over her shoulder to reveal the row of buttons down her spine. His hands shook, though his body was beginning to thaw, and when he grasped the first button of the blue fabric, his fingers scraped her neck, causing her to jump.

"I'm sorry, Your Grace, I…am out of practice."

She quickly shook her head. "It is not you, I assure you."

He was quiet as he worked down the line of buttons, baring first her shoulder blades and then the top of her chemise. It was when he reached the small of her back that he paused, and without thinking, ran the knuckle of his index finger down her spine in a soft, soothing caress. Instead of startling this time, Graecerys relaxed, and though he was certain it was a trick of the light, she leaned closer.

Elric swallowed, voice thick. "Is that far enough, or would you like me to go farther?"

She tilted her head enough to meet his eyes, her dress already slipping off the shoulder not draped in the curtain of her long, wine-colored hair. The firelight caught on the smoothness of her back, the gentle tremor of her shoulders, and the curve of her neck where a chain glinted. The sight of her took his breath away, and he found himself back in the training ring, inches from her face. He couldn't help but wonder what it might feel like to slide his hands along her skin, to pull her closer until they both warmed—to rest his head on her shoulder and just breathe her in.

Then he noticed the faint bruises on her neck, left by his own fingertips. Guilt and agonizing remorse gripped his chest, tightening his lungs until he missed a breath. Their exchange in the barn drifted through his mind. The cold had numbed the last bit of his anger, but when he reflected on their argument, he wondered if his emotion had been misplaced. If it had truly been meant for Graecerys, or if it was his own helplessness lashing out like a wounded animal, desperate for a scrap of justice in a place where mercy starved.

"You may go farther," she whispered, interrupting his thoughts. "With the buttons. If you are comfortable with that."

All of the air left his lungs, the dual meaning hidden within his words and the permission in her answer terrifying him to his senses.

He dropped his hand to his side. "I must change, myself. And then I need to try to call on my strands. We will not last long without food."

Graecerys nodded, her eyes coming back to life, as if waking from a daze, and she turned away, crossing the room to the cot and laying the tunic on it, preparing to change. Elric did the same in the opposite direction, removing his shirt, shucking off his trousers, and pulling on the dry pair that were far too long on him, but graciously fit well enough in the waist to clasp.

"Let me know when you are decent," he said to the wall, rummaging back in the trunk for the socks.

"Decent," she replied a few moments later. He faced her once more and blinked rapidly, trying to think of everything else in the kingdom save the woman before him in nothing but a man's shirt that stretched to her knees.

He handed her the socks and a blanket. "These will help keep you warm and will better cover your skin."

Her eyes flicked to his bare chest, and it may have been the dim lighting once more, but he swore he saw color return to her cheeks. "And your skin?"

"I have blankets until my cloak is dry," he replied, quickly grabbing one from the trunk.

Graecerys returned to the cot and slipped the socks on, then pulled her legs up beneath her and wrapped the blanket about her shoulders like a cape. Elric did the same, doing his best to cover his naked torso, and when he dragged a chair to the side of the bed and sank into it, it took everything in his power not to groan in relief.

"May I see your hands?" he asked.

She hesitated, then extended them out. He flipped them, palm up, laying them gently on his knees. He was exhausted, the very blood in his veins sluggish, but he needed to try one last time. Picturing the small lavender jar with the ancient runes etched around the mouth, he pulled with all his might, and with the faintest glimmer of blue dhust, it materialized in his hands.

He uncorked it, and then delicately brushed the balm inside from end to end across her palms.

She hissed in pain, and he clasped her wrists, holding them still. "I am sorry. Please, just, give it a moment."

Her stiff limbs relaxed, and by the time he released her, the balm was the only line shimmering on her skin. The frayed pieces of twine that had been embedded in the wound all collected in its pool, and the skin below was healed and new.

"How is that possible?" Graecerys asked, staring at her hands.

"Elfin folk have the oldest healers," he replied, standing and shuffling his chair to the opposite side of the room, closer to the fire.

She gawked at him. "You *stole* from the elfin folk?"

"More like I borrowed from an old friend," he answered, sinking back into the chair with a groan.

They both watched the fire in silence.

Elric did not realize he was nodding off until his chin smacked his chest. He bolted upright again, and glanced to Graecerys, who was still sitting up, gazing wide-eyed at the fire.

He was struck then by how small she looked. How normal, but also how young. Stripped out of her finery, in a cabin at the center of nowhere, it was all too easy to forget who and what she was. Unless it was her title that had been a lie. Unless, somehow, he was seeing who she truly was for the first time.

She blinked and looked away from the fire, finding Elric's eyes on her. "You may sleep here," he said softly. "I am prepared if the nightmares come for you, though I do not believe there are any around to hear us."

The weariness descended on her almost instantly. "None live this far north. Not in this province. The only ones who live here reside in the manor on the cliffside. It is where we must go."

Elric stiffened. "And you are certain it is safe?"

Graecerys, still bundled in the blanket, lay down on her side, her head resting on the pillow, though her eyes remained open. "It is the safest place I know."

Elric nodded, and when he moved the chair to lay on the floor, grabbing a second blanket from the trunk, the pillow hit the ground at his feet. He looked to Graecerys, who had curled up beneath the cot blankets and was now using the extra covering beneath her head.

"Thank you," he said earnestly.

"It is the least I can do for you putting up with me," she replied, a slight air of haughtiness bleeding into her tone.

Elric huffed a laugh. "Putting up with you is the most I can do."

"Do not make me take it back," she retorted. "And do not smother me with it either."

Elric smiled in spite of himself. "I would not dream of it. Rest easy, Your Grace. We shall see what tomorrow holds."

CHAPTER TWENTY-EIGHT

*E*lric awoke, warmed through and well rested. It was still dark outside, but he was unsure if it was the time of day or the storm that still raged. Graecerys had only suffered from one nightmare, and she now slept soundly in the cot, though he was certain she would not stay there for long if his stomach did not cease its grumbling.

He found his strands easily and summoned every food he could think of—bread, cheese, chunks of vegetables and meat that he put in the pot on the fire with a bucket of fresh water. He summoned proper kindling, a simple shirt for himself, and even a razor to shave his face. Peering into the cupboard, he realized what the bottles were filled with, and with a wide grin, set two out on the table.

The stew was nearly done when Graecerys's eyes fluttered open, and at the sight of the food, her stomach rumbled across the cabin.

"Help yourself," Elric replied, spooning out some of the stew and handing her a bowl.

She stared at it, as well as the goods on the table, and turned back to him. "You know how to cook?"

"I had to provide for myself often in Inflamel," he replied, spooning his own portion. "I am able to do much with little, though I prefer to do little with much."

Graecerys eyed the bread and cheese, grabbing a hunk of each. "I believe I like that logic."

They sat at the table, eating in silence until Graecerys asked, "What is in the bottles?"

"A fermented concoction that is as hard to find as it is strong. It is unlike wine, but not nearly as thin as ale or shocking as the spirits found in pubs. It is smooth and easy to drink much of, if you are not careful."

Graecerys nodded, her mouth full of stew, and then reached for a bottle. Elric called upon his strands, preparing to summon two glasses, but to his surprise, she yanked the cork from the top, lifted the spout to her lips, and tipped the entire bottle back. She took a long sip, then set it back on the table before swallowing, concentrating on the drink he knew would go down smooth, warm, and gentle—a deceiving lover that would be nowhere near when you awoke the next morning.

"Oh, I quite like that," Graecerys said, taking another swig, and when Elric reached for the drink, she pulled it away from him, wrapping her arms around it. "This is mine, that can be yours."

Elric looked at her incredulously. "Do you intend to drink an entire bottle this...." He searched for the right word. Was it day? Was it night? Did it even matter anymore?

"Yes," Graecerys replied simply. "There is no point in leaving while a storm blows so hard we do not know the time of day. So why not pass the time?"

He considered her words for a moment and then sighed. "You are not incorrect," he admitted, taking and uncorking his own bottle.

"Is it truly that difficult for you to say that I am right?"

"You have no idea," he murmured, but before the drink met

his lips, he found her eyes and asked, "You are not often left alone with your thoughts, are you, Your Grace?"

She watched him drink deeply, but instead of answering, suddenly said, "I believe we got off on the wrong foot."

Elric choked, coughing and sputtering as he set the bottle down.

"Did I say something amusing?" she asked dryly.

"Considering the terms of our introduction, I am curious what your idea of the right foot might be."

She thought for a moment. "Maybe something more diplomatic. With less kidnapping and imprisonment."

Elric stared at her, bewildered, yet thoroughly entertained. "You are amusing when you drink."

To his surprise, Graecerys broke into a huge smile—one that made the waves in her eyes dance. "Why, thank you. I appreciate the compliment."

"And I appreciate your apology."

The bottle stopped halfway to her lips. "I'm sorry, what?"

"Your apology," Elric said with a sly smile. "For the kidnapping and imprisonment."

She blinked once, eyes narrowing. "I don't believe that was an apology."

"It sounded like one to me." Elric shrugged, tipping his drink back again.

"And do you hear strange things often? I'm sure there is a tonic for that," she retorted sweetly, taking another drag from her bottle.

Elric flashed her a smile. "Only when you speak."

Graecerys froze, and then agonizingly slow, a smile spread across her face. "You're not afraid to say anything to me, are you?"

"In truth, the further we draw from the palace the more human you become, which makes it easier. However, when you've lived as long as I have, you fear very little, for you tend to have seen and survived it all."

Her smile faded, and when she took another drink, he could have sworn he saw a hint of sadness in her eyes. "What does it feel like being alive for so long? How do you hold so many lifetimes in your memory?"

"I do not," he replied. "I have pieces of memories, formative moments, and people and places important to me. I was unaware of how much I had truly forgotten, or hidden away in my mind, before I walked the palace halls once more. In truth, there is not much to recall. A life this long feels like being battered with wave after wave of give and take with hardly a moment in between for air. There is small wonder why I loathe the sea."

A cloud crossed over Graecerys's face. "That is a commonality we share, I'm afraid."

Elric paused, genuine surprise in his tone. "You do not like the ocean? Why?"

She thought for a long moment, as if searching for the reason, then drained the last of her bottle and set it on the table with a contented exhale, staring at a knot in the wood instead of meeting his gaze. "It betrayed me," she replied quietly.

He paused daring to tiptoe around a memory he almost never touched. "I knew someone once who loved the sea. The way she spoke of it was beautiful. But I never saw it the way she did. I never had the chance."

"What happened to her?" Graecerys asked carefully, her eyes full of keen interest.

Elric was quiet, then finally said, "I lost her."

Graecerys stilled and in the softest tone he had ever heard from her, said, "I…am sorry."

He watched her, taking in her uncomfortable honesty and the way she shifted awkwardly, and before he could stop himself, he said, "You remind me of the ocean."

She barked a laugh. "Why, because you despise it?"

Elric snorted but shook his head. "No. Because of your eyes. They are the color of the deepest waves. The dark ones you only ever see far from shore. The kind that keep you company until the current carries you home."

Graecerys's lips parted slightly at his admission, and Elric realized the words that had slipped out. He stood suddenly, knocking into the edge of the table, shaking everything on top. "What do you say to another bottle? I believe we have one more."

They moved from the table back to the cot, and Elric pulled his blankets and pillow over to the floor just beside Graecerys. They continued to talk, passing the bottle back and forth, their words becoming slurred and their laughs too frequent between questions. They spoke about nothing of importance, taking jabs at one another to their increasing amusement, and somehow it felt like everything.

Elric had not spoken so casually in years—since he watched his closest friend fall apart in the face of his loss. But Graecerys was easy to speak with, a good listener, and without inhibitions restraining her, her curiosity abounded, fueling question after question he knew she would be far too ashamed to ask were she not intoxicated. She was unguarded and genuine. Not a cold queen, an unfeeling ruler, but the woman who hid within the sarcophagus of both.

Perception, in tandem with her brazen violence against Jacian, had been the key to Graecerys's downfall, but had anyone once stopped to look at her? To extend a modicum of the grace her name begged for? Or to see beneath the skin that was so hardened, so thick, from the years she spent defending any tenderness that life had failed to strip away from her?

In this light she was a brash and unashamed reflection of all he felt—and so desperately fought to hide. Outwardly, they were collected and reserved individuals, bound to their duty in life, but inside, they were ancient creatures hiding and protecting reckless, youthful souls. They had aged so quickly, yet were somehow never allowed to grow up. He wanted to hate her still, but one thing was irrefutable: Had time treated them differently or had they been different people in a different world, they may have been decent friends.

The wood groaned beneath the mattress, and when he glanced up, he saw her gazing at the roof. A long strand of her hair dangled off the mattress like a string of rubies, and it took everything in his will not to wrap it around his finger. "What do stars count at night when they cannot sleep?" she asked. "Do you take inventory of your own freckles? Number the hairs on your arm?"

Elric paused. He'd been enjoying their drunken talk, but her question cut straight to his heart. Bliss never lasted alongside his truths. "Memories. We still look to the sky, we still count the stars, but they are not mere constellations to us. They're a reminder. Every one a memory. And we recall them as we drift away into slumber, sending silent wishes that our loved ones may join us there."

The cot creaked once more, and Graecerys's head poked over the side. "That is…terribly sad and morbidly depressing."

He shrugged. "It depends on the memory. They are all made to be kept. Whether sweet or bitter, I hold them in equal measure. They are dear because they are all I have left."

She stared at him, and he could have sworn he saw recognition in her eyes before she laid back down. "Then we shall make new ones."

He huffed a laugh. "We? When did we become a *we*?"

"When you decided to save my life, though you should've betrayed me like everyone else."

He fell silent, her honesty hanging like a new spring bloom—delicate and just out of reach. "Then I believe we have already begun."

"How do you suppose?"

"I would say becoming drunk in an abandoned cabin in the middle of nowhere suffices as a memorable time."

Graecerys laughed and the sound brought warmth to his face, but it was her next words that caused his skin to flame. "Is it among the sweet? Or the bitter?"

He swallowed, brushing off his nerves and summoning his courtly nonchalance. "Bittersweet. You stole the last dregs."

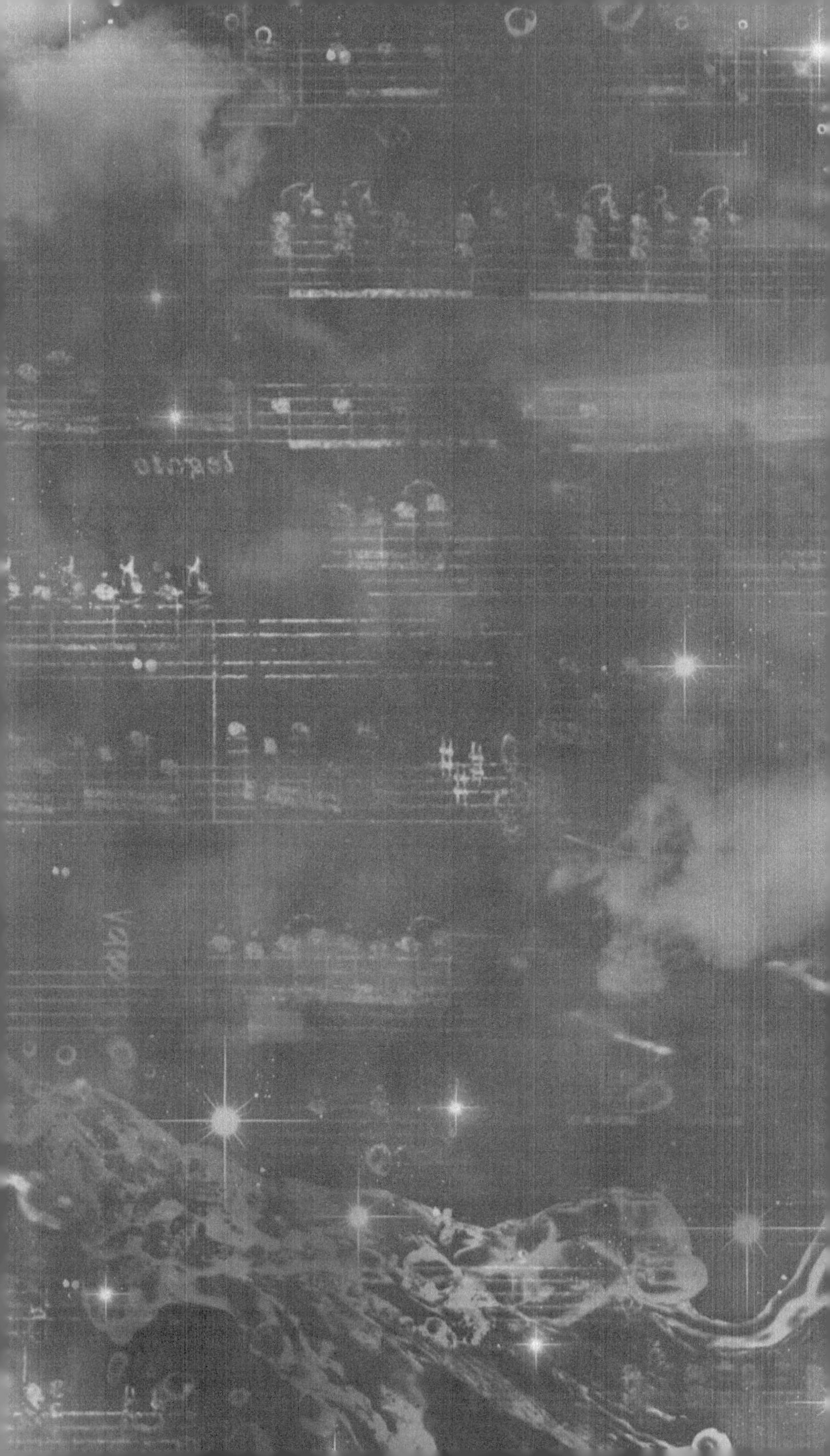

CHAPTER TWENTY-NINE

The sky was lighter beyond the cabin window, confirming that it was daytime. The storm had abated slightly, though the wind still howled, blowing the snow in drifts so thick and blindingly white that the world beyond a few paces was no more than a furious crystalline gyre.

And it was positively miserable.

Graecerys wretched one last time, and Elric let the coil of her tangled yet deceptively soft hair slip from his hand so she could lean against the wall for support.

He sent the rancid bucket away, then stretched out on the floor beside her, sliding his pillow over his face to suppress a groan. If anyone had told him months ago that he would be nursing the after-effects of a drunken night with the Queen of Obarian and going as far as to hold her hair while she vomited, he would have lost his own freedom staking everything on them having gone mad for the notion. And yet, here they were.

The sound of the creaking door and the rush of frigid air across the floor, along with the unimaginably loud howl of the wind, startled him from beneath his shelter, and he sat up slowly, attempting to blink away the pounding behind his eyes.

Slight color had returned to Graecerys's face, though her eyes remained half open from what looked like the same ache that resounded inside his skull. In her hand she carried a bowl heaping with snow, and he watched, mesmerized, when she slid the oversized socks from her feet and began to pack them with the frozen substance. After tying each one off with a knot, she handed him one, placed the other against her forehead, then swiftly tipped herself back onto her cot. A small, contented sigh snuck free as her head hit the pillow, and Elric couldn't help the smile that broadened across his face when he pressed the blissfully cold compress to his eyes.

"I may be the Isteriaeth, but this? This is true magic," he said thickly, lying back on his own pillow, still on the floor at her bedside.

"It is until it begins to melt. Then it is a mess," Graecerys replied in a dry and scratchy voice. "If the world did not waltz when I stood, I would far prefer to fill my stomach with it instead of stuffing it in a sock."

Elric's eyebrows lifted, shifting his sock down onto the bridge of his nose. "Consuming snow? I cannot imagine it would taste good. Or at the very least like anything more than painful water."

Graecerys snorted. "You do not eat it plain. And it is only painful if you are too greedy."

"Then what do you eat it with?"

"Wine. Spirits. Some other drink that gives you false promises of happiness, then forces its fingers through the back of your skull to squeeze your brain."

Elric groaned, his stomach churning at the thought, but Graecerys only chuckled. "It is a very simple treat to mix. You only need sugar and cream."

An amicable silence filled the cabin, the absence of noise an overwhelming relief to Elric, and though he knew Graecerys was probably dozing off—and that he should do the same—he could not resist the thought.

Sitting up slowly and with more effort than the action usually demanded, he walked to the table where the bowl of the remaining snow waited. It took a moment for the dhust in his veins to rouse in such a way that did not make the spots in his vision dance, but the moment it did, he summoned a small satchel of sugar and a modest cup of milk.

He searched around clumsily for a spoon, trying to determine where everything was—or rather where it had been left by the drunkards who had tidied the cabin the night prior—and after knocking over what felt like the hundredth item, Graecerys stood from her cot.

"What in the Thrones are you doing?" she asked, shuffling toward him.

He turned, spoon in hand, and watched the items sitting on the table register in her mind. Her eyes brightened, and though she kept it tightly restrained, a smile graced her lips. He held the utensil out to her. "Would you do me the honor of crafting your magic snow, Your Grace?"

She scowled at the name, and when she took the spoon from his hand, she gave him a good-natured smack on the arm with it before turning to the bowl.

He watched in amusement as she added small amounts of sugar and cream to the snow at a time, mixing thoroughly between each one, until she gazed with satisfaction at the consistency she had produced.

Elric handed her a second spoon, and she scooped a small amount out before handing it back to him, waiting patiently with her own until he raised the magic snow to his lips.

The sweet, creamy mixture was simple, yet somehow decadent in a way Elric had never experienced before. He helped himself to another spoonful, savoring the taste and trying to remember not to indulge too quickly, though he already craved more.

Graecerys frowned at her empty spoon. "It is not right," she said, studying the bowl like it might give her the answer.

"It is wonderful," Elric remarked around a mouthful of snow, but studying her growing frustration, he quickly swallowed. "Is there something missing?"

"I.... There must be," Graecerys muttered. "I know this recipe by heart. At least, I believed I did."

Annoyance and a flash of anger mounted in her face, the hard and cold mask of a queen returning. Only this time it was not directed at anyone other than herself.

"This is wonderful, Graecerys," Elric said quietly.

"It always was," she replied, shaking her head vehemently. "We made it so many times. I don't know how I could have forgotten."

"Maybe because you were running a kingdom," Elric offered, regretting the words when her eyes shot to him.

"Because I was doing such an admirable job at that," she fired back, and though her vitriol was aimed at Elric, he did not rise to the bait.

"I have no desire to argue with you while I have a headache, Your Grace," he replied tersely.

She stared him down, and he waited patiently, but instead of delivering another barb, she slammed her spoon on the table and marched back to her cot.

Elric took small satisfaction that the noise made both of them wince, but when Graecerys turned her back to him and dropped her already soaked snow-sock straight onto his pillow, his irritation coiled.

Striding over, he deposited the compress onto the bare floor, and after dragging his makeshift bed to the opposite side of the fireplace once more, he laid down. He tried and failed to summon another pillow to himself, resorting to resting his face upon his arm. The moment he found a comfortable position in which his eyes were shielded from the brightness, he fell into a deep sleep once more.

Whimpering. Soft, heaving breaths. And then—

"No," Graecerys moaned.

Elric sat up on his cot and stared across the dimly lit room. The fire had gone out, making the room far too cold and only slightly illuminated by the sheets of white streaking past the windows, but he could see Graecerys rolling in her bed.

He stood, thanking every star in the sky that his head no longer hurt and that the world did not pitch when he moved quickly to the fire. A flame sparked and he fed it the kindling he had summoned before their drunken meal, and when the flames finally licked and grew, he turned to Graecerys who still tossed restlessly.

Her hair glowed in the flickering light, an extension of the embers themselves, but it was twisted up in her fingers, her fists locked in their length. Her expression was contorted, pain-ridden, and as he watched her curl into a fetal position, her lips parted in a silent scream, as if there were something bearing down on her, agonizing her, and she were powerless to escape.

Her voice found life, and the scream that rent from her mouth struck fear in his heart.

Elric rushed to her bedside, sitting beside her and gently clasping her arms, stroking his thumbs along her inner wrist and guiding her to her back.

"Graecerys," he murmured, softly but urgently. "Graecerys, you must wake."

She paused under his touch, her limbs relaxing and the tension bleeding from her face only a heartbeat before she began to struggle. Her fists flew, but Elric deftly avoided them, carefully extracting her hair from their clutches while speaking calmly. "Open your eyes. Please. Graecerys, you are safe. I promise, I have you."

The last strand of hair fell safely away, her fists now free to swing unrestrained, but Elric moved faster. He pinned her elbows to her sides and hauled her up, locking her against his chest. Her fists beat against his back mercilessly, her cries urgent and determined to break free—to fend off whatever horror assaulted her mind—but Elric just held her.

"I have you," he spoke urgently into her ear, one arm banded around her, the other supporting her head and holding it to his heart. "You are safe, you can wake now. You must wake. I am not letting go until you do."

Her body slumped against him and her cry became a whine of exhaustion, but instead of striking him once more, her hands rested softly on his back. Then slowly, and ever so gently, she clutched his tunic and held on for dear life.

"That's it, Grace," Elric whispered. "You are safe with me. I have you, I will not let anything harm you."

Her head rose, and he loosened his grip, allowing her to pull back and see his face. Endless waves of broken devastation flooded her eyes, and though they did not focus entirely, they bounced between Elric's, searching them.

"You are safe," he murmured. He traced soft, soothing circles on her back and gently rubbed her scalp, finding all the places where the indentation of her nails remained. "You are almost back with me now. Have you found me?"

He did not move or break their stare, continuing his reassuring caresses and encouragement until her breathing returned to normal. And the next time she blinked, he saw the dark clouds in her eyes dissipate and register his presence.

"There she is," he said with a smile, but when he released her and made to move away, Graecerys wrapped her arms around him tighter and buried her cheek against his chest.

Elric froze, his arms suspended just off her body. He wasn't sure if he was more worried about her reaction or what she might do to him if he reciprocated while she wasn't fully in her own mind, but when he felt a small, damp spot grow on his tunic from her silent tears, he decided he did not care and embraced her fully.

They remained that way, holding each other in wordless comfort and reassurance, for what felt like an eternity. Elric's heart began to hammer, and his palms started to sweat. He worried that maybe his stomach was not as settled as he'd hoped, but then he came to the startling realization that it was quite the opposite. He *enjoyed* holding Graecerys. And though he tried to brush it off as a wistful longing for affection and the way he missed the simple, quiet moments that had accompanied a relationship, he knew at his core it was not purely circumstantial.

He liked the way she fit in his arms. And the epiphany left him unsettled.

"My mother taught me the recipe for the snow delight." Graecerys's words were monotone, drenched in exhaustion and the emotion she still clearly fought to pull in check.

Elric wondered if her words had anything to do with the nightmares that tortured her sleep but dared not ask. Instead, he found himself saying, "My mother told me every story I know. She used to pull me onto her lap, curl me into a blanket or shawl against her chest, and weave tale after tale. I never grew tired from the stories. I never wanted them to end." He paused, smiling to himself. "But it was her warmth, the scent of vanilla in her hair, that always carried me off to sleep."

Graecerys stiffened in his arms, and he braced himself as she straightened, but when he looked at her face, it was not angry. Her eyes were wide but bright, and deep in them, he thought he saw just a hint of relief. "Vanilla," she said slowly, voice full of gravel. "Extract of vanilla is the last ingredient."

Elric did not know what to say, but he suddenly became painfully aware that their faces were mere inches apart. His eyes fell to her lips, then quickly diverted over her shoulder. "You must rest now," he whispered.

Graecerys nodded sleepily, but when he moved to rise, she grasped his arm. "Will you stay near? In case I…."

"I will move my cot back," he reassured, but the hesitancy in her eyes made his pulse race again.

"Will you stay here?" Graecerys asked resolutely, sliding to the far left of the bed and tapping her hand on the small space she had made.

Blood rushed to Elric's face, but he swallowed and nodded wordlessly. They both shifted awkwardly, laying as best they could side by side in the cot without touching. Elric waited until Graecerys turned on her side, facing away from him, and rolled in the same way, keeping enough space between them to be a barrier between her and the rest of the room while still a comforting presence. He stared at the ruby strands of hair now resting on the pillow beside him, utterly perplexed by the woman they belonged to.

And that was where sleep finally found him.

CHAPTER THIRTY

The storm did not subside for what Elric counted to be another three days. And ever since he had awoken beside Graecerys—with his hands buried in her hair and her arms wrapped around his waist, as if they sought each other in sleep but could not get close enough—she had been like a caged animal, prowling and waiting to be baited with the right opportunity to strike.

Endless nightmares broke her rest, leaving her screaming and clawing at the bed as if fighting against an unseen foe desperate to steal her life. And the more her dreams tortured her, the more her condition seemed to deteriorate. She remained silent, unwilling to talk about what met her in the dark, yet in the daylight, she grew more agitated, and while Elric would have loved nothing more than to give her space, to be far away from her, there was none to be had in the single-room cabin.

It was midway through the day that she finally stopped prowling the space and slammed her foot to the ground. "This has gone on far too long. Do something, *anything*, with this storm."

Elric exhaled in frustration from his seat at the small table. "As I told you the last time you demanded, Your Grace, I have tried. There is no response from the elemental strand, and as of today, I hardly have enough dhust to summon food and drink to us."

"All the more reason to leave. We cannot stay here if you continue to starve us out."

"It is not my intent," he muttered.

"No, it is not. I apologize, I seem to have forgotten that I manage to be bound to the last Isteriaeth, who not only does not know what dhust he carries, but also cannot seem to control his own power."

"Do you ever tire of making the same useless arguments, or do you just appreciate hearing yourself speak?" he asked, leaning back in his chair with a devilish smile. He realized he was trying to make her angry now, but if she would not be tempered, maybe he might stoke her flames enough to burn out. Besides, part of him found some twisted sense of enjoyment tormenting her.

"I would not make the same arguments were they not the same problems over and over," she snapped. "And ever since you arrived, the recurring problem seems to be *you*."

"Because every problem in this kingdom—the revolution, the famine, the cold, the loss of your people—certainly ties back to my general existence," Elric deadpanned, staring at her darkly.

Graecerys smiled, and as he was learning, it meant nothing good was certain to come out of her mouth next. "Thank you for finally acknowledging it. I am grateful that if we're to ever agree on one thing, it is that this situation is entirely your fault."

Elric ground his teeth, any hint of his amusement gone. He needed to be away from this woman. Now.

As if hearing his thoughts, she took a step closer. "I didn't need to be saved. I didn't want to be protected. And if you hadn't done so, we wouldn't have needed to flee the palace and I wouldn't be trapped here with you."

"Good to know. Next time you are in mortal peril, I will leave you to die and spare you the agony of being near me."

"It sounds lovely in theory, but I don't believe you're capable of it," she mused, tapping her chin before counting each offense on her fingers. "You hate me. You blame me for the loss of your family—you admitted so yourself—and yet you could not deny your hero complex enough to kill me *or* leave me to rot."

Elric shoved to his feet, stepping before her, but instead of backing down, he only saw satisfaction in her eyes. She was goading him, and he was falling for it all. Worse, she was enjoying every second of it, and he wasn't sure what infuriated him more—his inability to best her, or the fact that she was a challenge that exhilarated him in ways he had never felt before.

"Be that as it may, Your Grace, you are alone with me," he murmured, leaning toward her. "So it would serve you well to stand down."

A smirk crossed her lips and she leaned closer still, the darkness in her eyes sparking with fire—a thousand stars burning to combustion in her stare. *"Or what?"*

Everything inside Elric writhed, stiffening and flexing against the cage of propriety he had shoved every last ounce of feeling into. The air was charged with their anger, their frustration, but also the days spent alone and separated from the world with far too much cornered emotion and nowhere for it to escape. He stepped back, turning away to pace the floor himself. "For the first time in your Thrones-forsaken life, just listen to something you are told to do," he warned.

The infuriating creature had the audacity to *laugh*. "You forget what you are, Isteriaeth," she said, shaking her head with a vicious smile. "Bound. To *me*."

The bars began to bend, his restraints fraying, and Elric whipped around to face her fully, hissing into the air rapidly thinning between them. "And you forget who I am. I fell from the stars above. I have lived hundreds of years. I could move this entire building if I wished. Summon your palace and your precious throne outside the door with a snap of my fingers. But this is not your court. I see none of your subjects or lords here, only me. I may be bound to your blood, but I will never sink so low as to fall at your feet. You are not and will never be my queen. Now do as you are told. Stand. Down."

The anger in her eyes burned hotter than the coals on the hearth, and by the damned Thrones, the woman sauntered to his side, knocking his shoulder with her own as she stepped past. "Summon whatever makes you feel better about yourself. I don't have to be your queen here, but as a woman, I do not deign to listen to your demands. I will do whatever I want."

Elric's hand shot out, finding her throat and sliding up the column to her chin, commanding her attention. The air shifted between them, the fire of anger smoldering to a low, consuming heat the instant their skin touched. Her eyes flared, but something else mixed with the loathing that crashed in their waves. The same thing that twisted the fire in his veins into knots, causing the hunger within him to salivate. And instead of extinguishing the inferno—pulling away, or laying him out on the ground for putting a hand on her—she leaned into his touch and her lips parted on a sharp, expectant inhale.

He froze, but she waited, and though he knew it would be wise to step back, to do the right thing and walk away, nothing in him wanted to. "If you will do whatever you want, then prove it."

Her mouth was on his in an instant, his hand slipping behind her neck, delving into her hair to pull her deeper into their kiss. Her fingers dug into his shirt, clawing fistfuls of the fabric to draw him closer. He deftly spun her on her feet, and swiped a hand out, clearing the table behind them, sending the cups and bowls clattering to the ground.

Graecerys pulled away, but he caught her bottom lip between his teeth, the roughness of his fresh stubble against her skin eliciting a small sigh, and then a whine that became a grunt of frustration as she ripped his shirt open. Buttons scattered on the floor in every direction, and she slid one hand across his toned core, tracing the muscles along his hip and up his back before digging her fingers into his hair and devouring his mouth once more.

He grabbed her about the waist and hoisted her onto the table, shoving her dress up her legs in the process, though it only served to reveal the layers she wore beneath. Cursing the Thrones-damned kingdom with their ridiculous cold and layers of clothing, Elric held his hand out in the air, and a heartbeat later, the soft, woolen material of her stockings weighed in his palm. In the next instant, they were in the fireplace, and with a snap of his fingers, they were engulfed in flames.

His cloak was still around his neck, but his shirt was now on the floor, his hands beneath her skirt and fingers gripping her hips before he dragged her undergarments to the floor. She clung to him, pulling him closer, her tongue now delving into his mouth, but he wrenched away, and she released a vexed groan. His mouth fell to her neck, and she dug her nails into his skin, their bite like fire, urging him on, but when he slipped a hand from her skirt to the buttons on the back of her dress, she swatted him away.

The action cut through his lust-consumed haze, and Elric froze, taking a small step back.

"Do you wish to go further?" he asked, chest heaving.

She grasped a handful of his cloak, trying to urge him closer, but he held the table firmly, keeping space between them. "Words, or I will stop."

Graecerys's needy groan turned into a laugh that set his skin ablaze. "I knew you secretly loved the sound of my voice. Do not stop. Do not make me wait any longer."

Elric smirked. "Any longer? And how long have you waited for this moment?"

She erased the air between them, her breath hot on his lips. "Do not make this more than what it is. You are burrowed under my skin as deep as I am buried in yours. I need you out."

His hand returned to her hip, pinning it in place, then he dragged his nails across the soft skin of her inner thigh. "As you wish," he murmured, swallowing her breathy cry when he brushed her heat with two fingers and curled them inside.

She moaned against his mouth, crying out against the wave he felt building within her, but he refused to let her go. He slipped a third finger aside the first two, and with a nip at her tongue, he finally pulled back enough for her to gasp in air and scream her release.

He took a moment, watched her flushed cheeks bloom hotter, soaked in her beauty. She was *breathtaking*—stunning fury and untamed violence. And somehow her unraveling was everything he had not realized he craved. Yet it still wasn't enough. He wanted more. He needed more.

He paused, waiting to see what she would do next, but when her gaze locked on his, flooding with heat, she took his hesitation to seize control. Unfastening his breeches, she plunged a hand inside and gripped him tightly. His eyes fell shut and he released a groan, leaning into her while she explored the length of him, finding his base and stroking all the way to the tip while peppering his neck with sharp kisses.

It was too much for him to take, his release building within him too quickly, and he almost relented—almost bent to her— but something in him refused. *Not like this.* He had not endured this woman for so long for this moment to end so soon.

In one swift motion, he gripped her hips and yanked her to the edge of the table, his pants falling about his ankles. She gasped and her hands shot up to clutch his shoulders, her eyes wide and filled with eager anticipation.

Elric paused and whispered against her mouth once more. "Do you want this?"

She answered with a rapid nod and pleading stare, but he shook his head. "I need to hear the words, Grace."

Her eyes fluttered shut, and to his surprise, instead of a witty jab or sharp comment, she smiled, then opened them once more. "I need this. *Now.*"

He did not wait a second longer to fully sheathe himself within her. Mouths barely a whisper apart, the silent cry of ecstasy and smile of satisfaction that graced her lips matched the screaming validation in his soul. And when their eyes met, fire for fire, there was not a single doubt in his mind.

He had met his match.

He started to move—setting a brutal, thorough pace—and their moans were one and the same, rising together. His nails dug into her skin to the point of breaking, and her teeth bit into his shoulder, threatening to do the same, but still they pushed on, united in their desperate need for more.

More of the anger that had ignited.

More of the passion that had exploded between them.

More of the fire that was swallowing them whole. But instead of destroying one other, they had found common ground at the center of the inferno. And instead of melting them to ruins, it was molding them into something new—something that threatened to never be separated again.

Release found Graecerys and with one last thrust, Elric stilled as his own sent him over the edge. His forehead fell to her shoulder, and she clasped the back of his neck, burying her hands in his hair and grinding her hips against him as they rode out the final waves together.

Barely waiting to catch his breath, Elric straightened, cupping her cheeks and brushing her hair back from her face.

There were a thousand words on his tongue, but none he

could say that came close to summing up the riot of feelings that threatened to collapse his chest.

And then, all at once, he realized what he had done.

Silently, he moved away from her, and with a flick of his wrist, he summoned the small towel he had used in his palace washroom. Handing it to Graecerys first, he righted his clothing, mumbled something about relieving himself, and then stumbled out the door and into the snow-filled night.

The bitter cold barely served to cool his boiling skin and certainly did nothing to ease the throbbing in his chest—the acute pain in his heart.

He had given himself to another woman. And to make matters worse, it hadn't even been someone he loved. It had been a reckless moment of passion, of weakness with someone he didn't even care for—who did not care for him. He had squandered some of his most private and sacred memories with Kathrina on a fling.

The wind howled, and though it bit his cheeks and the pelting snow stung his face, they blessedly covered the traces of tears that snuck from his eyes with a paralyzing guilt.

What had he done?

CHAPTER THIRTY-ONE

When Elric returned to the cabin, he was shocked to find Graecerys still sitting on the table. A small tin lay open beside her, and from it, she was drawing a spool of thread—a needle already pinched tight between her teeth, his shirt resting in her lap.

He knew he should say something, but when her eyes met his expectantly, waiting for his words, he only looked away.

He sent for a cold meal for them and two glasses of wine, and when he set the plate at her side, she reached for the glass and downed it in one go. He did the same, then stepped to the side and sat on the floor with his back against the table leg.

Sneaking a glance up at her from the corner of his eye, he watched her take a delicate bite of her sandwich, then resume her mending of his buttons, her brow drawn tight not from concentration on the task, but from irritation. He knew her well enough to know she wouldn't regret what had happened between them. But he was concerned that what set her on edge was the same subject that always seemed to coax out her claws —Elric himself, and his silence.

You miserable creature, do not hurt her pride because you are a wretch.

"You do not need to mend my shirt," he said quietly. "I am capable of sending for another."

She continued to thread the needle carefully through the buttonholes. "Believe it or not, I enjoy this sort of work. Stabbing things helps pass the time. However, on the subject of your dhust, have you noticed that it stops when you are drained of energy?"

"Yes. It has always been that way."

"But have you noticed it is effortless, in any form and regardless of how you are feeling, when we are not at odds?"

Elric paused, thinking over his struggles with the strands, pinning moments in his mind and examining them from multiple angles. "No," he said slowly. "I had not noticed, but...I believe you might be right."

The room fell silent once again, and Elric watched the flames dance, uncomfortable at Graecerys passing up the opportunity to accept the accolade of being correct, but also trying desperately to keep his eyes open. Why was he so tired?

"May I ask you something personal?"

Elric tried not to flinch, Graecerys's words so sterile for what had just transpired. "Of course, Your Grace."

She allowed the shirt to fall to her lap, and he tipped his head up to meet her gaze. What he saw relaxed his face, disarming him immediately. Her eyes were wide and earnest. There was no shrewdness, no cutting blade in sight. He was speaking to the inquisitive woman hiding in self-preservation, not the queen.

"What was her name?"

Elric swallowed but his mouth remained dry. Leave it to Graecerys to drive straight into the topic he had been hiding from in every second of silence.

"Kathrina," he said finally, silently sending for more wine in both their glasses.

She nodded, and then as if snapping from her own deep thoughts, returned to the shirt in her lap. "Was she the one you spoke of? The one who loved the sea?"

Elric shook his head, smiling softly to himself. "No, she was very different. She took a liking to flowers. Lilacs, actually. Though she never did see them for herself."

"How could she admire something she did not know?" Graecerys asked with a measure of curiosity.

"Sometimes it is easier to hold affinity for the idea of something more than the knowledge," Elric replied quietly. "Sometimes the dream you conjure is more powerful than even the weight of reality."

His chest constricted, choking his words and letting uncomfortable silence creep back in, but when Graecerys paused to knot her thread, he pressed on in a rushed tone.

"I apologize if it was unsatisfactory. It has been some time."

Her hand froze midair. "Do not do that. Do not debase yourself for the silence. You are allowed a moment."

"A moment for what?"

"To grieve."

Her words pinned him to the floor, her perception terrifying. "And why would you make such a bold assumption of my silence?" he asked picking at a groove in the floorboard beside him.

She hesitated for a moment, drawing his gaze once again, and it was the flash of reluctance in her face that terrified him more than the words she might flay him with next. "You are not the first for me either. I have seen guilt in a man's eyes. I've seen heartlessness, cruelty, and even prideful indifference. But what I saw on your face when you turned away was different, though an emotion I recognized just as well."

Elric stared at her, a cold trickle of dread pooling in his stomach, yet he still bit out the words. "What do you mean you have seen all of these things?"

Graecerys pressed her lips together, looking down at her hands where they had fallen palm up in her lap as if they might offer her the words. The silence stretched on, and with every blink, every word that formed on the tip of her tongue before slipping away unspoken, every light doused in her eyes, his fears were confirmed.

She met his eyes, and he found no sorrow or pain, just emptiness accompanied by a hollow laugh. "As it would turn out, being a young woman often unchaperoned in the palace, with a claim to the crown and innocence intact, makes you an attractive conquest for the wandering eye of noblemen. Logically, I cannot say I blame them. What easier way to find yourself a home on the throne than to compromise the virtue of a future queen and secure an heir for the kingdom?"

Something hardened in Elric, a vicious and burning fire, though it gripped him like ice. "And your father. Blenheim, none of them...."

"They never knew," she replied, fiddling once again with the needle and thread. "The king was already far too unwell, hardly ever present in his own mind, and Blenheim's duty was to my father until his death. It is why I sought help from the guards. Some of the older men— I suppose they figured out. Or learned through bragging drunkards. They stepped forward, a line of defense when possible, but they did something far better. They gave me what I needed to defend myself. For the times they could not be near me, they showed me how to protect my own destiny. They taught me how to fight."

Her words grew more resolute, her face set in firm lines, and for the first time, Elric understood just a fraction of the hardness, the armor that she donned, though even he failed to imagine its extent. And yet she had laid it all down, not in a moment of passion, but in a verbal and conscious choice. With him.

The weight of that revelation, of the trust she had put in

him, combined with the visceral anger at how brutally she had been failed by everyone around her, made him feel ill.

"How many have you been with of your own volition?" he asked, softening his tone but regretting the words as soon as they left his mouth.

Her eyes snapped to him, but no emotion betrayed her. "None," she replied. There was a long pause, and then she added, "Before you."

Speechless, Elric returned to studying the fire, folding his knees and resting his hands on them, watching the dancing embers. *None before you.* He had been the first man she gave herself to willingly. He had not been mistaken, then, for what he felt from her—that she had wanted him as badly as he did her—and while it was a relief, it terrified him all the more.

"It is like you said," she continued slowly, and though he dared not look at her, he felt her stare brand his skin. "Sometimes the idea of something, the dream of it, is power. You offered me the freedom, the safety to seize what has never been mine. You asked me and gave me the choice, and in doing so allowed me to claim something I only ever imagined. And for fear of sounding ridiculous, I will not thank you for it. But you deserve to know what you have helped return to me."

Elric straightened and turned, and at the vulnerability billowing in the waves of her unnaturally bright eyes, glistening in the flickering firelight, his voice caught in his throat. "It was my pleasure, Your Grace," he choked out, sketching a good-natured bow, but when he straightened, he met her gaze earnestly. "But you must know, you have always deserved the choice."

Returning to the fire, the riot of emotions in his chest stole all the words he tried to gather for a change of conversation, but before he could settle his thoughts, Graecerys spoke again.

"How long has it been? For you?" she asked, and he heard her glass scrape the wood.

He drained his with a humorless laugh. "Do you really wish to discuss my dead lover mere moments after you were taking my—"

"Yes, in fact, I do," she interrupted, and he was surprised to look up and see a slight pink flush to her cheeks.

"Why?" he asked, leveling her with a stare. "Is it a truth for a truth? You have confided in me, now I must trust you?"

"No," she said quickly. "I only wish to understand…why."

"Why what?"

"Why now?" And then she quietly added, "And why with me?"

He watched her carefully loop stitch after stitch. There it was. Her weakness. He had longed to see it, but now that he did, he despised its sight. He didn't want her to fear the rejection, the regret of something she had wanted—something delicate that she had finally held and given for herself, fierce as it was. He wanted to feel her warmth, and he wanted her to burn and glow with the hold she had on him, however fleeting it may be.

"Because…you are nothing like her," he replied softly. "You make me feel things that I did not know I was capable of feeling. My first love, she was safety and promise and the sweetness of home, but you? You infuriate me. You challenge me. And I masochistically crave the chase, the battle, even when I lose. You dare me to dance with fire when I hardly entertain matches."

Her eyes widened a fraction, then she cleared her throat. "You do not have to flatter me. It is okay to admit if I was no more than an itch to be scratched."

Elric rose to his knees before her, resting his hands over hers and stilling her work. He felt her small jolt, saw the surprise in her eyes, but it was the race of her pulse under his fingers when she searched his face that whispered the truth of her feelings despite the dismissive words.

"I hoped it might be," he admitted. "In truth, I feared I would become your regret. But while my grief feels like a scar I have torn open, trust me when I say I would do it all again. I have no regrets, but you have my apology for acting thoughtlessly as a man and forgetting who I am—who you are."

Graecerys searched his face, looking to find something, though he was unsure what. He did not move, did not look away, he only watched her and wondered what she was thinking.

After a moment, she straightened and moved her hands to rest atop his, leaning forward, and leveling him with a stare. "Do not apologize for what you do not regret. When did you ever last allow yourself to be free?"

Her eyes pierced him to his very heart, and Thrones help him, he wanted her again.

But he could not let that happen.

It would not happen. Not ever again.

"I'm not made for freedom," he replied with a tired smile. "Tethered, remember?"

"That's right," she said slowly, setting the shirt aside and slipping off the table to stand beside his kneeling form. "If you are bound to me, then you have no choice but to do as I command."

Crooking a finger, she beckoned him to stand, but even with the heat flaring in his veins once more, Elric was never one to listen to her too quickly. He took his time rising, and when he stood before her, she simply held his hand and led him to the cot.

"Lie down," she ordered, and he did so with slight confusion. To his shock, she pulled the blankets up to his shoulder and then sat on the bed by his side. Pulling her knees up beneath her dress, she reached out and began to run her fingers through his hair.

His eyes drifted shut in an instant. "I do not— I don't understand what is wrong with me," he admitted, more to himself than anyone else. "Why I crave sleep so."

"You are sated and you require rest," she replied softly. "So take it. I will keep watch. Allow yourself this night."

His breathing became even, his limbs leaden, sinking into the mattress, but in one last moment of weakness before he fell asleep, he whispered, "Thank you, Grace."

"Grace?" she said, her tone conveying a rare smile. "That is new."

"It will be my nickname for you," he murmured, words slurring.

"And what, pray tell, is a nickname? Is it another way of the stars?"

"It was something taught to me by a dear friend. A name given to those closest to us. One that says 'I care about you' in a single word."

His heart panged with the memory. Another time, another place, another loss of a different sort of pain, but it slipped from his mind as deftly as Graecerys's fingers slid through his hair.

"Sleep," she whispered. And when he was certain she had convinced herself he was asleep, she added, "Elric."

His name on her tongue was a sin. And though he denied it, it was one his soul demanded over and over again. And it was the last thing he heard before he fell into a deep sleep.

CHAPTER THIRTY-TWO

When Elric opened his eyes next, the sun was high in the sky, shining through the windows of the cabin and illuminating the world around them. Graecerys was cordial, though a hint of awkwardness lingered between them, and when they embarked across the drifts of snow and he reached for her hand, he could have sworn her cheeks reddened more than it had under the shock of the frigid air. Just as how he found himself sweating from nerves, despite the cold.

His dhust was easily accessible, and though he did not dare touch the strand responsible for shifting his form, he did play around with his elemental magic, sliding the snow back and forth in front of them to clear a small path.

They walked all day, the sun slowly dipping in the sky without another cabin in sight, but when Elric glanced to the mountains, he noticed they were farther away. "Are we traveling off course? Or are the mountains somehow moving?"

"Believe it or not, it is the mountains, not us," Graecerys replied, her breathing labored with the effort of trudging through the snow. It was becoming increasingly packed down—firmer to stand upon—and when Elric took another step and slid, he realized it was gradually sloping downward and hardening into ice.

"We are drawing closer to the coast," Graecerys said, her words filled with what sounded a lot like dread.

"You are concerned about what we will find there?"

She thought a moment, then shook her head. "No, I believe the people there are safe. And none at the palace would know to come here, save the eldest lords."

Awareness dawned in Elric's mind. "We are going to the province manor. Who is the lord over it?"

"There is none," she answered simply, and when he looked at her questioningly, she dropped his hand and began to walk ahead of him.

"How is there a manor, a province, with no lord over it?" he asked, falling into step behind her.

"It had one once. It has just been some time since they resided over it."

"And you said the people in this province all live within the manor?"

"There are not many, but yes. Stonestide Manor governs the land from the sea to the northernmost reaches of Obarian, at the end of the Trifolium Mountain range. There are cabins, should any travel for scouting or, in the olden days, for defense, but now the people simply reside in the manor and tend to the home and grounds."

Elric picked up his pace to match hers, but when he opened his mouth to speak again, a sharp whistle pierced the air.

Graecerys stopped in her tracks, and Elric halted at her side, dhust collecting in his palm and leaving behind the hilt of a sword. Before he could raise it, she rested a hand on his wrist and lifted a single finger to her lips. She looked around, and he did the same, though he was not sure what he was looking for.

And then he spotted them.

Two horses, unbridled, one sable and the other dark bay—

their long manes rippling and their thick, satin coats glistening in the twilight—galloped across the field far in the distance to their right. The air fogged about them, their snorts and exhalations creating small clouds that only enhanced their ethereal majesty against the endless landscape. Elric wasn't sure when his mouth dropped open, but he shut it quickly, shaking his head in wonder.

"Wild horses. Well, now I have seen it all."

He looked at Graecerys, but she continued to stare at their shadows fading in the distance, and when she blinked, a single tear slid down her cheek.

"Are you well?" Elric asked quietly, slight worry striking him that, of all the things he had seen her face, it was the sight of horses that visibly broke her.

She cleared her throat, nodded, then resumed her walk without a word.

They continued in silence until the sun vanished from sight. The temperature plunged, the sky almost fully night, and though a small breeze blew, what sounded like a roaring wind filled the air. Elric nearly asked if he should attempt to get them to another cabin to avoid spending the night in the snow, when he spotted a large, dark shape that appeared to be floating on the horizon, the land flattening perfectly behind it, leaving nothing but stars and the night.

"Stonestide Manor," Graecerys breathed, and her voice quivered, though her body did not. "We are almost there."

The closer they drew, the flatter, harder, and less snow- and ice-covered the land became. The roaring sound grew louder; however, there was an ebb and flow to it—the echoing howl fading into a crash that reached its crescendo, then diminished as gracefully as it rose.

It was when they reached a stone courtyard, blown over with a fine layer of frost, that Elric finally spotted lamps before the manor. And in the lamplight, shadows.

Graecerys stopped suddenly, turning around, but before Elric could ask what was wrong, the voice of an older male carried across the night. "Who goes there?"

Elric grasped her arm. "Why do I feel as though this is a mistake?"

Graecerys shook her head. "It is not. But that does not make it any easier."

The man was walking toward them now, his lamp held high. "Travelers do not come this far and live," he said curiously. "State your business, and know that if it is nefarious, I come armed."

"We are travelers," Elric replied carefully, realizing he did not know what to say. "We seek refuge."

"Refuge from what? And why?" the man asked, his steps slowing and his hand drifting to the sheath at his side.

Graecerys took a deep breath and turned. "Hello, Hubart."

The man stopped dead in his tracks, the lantern slipping from his hand and hitting the stone, though it somehow stayed upright, neither breaking nor extinguishing. "Grae... Graecerys?"

She strode toward him, both the man and Elric rooted to their spots, for what seemed like vastly different reasons, and when she finally stood before him—the man easily towering a head over her—she bent to pick up the lantern and held it aloft between them.

Hubart's face was old, pale, and wrinkled, his mustache almost entirely hiding his upper lip, but his eyes were bright green under bushy gray brows. They were wide in shock, but shone with hope, and when the light illuminated Graecerys fully, he broke into a smile that soon fell into a laugh, tumbling out of him with the tears streaming down his face.

"My dear girl," he cried, cupping her cheeks and then embracing her.

She wrapped her free arm around him, relaxing into the man's embrace in a way Elric had never seen her do before.

When they finally parted, Hubart took the lantern from her and lifted it, squinting at Elric. "And who might this be?"

"Hubart, this is my advisor, Elric. He…he is Isteriaeth."

Elric stepped forward, and the man's jaw fell slack. He first extended a hand, then resorted to dipping his head in an awkward bow, but Elric accepted his hand, shaking it firmly. "I am pleased to meet you, though I am unsure why you bowed to me and not the queen."

The words registered with shock on Hubart's face, but before he could bow, Graecerys laid a hand on his arm. "Don't you dare. I'm sure you have a lot of questions, and I will answer them, but for now we must get inside. It has been…a long journey."

Hubart shook his head in disbelief. "That does not feel adequate enough for the story I'm certain you will be sharing. Let's get you both warm and fed, and then after Arlys has her way with you, we will find where to begin."

He put his arm around Graecerys, guiding her to the manor. She wrapped her arm around his waist in return but turned back to Elric.

Their eyes met, his wordlessly asking question after question, and the look she returned was knowing, but filled with fledgling emotion, barely in check. She extended her hand back to him, and he moved to walk by her side, though he did not take it.

They reached the entrance to the manor, its large, rounded door thicker than any Elric had seen at the palace, and when they entered, he was shocked to find that despite the stone walls, the entire building was warm as any intimate home might be.

Graecerys looked around the entryway, taking in the walls, the floors, and he watched her draw in a deep breath not unlike those she did after her nightmares, and when she released it, it was anything but steady.

"Grace," Elric murmured for her ears only. "These people, this place. What are they to you?"

She hesitated, then reluctantly met his eyes. "This is my childhood home."

A short, stout woman with soft silver curls close about her head ran into the room, freezing in her steps and slapping a hand over her heart. Her face broke into sobs and though she tried to stumble forward, she sank to the floor instead. Graecerys strode to her with all the poise of a queen, then met her on the floor and wrapped her arms around her shoulders.

"Graecerys, my child," the woman cried. "My sweet, beautiful child."

"Hello, Arlys," Graecerys replied, pulling back far enough for the woman to grasp her face.

"Let me look at you, let me look at you. My dear, you look so much like them. How I never thought I'd live to see this day."

Graecerys did not reply, instead squeezing the woman tightly. It was then that she spotted Elric and her eyebrows shot up. "And you have brought home a king?"

"NO!"

"No, no!"

Graecerys glanced back to Elric, eyes narrowed as his wide stare met hers, both of them speaking too quickly at once. "He is my advisor," she replied. "An Isteriaeth."

Arlys looked between them, her gaze lingering just slightly too long on Elric, and when it returned to Graecerys, a mischievous smile wrinkled the skin around her eyes. "We can discuss that later. For now, allow me to show you to your rooms."

The staircase was square, not unlike the ones at the palace, though the manor was only two stories tall. At the top, they had the choice to go either right or left down the length of the building, and it was here that Arlys turned to Grace.

"Graecerys, dear, we have not changed anything…since. I would be more than happy to freshen up the main suite, if you would be more comfortable there. Unless you would prefer your old—"

"The guest quarters are fine," Graecerys replied quickly, turning her back on the right wing of the hall. "The adjacent ones, with the washroom in between. I…I suffer from night terrors and would prefer to keep Master Elric close. In case I am in need of his help to calm my nerves."

The older woman glanced out of the corner of her eye, her stare traveling up and down Elric slowly. "And just what sort of power does he possess?"

"Arlys," Graecerys hissed, but the woman merely winked at Elric and started down the corridor. "I will have the staff prepare the rooms for when you are done eating. And yes, you will be eating. Your face is too thin, and I do not want to think of the last honest meal you had. You may change in the washrooms." She paused, looking between Graecerys and Elric before hesitating once more. "Master Elric, I fear finding suitable clothing for you will be difficult, as our men run quite tall. But Graecerys, I am certain your mother's dresses will fit you. Unless…."

Graecerys was silent, grasping onto the rail with white knuckles, though she kept her posture at ease.

"I can summon a few of your dresses now that we are settled," Elric said to her, drawing Arlys's curiosity.

"No. No, I think I will be fine. I should like to see— On second thought, yes, Elric, just one for now. Something comfortable, if you do not mind."

Elric paused a moment, then with dhust tumbling from his palms, he pulled a long, light-green gown—fitted in the bodice, yet full in the skirt—and the gold-trimmed dressing gown in a shade of teal so rich it made her eyes and hair seem radiant. He handed them to Graecerys, and she took them, frowning.

"Why these?" she asked him, the recognition in her eyes showing she also recalled wearing it the night they met—the night he was bled to near death and bound to her.

"All else were ballgowns or the worn dresses you wore for training. I…thought you might be best comfortable in these."

"Atmospheric dhust," Arlys breathed. "I have not seen that strand since I was but a wee thing."

Elric gaped at the woman. "You saw dhust? You knew Isteriaeth?"

The woman shook her head sadly. "I saw it from a distance, in the final few Isteriaeth imprisoned. Such beauty to be so used and destroyed. I am sorry for all you have lost, but I am grateful to have you here beneath this roof. It would honor the lady of the house to know."

Graecerys slipped past the woman, carrying her clothes down the hall to the left and disappearing inside a door on the right.

Arlys sighed, then turned back to Elric. "There is another washroom down this way. Are you able to send for your own clothing?"

"I am, Lady Arlys, thank you. Please, lead the way."

The woman walked down the corridor to the right, considerably farther down than Graecerys had walked, and after passing a series of doors, they reached a long wall devoid of rooms. Lanterns illuminated the space, but what served to shine a light on the portrait that hung there were the windows directly across from it that allowed the night sky in.

Elric stopped before it, his breath catching in his chest at the image of the woman staring back at him. She wore a pale-ivory gown with billowing sleeves and a high, lace neckline. Her hair was a red-stained gold, but her deep eyes, strong jaw, and proud yet gentle smile were all things so intimately familiar to him now.

"The lady of the house," Arlys said softly with admiration in her voice, coming to stand beside him.

"She is beautiful," Elric said reverently.

"She truly was."

Elric hesitated at the truth he had already guessed. "Was?"

"I'm afraid she has departed this plane. You see, she is Graecerys's dearly loved mother. The Lady Auriana."

The air caught in Elric's chest, the name gripping him and threatening to shake the air from his lungs.

"*Auriana?*"

"Why yes, did you know her?"

Elric stared at the portrait, shaking off the jolt the memory sent through his body. "I did not. But I knew someone with that name once. A dear friend."

"A strong Obarian name at that. Though none carried it with such grace as the lady."

Elric paused, his mind reaching for an answer that lurked just out of his grasp. "Graecerys's father. He was the lord of this manor. Of the province."

"He was," confirmed Arlys. "When the throne was overturned from within, the seated lords voted for him to take the crown—to lead the kingdom."

"Why then do you refer to her as the lady of the house and not queen?"

"Lady Auriana was never crowned. But that is not something we discuss out of respect for the family, for who they are to us and what they are to the kingdom. We cared for them then, and we always shall. They are ours to protect." She stopped, studying him. "Did Graecerys never mention any of this?"

Elric shook his head. "She has not, though admittedly we have not always gotten along. I would not have expected her to share such intimate knowledge with me."

Arlys sighed. "I understand, but I must say, it concerns me. Graecerys…."

Elric looked at the woman, but she seemed to be grasping for words she could not find. When she noticed Elric's eyes on her, she smiled sadly. "She has endured much. I fear the reason she is here now and I worry for her future, but I am glad to see that she is in your company, amicable or not."

"It is my honor, Lady Arlys," Elric said, realizing that he truly meant the words. "And know, on my life, that Graecerys will always be safe with me."

He took one long, lingering look at the portrait, and before walking away, he whispered, "I promise."

$\mathscr{E}$lric did not know what time Hubart showed him to his quarters later that evening, only that he was asleep before his head hit the feather pillow. He awoke midway through the night, drenched in sweat, and upon stripping off the shirt he slept in, he did not open his eyes again until dawn.

He stared at the ceiling now, on a comfortable bed with fresh sheets and blankets, in a warm room, trying to wrap his mind around the last…well, he truly didn't know how many days. Or weeks. Having taken a long and much-needed bath the night before, he dressed and readied for the day, then pulled back the curtains and surveyed the world beyond in awe.

The manor sat a considerable number of yards back from a straight, obsidian rock cliff face, and beyond the cliffs was nothing but wide, open ocean. They truly had walked clear to the coast, and the mountains in the near distance to his left confirmed that they were at the further reaches of Obarian.

Somewhere on the other side of the water, just east of the northernmost shores of Tauriellis, was Inflamel—his home. And somewhere beyond the visible mountains to his left stood an abandoned Keep, and deep within the remnants of the past, the four Trifolium Thrones.

A soft knock on his door startled him from his thoughts, and when he crossed the room to open it, he was unsurprised to find Graecerys standing on the other side. She wore a simple black gown with long sleeves and a high neck, its delicate lace accents and ruffles giving it an elegant air despite its practicality. He realized then he had only ever seen her in bright tones, but there was something breathtaking about her in darker hues. Her hair was plaited in a braid down her back, but already strands had blown free, as if she had been outside and back that morning.

"May I come in?" she asked politely.

"You are still queen," he reminded her. "If you wish to enter, you enter."

She considered his words silently, and when he stepped aside, she walked in, immediately crossing the room to look out the window over the water. "I suppose you discovered how Stonestide was given its name," she said, turning back to face him.

"I did, though I am afraid I underestimated the proximity when you said the manor sat along the coast."

A small smile crossed her face but failed to reach her eyes. "There is a path cut into the cliffs that leads to the sand. We might walk down there, if you would like, though I understand if not. The sea holds painful memories for us both."

Elric watched her, surveying her intently and wondering the depths of her painful memories. How much did she truly hide behind the layers of protection she'd girded herself with as queen? Who was Graecerys, truly?

"I cannot say I have ever seen snow meet the sea," he replied. "The idea of it is, well, curious to me."

A smile broke out across her face, and though she tried to keep it reserved, it proved to be hard for her. He took her in:

the slight swelling of her eyelids; the dark circles cradling them; the way her very being was at ease, bleeding into her posture with a quiet, gentle confidence. And he realized just how much weight she truly carried. How tortured she was by the things she left unsaid. How he had never seen her this close to happy.

"There is not much to do here, and for that I apologize. But I might show you around," she added, stepping closer to him. "There are some rooms I cannot bring myself to enter yet, but I...I have missed this place. And I am glad you are with me. I don't know why, but it makes it all easier to face."

Elric swallowed, knowing how difficult it was for her to admit that, but also unsettled by how much it meant to him to hear it. "Your seriousness is terrifying, Your Grace. Surely you have something to insult me for this morning?"

Graecerys's smile vanished and she glared at him.

The sight transferred the grin to Elric's lips. "That is more like it. Thank you."

She exhaled sharply, looking to the ceiling. "Come along. Arlys has prepared breakfast, and she does not take kindly to food growing cold on the table."

It took longer than Elric expected to follow Graecerys down the beaten path, only wide enough for a single-file line. It was slick in spots, but she had been right in saying that the softer-soled boots she offered him gripped well. It was when the ground leveled and they stood upon the expanse of sand that his breath caught in his throat.

The ground in the direct shadow of the rock was covered in a fine layer of frost that crunched underfoot with each step. Then, midway to the water, it ended, curving in edges that reflected the places where the ocean had stretched on the shore.

But it was the colors, the view, that stole his breath. The sky was a soft blue, the lightest thing, though grayed over to dull the reflection and ease his eyes. And the diamond snow seamlessly melting into warm linen sand defied even the most uncanny of wonders in his mind. They should not exist together, the thought of both stirring the exact opposite vision, and yet there they were. A contradiction, but somehow perfect.

But all of it paled in comparison to the ocean that sprawled out before him. The deep teal waves crested, marbling into brighter shades as they rolled back into the sea, tumbling like pearls along its surface, then chasing the frills of white foam over the sand to kiss the snow before dancing away once more.

And at the center of it all, growing smaller as she walked on, was a woman in a thick black gown, more at home against the water-darkened rocks than the fair ground or bold, jewel waves. But even then, she did not fit, her long scarlet hair whipping from its restraint, over her shoulder and into the wind like a pennant of fire, a stream of garnet signaling the power and strength that followed her.

He was discovering that she, too, was a contradiction. She was like an ever-resilient rose, blooming in defiant spite of the ice encasing the world around her, wild even within the confines of the palace walls. Velvet-soft but armed to the teeth with the fiercest thorns, she was fair, yet deadly. Beautiful to gaze upon, but perilous to hold.

And as he stood on the snow and she on the sand, they also stood in perfect tension—a paradox, drawing closer to one another the harder they tried to push apart. He wanted to be rid of her, to be free, but even now he could admit that the thought of life without her seemed too quiet. Like an ocean with no waves.

"You can come closer," she turned and shouted, her voice dancing with the crash and froth of the tide on the shore.

"I am not sure," Elric called back, observing the way her ears, her cheeks, the tip of her nose were a darkened shade of pink. "It is cold enough without the water reaching me."

"There are incredible health benefits to a dip in a frigid pool, you know," she replied, catching strands of hair and pulling them across her forehead, back behind her ear.

Elric took one glance at the waves and shook his head again.

"At least reach the sand," she said firmly, a smile toying on her lips. "It is the best part."

Elric sighed and walked gingerly along the snow, pausing beside her when he finally reached the sand. It was surprisingly firm underfoot, easy for him to navigate in boots. Not like the heavy, thick churn that covered him in both dust and clumps in his memory, stuck inside his mouth and eyes and ears, burning his nose, bringing him to choke on the water that was not devoid of it enough to wash him clean.

"Join me," Graecerys said beside him, and before he knew what was happening, she had slipped out of her boots.

"Now I am certain you are mad," he replied, judging her with his stare.

"Maybe I am," she agreed, tugging her socks off. "But if I must touch the water, you shall as well. Now come on, boots off."

"I despise the water," Elric hissed. "I have no desire to touch it, thank you."

A sudden sadness filled her eyes, and she straightened, gazing out over it, then back at him again. "I apologize. I did not mean to dredge up poor memories. I simply...." She stared at it once more, and this time she didn't look away. "The farther I stray from the palace, the more strange I feel. Things I thought I believed seem far away, and things I thought were dreams and memories feel...."

She stopped, grasping for a word. "*Real*. They feel real and a part of me. And the sight of the ocean…. I believe I missed this. Or maybe I only missed the point of it before. It is bigger than me, more mysterious, with secrets too deep for us to ever know. And while that is terrifying, while it stole what I cannot get back, I find it easy to pretend that it is endless. It silences my head and my thoughts surrender to something I cannot surmount. Something I do not have to conquer. It is power, unmatched and vast, but it is also delicate and beautiful. It is proof that there can be both. That they can exist beside one another."

Elric watched her in awe, every layer of her words falling into his mind in waves of their own. "It is not the only thing," he said quietly, and though he didn't think he could be heard over the sea, Graecerys turned and looked at him with surprised eyes.

He sighed, then bent over to unlace and slip out of his boots. The ground was frigid and moist underfoot, but when he stepped forward, he understood what she meant. It glittered, shells of all shapes and sizes peeking up from the sand, slowly being freed by the tide rolling back and forth above them. The sand itself was grooved in shadowy, serpentine channels and divots, but the diamond-shaped pattern of the hidden treasures within made it look ethereal. So much so that Elric failed to brace himself for the water that touched his feet.

He gasped, jumping back and gulping in air. "It— It is freezing."

Graecerys covered her lips with the back of her hand, looking away to contain her smile.

No, not just a smile. She was *laughing* at him.

"I'm so glad I can be of amusement to you," he fired at her, rushing to pull his socks and boots back on.

She turned and walked down the sand parallel to the water, still laughing, but not before calling over her shoulder, "It is not a crime to steal a moment of happiness. What more do we truly have to lose?"

The weight of a memory slammed into Elric, seizing his breath and causing him to drop his laces and kneel upon the sand.

Would you not steal a moment of joy?

He had said those words before. What felt like an eternity ago, before loss cut him down at the knees and life marched on around him. When he had stolen those moments with Kathrina, who he knew inside and out without thinking or speaking. And now, in the silence, he realized that the details of her were washing away, like the frost on the sand. It had been slow at first but now…there was only so much he could hold on to.

What had her laugh sounded like? He could no longer hear it in his mind. And her eyes. He did not remember their exact shade. Had she truly smelled of lilacs? Or was that all that had remained with him when he left her in the ground? Would she have loved the sea as much as he did the sky? If it had been the other way, had their places been exchanged, would she have forgotten him already too?

He allowed his face to fall, and the pain to wash over him. He almost wished the water would rise to lift and carry him out to sea. But then those memories rushed back in, filling the small space around him too quickly and sloshing over his ears before dashing his world to pieces. But in that, everything came full circle. His past, those first cuts delivered by this very land and this ocean, were the reason he'd had the strength to survive his grief of losing Kathrina—he had already drowned once and survived.

Cold fingers rested on his wrist, and he jolted, opening his eyes to meet Graecerys's wide, endless gaze where she knelt before him.

Another contradiction—the woman in his heart against the

woman consuming his thoughts. One the calm, the other the storm. And somehow, he was finding parts of himself in both.

"I avoided this place for a reason," she said slowly, firmly. "This manor is a constant reminder of the greatest losses of my life, and I could not face them. But now that I am here, I realize it was foolish of me to deprive myself of what used to bring me so much comfort."

"Why are you telling me this?" Elric asked, his eyes searching hers.

"I thought you should know. So you do not face your loss alone either. I understand now what I missed. It was grief either way, but it never needed to be alone."

Elric swallowed, words failing him, and when Graecerys stood, she faced the sea once more. "Walking or standing?"

Elric rose and inhaled deeply, taking in the beauty again, letting the ebb and flow not drown his lungs with stringent water, but impart its cleansing strength—filling his cracks and letting him feel whole again, if only for a moment of fleeting peace.

He allowed his eyes to close and when he opened them again, with Graecerys quietly by his side, her own eyes shut and her face tipped toward the sky, he admitted the truth.

He did not hate her. He respected her, deeply. And while he knew he shouldn't, he found himself staring intently at the soft hairs—too short to stay restrained behind her ear—that quivered against her cheek in the breeze.

How would it feel to catch their strands between his fingers? What would it be like to see their fire curl against his skin, branding him with their mark like she had been a part of him all along? He could ask himself a million questions with no memory of an answer, or he could ask them anew.

"What else does Graecerys enjoy? Besides the ocean and the sky?"

She smiled, though her eyes remained closed, as if in a

dream. "Music. The only thing I love more than this place is a song that can carry me away."

"And have you been taught any music?"

She opened her eyes, her brow knit in concentration, and when she faced him, there was something unsettled within them once more. "I think so...but I do not remember."

CHAPTER THIRTY-FOUR

They spent the rest of the day walking along the shore, Graecerys finding and handing Elric shell after shell, and by the time they returned to the manor, he was wearing a satchel that he had summoned to carry them all.

It did not take long for her to guide him around the manor, showing him the expansive kitchen that resided beneath the house, its warmth rising through tunnels carved into the stone of the walls themselves to heat every room.

She avoided the wing to the right of the stairwell with deft care, and Elric did not pry, understanding full well from the night prior that it must be home to her childhood room and her parents' quarters. And though she was certainly wearing her mother's dresses—as the way she lovingly stroked the lace indicated—if she did not want to go there, he would not make her.

However, he was unable to shake the feeling that there was something more hidden within the manor. Too many things pricked at his memory, daring him to face his own darkness. Every time he asked Graecerys a question of her past, she was open and shared more than she ever would have before, yet she often failed to recall details. It seemed to concern her as much as it gave him pause, and while he wanted to believe it was a genuine lapse in memory, he couldn't bring himself to trust her implicitly.

She was still the queen responsible for the destruction of so many people, even if she was a woman trying to face past demons. Though he wanted to believe that she could not remember, he wondered if it was true, or if it was a ruse to protect herself. And if so, what she was hiding?

They sat at supper that night with Hubart and Arlys, the couple exchanging memories with Graecerys, who Elric watched in awe as she threw her head back and laughed with joy.

Unburdened by expectation and emotionless rule, she was changing before his very eyes. It was as if a curtain had been drawn back, and instead of admiring her through the gossamer veil, he was able to behold her true beauty, genuine and vibrant. And the warmth it awakened within terrified him more than the unknown ever could.

"Graecerys, dear, you must try to sleep," Arlys chided, watching her hide a yawn. "Do not think I did not hear you walking the house last night. I know that is when you retrieved your wardrobe."

Elric gazed at her, wondering how she managed to stay awake at all with how little she slept. She caught him watching, and at the small, reassuring smile he offered, she nodded. "I believe I will turn in. Goodnight, Arlys."

She pressed a kiss to Hubart's cheek, gave Arlys a hug, and then with one last glance at Elric, she slipped from the room.

Elric didn't realize he had continued to stare at the spot where she vanished until Hubart cleared his throat. He startled, catching sight of the couple exchanging glances, and in an effort to deflect the observation he was certain made him look like a forlorn puppy, he said, "She is different here."

"No, I'm afraid she is the same here," Hubart replied, his

mischief fading to a sad smile. "It just took her some time to remember it."

"Has she always struggled with her memory?"

Hubart laughed. "Far from it. She was a brilliant girl. Sharp-witted, observant, and very mature for her age. Always asking questions and giving the household a run. I do not doubt the loss of her mother changed her, but as for her memory, I cannot imagine it was dimmed."

"I have never seen her like this," Elric replied, more to himself than anyone at the table.

"That is because she changed when she left," said Arlys heavily, and Hubart laid his hand on hers, caressing the back of it.

"Changed?" Elric asked. "Changed how?"

The room grew quiet, and then finally Arlys replied. "I believe it was the palace that broke her spirit. I look at her now and it is as if everything about her has faded or been lost. I saw it the first time she returned as a child. She was but a ghost of herself. And then she did not return at all."

Elric turned in for the night, tired, but too restless to sleep. He discarded his vest, unbuttoning his sleeves and rolling them to his elbows, then sat on the chair before the small writing desk.

He thought a moment, long and hard, then reached for his strand of atmospheric magic, and the sapphire dhust unfurled. The book materialized in his hand, and as he leafed through it, he smiled. His page was still marked with his mother's notes, exactly where he had left off before.

Studying the words in his mother's handwriting, he wondered what the connection might be. The five-lined diagram alluded to the five strands of magic, yet the points of history and her carefully copied text about the Kollapsar forms led him to believe they had been the focus of her study.

Elric retrieved all three notes and carefully marked their original places in the tome before laying them out on the desk. There was a portion missing—whatever had come before the words "taken from within"—but all three had been written on the same piece of parchment.

Leaning back in his chair, unsure what to make of it, yet flooded with excitement at the revelation, Elric shut his eyes.

Axion, Vacare, Eoten, Hrotesk.

A host. Taken from within.

Had the Kollapsars been taken from within after they overthrew the Thrones, leaving Obarian to generation upon generation of Elérynd humans, all killing and seizing the throne endlessly? Or had his mother discovered something more? When had this been written?

Elric was so engrossed in thought that he almost did not hear the tapping on the washroom door, but when he did, he slid his chair back from the desk. "Enter."

The door clicked open, and Graecerys stepped in, closing it firmly at her back. His breath caught in his throat, and his jaw fell slack at the sight of her, standing before him in nothing but a silken slip the shade of soft-pink blooms, trimmed with hand-stitched lace. The straps on it were indecently thin, her shoulders practically bared to the night were it not for her hair, which hung soft and unbound. And when she walked toward him, her leg slid from the long slit in the skirt that extended well above her knee.

He cleared his throat, grasping for words. "What are you doing here?"

She shrugged. "I cannot sleep."

"Neither can I," he replied, turning back to his book for a desperate distraction. "So I am reading."

"More stories?" she asked, amusement in her tone.

"No, actually. I was researching the strands. For you."

Her brow furrowed. "For me?"

He hesitated, but pressed on, realizing she would wait for an answer regardless. "I have never had proper tutelage with my dhust. I am most comfortable with atmospheric, but the others and their odd blend of power are still strange to me. I was uncertain if there was a way to use them to keep your nightmares at bay. If there is not some way to break the hold this darkness seems to have on your memory."

The room grew so silent he almost dared not turn around, but when he did, the awestruck look on Graecerys's face stunned him. "I apologize if that is overstepping."

She shook her head slowly. "I have spent years sleeping only when I need, and mostly while the sun is highest in the sky in hopes that they would not find me. You are the first not to accept it as commonplace."

"I should not have been," Elric bit out, his words filled with venom. "You were failed, Graecerys. From the very start you were failed. I do not know your life before the crown, and I don't believe I want to as it will just serve to infuriate me more, but you deserved better. You still do."

She shook her head sadly. "That is where you are wrong. But I did not come here to argue with you."

Elric raised an eyebrow. "Then why are you here?"

She closed the space between them, placing her arms around his neck and sitting upon his lap. He hesitated, but the softness of her skin, the intoxicating rose scent of her hair, and how desperately his body craved her led him to wrap an arm around her and pull her closer. The skirt of her slip fell open, baring her leg, and he shook his head, resting a hand on her knee to ensure she did not fall.

"This is hardly appropriate," he whispered, afraid to be heard, though they were the only two on the second floor.

Graecerys shrugged, her nonchalance laying siege to his resolve. "Tell me to leave."

Danger. Each of his senses prompted the same warning, but

for some reason it only caused his hand to slip higher on her thigh.

"Tell me to stop," he replied, meeting her steel with iron. If she wanted to be stubborn, then two could play that game.

She tightened her arms about his neck, sliding her body perilously closer, and his grip formed small indentations on the skin of her thigh.

"No," she answered.

"Grace," he uttered in warning. "Tell me to stop."

"I will not."

"Say the words."

"I want this," she replied, fingers drifting into his hair, the opposite hand filled with the collar of his shirt. "I want you."

Dangerous. So dangerous. And yet...

He clenched his fingers and closed the final inch of space between them, locking her as tightly against his body as she had shackled him to her whim. "I will never forgive you," his voice rumbled. "The things you make me feel. They are all your fault."

"I'll take it," she breathed against his lips, into his soul. "Give me your hate. Give me everything."

"I do not hate you," he confessed.

She paused, drawing back ever so slightly to search his eyes, and then shook her head. "That is a mistake," she whispered, her lips brushing his with her words.

"Then it is mine to make," he replied, and when he wrapped his arms around her, she fell into his kiss.

It was different this time—not angry or violent, though desperate and starved all the same. There was a quiet defiance, neither willing to admit the truth about what was building between them, but also an understanding that in the end, it did not matter. And when Elric grabbed the hem of her gown and lifted it over her head, baring her completely before his eyes, he realized exactly how captive he was held by her.

He carried her to the bed and laid her down on the pillow,

stepping away just long enough to remove his clothing before easing onto the mattress above her.

She grasped his face, pulling him closer, and kissed him long and hard, but before he settled between her legs, he scooped her up and rolled, flipping their positions and allowing her to straddle his waist.

Her eyes widened at the control he had surrendered, and for the first time, she looked uncertain. He guided her slowly, showing her exactly how to command him, and it was no time at all before he was holding on to her hips as if it might do anything to stop him from coming apart entirely.

She cried his name as they both found release, and when she leaned down to kiss him once more with a proud and satisfied smile, he rolled her onto her side and tugged her close.

"Grace," he whispered, her name a prayer upon his lips.

"That is still not my name," she replied, smiling against his skin.

"But it is what you are to me," he rasped, leaning back far enough to stare into her eyes—to drown in her waves. "My grace, despite all odds, offered freely. A second chance. Graecerys may have been named for a throne, but Grace was born to show her people the way."

"You believe that," she all but whispered, searching his eyes. "After all you have lost, after what I and my people have done to you. After running across this Thrones-forsaken kingdom for our lives, you truly believe it."

The waves rose higher in her eyes, their churning darkness threatening to pull her away from him. It was too serious, too soon for what tenuous understanding they had. He was doomed by the weight of his own admission, it was certain to drag him under, but he shrugged it all away and kicked for shore. "I have no choice but to believe in you. I'll simply die if I don't."

She tipped her eyes to the ceiling and shoved him good-naturedly onto the mattress, rolling over and swinging her legs off the side of the bed. Her hair fell down her back, glittering like a waterfall of rubies between the soft peaks of her shoulder blades in the flickering lamplight. And though he was safely removed from her churning storm, the air was cold and he missed her comfort innately.

"Will you walk with me again tomorrow?" she asked, gathering her silk gown against herself and facing him.

Elric sat up and tipped his head, rolling his palm into his usual flourishing bow. "As you wish, Your Grace."

She shook her head, quickly turning and leaving—the washroom door latching behind her with a *click*. And if Elric didn't know any better, he could have sworn he saw her smile.

$\mathcal{I}$t was just past breakfast the next day when a storm descended upon the mountains, shrouding the cliff-side in a fog so thick Elric was unable to discern the difference between the sea and the sky.

And Graecerys was avoiding him.

She had taken her breakfast and later the midday meal in her room, and though dinner was now on the table, she was nowhere to be found.

"I sat with her a while this afternoon," Arlys said, still piling seconds on Elric's plate after he turned down another portion. And he was relieved for it because he was confident he could die inside the woman's pot pie and be content. "Physically she is well, though tired, but I fear many things have caught up with her now. She did not wish to talk about what ails her, she only wanted to reminisce—for me to tell her things she says she has forgotten."

Elric paused, his fork halfway to his lips, Graecerys's words on the beach and the look in her eyes returning to him. *I do not remember.*

Arlys had also stopped clearing the table, standing beside it with dish in hand and staring at a stain on the linen. "Master Elric," she said finally, "if I were to ask you what transpired at the palace...what brought you here...would you tell me honestly?"

Elric took a steady breath. "There is much I do not understand fully, but what I do know are things I would not dare repeat to you."

"I am an old woman," she blustered, forcing a small smile. "There is not much you could tell me that I have not already seen and heard in my lifetime. I did not always live away from the world. I have not always known peace."

Elric set his fork down, making sure it did not clink against the china, then met her eyes. "A girl so young had no right to be in a place so cold. As for our arrival, well, her people rose against her and sought to overthrow her. An attempt was made on her life, and though the man she held responsible was guilty of much, he did not commit the crime. Rather than face treason, he made a move on my life, and in return she ended his by wielding my dhust. The people attacked, many in her own army turned on her, and we fled."

Arlys was pale when she set down the dish, rubbing the place over her heart. "That is not her. Her father...he did lose himself. He was lost even to us. But her mother raised her."

Elric shook his head sadly. "She is not the same girl you knew. But I believe she may be trying to find her once more."

Arlys nodded, reassured by his words. "That is what I felt in my heart. But I fear what she hides that has forced her to abandon so much. Who would do such harm? Why would anyone break a child?"

Elric stared at the table, his pulse racing, the childhood memories he held locked deep inside his own mind rattling the bars of their prison.

"All goodness, anything worthy of redemption, left this

kingdom with the stars," Arlys said finally. "All we have known and embraced since is darkness."

Darkness. Hunger.

Belonging. Loss.

Pain. Resolve.

The pattern of his childhood.

How closely did Graecerys's match his own?

Elric's heart beat out of rhythm, and he rose from the table. "I fear the weather is paining my head. Allow me to help you clear and I shall turn in for the night."

Arlys laid a hand on his arm instead. "No, my dear, have your rest. I should have thought what this conversation would do to you. I know I am not responsible, and my word cannot mean much, but I am sorry for all you have prevailed against. I am sorry for what you have lost. And I am sorry that so much of it came from Graecerys's hand. Obarian has failed its children, both of this realm and from the stars. And I fear we are destined to collapse upon the bed we have made."

Elric swayed on his feet, tightness gripping his chest. A burn tickled his throat and eyes as he processed her words. All knew, yet none had ever paused to recognize his painful history, let alone apologized for it. Maybe the acknowledgement was something he had not realized he longed to hear. The admission that he had never been at fault in a world that stacked every odd against him before he drew his first breath. Perhaps being seen, even without full understanding, was simple enough to disrupt the pattern with a final cycle.

Endure. Live.

"Thank you, Arlys," he replied, his voice breaking.

The woman smiled, then brushed her tears away hurriedly and picked up the dish, disappearing into the scullery without another word.

Elric remained standing, alone, absorbing the weight her kindness had lifted from his shoulders, yet somehow feeling it split his heart at the same time. He made it to the second floor, nearly overcome by his emotions, when an old, familiar sound stopped him in his tracks.

The world froze around him, silencing not only his mind, but his heart as well, threatening to rip out the bars that imprisoned his deepest, most hidden memories. Before he could stop himself, he followed it down the hall.

He reached the room at the end, the last on the right, and stopped. Gentle *plinks* drifted under the door and he grasped the handle, pushing it open. Graecerys sat on a bench before a piano, her silhouette illuminated by the lamp flickering on the wall beyond, and she softly ran a finger over the ivory, one key at a time. She caught sight of him, turned on the bench to face him, and wiped her eyes quickly.

Elric stepped into the room, breathlessly looking between her and the piano. The cage containing the final broken piece of his past, the only memory he had failed to confront, crumbled to dust, and he uttered the five most terrifying words he had ever spoken. "Who am I to you?"

Graecerys shook her head, defeat in her eyes. "Another person whose life I have destroyed."

He startled from his trancelike state—the past growing dim, then vanishing—and looked about the room, at the shelves and the light-pink rug that the instrument sat upon. "Whose room is this?"

"It was my mother's," she said, smiling sadly. "She spent almost every morning and evening here. Even after she grew too sick, too weak for her hands to find the right notes. She had her bed moved there." She nodded to the opposite wall across the room, and when she met Elric's eyes once more, the tears began to fall. "This is where she died."

Elric stepped toward her, slowly, and she rested an elbow wearily on the wood bar where a music book sat, its pages coated in dust.

"How much of your memory is lost?" he asked quietly.

"Too much," she replied, brushing her eyes with her wrist. She wore a simple gown of deep wine, with sleeves that stretched over her knuckles. Small buttons were fastened the full length of the front, up the bodice, stopping at the scoop neckline where a chain was tucked inside.

"Is it why the nightmares follow you?" he added gently, and she nodded.

"Is it her loss that haunts you?" he asked, coming to kneel before her.

"It is darkness," she whispered. "No matter the dream, it finds me. It steals the beauty away and whispers that I am undeserving of it, but that *it* can hold me instead. My life is nothing but threads of shadow stealing my past and choking all that would comfort me. And that is not even the worst part. I used to fear it, to fight it, but now I believe it is right. Why should I sleep soundly when so many do not because of me? Because of who and what I am, and what I could not stop?

"But it no longer stays there. The fear, the torment, the pain, sometimes I see it all with my waking eyes. Each time it takes hold a little more, until I become weak and open my hands to allow it further in. I sink deeper and deeper, and I fear I am too far lost now. I wait for the day it will take me whole. When I will never come back from it again. They said my father died of madness. I did not believe it then, but this? I am not losing my mind alone. It is not enough for it to steal my mind. It will not rest until it consumes all of me."

Elric stared at her, horror pricking his skin with ice-cold talons. "How long have you fought this alone?"

"Since I was a child. Since—" Her voice broke off, and though he was desperate to know what haunted her so readily that she could speak of darkness but not recall the past, he did not press.

"I failed everyone I loved and then moved on to fail those

who hate me," she said, wringing her hands as tears welled in her eyes. "It is as if every step of my life was laid before me to be lost, to shatter me, and it has won. I am broken, irreparably so, and losing the will to fight because I know I am all too deserving of this fate. You were right to say that life is waves of loss, but I cannot face them any longer. I wish they would let me drown."

"I said there are waves of give and take, loss and gift," Elric said gently, rising to his feet and taking Graecerys's hand. "Not all waves are deadly."

"They are if it is all you can see. If you are unable to swim to the shore, if you cannot remember where to find it. And I am tired of fighting."

He watched her, powerless to change her belief, unable to ease the pain, but desperate to comfort her. He reached out and tipped her chin up, meeting tear-stained eyes that clenched his heart. "Did you have any other choice?"

She searched his face. "What?"

"The losses you suffered. The betrayal you blame yourself for. The pain you shouldered and carried all through your life. Was there ever any other choice? Were you independent enough to escape, or capable of turning away from it? Did you embrace it wholeheartedly and adopt the darkness as your own? Or did you do the best you could as a child trapped in a life that could offer you no more?"

She sucked in air, her tears falling in earnest, and shook her head. "There was no other choice. I tried, but there was nothing I could do. I did not know what else to do."

Elric nodded, bringing her to her feet and cupping her face, his own tears falling. "I would do anything to spare you this, but I cannot fix it or take it away. Yet I can and will stay beside you. You do not need to face it alone. It is okay to mourn what was stolen from you."

The resounding truth choked the words even as they left his

mouth, breaking Elric as much as Graecerys who crumpled in his arms. They both faced a brutal acceptance, standing before themselves with a lifetime of losses in the chasm between. And in the brokenness, they were finally learning how to reach a hand across and comfort the children they once were.

The youth they had sacrificed for survival.

The jagged pieces they pasted together to form the adults they were now.

The realities they had been powerless to prevent.

The things they could not change.

He held her tighter, closer while his own tears fell in earnest. "It's all right," he whispered, as much to himself as to her. "It will be all right."

Something jabbed into his chest, a sharp point of what felt like a needle, causing him to pull back, and when he did, Graecerys's chain hung between them, the pendant on the end stuck to his vest.

"I'm sorry," she hurried, fingers fumbling with it. "The pin must have come unclasped."

Elric looked down, realizing in the dim light that it was not a pendant, but a brooch that hung from the chain, and when it fell back against her dress, the sight of it brought his world to a standstill.

It was a brilliant blue stone, with a long, five-pointed white star on it and small diamonds surrounding it like a constellation holding together the sky for the one their world centered around. He would recognize it anywhere. It had been his mother's favorite.

"Some wonders are too precious to meet, and you, my dear, are one of them. Do not go where the stars cannot find you, and remember, I love you with my whole life."

His mother's final words to him resounded in his ears, his heart exploding into painful daggers that flayed open his heart. He stumbled back, hearing himself screaming and begging for her to stay, feeling her favorite shawl pressed into his arms, a small pack wrapped around his body, and her brooch tucked into his fist.

"Where did you get that brooch?" he demanded, chest heaving.

Graecerys's eyes went wide, and she clutched it, blocking it from his view. "I— I found it."

"*Where?*" he snapped, rising to his feet. "Or shall I ask *in what?*"

"What do you mean in—"

"Was it in a satchel?" he yelled.

Graecerys's eyes flared wide and she braced a hand on her stomach. "Why would you ask if it was in a satchel?"

Elric swallowed, though it did nothing to hide the painful rasp of his voice. "Because it is mine. It belonged to my mother."

Graecerys gasped as if she had been struck, like all the air rushed from her lungs. "Stargell?"

Elric froze. The name from his past, the boy he had pretended to be—first for protection and then for escape from the nightmare he did not believe he would survive—fell over him, not in a wave of cold and crushing grief, but a swell of soft, warm affection. He had let Stargell go on the shores of Inflamel, laying him to rest beside every other loss as if he had been another member of his family when he had, in truth, been the best parts of Elric. Hopeful. Innocent. The embodiment of his childhood. But there was only one person he had ever given that name to.

The girl who bore the same name as the woman whose portrait hung in the hall.

The one who had lost her own beloved mother.

The one who had vowed to save him.

The one who tried, though she had abandoned him when all he wanted in the world was to not be alone anymore.

"You told me your name was Auriana," he breathed.

"I gave you my mother's name. I hated my own and you were the only friend I had. I did not want...I didn't know...."

Graecerys began to visibly shake, holding herself tighter, but Elric's terror mounted, building with rage. "All you cannot remember. Was that your way of artfully lying? Of pulling me closer so you could stab what little innocence remained in my heart?"

"No, never!" she cried. "I do not remember, I cannot remember. The darkness has taken everything from those days. The only thing my mind held on to was you. But your ship was lost at sea."

"It was lost," Elric admitted. "All was lost. The crew on deck was dashed against the rocks, the ship broken to nothing, but... but you put me within a barrel. It filled with water, yet somehow I escaped it. I thought I would die, but I washed up on the shores of Inflamel instead."

Her chest heaved with a sob, and she took a step toward him. He took one back. "I thought I killed you. That it was my fault."

"You were supposed to come with me," Elric said, shaking his head. "I did not want to be rescued, I just wanted to not be alone anymore."

"I was bound for the throne. They would have never stopped looking for me."

"And how would I have known that?" he shouted, pain striking his heart as she flinched. "You said your parents worked at the palace. I thought you were a servant, I...I thought you died during the coup."

Graecerys shook her head. "The coup happened before I met you. It happened while you were there and you never knew. I am so sorry."

He shook his head, pacing, the frenetic energy making him feel ill. "Your mother died while we were together. You were alone. Why did you not just come with me, Graecerys? Why give me hope, then lie and betray me when you were all I had to hold on to? And why drag me back here after all these years? Help me make sense of it all."

"All I wanted was to leave with you," she said through tears. "But I had no choice. It was the only way."

"The only way to what?" Elric spat, his anger nearly uncontrollable.

"*To save you*," Graecerys yelled. "They found out about us and were going to hurt you. Letting you go was the only way I could save you."

CHAPTER THIRTY-SIX

THERE ONCE WAS A GIRL WHO HELD FAST TO THE TRUTH IN HER HEART, CLINGING TO THE FRAYING STRANDS OF CHILDHOOD, BEGGING TO HEAR THE MUSIC, TO FEEL THE WAVES, TO HOLD THE STARS. BUT THEN, SHE LIED.

"STARGELL, HURRY, OUR SHIP IS WAITING!" SHE WHISPERED, POURING THE LAST OF A TINCTURE INTO HIS FLASK. NOT THE ONE SHE HAD BEEN GIVEN FOR HIM, BUT THE ONE THAT TYPICALLY HELPED HER SLEEP. THE ONE THAT WOULD CAUSE NO HARM.

HE TOOK THE DRINK FROM HER HAND MOMENTS LATER, AND AS HE ALWAYS DID, DRAINED IT QUICKLY AND ALLOWED HER TO REFILL IT. WHEN SHE TURNED AWAY TO DO SO, HER EYES STUNG AND THE BACK OF HER THROAT BURNED.

HE TOOK THE FLASK ONCE MORE, THROWING THE STRAP AROUND HIS BODY WITH HIS PACK, THEN STUFFED HIS CAREFULLY FOLDED SHAWL INTO THE LOOP TO HOLD IT FAST.

THE GIRL SHIFTED HER OWN PACK ONTO HER SHOULDER, LIT HER CANDLE, AND THEN FOLLOWED HIM THROUGH THE DOOR IN THE WALL.

THROUGH THE TUNNELS, THEY STOLE DOWN LADDERS, TRACED AND RETRACED THEIR STEPS TO DRAW CLOSER TO THE GROUND,

AND WHEN THE SMELL OF HORSES FILLED HER NOSE, THE GIRL HELD THE LIGHT ALOFT WHILE THE BOY FOUND THE DOOR.

HE CRACKED IT OPEN TO THE COLD NIGHT, AND THEY SLIPPED OUT, TWO SMALL SHADOWS AGAINST THE STONE. SHE LED THEM ACROSS THE COURTYARD AND INTO THE BARN, PAUSING TO GRASP HIS HAND AND TUG HIM ALONG AS HE GAPED OPEN-MOUTHED AT THE SKY.

IT WAS ONLY WHEN THEY WERE SAFELY IN THE LOFT THAT SHE PAUSED TO LOOK AT IT TOO. SHE HAD LONGED FOR A NIGHT CLEAR ENOUGH TO COUNT ALL THE STARS, YET SHE FOUND HERSELF STARING AT THE BOY'S FACE ALONE.

JUST ON TIME, A WAGON PULLED FORWARD AND BARRELS WERE LOADED ON THE BACK. THEY SCURRIED DOWN, AND WHEN THE SAILOR PAUSED HIS TASK TO RETURN TO THE PALACE FOR PAYMENT, THEY HOISTED ONE ANOTHER UP, AND SHE HELD OPEN THE LID.

"YOU FIRST," SHE RUSHED. "HURRY, STARGELL, PLEASE."

HE YAWNED, AND HER HEART SKIPPED A BEAT, BUT TO HER RELIEF HE CLIMBED INSIDE. SHE HANDED HIM THE SACK ON HER OWN SHOULDER—THE EXTRA ONE SHE HAD PACKED FOR HIM—AND THEN DROPPED BACK ON HER HEELS, BRACING HERSELF FOR WHAT CAME NEXT.

THE BOY YAWNED ONCE MORE, SETTLING INTO THE BOTTOM OF THE BARREL, BUT HE FOUGHT THE SLEEP THAT WEIGHED DOWN HIS EYELIDS TO LOOK UP AT HER.

"WILL YOU BE NEAR ME? WILL YOU FIND ME ONCE WE ARE ON THE SHIP?"

SHE SMILED SADLY, HER VOICE SHAKING FROM THE BREAKING OF HER HEART. "I'LL FIND YOU. WHEREVER YOU GO, IN ALL THAT YOU SEE, I WILL ALWAYS BE THERE."

CONCERN KNIT HIS BROW, BUT INSTEAD OF PUSHING HIMSELF UP TO RISE, HE SLUMPED FARTHER DOWN, CURLING INTO THE BOTTOM OF THE BARREL AND FINALLY SUCCUMBING TO THE SLEEPING DRAUGHT SHE HAD GIVEN HIM.

NO LONGER ABLE TO STOP THE TEARS SPILLING DOWN HER

CHEEKS, THE GIRL CLOSED HER EYES TIGHT AND FORCED THE GOODBYE SHE KNEW SHE'D REGRET HOLDING BACK. WITH EACH WORD SHE SPOKE, SHE LET GO OF THE LAST OF HER CHILDHOOD, AND ACCEPTED THE FATE THAT LAY AHEAD.

"I'M SO SORRY, STARGELL, PLEASE FORGIVE ME. I NEED TO KNOW THAT YOU ARE ALIVE. THAT YOU ARE SOMEWHERE YOU CAN SEE THE STARS, WHERE THERE IS MORE TO THIS LIFE THAN EMPTINESS. AND I CAN'T KNOW THAT IF THEY KILL YOU. I HOPE YOU STILL THINK OF ME FROM TIME TO TIME, BECAUSE I SWEAR TO YOU, FOR AS LONG AS I LIVE, I WILL NEVER FORGET YOU."

CHAPTER THIRTY-SEVEN

They stood staring at each other.

Elric and Graecerys.

Stargell and Auriana.

And suddenly the chasm between them was an ocean. One that had ripped them apart, then slowly brought them back together.

All that she had just recounted of the night she saved him, all that he knew of her past—the life she lived between their parting and meeting—stilled the anger within Elric.

He had mourned a life of loneliness he didn't understand. He had grieved a friendship that had been his hope. But then he had found friends and a family and the love of his life. And though it was all gone once more, he had held it. He had known love.

But Graecerys had given everything. Sacrificed all comfort and safety and carried the weight of his loss—the burden of his life—before she could even properly grieve her mother. She was not given love, just a father who went mad. Lords who assaulted and violated her. And a darkness she had accepted *for him*—one that cursed her, plaguing her for the rest of her life, stealing her memories, and punishing her simply for saving her friend.

"Who?" he all but growled. "Who and what did they do to you?"

"I cannot remember. Only that the nightmares began the day I learned of your loss. I have tried so many times, in so many ways, to find answers, but everything was lost to me, fading in my mind until all that remained was the memory of you. So I stopped searching. Because if my saving you is what has brought this on me, then it was worth it," she confessed quietly, and the small tremor in her voice broke his heart.

Elric took a step toward her, and though she eyed him warily, she did not step back. "What the Augur practices is unnatural. And he admitted to using the dhust of my ancestors in his concoctions. There is no telling what has been done."

She nodded. "I was able to halt the worst of his crimes—his experiments. But the darkness, the nightmares. Nothing has stopped them since I lost you."

Elric stood just before her now, gently clasping her elbows, but she refused to let herself go, as if her arms were the only thing holding her in one piece. "You did not lose me. We lived entire lifetimes apart, but in the end, we found each other once again."

Her eyes fell shut, squeezing for a heartbeat before their endless sea met his once more. "I dared not hope, but I kept my promise. I never forgot you."

He wrapped his hands gently around her waist, and before he had a chance to pull her closer, she threw her arms about his neck and clung to him.

It struck him then how different it felt to have her in his arms. There had always been a familiarity between them, even with the hatred they felt for one another. It was the ease in which they spoke, how they acted around the other, their exchanges held without restraint, that had never made sense. But now that it did, there was a tenderness he could not escape, and a protectiveness he refused to deny.

As a girl, she had made a choice and unknowingly sacrificed her entire future to save him. And now as a man, he wanted nothing more than to give his all to protect her.

"Forgive me," she whispered. "I took everything from you."

"You saved me," he replied in disbelief.

"And then I became the very thing that hurt you in the first place."

Elric pulled back far enough to cup her face, to wipe away the tears rolling down her cheeks. "There are worse things than being bound to you."

She snorted. "You say that now that we know who we are to each other. But would you have said it a fortnight ago? A month?"

Elric thought a moment before giving her a roguish smile. "Roughly a fortnight ago you were mending my shirt, so yes. A month ago…no. But I have survived worse."

Her brow furrowed and she searched his eyes. "Will you share it with me? All you have survived since we parted? In time?"

Elric swallowed. "As I am able."

She rested her head back on his chest, letting her hands fall between them, clutching his vest as if she might lose him, and he took the opportunity to wrap his arms about her shoulders. "What do we do now?" she whispered.

Goose bumps raised on his skin and he recalled the girl who had been his oldest friend whispering the same words.

"We do not decide tonight," he replied. "We have much to determine of the road ahead, but first, we rest. *You* must rest. I shall see you to your room."

She pressed her lips together and, with eyes downcast, nodded. He gently took her hand, leading her back down the hall and to her bedchamber, but when he turned to leave, she did not release his fingers.

He paused, and she stepped into him, laying her palm on his

chest over the place where his heart beat wildly for her. "I am frightened, Elric. It is dark in my mind and there are faces—so many faces—but none of them are mine."

He tipped her chin up and her eyes met his, the pain in them threatening to carve his heart out. "Then find me within the dark, for as long as I live, the stars will know your face. Find them. Find me."

She searched his eyes, then finally whispered, "Stay with me. Please."

He paused, drowning in her waves, overcome by their depth, and when he felt himself being pulled to her, like a boat on the tide, her hands found his face and she kissed him. He returned it, gently at first, and then lost in the softness that had only flirted between them before. And when they parted, she whispered once more.

"Please?"

He did not release her hand as he closed the door behind them, nor when he lay beside her in bed and turned out the light.

And long after her breathing grew rhythmic, her heart a calm and easy pattern against his side, he held her still.

CHAPTER THIRTY-EIGHT

Graecerys opened her eyes to the brilliant sunlight streaming between her curtains, bathing the room in warmth, though the glass was frosted. They were still heavy with sleep, but she felt rested. Something that never happened.

Instead of rising and busying herself with another day, she remained, staring at the man snoring softly next to her. The burden, the grief, of her choices as a child had crushed her the day before, draining and exhausting her, while she recalled as much as possible of the night she had sent him away.

And now he lay beside her.

She didn't know how to articulate what he had brought out in her since the very first night he slighted her. From the beginning, he'd made her feel things she never had before. Powerful. Beautiful. In control, not as a ruler or even a tyrant, but someone who might grow and thrive, running far and fast knowing she was safe to do so. It is what had driven her to his bed in the first place, let alone back a second time. He was strong, brilliant, and all she admired, but he drew the greatest pleasure in watching her take the lead. She didn't understand why, she only knew she loved it and craved him more for how fully he helped her feel like herself again.

She reached out and tentatively brushed his warm-cinnamon hair back with her fingers to see his face clearly. To confirm that he was real. And though she was still too afraid to hope, she could not deny what his impossible presence signaled in her life.

He was tender, soft in ways she had not known since her mother's love, but he saw her and respected her as a woman—not a girl or a rung on the ladder of influence. He cared about her with an intensity that sent her heart racing with the wildest sense of abandon, but instead of stoking fear, he brought her to life. Everything about him felt old and familiar, yet new and beautiful. Even the scent of cardamom and reed that clung to his skin—like old parchment—returned her to days of safety and adventure. Since his arrival, she had done nothing but slowly lose the things she felt nothing for, what she wouldn't miss, but what little she had loved and lost was being returned to her in their stead.

She had become unrecognizable, while he was different, yet very much the same. He was unashamedly honest with his words and actions while she outwardly smiled and laughed when she wanted to draw her sword, raged as everything within her cried, and sobbed uncontrollably when consumed with joy.

Now there was hope. And she had never wanted to scream louder in terror before.

"If you think any harder, I fear your brow may permanently wrinkle that way."

She met Elric's sleep-drenched eyes, his voice still gravelly from slumber, and shook her head. "I was not thinking. I was... trying to remember."

"Remember what?"

"A time when you did not torment me day and night," she said with a devious grin. "You were far more silent as a boy."

He snorted. "I was. And then I met you. You see the influence you had on my life?"

"So it is my fault you are crass?"

"Do not feed me words. I remember the first moment we met as vividly as if it were yesterday. You asked me a dozen questions and then paraded me around the room like the royalty you were. I should have known then."

"Known what?"

"That you would own me someday."

She flinched. "I do not wish to. I would set you free if I knew a way."

"That is not what I meant," he replied, sitting up on an elbow and carefully lifting a strand of her hair, twisting it loosely around his finger. "You owned me the night you did not arrive by the piano. The days I spent wandering within the walls, listening to sound after sound until I knew I had found you."

Pain seized her heart, a fogged memory hanging just out of reach. "That was how they discovered you. You were heard. I truly was your downfall."

He shook his head. "I was fallen already. You simply helped me up again."

She stared at him, a warmth gripping her heart and making words difficult to speak. "I do not believe your pretty words. You are just trying to make me feel better."

"And I do not believe your assertion of men to be faulty any longer."

A smile played at her lips, and she almost dared to set it free. "Pray tell, what assertion might that be?"

"That all men are infants. Because I daresay I am helpless before you."

She was powerless to deny her smile now, and as it filled her face, his own mirrored it. He did not move, did not draw closer. The best of any man she had ever met before—save Hubart—he waited for her to move first.

But when she did, leaning in to meet his lips, a sharp knock on the door stopped her in her tracks.

"I am late to rise, Arlys, forgive me," Graecerys hurried, sitting up and nervously pulling on the covers, though she remained fully clothed. "I will heat my own food today, I promise."

"Arlys I am not, my queen," a slightly familiar male voice answered. "I am instead here at the palace's behest. Lord Blenheim has reached an agreement for your kingdom. You are to return for your coronation."

Silently, with wide eyes, Elric sat up and watched her. Mind racing, afraid someone might enter, she pointed frantically toward the washroom, but he shook his head firmly with a frown that caused her to roll her eyes skyward.

"I shall be down when I have refreshed," she replied aloud, letting a coldness bleed into her voice. One she had not used since she stopped believing herself queen.

"Yes, my queen. I will relay the message to the staff. We must depart at once."

Steps were heard retreating down the hall, and Graecerys lay back in bed, her heart thundering as she stared at the ceiling.

Blenheim had…reached an agreement? With the revolution?

"What agreement would need to be made to assure you the throne?" Elric asked, his voice even, though his brilliantly blue eyes were tinged with both concern and anger.

Graecerys didn't reply. She didn't dare to wonder. She did not want to imagine a scenario terrible enough to lessen the blow of reality.

Not when her heart told her it would be worse.

She dressed quickly in the nicest gown she could find, and when Graecerys exited her room, Elric was already waiting in the hall.

He cut a dashing figure in his perfectly tailored trousers, dark boots, crisp white shirt, and navy waistcoat, and she found her gaze lingering for just a second too long.

A smirk filled his face, but before he opened his mouth to say something she was certain would be inappropriate, she crossed the floor in front of him and moved down the stairs.

Both Arlys and Hubart stood by the doorway of the formal sitting room, eyeing her with concern, and when Arlys stepped inside, Hubart crossed the floor and took Graecerys's hands in his own.

"How did they arrive?" she asked.

"By carriage. A convoy sent directly from the palace with just a handful of guards. They said you've been missing for weeks, how did they know you would be here?"

Graecerys shook her head. "I am not sure. Blenheim knew of this place and of you. He was the one who came when my father sent for me. If he were searching for me, I suppose this would be the first place he would inquire."

Hubart nodded and glanced at Elric. The look they shared was nearly the same. "Are you to be safe, Graecerys?" the older man asked, his voice more serious than she had ever heard before, even when she was a child causing trouble on his grounds.

"You do not need to worry about me," she assured him. "I can take care of myself. I only wish I did not have to leave so soon."

He sighed, placing a hand on her cheek. His skin was gnarled with age and rough from the years he spent working the land, but his touch was gentle as any loving guardian's would be. "I wish you did not have to leave at all."

She leaned up, kissing him on the cheek, and when she passed him, she heard him speak in a quiet tone. "You will protect her?"

"With my life," Elric replied, and though her heart leaped

with happiness, her throat burned with unshed tears. She would never give him the chance. She would never put him in harm's way ever again.

She entered the sitting room, and Arlys dipped into a short, respectful curtsy, then promptly exited. Only one guard stood in front of her, the one she recognized as having always been with Elric. She believed his name was—

"Falchion," Elric said behind her, and before she had a chance to turn, he passed her and was clasping the guard on the shoulder. A motion the soldier returned with a broad smile on his face.

"You could not have thought me dead," he said with a laugh. "I am far too tenacious to be felled so soon."

"I am glad to see you," Elric said, relief pouring in his tone.

"And I you," Falchion replied, earnestness causing the hardness in his eyes to falter.

But when he turned to Graecerys, the mask of a soldier was donned once more, and he bowed low with his fist over his heart. "My queen. It is by the good fortune of the stars that you have survived and are well. I have come to bear you home—to the palace and your throne."

She nodded in acknowledgment, and when he straightened, she asked, "What are the terms of my return? You spoke of an agreement? What has happened since my departure?"

"The palace suffered great damage and many lives were lost. I fear the only lord who survived was Lord Blenheim, as he was the only one not present in the drawing room when the revolution breached the door."

Graecerys hid her flinch as he continued, "The leader of the people, a man they call Denfrin, agreed to an audience with Lord Blenheim where they spoke of the future of Obarian. They found that, despite their differences, both possessed an unyielding desire to see the kingdom flourish, united in peace once more, and after much discussion and deliberation an accord was made. Upon your arrival, the union shall be complete."

"What union?" Elric asked, his tone hard as stone as Graecerys turned the name over in her mind, searching her memory. The Moonrise Observation brought the recollection of the scarfaced man that Blenheim had introduced her to—the one she had shared a dance with—and her heart plummeted.

Falchion had the good sense to look nervous, and when he glanced to Elric, he murmured, "Do not summon a boulder to fall on my head, I am merely the messenger." Then his eyes met Graecerys's once more.

"The union between the nobility and the people's revolution —the marriage of you, my queen, to Denfrin, the new King of Obarian."

Silence fell on the room, and though Elric's eyes shot to her, burning into the side of her face like twin matches, she dared not look at him. "Marriage," she said, blinking slowly. "I have been used as a bartering token, sold to the people who would have seen me dead, and I am to be given to the man who led them as his lawful wife?"

Falchion swallowed. "Lord Blenheim was certain you would be unhappy. But you must know, he tried everything. This was the only way he could guarantee your safety. It was the only way they would not put a bounty on your head for treason."

She laughed humorlessly. "Well, that certainly eases my fears over my future husband. From execution to matrimony over conversation and a few glasses of wine."

"My queen, if I may…this Denfrin is not like many of the other men, in court or on the side of the revolution. He is hardened from the conflict, but he is a decent man. I believe this can be a good match. One that will strengthen Obarian, and if we are fortunate, grow in time to become the patriarchy we have failed to attain since before your father assumed the throne."

"Do you not mean monarchy?" Elric asked stonily.

Falchion shook his head. "Despite what I believe, or anything we have known before, the throne has not officially been filled since the loss of the king. The terms of the accord were clear, and Denfrin has already been crowned. It is now Graecerys who will be marrying onto the throne."

The blow struck Graecerys like a thousand waves at once, and she turned away, walking to the window to look out over the sea as Elric's angered tone questioned Falchion behind her.

She had lost crown, kingdom, future, and freedom, all while she thought she was in the process of discovering it. She had feared rule, denying herself the crown to protect the kingdom from the darkness waging war within her mind, but now she would not be free either.

It was when she spotted an Obarian ship weighing anchor along the shore that everything came rushing back to her. And suddenly she knew what she must do.

"Falchion, my household will ready the things I am to take back to the palace," she said, turning to face him. "Where shall I tell them to take my trunks?"

"To the ship, my queen. We arrived by convoy, but the ship shall carry us faster."

"I have no desire for speed," she said sharply. "We shall return by convoy instead. If Obarian is to be at peace, then I wish for us to also unite the realm. The ship shall go to Inflamel to parlay with their king. And my Isteriaeth shall go as my envoy."

Elric spun on her, his eyes wide as Falchion cocked his head. "I thought he was tethered to you. Shall he not remain by your side?"

"He is tethered and always will be," she confirmed, gathering every last bit of resolve she possessed to finally meet Elric's eyes. "But he was brought here to win the people, to strengthen my claim to the throne. If that is accomplished, then I have no need to keep him close. I have come to trust him in the weeks since we fled the palace, and there is no better representative of me to send forth. He has ties to Inflamel, so I see no harm in allowing him to return. In fact, I demand it."

Elric's lips parted, shock draining the color from his face, but Falchion simply bowed. "As you wish, my queen. I shall relay the message to my men and to the ship. We will all depart by nightfall."

She nodded to him, and before he left, she said, "Sir Falchion? Please close the door behind you on the way out."

His eyes flicked between her and Elric once more, and with a bow, he said, "Yes, my queen."

Then the door shut, leaving them alone once more.

CHAPTER THIRTY-NINE

"No," Elric said, staring at the woman before him in horror.

She shook her head sadly. "We do not have a choice."

"You always have a choice. You are a queen, Graecerys."

"I was, but I am no longer."

"It does not matter," he replied, pacing the floor, a desperate anger overtaking the fear at his core. "If I have learned anything over the last weeks and months in your infuriating presence, it is that you cannot be controlled. You cannot be made to do anything you do not want. What has changed?"

"Everything," she replied, gazing at a spot on the carpet, unable to meet his eyes.

"That is a Thrones-damned lie," he spat. "The nobility is the same, the lords are the same, the people do not love you any more, you are not magically endeared to the revolution. The only thing that has changed is what lies between us, which we have hardly had a moment to explore, and yet you have the nerve to attempt to send me away?"

She said nothing, and the sight of her—face emotionless and drawn, her shoulders slack and defeated—broke his heart.

He crossed the floor, standing on the spot before her, his boots in her line of sight. "You cannot send me away," he said quietly.

Her eyes drifted to a different place on the carpet, farther away from him. "I will not keep you here. If you return to the palace with me, you will be trapped just as I am."

"And I will not abandon you," Elric swore. "You are still in danger, from threats external and within. You are strong, but you should not have to face it alone. We are bound for a reason, and you will need my power in the coming days, if for nothing than to defend yourself."

"But haven't we always been bound?" she asked, finally lifting her eyes, their rolling waves tumultuous—restless. "I could not protect Stargell. I couldn't save him. But, Elric, let me rescue you this time. Let me try."

"It was never your responsibility to save me."

"But it was my duty," she said vehemently. "You told me once that you believed there was a reason why we remain—one beyond death and duty—and this is my reason. You are my purpose. And though in my heart I knew you would never be mine, that I would always lose you, I am taking your word as my armor, and I will not be swayed. Knowing you are alive and assuring your safety, your freedom, will give me a peace I never thought I would attain in this life. You have given me everything, Elric. Now please, let me save you."

"And what of *my* duty?" he asked, voice raw as bitter tears stung his eyes.

Her throat bobbed, but she fought back the tides rising in her eyes, and her voice remained strong. "Your duty is to Breteria. To the Isteriaeth and to the stars. To the kingdom you call your home and the people you call family. Do what you must. Find whatever has been lost there. And should you need aid in the future, I will ensure Obarian falls in line at your side."

Elric looked away, fighting to keep his composure, the ache

in his chest consuming him entirely, threatening to cut him down at the knees. "But what about us?"

Graecerys's eyes fell closed. "What about us?"

"You deny that there is something between us?" he asked, watching a single tear roll down her cheek. Yet when she opened her eyes, red-rimmed and broken, she smiled.

"There was only *us* for a season. And how lucky I am that I stole two in your arms."

Everything within Elric silenced. His resolve broke, and with it, his shoulders fell and he wavered where he stood.

Graecerys tugged the brooch on the chain over her head, then looped it around his neck, and let her hand fall to his heart. "Keep it safe this time," she whispered, kissing him softly on the cheek. Before she stepped away, he grasped her wrist, holding it against his chest.

"If things were different," he started, his voice thick with unshed tears, "if we had run faster, left sooner, escaped to a place without duty, would you be with me?"

Graecerys drew in a trembling breath and squeezed her eyes shut. He waited, hoping beyond everything for the answer he knew would not come. And when she opened her eyes once more, he allowed her hand to fall, her warmth to pull away, and a bitter loneliness to wrap his heart in ice.

"That place does not exist," she replied, taking a step back. "Not for us."

He nodded, and with every ounce of self-preservation he still possessed, walked to the door. But when he reached it, he turned to her one last time. "Grace," he said, clearing his throat.

She took a deep, steadying breath, and when she faced him, he forced a smile. "Wherever you go," he rasped, "in all that you see, I will always be there."

And before he could change his mind, before he could see her break, he left.

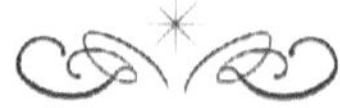

Elric stood before a small boat on the sand, the crew readying its oars and waiting to push off toward the ship that would carry him back to Inflamel. He watched it bob on the waves, his stomach twisting in knots at the sight, though the memories that plagued him were not of drowning or death, but of life and the part of him he feared leaving behind.

"I cannot help but envy you," Falchion said, standing at his side. "You traipse across the kingdom, avoid battle and imprisonment, then you take a holiday in a manor on the coast, and are now departing before any of the hard work begins. And you truly expected me to believe you hated it here."

"And *you* wish for me to believe that you despise your lot in life as the new commander over Obarian's armies?"

"Considering my predecessor is dead, yes. But I *believe* you owe me thanks."

Elric shook his head, unable to keep from smiling. "I am certain there is something I owe you, but I cannot say if you will like it or not."

Falchion chuckled. "You know you will miss me." Glancing around them, he stepped closer and lowered his voice for only Elric to hear. "But do not miss me enough to ever return. I do not think you should have ever faced what you have, and though I am grateful to know you, I am more glad to watch you go. Remain free. Stay far from here."

The sincerity in his words moved Elric, breaking through the stiffness in his spine, and he clasped a hand on Falchion's shoulder. "If you ever find yourself in Inflamel, I shall owe you an ale."

Falchion dipped his chin. "I look forward to it. So long as you do not lace it with anything."

Elric smirked, walking toward the boat and swinging a leg over the side. "I cannot make any guarantees."

Shaking his head, Falchion laughed. "May the stars guide you and the Thrones protect you, my friend."

Elric nodded to him, the boat floating on the water, and at the last minute, he turned and called over his shoulder. "Falchion! Protect her," he ordered, his voice carrying on the wind.

He did not hear if the soldier replied, he only saw him clench his hand into a fist, place it over his heart, and bow at the waist.

Elric watched the shoreline as it drew farther away, focusing on the land more than the water below, and when he finally climbed aboard the vessel and stood firmly on its deck, a weight on his shoulders—heavy enough to paralyze his steps—pulled him to the side.

There, at the top of the cliff, her dark dress and brilliant hair blowing across the manor that rose at her back, he saw Graecerys. He stared at the spot, saw her shrink in the distance, and long after the coast vanished entirely from his view, he still felt her eyes watching him leave.

CHAPTER FORTY

The ship was miserable, the ocean desolate, and though it was deep into the night on their second day at sea, Elric lay on the deck and stared at the stars. The sea was like a song now—melodic as the music that had flowed from the fingertips of a girl he once knew. The woman drifting farther from him by the moment. He twisted his mother's brooch, still on the chain around his neck, her words drifting back to him.

"Someday, I hope you behold them with joy and find rest in their skies. May you never go where they cannot find you."

There was nothing between him and the stars now. All locks had been broken, the doors thrown open, and there would be no walls to hold them from him again. Yet the farther they sailed, the more alone he felt.

He should be overjoyed at the thought of freedom, but he did not know where to begin. What would he find when he returned? How could he go back to the life he once knew now that he was forever changed?

The tether had not pained him once, but that in itself was an excruciating wound. It meant Graecerys had not needed him. She had not called for him. She did not want him.

"I did not forget you."

Would she forget him now? Would she remember to hold on to the hours they'd spent at peace? Or would the darkness—the unknown fate intended for him—claim her instead?

He sat up, stalking across the deck, but paused before descending below. He could not bring himself to do it. It was too far beneath the water.

Too far from the stars.

Yet remaining here, in the presence of the sea, he realized that in the dark it was the exact reflection of the sky—a midnight blue net filled with stars. The one above held them suspended, but the one below cradled their infinite beauty. And when he gazed at the horizon line, he was unable to tell where one ended and the other began. What he had loved most and what he feared, together, one and the same.

Just like him and Grace. He had drowned in her, swallowed so much of her into his lungs he couldn't help but sink further. Caught up in her darkness, he thought he was losing sight of the stars, when instead she reflected his own radiance, leading him to find them once more.

He *was* the star in her night—the last hope of the Isteriaeth and the final light walking upon the realm that his own kind had given everything to create and preserve. It was his duty to return to Inflamel, to save his friends, to find the Trifolium Thrones and rid Breteria of its darkness once and for all. But he knew now that all he wanted was to remain by her side, no matter what the future held.

But the stars didn't care what his heart wanted. They never did. They stared down at him from their grave markers in the sky, reminding him of the past, but all he could see was the girl who ran headfirst into nightmares just for him to live. And he longed to follow her.

He walked to the side of the ship and leaned on the rail, resting his head in his hands. Who would be there when she had nightmares? When the darkness gripped her, who would remind her who she was?

He slammed his hands down and stalked back to his corner, lying once more to face the sky. Only this time when he tried to sleep, he did not see the stars. He did not hear his mother's voice. He pushed all thought of Graecerys from his mind. And he only knew he had drifted off when a soft hand rested on his cheek, and he opened his eyes to see Kathrina.

He reached for her, but she shook her head. "Do you remember what I told you?" she asked.

He frowned but did not answer.

She gave him a chiding smile. "You promised me you wouldn't forget."

His eyes snapped open, and he scraped a hand down his face, her forgotten words echoing in his head, shaking his heart within his chest.

"Promise me you will love."

He rose again but did not look to the sky. He stared at the waves. They were dark and fathomless, but graceful as they rolled—their whitecaps delicately catching any light the night cast down on them.

What was the ocean without the sky to balance it? And how would anyone navigate the sea without stars to guide their way?

He looked at the brooch once more, then to the horizon where his home waited for him. And then, with a silent apology, he turned back and fixed his eyes to the north.

He knew what he must do.

PART III
THE STARS

CHAPTER FORTY-ONE

The days it took for the ship to change course and return to the port in Obarian felt like a lifetime, though no amount of time would prepare Elric for the sight that greeted him when he stood before the palace gates once more.

Damage was still visible, some windows were covered with boards and the labyrinth of hedges was half-gone, but the doors were open and people milled about as if a gala were in progress.

His heart thrummed in his chest, his nerves threatening to break him down, yet the feeling of striding through the door, down the halls of his own volition was empowering. He looked a mess, he knew it. He should summon fresh clothing, a razor at the least, but instead of self-preservation, he found himself craving recklessness. Let Grace see the way she unmoored him. Let it remove all doubt of what he was choosing—who he was standing for.

When he finally reached the banquet room, he froze.

Seated at the head of the room, before the dancers and revelers, was the man he recognized as Denfrin—a cloak of fur on his shoulders and a gold circlet on his head. And seated by his side, her hair caught up in an intricate braid about her head, though no crown adorned it, was Grace.

He met Denfrin's eyes, and the man stood, extending an arm to silence the musicians. "Master Elric," he boomed. "Is that you?"

Grace's attention snapped to the door, and though he saw her eyes widen, she did not move. She just pinned him to the ground in her emotionless, commanding way.

And oh, how he had missed it.

"It is, Your Majesty," Elric replied with a smile, striding through the room and stopping before the throne. He bowed to the king, and when he straightened, Denfrin was already halfway down from the dais.

He clasped Elric on the shoulders, holding him at arm's length. "Long did my friend Jacian speak of your loyalty, of your dedication to Obarian. I admired you then, but now? To know you protected my betrothed, kept her safe and alive through the most desolate parts of this land, it is beyond loyalty and dedication. I do not know why your course averted from Inflamel so soon, but I am thankful you are here and honored to be in your presence."

Elric was at a loss for words, the man's reception of him unexpected, and when they embraced, he met Grace's eyes over his shoulder. They narrowed, and though the position he found himself in before the king was uncomfortable, he could not help but wink at her.

"It is...too soon to open discussion with Inflamel," Elric replied as Denfrin released him and took a step back. "So, as Advisor to the Crown, I returned as quickly as I could. To guide you in this fledgling time of peace."

Grace snorted imperceptibly, but Denfrin smiled. "We shall need your counsel in the coming days, of that I have no doubt. But for now, we feast. Wine for the Isteriaeth!"

Elric accepted the wine, allowing Denfrin to escort him

about the room, introducing him to both members of the nobility he had seen but never known and faces of the revolution alike. He did not see Blenheim or Falchion, or even Augur —who he intended to track down at first chance.

But it did not matter where he moved, he always felt Grace's stare on him.

After some time, he feigned drowsiness, thanked Denfrin for his hospitality, and retired to his quarters for the evening.

Once inside, he waited.

He stood by the door in the wall—the very thing that had led him to Grace what felt like a lifetime ago. The girl who saved him, then stole him, and then set him free all so the waves might carry him back to her once more. He was so nervous he thought his heart might burst, that his stomach might reject everything in it, though he didn't know if it was from fear of his own actions or worry of what Grace would do—how she would react to his return once alone.

He waited until he heard a door *click*. Soft shoes crossed the floor. And then he knocked.

There was no answer, no sound on the other side, so he knocked again, repeatedly, and paused, listening for an answer before beginning again.

"Leave me *be*, Elric," Grace finally said over his rap, exasperation filling her words. But it was the hint of a tremble that seized his heart. The tears hiding along the edge of her voice.

He pictured her—the long blue gown she wore. The way the pearlescent fabric draped off her shoulders, surrounding her like starlight. And before he could think twice, he pushed against the door, his heart stuttering to find it unlocked, and strode through.

Grace stood in front of her dressing table, her shoes removed and the net from her hair sitting on its surface, though she still remained in her dress. And when she met his eyes, all hint of anger vanished from them, replaced with worry, and below it, a welling joy.

"You did not take the ship," she sighed, hopelessness and happiness dampening her words.

"I couldn't," Elric replied, taking slow steps toward her.

Her lip quivered, but she kept her tone even. "You should have."

"I did not want to."

"I don't believe you were given a choice."

"And you do not command me," he retorted, finally coming to a stop before her.

"But I do," she said, an indignant heat flaring in her eyes.

"Then make me leave."

She opened her mouth to speak, but turned away from him instead, removing pins and letting her hair fall before furiously unwinding the strands. "You are here, I do not control you, so be it. But why are you in my quarters? You should not be."

Elric pulled the chain from around his neck, then carefully placed it around Grace's, allowing the brooch to fall onto her skin. She froze, staring at it in the mirror, and he watched as her fingers lifted slowly to caress it.

"None survive the sea on wind and ship alone. They need the stars to guide them," Elric murmured. "I have come to realize that, though I am bound to you in every way, I would not change it. You saved me, not once but twice, only now where I go is my decision alone. And I choose to stay with you."

She pulled her hair through the chain, letting it cascade over her shoulder, but did not move. She did not turn, but she did not walk away either.

All Elric wanted was to wrap his arms around her and hold her close, so that is what he did, stepping forward and resting his hands upon her waist. She stiffened instinctually, then her body relaxed into his chest. "I am to be married," she whispered.

"I know."

"What we shared," she glanced up, meeting his eyes in the mirror, "it is over. It must be, or we will bring down this entire kingdom."

"I know," Elric repeated.

Grace turned in his arms, staring into his soul, searching it desperately for something, though he did not know what. "Yet you stay?"

"If you are surprised, then I am wounded already," he said with a teasing smile.

"But why?" she asked, desperation in her voice, and Elric realized it was not a lack of her understanding, but a pleading for him to speak the words. She knew why he was there, but she needed to hear him say it.

"Because I…." *Would rather spend a lifetime with you just out of reach than say goodbye.*

The words failed on Elric's tongue, his mouth drying instantly, swept away with his courage now that he stood before her.

"Yes?" she prodded, her eyes too wide, too bright. Too hopeful.

"I am here because…."

"Yes?" she asked, somehow slipping closer, consuming all the air between them.

Because my heart is yours to claim.

He could not do this. He could not let her hope for the future if he had no solution to offer. And right now, there was none.

Not yet.

"Because you saved me. And I will not rest until I know that you are safe from whatever steals your memory in the dark of the night."

Her eyes fell, darkness hooding her gaze, and when she turned away, her tone was cold. "I will forget everything soon enough. You cannot save me, Elric. And I do not need you to."

"I know. And yet here is where I will stay."

"And I still do not understand why," she snapped, glaring at him. "It's foolishness. It will not matter in the end, you must know this."

"It matters to me. And if it did not matter to you, your door would have remained locked."

The accusation silenced her, but her lips parted. What seemed like a thousand words danced on the edge of her tongue, yet she only exhaled, her shoulders falling, her eyes growing tired once more.

He closed the space between them, but this time, he simply took her hand and lifted her fingers to his lips. "Will you sleep tonight?"

She blinked, as if snapping from a stupor, and when she spoke, her voice was soft. "I shall try."

It took everything in his power to release her, to let her go, but he did. Before he returned through the wall, he nodded and forced a smile. "I will be here if you need me."

CHAPTER FORTY-TWO

Grace, in fact, did not need him. She had departed her quarters long before he rose the following morning, though he suspected she had slept far less than he did. However, when he spotted her from the window, walking through the courtyard on Denfrin's arm, she looked well rested—joyful, even. And when he approached to accompany them about the grounds as they examined the repairs being made from the assault on the palace, he found that he couldn't help the twinge in his chest watching Denfrin dote on her, and how she accepted it so openly in return.

"Good morrow, Master Isteriaeth," the king greeted him jovially.

Elric regained his wits and quickly bowed. "I hope your night was restful," he said, addressing the king, though the words were meant for Grace.

"Quite, though I suspect they will become better in the near future," Denfrin replied with a smile directed at Grace.

Elric's strands grew taut against his skin, his palms heating, but he wrestled the dhust under control, folding his hands behind his back—the only thing that stopped him from tearing Grace away from the man.

Or possibly summoning his eyeballs from his skull.

She smiled back demurely, and when she tipped her head to the king, he grasped her fingers and lifted her hand to his lips, pressing them to her knuckles.

The same ones Elric had kissed the night before.

Denfrin regarded Elric warmly, involving him in discussion, but Grace would not so much as meet his eye, keeping her focus solely on her husband-to-be. As she should, he knew this. After all, had he not said he only returned to be near her? To help her break free of her curse? He held no claim on her outside of a few nights of weakness and a complicated past.

But, if that were true, then why was there a burning guilt in his chest that he could not rid himself of? And why did the fire of a thousand coals scald his skin every time she touched Denfrin's arm?

It was when they walked ahead of him and Denfrin stopped, tentatively taking Grace's hand in his own and pressing a soft kiss to her cheek—that she answered with a blushing smile— that Elric realized he had made a grave mistake returning at all.

"Your Majesty, I fear I must return to my tower now. There is much that needs tending in my absence," he said with a bow, drawing both Denfrin and Grace's attention.

"As you wish, Master Elric," Denfrin said with a polite nod. "However, before you depart, there's a matter of importance I wish to discuss. One which I hoped to get your opinion on, and in turn, a favor I must ask of you."

Elric cocked his head. "How intriguing."

Grace's eyes narrowed on Elric, but Denfrin, none the wiser, pressed on. "We are to be married upon the next Moonrise, a few short weeks from now. I believe it to be a strong show of unity, bringing nobility and commoner together as they once were, but in a fair and equal status. I also hoped it would bring honor and blessing on our great history, and from the stars themselves. And you are a star, are you not?"

It took everything in Elric's power to temper his breathing, to control his movements. "Last I checked."

"Then would you do us the great honor of facilitating our marriage ceremony? I do not have any expectation that the stars might bless us, but it is my hope that if they see our dedication in returning their land to the greatness of old, they will honor our union. And that the people may see it and know it is one never to be broken."

Elric opened his mouth to speak, but no words came out. He licked his lips, cleared his throat, and forced a smile. "It would be my greatest honor."

Denfrin beamed. "The honor is ours. I cannot thank you enough."

He turned, taking Grace with him, but before they walked away, he called over his shoulder. "We shall see you at our table this evening for dinner, Master Elric. I insist you join us."

Elric bowed to their backs. "As you wish."

Without another thought or word, he turned on his heel and strode away. He did not stop until he reached the familiar corridor, the room he had not forgotten, and he did not bother to knock before striding straight into Augur's apothecary.

But it was empty.

The tables remained, the shelves too, but no vials lined the shelves. No papers lay on the tables, and no books were scattered about. The waif of a man was gone.

"I am sorry you needed to learn this way," a voice drawled from the doorway.

Elric turned to stare at Lord Blenheim, the man's eyes cold and his posture stiff. He paced inside, hands clasped behind his back. "I was unaware that you and Augur were friends. I suspected your first impressions were not fond enough to endear you to one another."

"Where is he?" Elric asked, cutting all pleasantries.

Blenheim stopped his pacing. "He is dead. A casualty of the revolution's attack on the palace."

The wind knocked from Elric's sails, though he did not let on. "How unfortunate. I had meant to inquire about some books in his possession."

"I'm afraid the room was destroyed in the struggle. As you can see, there is nothing left."

Elric nodded, pasting a pleasant smile on his face. "How unfortunate. Thank you for letting me know."

"It is my pleasure. And also, if I may, welcome back. It is an honor to have you *grace* our halls once more."

Elric stared at the man, the emphasis on the single word sounding alarm bells in his mind, but Lord Blenheim only smiled and inclined his head. "Have a good day, Master Isteriaeth."

It took everything in Elric's power to maintain his composure while walking away, but when he reached the staircase, he found himself bounding down them two at a time, his feet racing to keep up with his pulse.

Augur was gone. His one link to whatever evil had been meant for him, whatever perverse power had infected Grace, was gone. And though he did not count Blenheim as innocent in his intentions, he was a man without dhust. He stood to gain far more at her side than he would if he lost her—as his arrangement of her marriage confirmed—so while he was a foe, he appeared to be one necessary for Grace's safety.

For now.

Elric was so lost in his thoughts, coming to the end of the staircase, that he failed to see the door open beside the landing. And when an arm reached out, grabbing him by the back of the vest and tugging him inside, he did not have time to react.

The door shut, and as starlit dhust pooled in his palms, bringing a dagger with it, a soft hand slapped over his mouth. In the blue glow, Grace's stern face glared at him. He sent the blade away and quickly called a candle to his opposite hand, sitting it on a shelf at their side to properly light the space.

"What do you think you are doing?" she hissed, removing her hand from his lips.

Elric glared at her. "I was walking. My apologies if it offended you."

"In a foul mood today, aren't we?"

"I can't imagine being in a good mood, though it seems you are."

Grace reared back as if slapped. "What would give you that impression?"

"Possibly the smiles you offer Denfrin. The blush that creeps up your cheeks when his lips touch your skin. Or the way you fawn over his general presence."

"The king? *My betrothed?*" she fired back. "And how do you suppose I should act?"

"With any of the smallest sense of decorum and decency would be appreciated, considering you have only been with the man a matter of days."

Grace smiled with a low laugh. "Jealousy does not become you."

"I am not jealous in the least," Elric scoffed. "There is nothing for me to envy, you were never mine."

The words pained him, a self-inflicted wound, though they seemed to anger Grace more, her nostrils flaring when she spoke. "I sent you away for a reason. It was your choice to return, so what your emotions dredge up is your own fault. You are more than happy to remove yourself at any time you see fit."

Elric paused, then let a hint of barbed amusement seep into his words as he leaned closer to her. "Does it bother you?"

"Your general presence? As a matter of fact, it does," Grace replied without venom, trying to step back, though there was barely space for a mop and bucket in the room that now contained two people.

"Well, that is a new development. I thought we surpassed that by our second night at the manor."

Her eyes narrowed, but even in the dim light he saw the color creeping into her skin. "You must stop."

"Why? Because it is inappropriate? Unfit?"

"Very."

Elric laughed. "Rich, coming from the unaccompanied woman who pulled me into a dark closet. Are you certain it is not because you're unable to handle the memories it brings to your mind?"

She shook her head, her eyes filled with so much fire Elric swore he felt its heat. "This is unfair."

"In what way?" he asked innocently.

"It is unfair to you, it is unfair to me, and it is unfair to Denfrin, who cannot help what transpired between us when none of us had enough propriety to consider the future."

"Then you regret it?" Elric blurted, the pit of his stomach souring.

"That is not what I said," she snapped before pressing her lips together. Her anger dissolved before his eyes, leaving behind a well of defeat, and then she continued. "As it would seem, all I am meant for is duty. And if it will save my kingdom, if I can be known for protecting my people instead of persecuting them—if it will keep *you* safe—then I will do it."

Elric stared at her, the pain her words brought to his heart acute. "Then you have given up already? You have accepted this, truly?"

Her eyes searched his, their waves endless but no longer terrifying. In them he saw the cliffs, the coast, the girl who loved them, and the woman he—

He stopped himself. Love was a line he was not willing to let himself cross. Not if she was truly moving forward without him. Not if this was where they parted.

Grace only sighed, eyes glistening with the tears she held in. "I did not say that either."

Something within Elric snapped, and he reached out, wrapping his arms around her waist and pulling her to him. Her hands shot out, her palms flat against his chest, forcing space to remain, though he knew she felt every inch of him from the waist down.

"I fear I've made a mistake in returning to you, Grace," Elric murmured into her ear. "I wanted to remain by your side without condition until you were free, but I fear that for me, it will never be enough. And I suspect you feel the same as well. Regardless of what your head tells you it wants."

"My mind lies," she replied, shaking her head "But I believe my heart may be an even better liar."

"Is it?" Elric asked, gaze burning into hers. "Or are you simply afraid of what it is saying?"

"Do not act as though you know my feelings," she hissed. "You cannot, especially when I am not certain of them myself."

"You say you are not certain, yet you did not hesitate to open the walls between us. The one we defied as children, and the one we stand before now. I think you know exactly what you want but are too fearful to admit it."

"What I know is that I cannot love you," she bit out, exasperation filling her tone.

Elric's eyes widened, searching hers, and he could not help the slow smile that tipped up the corners of his mouth when he leaned closer—her hands providing no resistance—and whispered against her lips. "Is that why we are discussing this in a closet, where eyes cannot find us? Where the stars themselves cannot hear us whisper? So that if the truth slips, none will know?"

Grace swallowed, but she didn't move, either to pull away or close the space between them. "Let another shackle their future to my unfortunate soul," she whispered, vulnerability seeping through. "I am doomed already."

"You are not, Grace," Elric replied, shaking his head. "Not for as long as I live. I will free you from the darkness that claims your mind, but if I may be so bold, I would lay claim to your heart and soul as well."

"I cannot handle that," she rasped, her eyes wide and unblinking, though tears dripped from her lashes in earnest. "I do not want it."

"Then you would see me leave?" Elric asked fearfully.

She groaned at his words, viciously swiping away the tears as if they offended her, then leveled her shattered gaze on him. "You stupid, foolish man. Do you not realize what it did to me to let go of you once? Do you understand what it took to do so again? I do not have the strength to release you a third time, and it is not because of the magic in your veins. It is because you are the boy who slipped through a wall and brought music back into my life. I gave everything to save you because when I lost you, I lost myself as well. The better parts of me, my soul and my heart, are yours. And they always will be."

Before Elric could absorb the full weight of her confession, Grace stormed from the closet and slammed the door in his face.

CHAPTER FORTY-THREE

*D*inner was miserable. And while Grace acted as though their conversation never happened, and failed to acknowledge Elric all evening, he found it easy not to wear his heart on his sleeve. At least until he was alone. The next day, however, he could not bring himself to seek them out and instead returned to the Diviner's Wing.

He immediately began to scour the texts on vows and tethering, wondering if he had been incorrect to assume that the research being conducted was meant for him. But none of the texts described spoke of darkness, madness, or losing oneself entirely. And nothing mentioned dreams.

Elric stood and started to pace. What corruption intended for him would have been so easily turned upon an innocent girl who possessed no power whatsoever? What force, meant to siphon his dhust, would drain her memories instead?

No, it was beyond that. Madness had taken the king before her, yet even Grace herself had said how much her father withdrew. He looked out the window, at the scorch marks on the walls, the bloodstains still on the stone. It all had been born from what the king had done—or rather refused to do—for his people. But if Arlys was to be believed, that was not the sort of man he was either. He had been picked by the lords for being well loved, then slowly withdrew even before the loss of his wife, taking the prosperity of the kingdom with him. So was it possible that what held Grace captive was not a result of her saving Elric at all, but from her lineage itself?

As if summoned by his thoughts, Grace's voice carried up into the tower, causing him to whirl around and face the small set of stairs.

"Your Majesty," someone said in greeting, and Elric's stomach plummeted as the door opened and Denfrin's face came into view.

"Master Elric," he said in a warm tone, and Elric quickly bowed. "I apologize for the surprise visit; however, this is the only place in the palace I have not yet seen. Since you were absent at breakfast, I supposed we'd find you here, and who better to give us a tour."

Elric forced a smile that faded quickly when Grace appeared from behind the king, looking everywhere about the room except at Elric. "I am flattered, Your Majesty, but I'm afraid that unless you seek books on history, this wing will not be as inter-esting as one would hope."

Denfrin hummed, walking the perimeter of the room and gazing in awe at the books and parchment tucked onto every shelf as high as the eye could see. "History does fascinate me, though I must admit the future interests me far more than the past."

"I told you there was not much to be found here," Grace said, running her finger along the spine of a book the same shade as her deep-teal dress. It was not unlike the sea, with delicate white lace trimming the bodice and sleeves, and when Elric's eyes traveled to her throat, he caught sight of the chain around her neck.

The chain that held a brooch concealed close to her heart.

"Your Majesty," came Falchion's voice, slightly out of breath as he bounded up the steps, stopping short to bow. "Forgive the interruption, but you are needed outside."

Elric glanced out the window in time to see two soldiers at the center of a small training circle throw down their weapons and start to pummel each other, collapsing into a heap on the ground.

Denfrin moved to his side, looking out, then groaned. He turned to Grace. "It would appear I must facilitate training... again. Will you remain here until I return?"

"I can accompany you," she said, a spark lighting up her words. "I am well-versed in their training—"

Denfrin's laugh interrupted her. "Swords have no place in a woman's hand, especially not one of nobility. You will remain here."

Graecerys bit her lip but dipped into a small bow. "As you wish."

Denfrin faced Elric and lowered his voice. "I trust my people to obey me, but I am not yet convinced I would trust them with my betrothed. Will you keep her safe for me?"

"With my life," Elric replied, and it was the easiest promise he ever made.

Denfrin nodded, smiling with gratitude, then stalked from the tower with Falchion on his heels, leaving the door ajar.

Elric glanced over at Grace flipping through a book she had pulled from the shelf and ignoring his presence intently. "You appear well rested this morning, Your Grace," he remarked.

Her eyes tipped to the ceiling. "Odd. I am actually quite tired."

She snapped the book shut, replacing it on the shelf before striding across the room to pick up a bright book with swirling letters on the front—ones that spelled out none other than *The King of Wishes*.

Elric grinned and moved to the shelves opposite her,

absently pulling one off the shelf and leaning on the desk. He leafed through it, though his eyes never left Grace. "Are you looking for something in particular?"

She released a low laugh. "No, I believe I am fine."

Elric paused mid-page turn. "Are you?"

Grace shifted, meeting his eyes for the first time. "I am. I am only disappointed the king was unable to stay, as I was the one who insisted you give him a tour of this wing."

She sauntered away from Elric, and he watched her go with a smirk on his face. "Just when I think I am the one preying upon you, I realize I am simply enjoying the bait in your trap."

Grace stopped before the next shelf, turning back to stare him down. Then the beautiful monster had the nerve to lift her chin in haughty defiance. "This isn't a trap. It is just another chase. If you're willing to pursue."

Thrones-damn it all.

Elric stalked across the library, erasing all space between them, and slipped his fingers around her bared neck. He applied just enough pressure for her skin to blanche—to summon the memory of their time in the cabin—then slid them north to tip up her chin.

Her eyes flared, but her expression did not falter, and though there was a flex in her jaw followed by a small gulp, she held his stare with a hungry fire.

"I expect better of you, Your Grace," he murmured, leaning down to place a slow kiss against the skin of her clavicle. "Everyone knows a hunter would go for the neck."

He tipped her head to the opposite side, nipping at the lobe of her ear before running his tongue along its curve and pressing another kiss to the skin below. "An instinctual predator would know their prey enough to understand their point of weakness," he whispered, leaning back, his mouth a fraction of an inch from her own.

Her gaze dipped to it for a heartbeat before she locked eyes with him again. And though he saw her try to resist, her lips parted.

"Going in for the kill is only an expeditious end when you are wiser than the unfortunate soul on the receiving end," he continued, tracing a line down her jaw to where her pulse raced. "But it's easy for them to make you a fool. It is better to be patient and cut them down where it will hurt the most."

Another swallow. But this time a smile crept across her face. "And what would an ancient and benevolent power know of such dark and violent ends?"

"Everything," he replied, letting his fingers slide from her neck before he stepped back and inclined his head with a small, flourishing bow. "And I have you to thank for that."

Her eyes were ravenous when she lurched toward him. He caught her, their lips colliding in unrestrained fury, a storm of tension finally combusting. He guided her back until they hit the shelves, holding her against them as she pulled her skirt up enough to wrap her legs about his waist.

He was locked in her grip, she was trapped in his grasp, they were both hunter and hunted, playing a dangerous game with fate, drowning the risk of their tryst in the silent gasps between kisses.

Elric finally pulled back, gulping in air as Grace gasped for it, her forehead falling against his, her legs still wrapped about his waist and her arms around his neck. He had never seen her so undone. And she could not be any more perfect.

"I love you," he whispered.

The words slipped out. The truth. And when she pulled back, when her broken eyes met his, she shook her head profusely. "You did not mean to say that."

"But I did. I do, Grace. I love you. With all my scattered mind, heart, body, and soul, I am yours and you are mine."

"I'm not even my own," she said, her voice cracking. "How can I be yours?"

"Because you are powerful," he murmured, banishing the air between them and whispering against her lips. "So powerful you hold command over a star, and in turn, I have fallen for you. Much has been decided for you, even more stripped away, but this choice is yours. Tell me I am not alone in this. Say you love me, even in the slightest, and lay my heart to rest."

She paused, but the sound of boots pounding down the hall sent them scattering apart. Grace yanked her dress into place, fixing the back of her hair while Elric smoothed his clothes and turned away from the door, clearing his throat and willing his body to calm.

"Graecerys!" Denfrin called up. "Come along, we have a meeting with the kitchen to discuss the meal that shall follow our wedding."

The words broke Elric's heart all over again.

"I am coming," Grace replied, her voice controlled, but she strode to where Elric stood across the room, safely out of sight, and threw her arms around his neck, kissing him as if her entire life were dependent on it.

"I want to," she whispered in his ear. "I want to love you. For the rest of my days. If it were my choice, my heart to give, I would give it only to you. Do not forget that. Even when you let me go."

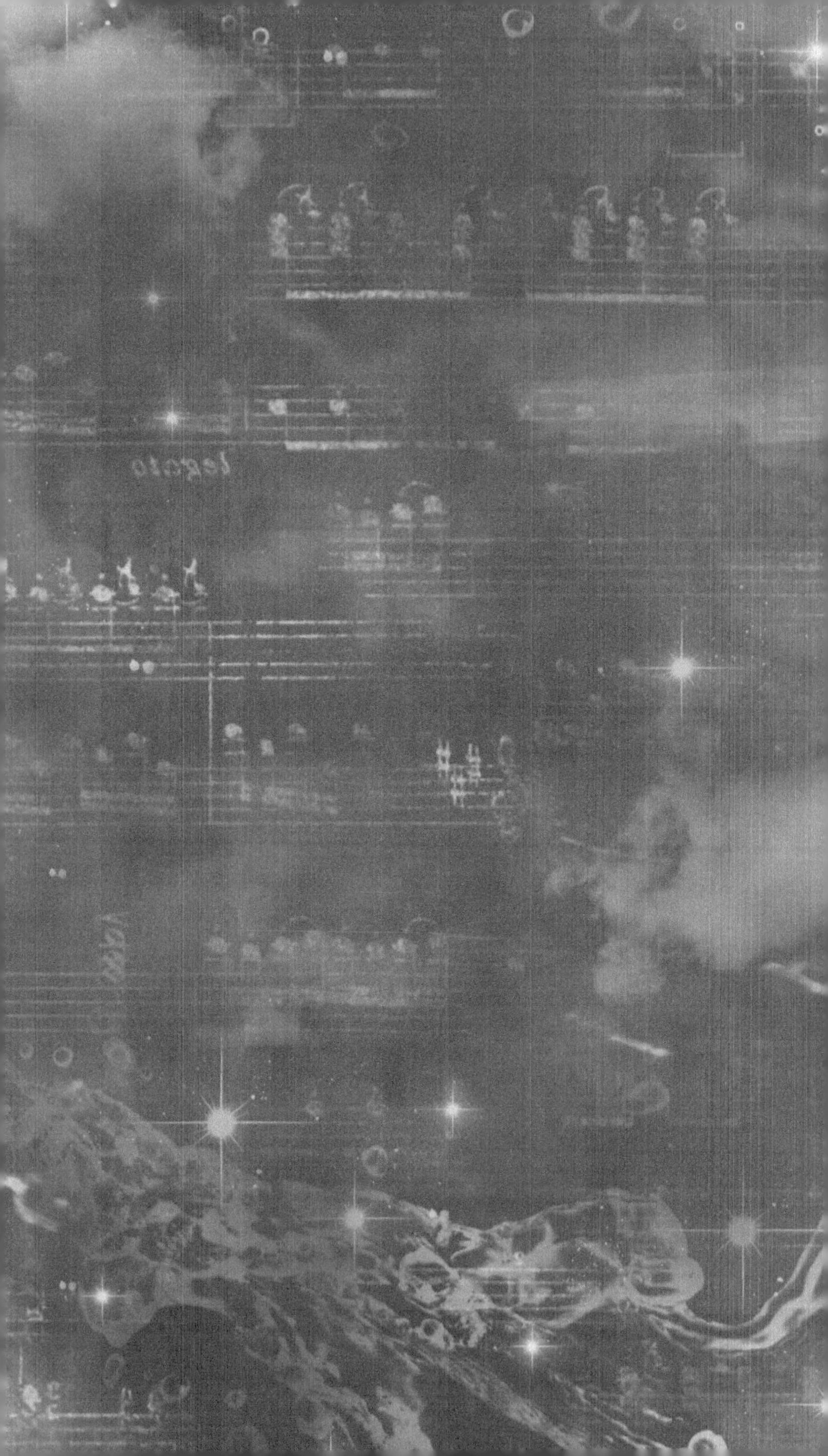

CHAPTER FORTY-FOUR

"Exactly how many bottles of wine are in your stomach right now?" Falchion asked, eyeing Elric's haggard appearance. Elric knew he should be grateful for the good-natured ribbing. They had hardly spoken since his return, the soldier more than displeased with his reappearance at the palace. But then he showed up in the hall outside Elric's quarters and waited until it was time to attend to the banquet hall, extending a silent olive branch.

"Sadly, none," he replied flatly. He had stayed in the Diviner's Wing after Grace left, pacing, then returning to his books for distraction, but nothing had helped. He then moved to his quarters where he remained restless, unable to escape his frustration over not being able to locate a source for Grace's darkness—and the torturous memory of her body wrapped around his.

Falchion halted, stopping short on the stairs. "Is that something we must fix?"

Elric snorted. "I am simply adjusting to life and its… changes."

Falchion nodded. "It has been quite the year. Nearly two."

Realization of the time he'd spent in Obarian hit like an anvil to Elric's heart. And though guilt surfaced anew—considering his willing abandonment of Inflamel—he was also weighed down by the bleak future he faced in the palace.

He would watch Graecerys live out her life belonging to another man. Over time, he would see her fall in love with him. Become a mother. Raise the future king or queen. And then turn into no more than a wave that battered his memory, constantly threatening to carry him away, though he would never be moved. They may have looked the same within the peaceful night, but when it all ended, the stars would be the ones to hold him. The ocean never would.

The banquet hall was already bustling, faces familiar and unfamiliar all eating together, though tensions were still present. And at the head was Denfrin with Grace on his left and an empty chair to his right.

The king waved him over, but when Elric began to cross the room, a woman with dark hair and fair eyes approached him, wearing a simple black gown that hung loosely about her waist. Her frame was delicate, yet she walked with strength, and though her countenance was pale, her cheeks were warm with life.

"You are the Isteriaeth?" she asked tentatively.

"I am," Elric replied with a respectful dip of his chin.

The woman swallowed, and when she met his gaze, she looked nervous. "I wanted to meet you. And to thank you. You do not know me, but you knew my husband, Lord Jacian."

Elric's eyes widened as she continued, "I was told of your kindness to him, and he spoke highly of you. I know it did not matter in the end, but I wanted you to know how much it meant to me."

Elric cleared his throat. "I am honored to meet you. And I am deeply sorry for your loss."

She smiled sadly. "The king has assured me I will always have a place within his court, and though I would rather it be by my husband's side, I am grateful. Should you need anything, please know that you have a friend here."

"Thank you, my lady," Elric said earnestly. "Your husband had a good heart. You should always remember that."

She bowed quickly, hiding the tears that threatened to spill over, and returned to the table, allowing Elric to regain his composure and continue to his place at the right hand of the king.

"Are you well, Master Elric?" Denfrin asked, peering at him over his wine.

"I believe I am," Elric replied truthfully, staring far too intensely at his food to avoid looking at the woman sitting before him in a shade of green so deep it made her eyes and hair appear radiant as jewels. "I am just weary."

Denfrin watched at him, his gaze piercing, then slowly set his glass on the table. "Many are the experiences that a man can handle, but even we have our limits," he said softly. "What you have seen and endured since your arrival is no small feat, and you still had a lifetime before. I hope you are able to allow yourself space for healing and that, in time, you find the happiness and peace you deserve."

"Thank you, Your Majesty," Elric replied, placing a sliver of meat in his mouth. It tasted like parchment, the texture like glue on his tongue. He had nothing against the man seated beside him, and in truth, he seemed decent as Falchion had said. But Elric wasn't sure which was worse, knowing that the cause of his misery was the woman meant to be Denfrin's wife, or that he was lying to Denfrin about it.

"Lady Lyra," the king continued, nodding to Lord Jacian's widow seated a ways down the table. "She is a good woman. One of the most honorable women I have ever had the pleasure of meeting. It was too soon to know, but when she lost Jacian, she was already with child. She is stronger now, with more health and care, but I am certain she will have her hands full.

Should you find that you enjoy her company, it is a match I would wholeheartedly approve of."

A fork clattered onto the table, and Elric jumped, looking up to meet Grace's wide eyes. "Apologies, my lords," she replied with a hasty smile, quickly picking up the utensil.

"I understand the topic is not one suited for you, but you might at least refrain from causing a scene," Denfrin said, his tone sharp as he stared Grace down.

Elric stiffened, having never heard him take anything but a jovial tone with her, but Grace only blinked twice, unfazed. "And what would give you the impression that I cannot handle talk of the future?"

Denfrin smirked, a thread of malice creeping into his eyes, causing Elric's hackles to rise. "Lady Lyra's plight resides on your shoulders. Her husband's blood stains your hands. I believe our union will grow to be something we enjoy, but do not think I have forgotten who and what you are. I extend you my favor, but I will not tolerate anything less than your penance. As I said, there is always space for healing, for happiness, for peace, even for forgiveness. But not even time itself can erase the harm you caused."

Grace smiled demurely, then picked up her wine glass. "Space and time, how aptly put. My lord, have you ever heard the 'Ballad of the Great Three'?"

Denfrin's eyes narrowed in confusion, but Elric shoved another piece of meat into his mouth nervously.

"The Great Three," she pressed on. "The Warden of Time—time in this instance—and the Muse of Darkness, composing music in the expansive space of the heavens itself."

Elric's heart hammered, threatening to explode out of his chest. Grace was sharing the story of the stars. But why? Denfrin leaned back in his chair, unaware of Elric's panic, his stare growing colder. "Did you mean the Great Two?"

"I meant what I said." Grace sipped her drink before continuing, "According to the tale, all that was needed to bring wholeness to the world—to form the realm we dare call our own—were the Three. I believe, between us, we have it all."

Denfrin chuckled darkly, shaking his head. "If time and space are lacking for you, my lady, then I fear that means I am the one to hold it all."

Grace set her glass on the table and rose. "One might think so, but as it would turn out, I have no need for either. All I need to be whole, for happiness and peace, is the third. The only thing I need are the stars."

Denfrin froze, but Grace simply dipped into a curtsy, then walked away.

Elric gripped his glass too tightly, willing his heart to slow as he drank. Denfrin watched her leave, then drained his wine, sighing in frustration and turning to Elric. "Find happiness and peace, Master Elric. And a woman who is soft. Not one you must break."

"Aye, but you'll have fun breaking this one, m'lord," a voice called from down the table.

Jeers sounded, glasses raised, and Elric sat frozen at the implication of the man's words, but it was what Denfrin said next that horrified him most.

"You are not incorrect, good sir, but I would be remiss not to raise a glass to the bitch. Were it not for her moment of weakness sending food to the Province of Stragium these many months ago, we would still be beyond the palace gate arguing the way forward."

Agreement chorused, but the man down the table spoke once more. "Credit where credit is due, Your Majesty. It was Lord Jacian, rest his soul, who made sure the bread never made it. Hard days they were, but it was a worthy sacrifice our bellies made then to have all that we do now."

Resounding confirmation surged in the room, and Elric

searched until he found Lady Lyra, eyes sparkling with unshed tears, though her smile remained wide and proud.

"Then we raise a glass to them both," Denfrin declared, rising to his feet. "And to the souls in the north who made the ultimate sacrifice to ensure a bright future for noble and revolutionary alike." He held his glass high, turning in place to face the room. "To the breaking and the taming! And may heirs be swift."

Cheers rose as Elric sliced another bit of meat, shoving it in his mouth for a moment to gather his wits, though it turned to ash in his stomach. Memories flooded his mind—Graecerys's confusion over the people's rejection of aid. The Province of Culwyrt in the north. The way the soldiers had turned on her there, and the look in Grace's eyes when she realized an entire province had perished. She had believed she was the cause. Everyone had. Yet while her hands were not devoid of blood, she was not the villain. It was all a lie, carefully orchestrated by the leaders of the revolution. And the price of their victory?

The lives of their own innocent people.

Only a heartbeat too late, Elric realized he was still staring in silent disgust at the king. Denfrin, none the wiser, clapped him on the shoulder and refilled his glass. "I apologize for every second you had to bear her presence alone. I know you are bound to her, but you will have to guide me. I must know how to survive her. You will help me, yes?"

Denfrin's eyes were wide, imploring, but Elric was desperate for the meal to end. He longed to rise and follow the woman who had claimed the stars as her own. And he could not wait to free her of the man, the wretch, that stood before him.

He washed the food down with a splash of ale, and with a tight smile, dipped his head and turned up his palm with a flourish. "Of course, Your Majesty."

CHAPTER FORTY-FIVE

Elric stepped inside his quarters, closing the door and sliding his back down the wall to the floor in exhaustion, but before he could rest his head in his hands, a rapping sound drew his attention.

It was tapping. Not on his door, or the wall, but from the balcony.

He pushed himself to his feet and crossed the room, opening the doors and exiting into the night air—a cold relief to his overheated, stress-ridden body.

Grace stood a short distance away, still wearing the same dress from dinner, though her hair was unbound now. It shone like silk in the starlight, her eyes like sapphires, and despite the inescapable horror he felt closing in on them at every turn, the tension bled from Elric's shoulders and he smiled.

"You are breathtaking."

Something in her face broke, and she ran to him, her hair floating on the air behind her in perfect waves, and before Elric could blink, she threw her arms around his neck.

He caught her—he would always catch her—and her body melded into his. He held her tighter, breathing her in. It was dangerous, and it terrified him, but it was becoming harder to deny how it made him feel to have her in his arms.

"I thought earlier, in the tower, when you said—"

"I didn't know what I was talking about," Grace cried, pulling back to clasp his face in her hands. "You were braver than I, but I have made my choice. You are all I want. All I need are the stars."

His mind silenced. His world silenced. And for the first time since flirting with freedom as a young man under the trees beside his first love, Elric knew peace. His life was an endless, violent storm bent on breaking him and tearing him away from all that he loved, but the woman before him now was fiercer than it all.

And she was his.

He wanted to sink, to be lost in her. Even if it meant he could no longer see the stars, he would go willingly. For her he would live. For her he would die. If it meant she thrived, he would lose it all. He had made that mistake once before, not being enough to save those he loved most, but he would not breathe without the woman in his arms.

He rested her feet on the ground once more and pressed a soft, tender kiss to her lips. She pulled him tighter, crushing his face against her own, then pushing away when he resisted.

"Do not do this," she warned. "I do not want soft, I do not want tender. I want to feel something. *Anything*. Take me, Elric. I need you. Right now."

He shook his head. "No."

Her eyes flashed, and she tried to step away, but he only drew her closer.

"I don't want to *take* you," he replied. "You are not here for the taking, you are not a horse to be broken or tamed. You are wild and beautiful and everything I did not know would bring my soul to life. But if I may be so fortunate, may I have you? Your hand. Your body. Your heart. Your storm against my shore. Your music in my silence. Your darkness amid my stars."

Her face crumpled and she collapsed against his chest, surrendering, hiding in his arms, even if for a fleeting moment. But he would steal it like the thief he was, and he would find a way to make it last forever.

"You already have all of me," she swore. "I love the stars too much to ever fear the darkness. Never let me go."

And he did not. He held her, turning her into the shadows of the balcony, pressing her back to the wall, and shielding her from the night as he swallowed her breathy cries, giving her all that she begged for.

He did not let her go when he carried her back into her quarters, not trusting his own to be undisturbed. He laid her across the bed, reverently kissing, marking, claiming every inch of her skin, then allowing her to do the same in return. And when she sat astride him and leaned down to press a kiss to his lips, he held her still, and whispered, "I think I love you the most like this."

Her face flushed, her brow creasing in amusement. "What do you mean?"

"Choosing for yourself. Powerful. Free."

Tears rimmed her eyes, and when she settled into Elric's side, he smiled. "And happy."

"How do you know I am happy?" she asked breathlessly.

"You cry when you are happy. You rage when you are heartbroken. And when you smile and laugh? All should run for cover."

Grace threw her head back and laughed, though her eyes widened quickly and she slapped a hand over her mouth.

Elric chuckled softly, cupping the back of her neck and pulling her face to his. "Except for then."

"Good, because there will be no running for cover for you," she replied, peppering kisses along his jawline toward his ear.

"I have no desire to go anywhere," he murmured back, burying his face in the curve of her neck.

"Would you go somewhere? With me?" she whispered in his ear.

He stilled, and at his silence, she pulled away to meet his eyes. "Will you come with me this time?" he asked, vulnerable enough to fear the answer.

She nodded. "Right now. Summon your dhust. Carry us far from here, and I will never look back."

Elric smiled sadly. "I have not seen nor felt that strand since I expended it carrying us to the mountains, or else this place would be a distant memory."

Grace's face fell, and she nestled closer into his side. "The we leave as we always planned. It will truly be *our* boat this time."

Reality seeped back into his mind like a cold current slowly rising in his chest. "They will still not stop until they find us, will they?"

She shook her head, words failing, though her face fell, shadowed with worry and fear.

Elric nodded in silent acceptance. "Then we best hide well. How do you feel about living within a tree?"

They remained in her bed until the sky began to lighten and the sun threatened to shine on all they had hidden in the dark. When Elric finally dressed and opened the door in the wall, Grace laid a hand on his arm.

He turned back toward her, wrapping his arms around her waist and pressing a kiss to her forehead. "We must find a way before Moonrise," she said. "I am ready when you are."

He pulled away, caressing her cheek and losing himself to the waves in her eyes. "I will not leave until I find a way to free your mind. Until I break whatever hold the darkness has on you. And when I find it, I swear I will stop it once and for all. You found me in the dark. Saved me and reminded me who I was. I will do the same for you. This is only the start."

She met his eyes once more, then reached up and slid a finger down his cheek, as if she wished to memorize every inch of his skin. "I love you," she whispered.

He froze. His mind silenced. The stars stilled in his veins.

"I love you," she repeated. "You are all that I have, Elric, all that I want, and the only thing in this Thrones-forsaken world that I love. I'm scared to death of the future, of the darkness consuming me whole, but if my heart will know safety anywhere, it is in your hands. With my entire broken and tormented soul, I love you."

He held her close, clutching her tightly to him, his heart racing at her words, and when they parted, she pressed one final kiss to his lips and whispered, "Please hurry."

Exhausted, yet sated, Elric shut the door in the wall behind him and collapsed across his bed. He knew he needed to rest for a few hours, but everything in him spurred him to keep searching, to find answers faster and get Grace as far away as possible. Allowing himself to dream of the future, of what it might be like to be free with her by his side, he found himself slowly drifting off to sleep—

He gasped and sat up with a jolt.

The darkness was *consuming* her.

Grace was not cursed. There was no dark magic at work within her as she carried no dhust. She was being *consumed*.

Sapphire dhust poured from his hand, the tome and his mother's notes tumbling onto the bed beside him, and he ripped the papers out, surveying them together in awestruck horror.

He did not know what led his mother to study Kollapsars, or how she would have determined that the only demon faceless and unknown to Breteria existed as a host within a living being, but she had left him exactly what he was looking for all along.

Grace was not being lost to madness.

Grace was slowly being devoured by a Vacare.

CHAPTER FORTY-SIX

The girl who had grown up in the presence of the Trifolium Mountains—the very ones the Kollapsars hid within before they rose to destroy the Thrones—was being consumed from the inside out, *taken from within*, by the most mysterious and deadly form of darkness known to Breteria.

The truth thrummed in Elric like a current, driving him to read faster and faster, burning through the shelves in the Diviner's Wing, though he had missed dinner and the sun had long since vanished in the sky.

Now that he knew what subject to read, he had found more of his mother's notes. They confirmed that the Vacare were known only as formless and shapeless. Some had suspected they could indwell beings, but there had been no proof. It was believed they had disappeared with the rest of the Kollapsar forms when their leader was felled at the Trifolium Keep, but following his mother's trail had led him to deduce that the Vacare had never left Obarian. Instead, they slipped through the ages undetected, a single host existing to consume and ulti-mately control other beings one by one until they amassed an army for the Kollapsar. They had always been there, orchestrating the rise and fall of so many Obarian leaders, fueling unrest, trying and failing to claim the greatest source of the dhust that sustained their life—the last of the Isteriaeth. But instead of capturing Elric, they ended up with Grace.

Grace, however, had not fallen. She had sacrificed herself, held on to her humanity—to her memory of Elric—and avoided being taken fully. Which meant that the host still existed. But if Augur had in fact been the host, and he was now dead, would that not have set her free?

Elric pushed away from his desk, pacing the floor furiously. They were running out of time in more ways than one, only now he did not need to learn how to break the hold of a curse. He needed to know how to find and defeat an ancient darkness.

The door to the wing opened with a *bang*, and Falchion entered. "Your presence has been requested immediately."

Elric froze, fear seizing his heart. "Is there something wrong?"

Falchion did not meet his eyes but nodded. "Indeed. The king must see you at once."

Elric followed him, the soldier unnaturally stiff, and when he led Elric not to the throne room but directly to the king's private quarters, his stomach plummeted. He had never been to the royal chambers before.

Falchion knocked on the door, then inclined his head to Elric. "I am to wait outside."

"Enter," Denfrin's voice said from within.

Elric nodded to Falchion and then, taking a deep breath, entered the room. It was easily three times the size of his or Grace's quarters. He tried not to look at the enormous four-poster bed, to think of what he risked transpiring there if he did not find answers in time, but instead turned to the round, wooden table opposite it.

Denfrin stood behind it, his chair pushed back, leaning on his knuckles on the surface, his anger palpable and his stare severe. And sitting in the chair at his side was none other than Lord Blenheim.

Elric bowed. "Your Majesty. My lord. How may I be of assistance?"

"Explain to me your tether with Graecerys," Denfrin demanded. "How does it work?"

Elric tipped his head to the side. "I am not sure what you mean."

"Can you speak to each other? See inside one another's thoughts? Anything of the sort?"

Elric gave credit where credit was due—Denfrin was an intelligent man. And despite his disdain for the books on history, he seemed to know it quite well. "We cannot. Because the tether was seized and not shared, we are inexplicably tied only. She may draw from me whatever she wishes, but I did not willingly enter into the tethering, so I cannot draw anything from her."

Blenheim's stare bore into him, unblinking, but Denfrin simply exhaled and dipped his head, staring at the table. Elric waited in silence, and when the king lifted his head again, there was a weariness in his face that Elric had never seen before. "Tell me, Isteriaeth, can I trust you?"

Elric's throat constricted, his guilt threatening to choke him, but he rallied his courage, knowing in his heart that he would not change a thing where Grace was concerned. "Of course, Your Majesty."

Denfrin opened his mouth, then closed it again. He stood straighter, shifting as though he might pace, but sat instead, resting his elbows on the table and clasping his hands before him. "I have reason to believe Graecerys may be unfaithful."

Elric felt the color drain from his face, knowing that Blenheim did not miss it, but unable to stop it all the same. Denfrin saw it too, but he just nodded. "I know. I do not know what to think. I want to rage, I want to storm her chambers, I want to wring her neck, but at the same time, I am simply hurt. I did not expect her to embrace this arrangement right away, I did not wish her to feign love for me. But I thought she would at least respect the crown, the throne she fought so desperately to hold, and not make a mockery of this union. I thought we may at least make it to the altar."

"I…am sorry, Your Majesty," Elric said, his sincerity real.

Denfrin shook his head. "You have nothing to be sorrowful for. It is still rumor. I had simply hoped you might confirm or deny."

"The guards confirmed that she was seen slipping about the palace, in dark closets and the shadows of her own balcony, presumably with a lover," Blenheim said, addressing the king. "Do you believe they would seek to sow disunity between you?"

"I do not doubt it," Denfrin replied, his tone laced with defeat. "It is as if the entire kingdom is against us, the very soil and air fighting to prevent peace from finally being won."

"Then might I make a suggestion, Your Majesty?" Blenheim said, shifting in his seat so he faced both Elric and the king.

Denfrin nodded, extending a hand. "Please do."

"I know the significance of the Moonrise, but I daresay waiting will only breed trouble. The wedding must be moved. You must marry as soon as possible. Before you tour the kingdom, so that she may join you and not fall into another's bed."

A hollow echo was all Elric heard in his ears, watching the men discuss the arrangements, the implications on the kingdom, and what might come of a quicker union. He replied when spoken to, nodded when asked for his acquiescence, and when both men finally stood with smiles on their faces, he smiled too.

Denfrin crossed the room, laying a hand on his shoulder. "I cannot thank you enough, Master Elric. And with the wedding now days away instead of weeks, perhaps we might find you some peace as well. There will be no need to watch her once I have control of her. It is not full freedom, but it will at least somewhat mend the agency stolen from you."

Elric nodded, bowing his head to avoid the king's eyes. "It is my greatest honor, Your Majesty."

He exited the room, stalking down the hall past Falchion, who jumped off the wall and followed in long strides to catch up.

"What is it?" he asked, but Elric said nothing.

"Surely it is something," the guard went on, but Elric ignored him. It was not until they had reached the long, dark hall leading to the Diviner's Wing that Falchion grasped his arm, forcibly halting him.

"Elric, say something, please. I am concerned for you." The earnestness, the fear in his eyes, softened Elric's heart, and he shook his head.

"All is well. The wedding is to be moved. It will take place in two evenings' time."

Falchion's brow furrowed. "But that is good news."

"Very," Elric replied. "Now if you'll excuse me, I wish to return to my studies."

But Falchion did not release his arm. "I fear I must ask you a question," he said quietly, as if afraid someone might hear. "All that I ask is you reply honestly."

Elric swallowed. "Falchion, do not ask me to do what I cannot."

The soldier dropped his elbow and took a step back. "Something did transpire, then. There was a difference at the manor, but I...I did not think...."

Elric said nothing, but he did not move either. He did not have the strength to walk away.

Falchion shook his head, and to Elric's surprise, he stepped forward and rested both of his hands on Elric's shoulders. "I am sorry. Deeply. But it must end. I know it will break you, and I daresay it will mar both your hearts for the differences I have seen in her. But 'tis better to live broken than be lost forever. Take heart and let her go."

Elric cleared his throat, straightening. "I already have. I am many things—hopeless, a fool—but I will not seek out another man's wife. She is to be our queen. I will not interfere with that."

An ironic sorrow filled Falchion's face. "You are even worse off than I feared, my friend. Giving up is unlike you."

Elric stepped away, shaking his head. "There is only so much unfairness one can fan into rage before the air that once fueled it chokes instead. It is over, Falchion. You have nothing to fear."

He began walking again, then paused suddenly and turned back. "When is the next trade ship departing for Inflamel?"

"I believe there is one set a few days from now. Two beyond the wedding." Falchion hesitated. "Do you have need of it?"

Elric took a deep breath, steadying himself, then he exhaled once more. "I do. Let them know there shall be more cargo aboard."

CHAPTER FORTY-SEVEN

The news descended on the palace with a flurry of excitement. Couriers were sent to the provinces, royal carriages accompanying them to bring all who might wish to witness the accord between the people and the crown. But Elric kept to himself, avoiding his quarters and refusing to emerge from the Diviner's Wing, claiming preparation for the wedding ceremony.

And it was not a lie. Entirely. He was trying, though he did not believe there was an amount of time that would prepare him to witness the woman he loved marrying another—nothing in the realm he could summon to help him survive being the one who bound her to another. His heart could not take it.

The door handle jiggled and then someone banged on the door.

"Elric. Elric, I know you are in there."

His head shot up, Grace's voice like a siren call to his heart.

"Elric, I must see you. I must speak with you."

He closed his eyes, squeezing them shut. "I am busy."

"Then meet me tonight. On the balcony. It is…it is my last night in my quarters."

Elric swallowed. "I do not know if I shall return to mine this evening."

"Elric, please," Grace urged, panic rising in her voice.

"I cannot, Grace," he snapped. "My heart cannot. It will perish on this ride. It is already failing and still has yet to face the end."

"And I will perish if you do not meet me one last time," she pleaded.

He ran his hands down his face, then pushed them back into his hair, squeezing it in fistfuls. "As you wish, Your Grace."

He remained in the wing for as long as possible, then finally —when he knew he could avoid it no longer—returned to his quarters. He crossed the floor in the darkness and looked outside, finding where Grace waited for him, her soft-yellow gown and silken red hair flowing out behind her in the night breeze. It was nearly impossible to breathe through the pain of losing her again, but with all the strength he possessed, he steeled himself and stepped out on the balcony.

She turned at the sound of his door, her eyes alight when she saw his face, but she did not run to him this time. She simply folded her arms about her front, though he was unsure if it was to stave away the cold or hold herself together.

"I believe I have discovered why your dreams plague you," he said quietly. "I dare not tell you now, but I will save you as I promised. And when the root is gone, I will depart. Just as you ordered."

Her throat bobbed and she looked away, tears filling her eyes when she stared into the night, and then—as only Grace would —she began to laugh. "So that is it, then. Just like that. I never had high hopes for love before, but I thought coming from you it might have meant something stronger."

Elric stepped toward her slowly. "It means everything."

"Is that supposed to be funny?" she asked incredulously, meeting his eyes with a flash of anger. "You who claimed to have lost everything. Am I now just another one of those things?"

"I am allowing you to keep your word, and I am honoring mine," Elric said evenly. "And if bound is all we are meant to be, then know I will die a prisoner to you. Heart and soul, the galaxies in my veins will shine for you alone."

"And what if that is not good enough?" she demanded. "What then? You claim you can save me, but who will keep me from the dark until then? Who will chase the shadows from my mind when I cannot remember who I am?"

Her eyes shone, the waves cascading down her cheeks, staining her skin in tracks much like the tide had done through the sand they'd stood upon the moment his heart knew he loved her.

"It must be good enough," he whispered. He couldn't find the strength to speak firmly, and even after he swallowed and cleared his throat, his traitorous lip quivered. "We are strong, not because we were born to be, but because we have to be. We must be bold, if not for ourselves, then for the people who rely on our power. And that is what you will bring, Grace. Power. As a queen. In your rightful place."

"And what about who I rely on? Who you rely on? Did we come this far to be nothing more than powerless children once again?"

He stepped toward her slowly. "We knew, Grace. We dared to hope for more, dream as we had once before, but deep inside, we knew. Our love will never fade, but it was made of stolen moments that departed too quickly. At least we both shall survive in the end."

Her face collapsed in bitterness, her eyes squeezed shut. "I know duty supersedes death, but love is greater than either. You might have changed your mind, but I will never change my heart."

He caught her chin, lifted her eyes to his, brushed her tears away, and then pressed the softest, most tender kiss to her lips. She returned it, clinging to him as if he was the only thing grounding her to earth. And even after their lips parted, she held on, safe in his embrace.

He wrapped an arm tight around her shoulders and buried the opposite hand in her hair, his fingers caressing her scalp in the places he knew the pins had gripped too tight. He held her until her breathing became even, until both their tears stopped falling, and then he stepped away.

Placing one hand behind his back, he clasped the balled fist of the other to his heart, and when he descended to one knee before her, he offered her one last glance filled with all the love and pride in his heart, then bowed his head deeply.

"My queen."

CHAPTER FORTY-EIGHT

Grace stood before the mirror, excited chatter milling about her as maids pinned her hair, adjusted her dress, powdered her nose. She gazed at herself, unsure if it was real or not. If *she* was real or not. There were many days when she had wondered if life could be worse than the darkness that haunted her sleep, but now she knew they were one and the same. Except the darkness was comforting. She was alone there. She had not considered choosing it above life in some time, but now, facing the truth of what lay ahead of her, maybe she would.

The door opened and the women around her stood, all curtsying. She braced herself to see the king, but met the eyes of Lord Blenheim instead.

"Leave us, please," he addressed the maids, and when the last had filed from the room, shutting the door behind her, he faced Grace and smiled.

"You look lovely."

She turned away from him, back to the mirror, without saying a word.

"Oh, come now, Graecerys. I understand you are angry with me, but we both know this is for the best."

She did not speak. She refused. Her silence was one of the final things she could wield as a weapon, and she would use it to guard her life.

Blenheim stopped by her side, both their frames filling the mirror now. "I know it does not seem like it, but I have always wanted what is best for you. Since your father entrusted you to me, I have sought to make you great, and I will. You need only trust me for a little longer and forgive me for taking these matters into my own hands."

Something stirred in her, rising, responding to his words.

Something she knew.

Something she feared.

The weight of the memory slammed into her, the pain slicing through her mind, stealing her breath away....

THE COLD MAN WAITED FOR HER. LORD BLENHEIM WAITED FOR HER.

"WERE YOU SPEAKING TO YOURSELF LAST NIGHT, OR HAVE YOU A GHOST IN YOUR QUARTERS?"

THE HAIRS LIFTED ON HER ARM, PANIC SEIZING HER HEART, THOUGH SHE REPLIED HAUGHTILY, "IMAGINED FRIENDS ARE THE ONLY ONES I HAVE TO TALK WITH HERE."

"THAT IS A RELIEF. THOUGH I DON'T BELIEVE FIGMENTS OF YOUR IMAGINATION CAN TAP FROM WITHIN THE WALLS UNDER COVER OF DARKNESS, CAN THEY?"

SHE FROZE, MIND SPINNING. STARGELL HAD TO KNOW THE RISKS HE TOOK TO FIND HER. SHE DID NOT HAVE TIME TO WONDER WHAT HE HAD BEEN THINKING, AND IN THE END, BENEATH THE COLD MAN'S STARE, SHE DECIDED SILENCE WAS BEST.

"IF YOU FIND THAT THIS FRIEND OF YOURS IS A BIT MORE... LIVELY, I SHOULD VERY MUCH LIKE TO BE INTRODUCED. AND IF

THEY ARE WHO I SUSPECT, THEN YOU NEED NOT FEAR. YOU TWO WILL CERTAINLY REMAIN CLOSE." HE PULLED A VIAL FROM HIS JACKET AND PLACED IT IN HER HAND. "SHARE TEA WITH HIM AND GIVE HIM THIS. I SHALL HANDLE THE REST. NO ONE SHOULD ROAM ALONE IN DARKNESS. YOU BOTH DESERVE FAR BETTER."

SHE STILL SAID NOTHING, WAITING UNTIL THE MAN WAS OUT OF THE ROOM BEFORE RELEASING THE AIR FROM HER LUNGS.

"OH, AND *AURIANA*," HE SAID FROM THE HALL, THE NAME SHE HAD ONLY USED IN SECRET CHILLING HER TO THE BONE. "DO NOT MAKE ME WAIT, ELSE I WILL TAKE THESE MATTERS INTO MY OWN HANDS."

Grace shook her head. "No."

Lord Blenheim's eyebrows lifted. "No? My dear, when did you start believing you had a choice?"

The darkness seeped into her vision now. Her fear drew closer, threatening to strike, but then she saw something glisten. Just the thinnest strand sparkling in the dark. She tugged on it, and it cut through the shadows, warming her and filling her with strength.

"I know who I am," she said firmly. "And I will always have a choice."

Blenheim's eyes were hard, cutting through her armor to her very heart, and though Grace refused to let her determination waver, she worried he could see straight through her.

"You were always stronger than your father," he mused. "The better leader. The more moldable mind. You leaned on me as much as I poured into you. Resistant at first, then all too willing to escape your own living nightmare. The guilt. The betrayal."

Grace closed her eyes, searching for the strand again, looking for her star in the dark, but when cold hands seized her roughly by the arm, pulling her ear to Blenheim's lips, she flinched.

"Have you forgotten why your mind tortures you the way it does?" he whispered. "Do you remember what you've done?"

The world spun around her, the darkness churning whether her eyes were open or shut. She wanted to refuse it, but it all came rushing toward her.

SHE WATCHED THE HORIZON FOR AS LONG AS HER EYES WOULD STAY OPEN, THEN RETURNED TO BED. THE NEXT WEEK BROUGHT DAYS MORE LONELY THAN ANY SHE HAD KNOWN BEFORE, BUT FREEDOM WAS JUST WITHIN HER GRASP.

SHE WOULD RETURN TO THE MANOR IN THE SUMMER, ALONE, AND FROM THERE, SHE WOULD VANISH.

BUT THE WEEK BEFORE HER DEPARTURE, SHE ENTERED THE BANQUET HALL TO FIND LORD BLENHEIM WAITING FOR HER.

"YOU BETRAYED ME."

"I DID NOT."

"THE BOY IS GONE, AND I KNOW YOU HAD A HAND IN IT."

"I DO NOT KNOW WHAT BOY YOU—"

"THE BOY HIDING WITHIN THE WALLS. THE ONE WE HAVE BEEN SEARCHING FOR LONGER THAN YOU HAVE BEEN ALIVE," HE SHOUTED.

THE GIRL SNAPPED HER MOUTH SHUT, AND IN THE RINGING SILENCE, SAID, "HE WAS GONE BEFORE I COULD ACT ON YOUR WORD."

LORD BLENHEIM STARED AT HER, THEN LET OUT A SHORT EXHALE AND DABBED AT HIS BROW WITH A HANDKERCHIEF. "THEN I SUPPOSE YOU ARE ABSOLVED ON ALL COUNTS. YOU SEE, HAD YOU BROUGHT HIM TO ME AS INSTRUCTED, HE WOULD STILL BE HERE. WITH YOU. NO LONGER IN HIDING, BUT FREE TO BECOME ALL HE WAS BORN TO BE. INSTEAD, THE SHIP HE STOWED AWAY ON MET A STORM ON THE STRAIT. THE BOAT AND ALL ITS CARGO WERE RUN ADRIFT ON THE ROCKS, THEN CLAIMED BY THE SEA. THE REMNANTS HAVE BEEN WASHING UP ON SHORE FOR DAYS. INCLUDING THIS."

The girl jumped as Lord Blenheim threw a pack on the table. A small leather one. The one that had never left Stargell's body, save once in her room on the worst night of her life.

Her heartbeat roared in her ears, and she grasped the table for purchase, gasping for air. "He— He is…."

"Dead. All because of you."

The music stopped.

The world grew quiet, more than it had ever been before.

And when she reached out to grasp the pack, to pull it to her own chest, she did not think of her position, her place, or her name.

She simply fled, ignoring the calls and shouts after her, the admonishment for her running through the palace halls.

She did not stop until she reached the music room. Dropping the pack on the floor, she climbed onto the bench. Her fingers attempted to grip the ivory, to grab onto it like a life raft, and she gasped for breath like it was her own lungs filling with water. It should have been. She should have been right beside him. It was all her fault.

"Stargell?" she whispered, though she knew he wasn't there. He never would be again.

"I'm sorry. I'm sorry. I am so sorry," she sobbed. Her chest caved in and her shoulders heaved. Trembling uncontrollably, she bent forward, resting her head on the piano, allowing the cool keys to move against her cheek.

It was the only caress she would receive. The sole comfort that would hold her while her heart felt as though it were dying in her chest. It had somehow survived one unimaginable loss, it was unfathomable for it to hold another.

She sobbed her apologies, their cries wailing from her

The sob in Grace's chest turned into a scream. Her body was racked with pain, tears streamed down her face, but she whirled to face Blenheim and shoved him away. "Get out."

His smile was cruel, and he shook his head. "I'm not through with you yet. Almost, but not quite."

"But I am finished with you," she spat back, and instead of searching for light, she seized the very darkness that had plagued and tortured her for most of her life. She harnessed it, letting it bleed into her eyes and flare from her nostrils.

Blenheim's gaze turned to stone, then a violent anger filled his face. "You were nothing more than broken pieces of a girl when I took you under my wing. I should have known you would grow into an ungracious mess of a woman."

"I was never cared for by you," she growled back. "You left me alone, you kept me from my father, and then you allowed the court to have their way with me. You tried to break me, but I owe every bit of the woman I am to the one who taught me how to survive. The one who showed me how to fight every second for what is good and bright in this darkness. I owe my life to my mother."

Blenheim laughed haughtily. "The one who let you go?"

"The one who died believing I was everything she thought I could be. I honor her in all that I do, every breath I draw, and when I am finally free of this place—when you search and can no longer find me—I will be somewhere fighting for the beauty left in this realm. And I will not stop until you suffer the same fate as every other man who sought to destroy me."

Blenheim stared at her, his face transfixed in rage, but it was his smile that made the darkness flee, stealing her confidence with it. And once again, Grace knew true fear.

"Be careful, little *Auriana*. I would so hate for your star to find his way to the bottom of the Grimm Sea."

Fear and rage in tandem gripped her, but she matched his cruel, heartless smile. "Touch him and I will kill you myself."

Blenheim laughed, shaking his head, then turned away. "I should like to see you murderous. It is a sight I have waited a lifetime for. I will see you at the ceremony. Do not be late."

CHAPTER FORTY-NINE

$\mathcal{E}$lric felt as though he stood inside a memory. Or was it a nightmare?

The throne room was filled with people, all watching, all eagerly awaiting the long sought-after peace promised to them. And he had been there before. In a different kingdom, a different age, and what seemed like a different lifetime. He had stood beside his brother, his friend—consumed with joy and finally whole—and facilitated his marriage to a woman who had felt more family to him than the distant stars in the sky.

Only now, a king stood next to him, resplendent in his armor, not unlike the warrior kings of old. He was not evil, yet not a good man either, and somehow that made him worse.

After a few moments, when a hush fell over the crowd, the doors at the back of the opulent room opened and the darkness and memories alike all faded, leaving only Grace before him.

She was breathtaking, her gown an ethereal gold, with strands of pearls that dripped from the front, framing her flaw-less figure and swaying as she walked. Her sleeves flowed off her shoulders, billowing around her in sheer folds, and the blue silken sash that cinched her waist matched the thin one braided through her hair. On her head was a crown, tall but delicate, reaching to the sky and suspending strand after strand of starlit diamonds. She was the embodiment of the land, the sky, and the sea, all in one. Elric's entire world. She was the brightest star in her own universe and the lone light inside his.

And like a star near death, she was ready to burst and fade away into something more beautiful—something far greater than even he. There would be no more pretending that the future might be theirs. She was gone. This was the end.

Elric held his face controlled, refusing to see the ghosts that accompanied her. The loves he had lost before, paving her path forward, beside her as she walked both to and further from him with every step.

His mother, promising him wonder for as long as he found the stars.

Timothius, consumed with joy and then madness, cursing them for their ruthlessness.

Kathrina, dreaming of a future by his side and claiming the entire sky for herself.

And now Grace.

All the pieces of his heart that he had removed in order to survive, the losses he was never strong enough to carry alone, he would now lay to rest in the grave beside his love for her.

Yet he would remain. He always did.

Grace reached the dais, and when Denfrin extended his hand to her, she took it, stepping up before him and beside Elric. Her chest rose and fell in steady rhythm, and she offered Denfrin a polite smile, dipping on her heel in a curtsy. He bowed in return, and then they both turned their attention to Elric.

Avoiding the blue waves that he would sacrifice his dhust to drown in, he faced Denfrin and summoned a rope of alabaster velvet. He bound it to Denfrin's wrist, then after speaking a few words over it in the tongue of the stars, he met the king's eyes.

"His Majesty will now recite the vow set forth by the stars for binding in blessing."

The king cleared his throat, faced Grace, and then spoke loud and true.

"From strands to dhust, of this union I proclaim—

"Our fate bound by the stars and sworn by my name."

A soft cloud gathered, fading the world's edges with a glimmer of soft starlight—the presence of Elric's parents, his siblings, his loved ones, and the generations before.

His first loves. His first losses. His final failure.

Resigned, he faced Grace once more, taking her hand, and fastening the opposite end of the rope to her wrist. On the surface, her confidence was assured, but he saw the panic dancing behind her eyes, her mask slipping, those vulnerable waves threatening to break through. She never cracked or bent for anyone. And seeing her falter, watching her break?

Something within him burst, and the force of a thousand stars rushed from his chest into his veins.

"It is your turn," Denfrin prodded, whispering to Grace and drawing her attention. "We are almost finished."

She blinked, her chest starting to rise and fall faster. "I... I...."

Concern crossed the king's face. "Are you not well? You look faint."

"I am...I just...I cannot remember the words."

Her eyes found Elric's and the knife in his heart twisted deeper. "Then repeat after me."

She looked down, her breathing growing erratic, and as the crowd began to murmur and Denfrin turned to silence them, Elric leaned forward ever so slightly, and whispered, "Grace."

Her breath caught, and she looked up at him as a single tear fell from her lashes. He nodded once, wordlessly reassuring her, and when she inhaled again, she nodded in return.

"From strands to dhust," he murmured.

"From strands to dhust," she echoed, her eyes tracing his face.

"Of this union I proclaim."

"Of this union I proclaim."

"Our fate bound by the stars," Elric whispered, his attention never once wavering from her.

"Our love bound by the stars," Grace breathed, and before Elric could correct her, she finished. "And sworn by my name."

He nodded, smiling softly, even though his heart bled. "And sworn by my name."

It was as if the world ceased moving. The dhust, the starlight surrounded them, sealing them in and hiding them from the world.

"*Grace*," he whispered, but his lips did not move. And though he swore the words were not audible, he heard her reply.

"*Elric*."

Something burned on his arm, as if he were being branded, and he flinched. He saw Grace do the same, their eyes meeting for a heartbeat in confusion and panic, but when he caught a glimpse of her skin, Elric ceased breathing.

Stars, golden and shining, twined around her arm in a delicate band just above the crook of her elbow. They coiled like a ribbon, then a strand tumbled into the air between them, and from his own sleeve he watched another unfurl. The halves met, and a cage within his chest clicked open, the key thrown away and the doors flung wide.

The strand grew taut between them, binding them to one another, and then it disappeared into nothing more than a cloud of gilded dhust—the only sign it had ever existed were the stars that shone on both of them, etched forever into their skin.

The mark of the star-blessed tether.

Sacred. Unbreakable. Everlasting.

Elric rushed to utter the final words, feeling the sting of the brand and a soft flutter against his heart all at the same time. He warned Grace not to speak with a glance, her face slack with disbelief, and when Denfrin opened his eyes and pressed a chaste kiss to her cheek, her eyes never left Elric.

Even when they turned and walked back down the aisle as husband and wife in the sight of the people, she glanced over her shoulder and lit up his skies with her hope.

The stars did not lie, and now Elric and Grace were forever bound. In the eyes of the stars, he had just taken the Queen of Obarian as his wife.

CHAPTER FIFTY

The celebration lasted unbearably long, Elric occupying the wall as the couple danced and were showered with gifts—small trinkets and flowers from the children of Obarian.

He disappeared only for a moment, long enough to seek shelter and rip the shirt from his arm, revealing his cuff of stars to the air.

It was real. It was all real.

He leaned against the wall, relief and terror gripping him at once.

Grace was his wife, but the man who believed he was her husband was about to take her to their marriage chamber. He could not— He would not allow it to happen. She was his. Truly his now. And as such, pain would never come to her again. Sacrifice would never touch her. Her duty would be to be loved and cherished until she took her final breaths. And even then, he would ascend to the sky and protect her. Beyond life, beyond the grave, she was his.

He watched closely as Denfrin moved back to the throne. A table sat by its side, some food laid out for the king and queen to have refreshment. And though a small part of him felt guilt, he summoned the king's meal to himself and replaced it with the meat from a few nights prior, refilling his glass with an odorless tonic that would speed the effects of the rancid food in his system.

Grace danced, passed hand over hand to different men and ladies, all wishing to pay their respects and offer congratulations, and Elric slipped in among them. When he grasped her fingers and she turned into his arms, she gasped.

"Do not touch the food," he uttered under his breath. "Trust me."

Her brow furrowed slightly, but she kept her fake smile in place, and when he handed her off once more, he vanished from the room.

He found Falchion in the courtyard with ale, the soldiers in his care coming off watch and milling about with the same. He saw Elric and lifted his drink in salute, then grabbed a bottle off the wall and threw it his way. Elric snatched it from the air, and though he uncorked it, he did not take a drink. He would not be drowning his sorrows tonight. He wanted to remember this day for the rest of his life.

"My friend, here is to you," slurred Falchion. "And here is to me. And here is to every other sorry lot not yet fortunate enough to find happiness in this life. May it come quickly, with a fine woman and a strong drink."

Elric raised his bottle. "I shall drink to that."

Falchion drained his and discarded it, reaching for another before remembering it was in Elric's hand. "I love a good celebration," he sighed. "But I do not appreciate the reminder that I am sad and alone."

"Understood," Elric replied, casually tipping his bottle into the hedges to drain it.

He offered the remainder to Falchion, who frowned. "You cannot be done, Isteriaeth."

"This eve I am," Elric answered. "I should not want to be ill for days as you are certain to be."

Falchion accepted the drink and smiled. "When you are a bachelor such as I, there is not much more to look forward to than some reckless indulgence or a day off."

Elric watched him then, realizing for the first time how young Falchion was. Truly, he only appeared Elric's age, but where Elric had been alive for centuries, Falchion had seen mere decades. And though Elric had untold time before him, with a world still filled with unrest, his friend may have already seen his half-life pass him by.

"What would you look forward to?" he asked curiously. "What is it that Falchion, the great Isteriaeth abductor of Obarian, wishes for beyond his illustrious reputation and continuous honor?"

Falchion's smile faltered. "What I want most, none can give me. Though I still think of my family on days such as these. I wonder what my sister might've worn for her wedding, or if she would have married at all. I like to believe she would have made me an uncle, of which I am certain I'd have been the greatest, but that is a truth I will never know."

He paused, the weight of his words driving him to drain Elric's bottle, which he deposited on the wall at his side before continuing. "And if I cannot have truth, then I will live in legend. I wish to be unforgettable—impossible to leave behind. I will have renown, and I dare say I am close to arriving on the top of that mountain, and yet...I think it would be better were there someone to share it with."

Elric opened his mouth to reply, but Falchion pushed off the wall. "Then again, I enjoy my freedom too much. And the view from here has already grown stale. I want more. I want to climb higher. The palace is not enough. I want all of Obarian to know my name. No, I want the farthest reaches of Breteria to know who Falchion Drisbane is!"

He shouted the last bit into the night, and from across the courtyard, a few soldiers heckled him.

Elric chuckled, shaking his head. "You are definitely off to a fair start if you insist on shouting like that. But maybe consider what life might be like if you had both. There is no harm in not wanting to be alone."

Falchion, who had begun to stroll away, paused and turned on his heel, attempting to press his fist to his chest and bow. It ended up before his forehead, and he crossed his feet at the ankles in an awkward rendition of a curtsy instead. "I will be infamous, and I shall have you as a friend. I could ask for nothing more in this life."

He had just disappeared from view when shouts rose from the palace. Soldiers rushed inside, and though Elric hid, stealing away to the small room beneath the stairs, he heard the chatter of guests quickly leaving.

"—king is ill."

"Such hurried, violent sickness."

"…returned to her quarters, to not further the spread."

He smiled to himself, and once the hall quieted, he slipped up the staircase and returned to his room. He locked the door firmly behind him, but instead of striding to the balcony, he moved to the wall. Before his knuckles could touch the surface, the lock clicked and the door swung open.

Grace fell into him, her arms thrown about his neck, and he scooped her up off her feet and spun her around.

Mine, mine, mine. His head, his body, his entire being danced and screamed the word, drowning out everything, save their relentless craving for the woman in his arms. Her words in return were a whispered vow, rhythmic waves beating against his heart over and over, and when he pulled away, he grasped her face and silenced his own torrent of emotion with a kiss.

"I love you. I love you. I love you."

The pledge from her lips between kissing echoed in his head, and they parted, both staring at the other in wonder. Realization dawned in Elric's mind. "A star-blessed tether. It would supersede the seized."

Grace's eyes grew wide as Elric beamed, clasping her cheeks. "You set me free after all."

She hesitated a moment, then asked, "If my life is tethered to yours, does that mean…."

"Yes," Elric nodded. "You will live for as long as I am breathing. Not a day less."

Unrestrained joy broke across her face, though when she reached for his vest, ready to remove it, Elric caught her hand.

Blue dhust fell from his palm, and in it, the cord of alabaster velvet appeared again. Grace looked at it with wide eyes, then back to him imploringly.

"I wish to do this right," he whispered, coiling the strand first around her wrist and then around his. She helped him tie it, but instead of standing apart, they came together, and whispered their vows softly into each other's ears, the stars on their arms shining brightly.

They fell together once more, a torrent of love and passion, fearless and unrestrained, husband and wife, bound by the highest order and the deepest, oldest rule. Their bodies knew each other. Their hearts did too. They had for an age, and they would forever.

Elric did not stop to think, barely stopped to breathe, until his claim was laid on her body and the dhust in his veins hummed in contentment. Grace lay sated in his arms, a smile on her face, her gasps hot against his lips.

Elric leaned away and forced her to meet his eyes. "I…meant to move slower. I'm sorry it did not last."

She laughed softly. "No, you are not."

"No, I am not."

"Good," she replied, pressing a kiss to his lips, then brushing her nose against his. "You shouldn't be. And now we must simply go again."

Elric hesitated, but when Grace raised an eyebrow, he spoke sheepishly. "I poisoned the king."

Grace stared at him, wide-eyed, and then threw her head back and laughed. He had never heard a sound more beautiful. Only when she stopped did the spell break between them and her gaze grew serious. "You will not be able to do so forever."

He shook his head. "That is not for you to worry about. He will never have you, because we are leaving. There is a ship set to depart for Inflamel in two days' time, while he is touring the province. And we shall be on it."

CHAPTER FIFTY-ONE

The king was recovered by the next day, the caravan ready to tour each province of Obarian waiting in the courtyard, and as Elric stood by the door, he heard the whispers before Denfrin stormed out of the palace.

"The queen has contracted the very illness that found me," he grunted in displeasure when Elric fell into step beside him on the way to his horse. "I would delay my travels, but I wish to go and return quickly. And I do not have a desire to consummate my marriage in a tent surrounded by soldiers."

Elric said nothing.

Denfrin stopped short and grasped Elric's arm. "Do you think it odd that I fell ill, preventing me from sealing my union with the queen? And now it shall be further delayed a near fortnight?"

Elric shook his head. "Oftentimes when the right thing is done obstacles will arise. Do not lose hope, Your Majesty. All must come to an end."

Denfrin nodded, then pinned Elric with a stare laced with daggers. "I want her watched. None enter a room with her, and certainly none go to her private quarters for any reason. Not even you. If there is anything afoot, I will discover it. And Thrones help any who think they might steal what is mine."

Elric bowed, holding his face in check. "Yes, Your Majesty."

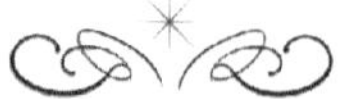

Night descended, and Elric found himself standing on the balcony before the sky, doing everything in his power to will time away. To arrive at the next night. To flee this kingdom once and for all.

He did not hear Grace approach, but when she did, she wrapped her arms around his waist and slid into his embrace. Concern crossed her eyes at the look on his face. "What did he say to you?"

Elric pressed a kiss to her lips. "He informed me that, advisor or not, I am no longer permitted to enter the queen's private quarters. His feathers are quite ruffled that he has not yet bed you, and he wants to ensure your interests remain with him."

Grace paled, but Elric kissed her again, harder this time to banish both their fears, and when they parted, a smirk crossed her face. "I see that has deterred you."

Elric barked a laugh, taking her hand and walking her back toward his quarters. "I am simply amused that he thinks I require a private room for time alone with my wife."

He slipped the shoulder of her gown down, exposing her collarbone to the light snow that fell across her skin, leaving bumps in their wake, but before he lowered his lips to warm it, a heavy fist banged on the door.

Grace's door.

They leaped apart, and Grace met his eyes briefly before turning to march inside. Her hair was damp from the flakes of snow melting into it, her skin cold flushed, and Elric knew she would have no excuse for being alone on the balcony. He moved without thinking, but when he tried to follow, she turned and shut the door in his face, locking it from the inside.

Worry seized his heart, and he spun, striding back into his room and pressing an ear to the door within their wall. The voice he heard, however, struck fear to his very core.

It was Denfrin.

"...snow on the highway. It does not matter why I am here, only that I am. There will be no more excuses. No more games. You will attend my quarters tonight, or tomorrow you will hang for treason," he hissed.

"You cannot make—"

A slap sounded in the air, and Elric was through the door in the wall and in Grace's room in a heartbeat. He stepped up to her side, her hand shaking, holding her cheek that bloomed red.

His eyes narrowed on Denfrin, and all he saw staring back at him was cold and horrified malice.

"*You*," the king said, pointing a shaking finger at Elric. "I should have known it would be you."

Two soldiers rushed in at his back, but Denfrin only lifted a hand. "Leave them," he ordered. "Wait outside and bring me the queen when she is ready. I understand we possess a ship with a hull built for containing an Isteriaeth. I want him in it, and I want it cut free in the Grimm Sea. Let him meet his eternal fate in the horrors that live beneath the waves. Let the stars have their way with him then."

He strode from the room, the soldiers following, and with a *click*, the door locked from the outside.

Grace spun in Elric's arms, grasping his elbows. "Leave," she begged, her eyes wider than he had ever seen before.

"Absolutely not."

"It was not a request, Elric. When I go to him it will give you enough time to run. I cannot bear the thought of you dead. I will not survive it. We are bound by the stars. They led us back to one another once, they will do so again."

He protested, but she turned from him, tearing her braid loose and stripping her gown away, replacing it with a white chemise and the same teal robe from the night he first laid eyes on her. She had bound him to his fate wearing it then, and she would be condemned to hers in the same.

Everything within Elric raged. "Grace, you cannot do this. You will not do this, I won't allow it."

She shook her head, facing the mirror and quickly brushing powder over her cheek with a shaking hand. "And you know better than to control me."

"I am not trying to control you, I am trying to save you. I know what it is to accompany someone I love to their fate. I lost Kathrina because I could not protect her, because I was too late to save her. I refuse to feel you slip from my life as well."

Grace spun on him and a venom-soaked darkness filled her gaze, causing him to take a step back. When she spoke, her words were labored, as if she were fighting an invisible force to keep her rage restrained. "I cannot, and I will not, become a martyr for your mistakes. I do not need to be saved. I have lived through a host of darknesses, and I will survive this one too. I will surmount it."

"You will not," Elric bit out.

"I will. And I refuse to be debased to nothing more than a penance you feel you must pay because you failed to save the woman you loved."

"She was my love, but you are my *wife*," he shouted, his bellow silencing the room and wiping all malevolence from her face. "I loved her with my whole being, but it is you my soul has searched for all my life. I will not stand aside and allow it to be cleaved in two. Not now that I am yours. There is nothing—" His voice broke, cracking under the weight of his own emotions and the tears that dripped from her eyes. "There is nothing I would not do for you. You are worth more than my life. Do you understand?"

Tears rolled down her face now, but her eyes only grew darker and darker. "You cannot allow me to push you away. Not even when it will save you."

"You were what saved me," he retorted. "You alone. Then, now, and forever. You found me, remember?"

His words stilled the churning in her eyes, and her tears stopped falling, but before he could go to her, before he could say anything, a guard opened the door.

Dhust pooled in his palms, ready to strike, to defend, to claim what was his, but with one look from Grace, his body froze. His strands fell silent, and he felt it then—the burning, pulling force draining them. Fear took hold alongside the realization that the seized tether no longer existed between them, so Grace was not claiming his dhust.

The darkness within her was.

She was no longer fighting it—she was embracing it.

The pain was worse than it had been the day he was forcibly tethered to her, only now he was being drained to his bones in a matter of heartbeats and not minutes. Something held him at bay, allowing his dhust to be torn away while he simply waited, paralyzed. His pulse stuttered, his limbs fell slack, sending him to the floor like no more than a ragdoll.

Then as quickly as it started, it stopped.

Elric's eyes widened and he gasped for breath, his body boneless and limp, fighting for strength against the immeasurable force of gravity. He watched helplessly as Grace turned away, taking his power with her, imprisoning him and sealing her own fate. But before the door could shut, before he lost her for the very last time, she paused, and in his mind, he heard her whisper.

"I will never forget you. And I will find you in the dark."

CHAPTER FIFTY-TWO

There once lived a woman who longed for the sea. Its waves, the wind, the storm.

The land called her heart even more, with its rolling hills and small bluffs hiding secrets and teasing life entrapped beneath its dead and frozen ground. The horses that ran wild. The sights she never got to see.

She cared about her people—the ones who remained long after she hurt them. She wondered if they would ever look upon her again in the way they had long ago.

But none of it mattered, for she loved her star the most.

And every last thing she held dear, each one of those moments led her to this. To the final giving over of herself.

It had always been inside her, waiting, whispering. Crawling from her thoughts, making home in her mind and bleeding out into the world before her eyes. Now, blessed by the stars and filled with the power drawn from her beloved, the darkness welcomed her with open arms.

The world, her life, vanished, disappearing into the

ENDLESS NIGHT CONSUMING HER. AND WHEN IT FINALLY REACHED HER HEART, SHE LOOSENED HER GRIP AND SURRENDERED.

FOR THE FIRST TIME, EVERYTHING SILENCED.

IT WAS CALM IN THE DARKNESS OF HER MIND. SHE STOOD ON AN OBSIDIAN SHORE, ON ONYX SAND, BEFORE DARK WATERS. SHADOW WAS ALL SHE COULD SEE, HEAR, AND FEEL. AND SHE REMEMBERED NOTHING.

THE DARKNESS GUIDED HER ACTIONS. IT MOVED HER HANDS; IT LIFTED HER FEET. IT FLUTTERED HER HEART AND TIPPED UP HER CHEEKS IN A DISARMING SMILE.

BUT BEFORE THE LOWLY MAN COULD LIFT A FINGER, BREATHE AGAINST HER SKIN, OR MUSS HER CLOTHING, SHE OPENED HER EYES AND LET THE DARKNESS CREEP OUT.

THE NIGHTMARES DANCED IN SHADOW AROUND HIS DISORIENTED FORM AND LULLED HIM TO REST ON THE PILLOW. AND THOUGH A VOICE FAR AWAY CALLED HER, REMINDING HER TO FIND HIM IN THE DARK, SHE DARED NOT ANSWER.

SHE DID NOT WANT HIM TO SEE HER LIKE THIS.

DID NOT WANT HIM TO REMEMBER HER THIS WAY.

THE DARKNESS STILLED, AND SHE SMILED. THEN SHE HELD THE BLADE OVER THE MAN SLEEPING SOUNDLY BENEATH HER AND DID NOT FLINCH—DID NOT FALTER—WHEN SHE PLUNGED IT DOWN AND SEVERED HIS THROAT.

CHAPTER FIFTY-THREE

Elric lay motionless on the floor, fighting movement back into his limbs one foot and then one hand at a time. But within his mind, he raged like a caged animal. His dhust was gone, he was powerless, and though he knew there might be a chance yet to regain his strength and run—that the passages in the palace would carry him out and far away before he could be spotted—he refused to go.

He would not leave without his wife.

With a groan, he forced himself onto his side, then rolled flat on his stomach with a grunt of frustrated exhaustion. Pressing his cheek to the cool wood floor, he caught sight of himself in Graecerys's mirror. As a star that descended to the realm, born to a mother who had raised him to the tender age of ten, and provided for him for hundreds of years after until she was lost to him, loneliness had always been a fleeting inevitability. And here he was.

The only. The last.

If he were able to convince himself this was truly the end, maybe he would find peace after all. Maybe after trying and failing to run, fight, and live, it was time to give in and let go.

But there was an ancient darkness to defeat first.

The door flew open, but before Elric could react, Falchion stepped inside. "There is not much time," he rushed, wildly looking about the room before locating Elric flat on the floor. He rushed to kneel at his side, concern marring his features. "We must go now."

Elric shook his head. "I will not flee, but I do need your help, if you are willing."

"This is not the time," Falchion grunted, heaving Elric off the floor. "You should have never returned, but it is not too late. I stole you here, I can smuggle you out."

"No," Elric all but growled, the vehemence in his voice bringing the soldier to pause. "If you ever considered me a friend, if you ever trusted that you were one of mine in return, then you will not refuse me this final favor."

Falchion hesitated, and Elric watched him war between the duty, the greatness he longed for, and throwing it all away for the friend who might cost him his life.

"Please, Falchion," he asked, bracing himself for the worst.

The soldier shifted his hold on Elric, but instead of dragging him from the room against his will, he lifted a fist to his chest and bowed his head. "Whatever you need."

They stole through the halls, the guard supporting his weight up the staircase and down the corridor to the Diviner's Wing.

"Secure a way out," Elric whispered to Falchion as his friend helped him lean against the bookcase, his legs finally steady beneath him, though he remained weak and devoid of dhust. "If you see Blenheim, follow him. Otherwise, wait on Graecerys. When you have her, whether I am there or not, you must run."

Falchion's eyes widened, protest rising on his lips, but Elric shook his head firmly. "Go. Quickly."

Disappointment wrinkled the soldier's brow, but he nodded, then turned and ran from the tower.

Elric took a deep breath, steadying himself in the stillness of the room, then he closed his eyes and searched within for his strands. Emptiness, cold and silent, met him, and when he loosed a shaky exhale and opened his eyes once more, they caught on a shadow on the floor. Straightening, he forced his feet forward, but after two steps the flickering light revealed that it was not a shadow.

It was a great gray bird with unnatural green eyes. And it was lying in a pool of blood.

Red dhust began to cloud around the animal, and Elric stumbled as quickly as he could to the corner of the room where his sword had been left abandoned. Grasping the hilt of the blade, yet angling to keep it from sight, he turned in time to watch the air clear—and to meet the eyes of Augur.

A thirst for vengeance flared in his chest. "It was as I thought. I did not believe a Kollapsar hidden in plain sight to be so easily felled, and here you are, alive."

Augur stepped forward, resting a hand on the table for support and revealing his bloodied arms and side. "They are not when there are many. 'Tis why the Vacare keep their number few. But what is seen is not always how it appears."

The man stepped forward again, and with all the strength Elric could muster, he raised the sword with both hands. "That number will be smaller this night. You will not take Grace."

The man stared at him for a moment, then began to laugh, his cackle echoing in the tower. But before Elric could move, the blade vanished from his hand—appearing in Augur's.

He froze, watching the sapphire stars glint as they fell from Augur's hand to the floor. "Atmospheric dhust?"

Augur shook his head, his chest still rumbling with laughter. "We are far more alike than you realized. Do you wish for me to show you now?"

Elric fell back a step, but his brow creased as he watched the man move, shuffling across the room and using the sword as a staff instead of a weapon.

"You are correct as you are incorrect," Augur continued, his breathing more haggard now. "The girl resisted, stronger than any before her, but she has accepted the nightmare. The darkness shall claim its throne this night."

Elric stumbled backward again, keeping distance between them and desperately pulling on his strands, begging something —*anything*—to come to his aid. "You will not get far," he hissed. "You may have hidden this long, but when you fall, she will be freed."

The man laughed. "I have already fallen. The Vacare have consumed ruler after ruler of Obarian, fueling revolt and revolution, turning brother upon brother and feeding them all to ruin, though none brought forth the power they seek. I did not recognize my own madness for what it was until it was too late. But your mother did."

Elric froze. "My mother?"

Augur lifted the sword, holding it out toward the window, and in the blink of an eye, the snow beyond stopped. The wind ceased its blowing. The tower grew silent.

Elric's eyes widened as the man brought the sword back to the floor, leaning on it as if the act took nearly all he had left. And yet, green dhust still trickled from his palms. "Your mother. She suspected there was more. Even after I faded from sight, the Vacare pursued my dhust. It was she who studied the text to find how a greater number of strands together might lure the darkness from the earth to feed. She alone discovered the Vacare's form and how they were drawn to me. It was too late to spare me. But it was not for you."

Elric's legs gave out, and he fell against the bookcase at his back. Instead of advancing on him, Augur slumped forward on the sword—now stuck firmly in the floor beneath his weight— and moved no farther.

"Who are you?" Elric asked, his words too feeble.

Augur lifted his eyes, but this time they were a bright and familiar shade of blue. Elric watched his skin and wrinkles fade, and the harsh, sharp lines of his face soften to reveal the figure of a man Elric recognized instantly. Gevallester—the first King of Obarian.

Gevallester fell to his knees, coughing blood across the tile, and Elric instinctively lurched forward, dropping at his side to hold him upright.

"I thought I could defeat it," the king of old wheezed. "Bind it to myself. Stop it from ever seeking your strands—all three. I only gave it power, and a path forward that would destroy us all. But it was not for nothing. For while your mother was too late to save me, she concealed your strands. Hid you. Saved you."

Elric's mind spun as the man folded beside him. He guided him to the floor, supporting his head, though the king of old refused to let go of his hand—his grip clenched like a vice. Then with faltering strength, he raised his fingers to Elric's face, softly cupped his cheek, and smiled. "My boy."

Elric's mouth dropped open, and when Gevallester's hand fell away, he clutched it. "You are Isteriaeth?" he whispered. "You are my father?"

"And you are a wonder so precious that even the darkness let me to live long enough to lay eyes on you."

Elric shook his head in disbelief, oxygen failing to fill his lungs as Gevallester dissolved into a coughing fit before pressing on through slurring, weakened words. "Three strands, knotted, a beacon for darkness. They consumed me, so I gave away my kingdom. But the Vacare still sought you. Love saved you, but in its cruelty, fate returned you. And though the darkness came for you once more, you found what I could not."

"What is that?"

"What your mother found. The host."

His eyes fell shut, his breathing labored, and Elric lifted a trembling hand, resting it on the man's cheek. "Father," he whispered, and Gevallester opened his eyes, smiling, though Elric knew all too well his final moments were near.

"I was not the last?" he asked, voice breaking through tears.

"Never. And you shall never be. You will now be the first of generations to come. You are star—and you are king."

Gevallester's dhust filled the space between them, brilliant stars of green, blue, and red—their shared strands—and all at once, Elric felt the same power reverberate beneath his skin, flooding his body and veins with a strength unlike any he had known before. There was no hesitancy in his strands now. They were no longer tainted, twisted, or flawed. It was not only the full force of his own power that had been restored, but his father's that was given to him as well.

The dhust dissipated and Gevallester's eyes focused on Elric once more. He beamed, gazing proudly at his son's face. "'*When magic doth bind Isteriaeth to king, the strands shall sing with stars' blessing.*' We are now forever bound, together, your dhust and mine. May your reign be blessed from the sea to the stars."

As he breathed his last, his eyes stayed fixed on Elric, love pouring from them for the son he had clung to life, to humanity, to see. Elric's face crumpled, and he gently closed the man's lids, pulling him close. It was a grief familiar to him, but it was also overwhelming gratitude. A piece he never knew was missing that had somehow sealed the scar time had torn open over and over again.

He was not the last. He had never been alone. *And* he was now the rightful King of Obarian.

The world beneath his very feet shuddered, snapping him from his stupor.

Screams and shouts sounded from the floors below as the palace shook to its very foundation, and when he gently laid Gevallester on the floor, he hurried to the window and looked out across the torchlit courtyard.

Soldiers rushed from the palace, citizens pursuing and raising arms against them. War was ensuing everywhere, coming from within the palace itself.

He fled the tower, running down halls and stairwells, and when he finally reached the first guard, he slammed to a halt. "What has happened?" he called after the man who could barely be bothered to stop running.

"The false queen!" he shouted. "She murdered the king. The nobility cursed us and killed our king. He must be avenged!"

Terror seized Elric's heart. He turned toward the throne room, hearing the shouts and cries for justice coming from within, and whispered, "Grace."

And then he ran.

CHAPTER FIFTY-FOUR

Elric burst through the door. The room was in chaos. Soldiers battling their own. Citizens fighting soldiers. Servants fleeing for their lives. Nobility scrambling to hide, only to be cut down by a hacking blade.

And in the middle of it all was Grace.

A rope bound her hands before her, her ivory chemise was splattered in blood, and though her hair was tangled and wild, her eyes held no pain. Only vicious pride, fathomless vengeance, and endless darkness.

She had been villainized for so long and had finally succumbed to everything the kingdom believed her to be.

Heartless. A monster. A murderer.

Yet all he could see was the friend who saved him. The girl who pulled him from the shadows. His wife. His Queen. The woman he loved.

And he was enraptured to know she was wholly his.

A sword swung for Elric's neck, and he ducked, reaching for his strands and realizing that while they had been restored, he was unable to use them. Thinking back to each time on their journey that his dhust had failed, when he and Grace were not united, cast fear into his heart, but it was quickly stolen away by the beautiful creature using her very bindings to choke the life out of a soldier who had tried to stab her.

He spotted a sword on the tile and scooped it up not a second too soon as a soldier lunged for him. They immediately locked into battle, fighting until he impaled the guard on his blade, and then his eyes searched the frenzy once more.

Grace's hands were free now and she held a sword, but the more he watched her, the more he realized her actions were not her own. She had given herself over. Her humanity was gone.

He needed to find the Vacare host.

And there was only one person left who had remained through it all.

Elric fought his way to Grace, but before he could speak to her, she swung her blade on him. He blocked it high over their heads, shocked at the strength she wielded.

She stared at him with unseeing eyes, and when the blade started to descend on his head, Elric shouted the only words he could think to say. "Find me, Grace! Find me within the dark!"

She froze, and he watched the unnaturally still shadows in her eyes start to move—rolling like soft waves. And when she blinked, though the darkness remained, there were pinpricks of blue within, and her eyes registered his presence.

Grace gasped, dropping the sword to her side and throwing her arms around his neck. "I love you. I love you," she swore.

"And I you," he replied. "But we must find the Vacare."

"Blenheim!" she yelled above the chaos. "It is Blenheim, it always has been."

Elric nodded. "Then we kill him. We free you. We end this."

Grace nodded furiously, but before she turned out of his arms, he grabbed her wrist, stopping her. "You killed Denfrin? Did he harm you?"

Her smile was vicious—deadly, yet brilliant. "I told you I am capable of taking care of myself."

His pride overwhelming, he gripped her face and crushed her lips to his own. Not a heartbeat later, they were back to back, fighting any who came at them, all the while searching for Blenheim.

The doors flew open and a new wave of soldiers rushed in, though it was impossible to tell who was for them and who against. The room barely held the warring sides and all the bodies, and when Elric spun, he realized Grace was nowhere to be found.

He shouted her name above the crowd, rushing to the dais and climbing upon the throne, looking out over the room to find her.

And when he finally spotted her, his chest seized.

She was fighting her way through the center of the room—battling toward Blenheim, who was engaging a soldier on the fringes of the melee.

Elric leaped off the throne and began making his way toward Blenheim. Grace may reach him first, but he would not be long after.

A guard blocked his path, but he felled him quickly, flinging the corpse off his blade and catching sight of Grace doing the same.

There were none left between her and Blenheim.

She froze for a moment, and Blenheim's eyes found her, both of them staring at each other as if they were the only two in the room.

"Fight, Graecerys." Elric whispered the words in his mind, pushing against the dhust fighting to come to life in his bones, willing the words to her. As if she heard him, she snapped from her stupor and, with a cry, lunged for Blenheim.

A body collided with Elric, sending him hurtling to the floor. The man on top of him brought his sword point down, and Elric barely dodged it to the right, then back to the left. The third blow glanced off his forehead, the sting sharp as fresh blood poured down into his eye. The man threw a fist at Elric's face—once, and then again—dizzying him, and through the haze of pain and blood, Elric saw the blade rise over his head once more.

But then the man vanished.

Firm hands gripped Elric, lifting him to his feet before Falchion said, "Fancy seeing you here," then cut down a fellow soldier who was running toward Elric with his blade held high.

"Grace," Elric grunted, spitting a wad of blood on the floor. "Get to Grace. Blenheim is Vacare. We must kill Blenheim."

Elric ducked, shoving his own blade out and disemboweling a man who was rushing at Falchion with an axe. They engaged, fighting axe to blade, the force of his blows shuddering down Elric's arms. A hint of warmth tingled in his veins. He blinked, and suddenly, he held the man's axe, sapphire stars dissipating in the air. He swung, cleanly removing the man's head, and as it hit the floor, the sight beyond him sent Elric's heart plummeting into the pit of his stomach.

Lord Blenheim, arm outstretched, had his hand wrapped around Grace's throat. The murderous hate in his eyes turned them wholly black, and every wrinkle and groove of his rage-filled grimace looked like cracks of shadow bleeding from a pale and lifeless corpse.

The Vacare was formless no longer.

He lifted Grace from the floor, and her feet kicked frantically as she grappled with him, trying and failing to strike, to loosen his hold on her.

Elric's feet began to move, Falchion already strides ahead of him, but each path he took he was deflected—blocked and intercepted. He reached for his dhust, but it stuttered, the strand breaking off in the grasp of his wavering concentration. He felled another soldier, then spotted Falchion once more. He was almost to them.

Elric's adrenaline surged, and he rushed forward. Falchion

broke free from the battle, his course set straight for Grace, but Lord Blenheim spotted him first. The shock on his face caused the shadows to falter, knocking him off balance. Grace seized the opportunity, landing a kick to his ribs that sent her feet slamming back to the floor, though Bleinheim's hand still gripped her neck.

Elric's heart surged with pride, with hope, and he locked blades with the final guard between him and his wife. The guard stood head and shoulders above him, using every bit to his advantage, but as Elric cut him down at the knee, and the man sank, he saw Lord Blenheim's face swing to his own.

Their eyes met for a brief instant.

Falchion swept into the clearing, sword raised high.

And when Lord Blenheim rolled his hand, sketching Elric's own bow to him, he released Grace, stepped back, then smiled.

Grace's scream of agony split the air inside the room. A sword firmly lodged between the ribs in her back, protruding from her heart, cleaved Elric in two, stealing the air from his lungs and renting an agonized cry from his throat.

Falchion ripped the blade free from her back in one swift motion, and her legs immediately gave way. Shock leached all life from Elric's limbs, his mind wondering how such a horrible accident could have happened....

But when his friend caught her only long enough to toss her body to the side, he knew the fatal mistake had not been Falchion's—it had been his.

The guard stared down at her with a look of pure disgust, and when he stepped over her body, he spat, "You chose the wrong side, my queen."

Blenheim laughed, the cold and jarring noise filling the air, and when he reached out and grasped Falchion's shoulder, they both disappeared in a cloud of obsidian dhust.

Elric rushed to Grace's side, hauling her off the ground and to his chest. "Grace, please."

But there was no reply.

"No," he grunted out.

She didn't answer.

Didn't move.

He bellowed the word at the top of his lungs, screaming even after his voice cracked and broke into raw and broken shards, but there was no reply.

And when he collapsed into sobs, begging and pleading with anyone who might listen, his head fell and he pressed his forehead to her own. "Grace, please. Come back. Find me."

Her eyes shot open and he jumped, nearly dropping her, but when he met them—entirely black and empty—a cloud of darkness fell, engulfing them whole, and the world vanished.

CHAPTER FIFTY-FIVE

Obsidian shore. Onyx sand. Dark waters.

Grace had always loved the sea, but now she was lost to it. It had claimed her, swallowed her whole, and though her heart ached at the thought of giving up, the waves were soothing. So she floated in their arms.

"Grace. Please."

The words broke through, clear as day, though her ears were underwater.

And then she heard it.

The song she had forgotten.

It was deep within the depths of the sea, the echo of plinking notes waiting for her reprise.

She only needed to descend and find it.

She fought to draw a breath so that she might swim down, but her lungs refused to pull in air. Not that it mattered. She would sink anyway.

"No."

That voice stilled her again. Music below, the waves above, and though she loved them both, though they were a comfort to her, there was something else....

Something she needed to find.

"Grace, please. Come back. Find me."

She lifted her head from the water, looking around the endless darkness. Finding nothing.

"Where are you?" she asked, her own voice sounding foreign to her.

"I'm right here," it replied. "Can you see me?"

Panic rose in her chest. "I see nothing," she said with heartbreak, though the words that came out of her mouth sounded vicious and full of hate.

"But you can hear me?"

"Yes," she replied cautiously, though it loosed into the air like a hiss.

"Then I will tell you a story."

"There once was a girl, free as the wind that soared through her hair. Wilder than the sea, she was loved by all who knew her. But the world could not handle it. It could not contend with her strength, so they locked her away and sought to break her spirit.

"But that did not stop her. It did nothing to harness the music in her very soul, and through it all, she managed to be a song within the silence.

"Then one night, she found a boy. One who carried the stars that would color her world. She taught him the song of her heart, and he lit her darkness, and together they decided they could conquer it all."

Elric brushed the hair back from Grace's face, her eyes still unseeing. He did not know where she was, if it was even possible to pull her back from the darkness alive inside her, but he would never give up. He would never let her go.

"The darkness rose against them, hungry for the boy's stars and the girl's strength, and though they were better off together, the girl made a sacrifice—she gave herself up to save the boy. She was no more than salt air and gentle song, but she honored the timeless stars by showing mercy to the one they gave their lives to protect. The one who might one day unite a kingdom.

"Years went by. The darkness stole all from the girl, save the secret she hid in her heart. And it was safer there than anywhere else in the world.

"Against all odds, the stars brought the boy back to her, and despite the dark, she held on to his light."

Elric became innately aware that the world had quieted around them, and when he looked up, he realized that the darkness surrounding them had faded. Everything had stopped, as if time itself was frozen. The hairs raised on his arms, but he focused on the woman he held. And that was when he saw it. The soft glittering of the star-blessed tether on her skin.

"The boy did not know her. And though she had forgotten all else, she remembered him. And when the tables were turned, when she had expended all her strength with none left, instead of betraying her, the boy had mercy and saved her life, sealing their bond forever.

"Their love grew without light. It thrived in the storm, it survived being lashed apart, then it defied a world. The boy's fear of loss became the foundation for his fight, and the girl's loss of innocence, of the softness she was worthy of, became the reason she survived. Because you are alive, Grace. You're alive and you remember me, and I know you can find me."

She did not move, did not breathe, did not blink, even as he pressed a kiss to her cold, pale lips.

"Find me within the dark," he whispered.

And when he pulled away, she blinked.

Grace rose from the water, staring at the single star in the sky illuminating her world of darkness.

The story resonated in her bones. She knew it. She had heard it before. What had saved them? What was it she was missing?

"Color," she said excitedly, though her voice was monotonous.

The voice was silent, and then, "What color?"

She thought a moment. *What color?*

She looked around, but all she knew was darkness. How could she remember what she never had? How could she find the words for something she did not know?

Finally, she looked back to the star. "Yours."

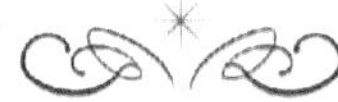

"Yours."

His colors. His dhust, his strands.

Elric did not hesitate, and though warning bells told him the darkness would steal his magic, in his heart he knew this was not the Vacare talking to him. This was Grace. And he would save her this time.

He reached within, scraping at his flesh and bones, ripping and tearing the strands his father had died to return to him, begging them to shine, and when he felt them come to life, he almost cried with relief.

He pushed the dhust out, the colors pouring from his palms, surrounding him and Grace.

Green.

"To drive away the storm."

Red.

"To fly from darkness."

And blue.

"To call you to me."

He watched, holding his breath, letting the stars rain down on them both. He would release their dhust until he had no more. He would pour it out until he was only a husk by her side.

The world grew bright around them, and when Elric glanced up, he drew in a sharp breath. The darkness that encased them was fading. No, not fading—it was being pulled back. His strands were binding it, their brilliant shine radiating light in coils lashed around the writhing venom.

The darkness persisted, but he watched in awe as it was stripped away from them. And when he looked at Grace, he saw thick shadows, dark as an endless void, seeping from her skin like poison. The dhust was drawing the Vacare's claws from her. It was setting her free.

The last of the darkness bled into the air, the trident dhust banding around it, but try as it did to suffocate the force it imprisoned, it was not strong enough. Some tendrils escaped, breaking away from the stars, and fled, vanishing once and for all.

Elric became acutely aware of the shocked stares of the world that had slowly returned to life around them. But there was only one face he wanted to see. He looked down at Grace and held his breath. She did not speak, but ever so slowly, the clouds rolled back from her eyes like a fog until all that remained was their beginning.

The boy, the girl, the stars, and the sea.

And the next time he leaned down to whisper in her ear, his words were filled with the power of every Isteriaeth in the sky. "I found you, Grace."

Her fingers brushed against his cheek, tentative yet alive, and then her velvet voice filled his ears. "And I will never forget you again."

CHAPTER FIFTY-SIX

Silence descended upon the kingdom of Obarian, only now it was not in death and darkness, but peaceful rest.

It had been five weeks since the people of Obarian were roused from a mindless fight to the unnatural departure of Falchion and Lord Blenheim. The tenebrescent dhust left in their wake served as a confirmation for some that a Kollapsar had been at work in their midst, but it was the banishment of the same dark curse from the queen lying lifeless on the floor that brought them all to lay down their arms. And at the three distinct strands binding the last Isteriaeth in Breteria to the Queen of Obarian, breaking the hundreds-year curse before their eyes, the unrest in Obarian was brought to its final surrender.

For the first time since the Fall of the Thrones, the kingdom would know freedom from darkness. They would once again be blessed by the stars. They did not know that the true meaning of the words ran far deeper than the dhust in Elric's veins.

Gevallester, the first king, was laid to final rest privately before the fountain—hidden deep within the labyrinth—that depicted his love and union between the land and the stars. But now, a second statue appeared with him. A woman stood at his back, her smiling face lifted to the sky. One hand was clasped around her husband's wrist, his hand holding the crown, and the other was outstretched, a precious stone inlaid with stars cradled in her palm. Their love cost them everything, but from it, Obarian's hope for the future was born.

"Have you seen the courtyard?" Grace asked softly, standing at Elric's side before the fountain.

He looked at her, brow knit in confusion, but she only smiled. "Growth has begun to sprout from the cracks in the stone. Clovers."

Clovers. The very symbol of the Trifolium Thrones.

Exactly the confirmation Elric had been searching for.

"There is a matter I wished to discuss with you," he said, turning to face his wife. "Before the coronation ritual."

She raised an eyebrow at the seriousness of his tone but did not reply, instead waiting for him to continue.

Elric swallowed. "I do not want to rule. I do not want to control a kingdom. You were right when you said that my duty is to Breteria, and I will not rest until the Trifolium Thrones have risen once more—until the realm is free of the Kollapsar once and for all. But in order to serve Breteria well, I do not need to be King of Obarian."

Grace's eyes widened, but Elric continued.

"You were born for the throne. Named to be the most powerful ruler since my father. One who rules with grace and mercy, bound eternally to the stars. While I will be crowned a High King of the Trifolium Throne, I wish to be known in Obarian as consort only. Consort to the rightful Queen of Obarian. If that is what you wish."

He waited for her reply, but despite the joy in her unshed tears, Grace's smile faltered. "I know you view the future with hope, but I do not know if I can. I cannot ask the people to ever trust me outside of you—I would not expect them to."

Elric took her hand, lacing her fingers with his own and lifting them to his lips. "The sea needs the stars, as the night reflects the waves. There will never be one of us without the other. Not ever again. Everything is going to be fine."

Tears streamed down her cheeks, and when Elric cupped her face, kissing them away one by one, she fell into his embrace and drowned him with her endless tide of happiness.

"But is that still what you want, Grace? To be your own queen?" he asked, pulling back to search her eyes.

"It is." She smiled, kissing his lips firmly. "But there is one more thing I need."

"And what is that?" Elric murmured, smirking at the glint in her eye.

"A consort is fine, but I will also need an advisor."

Elric laughed, kissing her once more, then rested his forehead to hers. "As you wish, my queen."

It took another year to recover Obarian. To secure her borders and start to rebuild her broken people. But with the rightful king set to ascend the Trifolium Throne and the queen—a true daughter of Obarian—free to reign for her kingdom and not the darkness, it was as if every curse they knew melted away, pulling back the bitterness that had frozen the ground to make way for life again.

Every field and bluff was carpeted in clover now, and Elric would never tire of seeing it all. But though he loved the sight, he did not bother to take horse or carriage to his destination, choosing to vanish in a cloud of red dhust and soar to the cliffs above the ocean instead.

"Where is my wife hiding these days?" he thought.

"Where do you think?" her voice returned in his mind.

He scoured the sand and found no one, so it left only one other place she might be. He crossed the frost-covered ground and entered Stonestide, shaking Hubart's hand and waving to Arlys in the dining room. He had hoped there would be more time before dinner, but she already had a dish in her hand…and they all knew how Arlys felt about food growing cold.

He strode down the hall to the right, into the second to last room, and there before the piano, he found who he was looking for. Coming up behind her, he waited patiently, but the second the song ended, he wrapped his arms around Grace's waist and pressed a kiss to her neck.

"All is well at the palace?" she asked.

"More than," he replied. "The residents of the second floor may be ready to return to the north. And the third should not be far behind, now that the city beyond the gate has been built."

The first thing he and Grace had done after their coronation was open the palace, allowing all who could reach them to live within the walls and weather the winter as the world thawed around them. Now, with the help of Elric's dhust, they had rebuilt nearly every province in Obarian, and the people were ready to return home.

Home.

Grace searched his eyes, as if hearing his thoughts, and nodded. "It is time, you know."

He swallowed but nodded.

She laid a hand on his arm, pressing a soft kiss to his cheek. "I will be beside you every step of the way."

"I know. I just…am not certain what we will find."

"It does not matter," she replied. "We have faced the darkness once. We will do it again. However many times it takes to bring your friends back to you."

Elric nodded, glancing out the window at the mountains

before him. "Then we find the final two Thrones and forge a path through the mountains. To the Trifolium Keep."

He sensed her hesitation and met her eyes, knowing the question before she voiced it. "Have there been any more sightings of…."

"None," he replied. "Scouts say there is darkness gathering close to the ruins of the Keep high in the mountains. They've also brought word that a restlessness is coming from the islet at the center of the Grimm Sea too, so it would appear as though we are being surrounded. I do not know what they are planning, but something grows in the darkness. And the Trifolium Thrones must rise again before they do."

"They will," Grace replied, standing from the bench. "I have faith in you."

He caught sight of the falter in her eyes, the cold uncertainty and vulnerability she reserved for the quiet moments when they were alone, and slipped an arm back around her waist. "It is my duty to love you and my honor to protect you. The Vacare will never touch you again. I will make sure of it."

Brilliant warmth and light consumed the fear in her eyes, and she pressed a long, lingering kiss to his lips. Before Elric could make another move, Arlys's voice called for the house to eat.

He released Grace with a promise of more later, and she wrapped her hands around his arm, walking beside him from the music room and down the hall.

"So, Inflamel," she said with an air of mischief. "I suppose you will want to travel by dhust?"

Elric shook his head. "I thought we might sail instead."

"On a boat? On the sea?" she asked slowly, an eyebrow lifting.

Before she stepped onto the stairwell, he spun and scooped an arm beneath her knees, lifting her easily into his arms. "I thought a few uninterrupted days at sea prior to our rushing headlong into another war might be nice. I have it on good authority that one has a piano aboard."

Grace smiled, shaking her head. "I do not care, so long as you are there."

Elric kissed her soundly, brushing her nose with his own. "Everywhere you go. In everything you see." He paused, then added with a wink, "But especially in the dark."

Grace laughed, her eyes dancing with a life and fullness that Elric knew he would never tire of. "I love you, Stargell," she whispered.

"And I, you, Auriana."

WARNING: YOU ARE ABOUT TO READ THE EPILOGUE

There is no going back once you turn this page.
While Elric and Grace will firmly remain in their happily-ever-
after, what comes next will be far from light and lyrical. The
next chapter in their story **will contain spoilers** for the
epilogue of *The Cadence of Crowns*, so if you have not and do not
intend to read it (yet), I highly suggest you complete your
journey here.

However…
If you are a risk taker and a lover of chaos who enjoys plunging
off the side of a cliff for the long scale down to closure far, far,
far at the bottom, then by all means continue on!

Either way, I will see you on the other side🖤

*H*oofbeats thundered along the road across the meadow, the torchlights on the wall of Inflamel City reflecting off the weathered helmets and gilded bridles of the steeds.

A lone figure led the way with another on each flank, their hoods of elfin green pulled over their heads and around their mouths like a scarf, protecting their skin from the breakneck pace.

The howl of wealdwolves echoed from the trees, but the horses' gaits outpaced their hunt. The drawbridge lowered, rising once all three riders cleared the gate—before it could even touch the ground.

The trio cantered across the city, trotting before the castle keep, and only when the elfin guard stationed before the castle's door identified their leader did it open.

On silent boots all three figures dismounted, stealing through the darkness to emerge in the castle's great hall, the flickering flames illuminating the Trifolium sigil emblazoned on every pillar banner.

A tall figure bled out of the shadows, her raven hair long

with soft braids twisted back to keep her face unobstructed. Her shining golden eyes narrowed, and her hand drifted to her weapon as the first man removed his hood and bowed to the Guardian.

Nelluenya nodded to him, but her eyes never moved from the other two figures and her hand never left her blade.

The second figure removed his hood, the third following closely, and with a small gasp, Nelluenya released her sword and took a step back.

The firelight glinted off Elric's circlet, danced against Grace's diadem, and when she took in the sight of them both, the King and Queen of Obarian, she clasped a hand across her chest and began to sink to one knee.

Elric did not allow her to get that far. In four long strides he was before her, his arms around her neck, holding her to him.

"Elric," she whispered, her voice cracking in a mixture of gratitude and tear-stricken joy as she clutched him. "We thought you were lost to us."

"I believed I was," he admitted, relishing the embrace of a lifelong friend. "But I have returned as consort to the Queen of Obarian...and heir to the Trifolium Throne."

Nelluenya pulled back, eyes wide and searching his own, and when she found what she was looking for, only then did the tears fall from her lids. She laid a hand on his cheek and beamed, and though words failed her, Elric whispered, "It is so good to see you, Enya."

He turned, extending a hand, and Grace stepped forward, a starry look in her eyes as she surveyed the Elfin Guardian. Her graceful strides parted the skirts tied loosely about her waist to reveal the leather riding trousers molded to her figure. She had never looked more comfortable in her own skin, and Elric had never seen her appear more of a queen.

His queen.

"Queen Graecerys," Nelluenya greeted her, extending a

hand. Grace took it and bowed, pressing her forehead to the back of it. When she straightened, Nelluenya shook her head. "It is I who should bow to you. For only a queen and a mighty warrior could bring this one back from the depths of his own exile."

"Guardian, I…was the sole reason for his exile," Grace replied slowly, vulnerability bleeding into her words despite their strength.

Nelluenya smiled. "That is not the exile I refer to. You have returned him to us in more ways than one. And you may call me Enya, for we are now friends."

Grace's face softened, and when she nodded, her sparkling eyes met Elric's. And all he saw in them was the depths of her love, wide as an ocean for him.

He took a steadying breath, preparing himself for what came next, then faced Nelluenya. "How is he?"

A shadow passed over her face, and she exhaled slowly, turning to look up the stairs at her back. "I wish I were able to say unchanged since you were last with him, but I am afraid…he has grown worse."

Elric flinched, closing his eyes for a heartbeat, but Grace's hand in his own rallied him to open them once more. "Will he accept visitors?"

Nelluenya shook her head sadly. "He will, but only because he no longer recognizes any. We have kept him closely guarded, protected, as the kingdom is vulnerable without him and knowledge of his condition would invite chaos back to our shores. But his mind is absent. I do not know if he sees or hears at all."

Elric swallowed, glancing at Grace, then returning to Nelluenya. "I will go to him."

She nodded, then clasped both his hands in her own. "You know where to find him."

Elric ascended the stairs with Grace by his side, Nelluenya

remaining behind with her kinfolk. Nearly at the top, Grace squeezed Elric's hand and prompted him to stop.

She leaned in and kissed him soundly, yet softly. He sank into her lips, his hand slipping into her hair and around the back of her neck, holding her close. For that moment, that heartbeat, they were alone—safe inside the pocket they'd carved for themselves in the storm that still threatened to bring the world down around them.

They separated, foreheads touching, noses brushing, and finally Elric leaned back with a small smile. "There is much I wish to show you. Though it might be better if we leave the crowns here."

"I believe that can be arranged," Grace replied. "So long as you wear the crown when we are alone in our rooms."

He winked at her, ascending the last of the stairs and making his way down the hall to the center door. With a rallying breath, he clasped the handles and pushed them open.

The sitting room was just as he remembered, cold and impersonal, but instead of being empty, a lone figure whirled to face him, blade in hand, ready to strike. However, when he recognized Elric, he dropped it, and as a broad smile broke his stern gaze, Elric realized exactly who he was.

"Milo."

The boy, now well on his way to being a young man, nodded. "Elric. We hoped you would return. When word reached the castle of all you have done in Obarian, we were encouraged."

"Where is Reginald? I expected to see him here."

Sadness filled the boy's eyes, and though he stiffened his shoulders, his voice trembled with barely restrained emotion. "He was leading our fleets to the south, defending our ports against the infestation of mercenaries from Tauriellis. We were losing too many men, and Reg was injured in a skirmish. He was not the same after he healed, convinced he was unfit for his rank, so when he returned to command, he took a fleet of our best men straight to the Bay in Tauriellis. Only, they never made it. Pieces of their ship washed aground in the Brumal Forest, and still more was recovered at sea, but no survivors. If there were any, they either ran afoul of pirates or they are lost to us forever. In Grimoira."

Elric felt the blow land squarely in his gut, and though the revelation left him speechless, he grasped the boy's shoulder.

"I have been here ever since," Milo continued, sniffling and clearing the emotion from his throat. "Taken his post. It is what he would have wanted."

Elric nodded, and after a long moment gazed at the door beyond.

"Has there been any sign of *her*?"

Milo shook his head. "None. But the wolves remain constant."

Elric turned, Grace's sorrow-filled eyes looking up at him before he returned his attention to the boy. "Milo, there is someone I would like you to meet. This is my wife, Graecerys."

Milo's eyes widened, and when he took in her smile, the mask of a responsible guard slipped to reveal the boy who had once frolicked through the fields of Inflamel. "You are beautiful," he whispered, awestruck.

To Elric's surprise, Grace closed the space between them and hugged him. And though Milo's shoulders fell slack, Grace's remained strong, filled with compassion and understanding. "I am so sorry for your loss."

"Thank you, my lady," he replied softly.

Elric did not speak again until they separated, Grace leaving a reassuring hand on the boy's arm, and then he uttered the four words he feared the most. "May I see him?"

With Milo's nod, Elric left the two outside the room, closing the door at his back. Light filtered in the great windows, the sky beyond the castle breaking with the dawn, but the bed was still made. The food on the platter remained untouched. And in the center of the room, a single high-backed chair stood, occupied by a lone form.

Elric crossed the floor, coming around the chair to survey his brother's face. It was old and haggard, nothing near what his age should have beheld. Wrinkles marred his skin, his eyes were sunken in, and though they were wide and staring at nothing, his pupils were surrounded by rings of glittering black.

"What has taken hold of you, brother?" Elric whispered, his heart breaking. Timothius showed no sign of life, no hint of recognition. He was alive, breathing, but though his heart beat steady, he was lifeless.

His heart.

Wren's heart.

Whatever the mage had done to her had infected him. His descent into madness was the very thing that drove a wedge in their friendship. It was what had driven him to cast Elric out.

The night where his journey started.

Yet here he was, back at the beginning, with more power than what he had left with, and now two crowns between them.

"I will not leave you this time," he swore. "Obarian will assure your people are safe. That you do not lose any more men to mercenaries or other threats. And I, I will keep *you* safe. I will find Wren and I will save you both. And mark my words, brother, I will ensure that every drop of life that bleeds from that witch's dark, cursed heart brings back all that she has stolen from you. I will not rest until Wren is returned and you are restored. I will not rest until the Isperi Mage is dead."

ALSO BY

The Virtues Trilogy

Flight (Book One)

Fight (Book Two)

Free (Book Three)

Legend of the Trifolium Thrones

The Cadence of Crowns

The Rebellion of Stars

The Ashes of Fate - October 2026

ACKNOWLEDGMENTS

Well hello, thank you so much for reading The Rebellion of Stars! Whether this is your first introduction to my writing, or you're returning as a friend I am SO grateful for you and thankful that you've given my words your time, my stories a place in your mind, and my characters room in your heart.

Thank you so much to my incredible Alpha and Beta readers, Street Team, and ARC Team for embracing Elric and Grace and their journey…you came for the Anastasia vibes and stayed for the emotional damage and it makes doing my job so much easier knowing you are rallying behind me every step of the way!

To Erik and my babies, my loves, my life, I feel like every book I get into this adventure demands more and more of me, but you never ask me to stop. In fact, you cheer even louder now than when I started!! I couldn't do this without you. I am a better person and writer because of the way you love me. You're the stars that guide me home, and the music that fills up my head when I feel alone and don't think I can do this anymore. I love you with my entire heart and soul.

To my parents for being my biggest fans and for being just as excited and anxious as I am for every book release (even when I make you cry)!!

To Megs, Ashley, and Talia for reading this book a thousand times over at every stage just to ease my mind and help me keep my story threads straight. The way you just GET me is terrifying and honestly the best. Thank you for making me better with every comment and note, and still coming back for more even though I'm inevitably going to hurt your feelings.

To Ashley, because this book would NOT exist without you!! Thank you for the hours of voice messages, the rants, the five stages of grief that I cycled through on an hourly basis, for ALL of the "we're going to get through this" and the "let's work it out" chats, and for staying on the wall of my brain until I found my footing and clawed back out of my mental ditch with a book I'm still so very passionate about. I…might let you conspire with A+E about future events now. Maybe.

To Lex with Selkkie Designs, for my incredible cover and for continuing to build an entire story with your art. You are brilliant and keep outdoing yourself and I cannot thank you enough!!

To Maryia, for the incredibly stunning map of Breteria. I am obsessed every time I refer back to it.

To Chinah, for once again helping my words shine and for pushing me to grow and be the best version of my author-self possible.

Brittany, thank you for always always always being in my corner, for never being more than a text message away, and for coffee on Saturday mornings even though our schedules are insane. You remind me of the value in my art and my words when I need it the most and you don't even realize it. I don't know what I'd do without you!!

To my QoCs, my sisters, my found family, I have no words for how much each one of you mean to me!! Thank you for making me laugh out loud when I want to cry, for crying with me when I need a good one, and for reminding me all of the reasons why I shouldn't give up on a weekly basis. I don't deserve you, but I'm eternally grateful that I get to exist in the same lifetime as each of your beautiful selves🖤

To Rory Pond for being the literal best emotional support floof in the world. You're a menace, but you're our menace, and as long as you purr and help me fall asleep when my brain won't stop, I'll let you sleep on my timeline when I'm trying to take notes.

And last but certainly not least, if you've made it this far, I have a surprise for you... Come on, you didn't ACTUALLY think I'd kill off my sweet baby Reginald, did you?? No, I have much, MUCH bigger plans for him. See you in Grimoira😎

Coming October 27th:

Preorder Now on Amazon

ABOUT THE AUTHOR

R.V. Wilbur has been in love with reading ever since she received her first Little Golden Book library at the age of two. A love of words soon followed and, after publishing selected poems, she drafted her first book at the age of thirteen.

Despite all of this she is still somehow terrible at writing blurbs, so this is about all you get. She currently resides in North Carolina with her husband, two children, and of course her black cat Rory Pond. And she's probably drinking coffee.

No, she is definitely drinking coffee.

facebook.com/RVWilburAuthor
instagram.com/rvwilburauthor
amazon.com/author/rvwilbur